P9-BBP-981

Alec began to drag Katherine's glove off.

"No!" she hissed under her breath.

"Yes." He smiled, the way Alexander the Great must have smiled when he chose the first land to conquer.

Katherine tried to jerk her hand free, but he held on to it and began to strip her glove off each finger, inch by inch, the way Alexander had probably stripped the female captives he'd made his wives.

Heat rose in her cheeks as Alec bared her hand. He tossed her glove into her lap. Then, resting the back of her hand on his warm thigh so the soft palm lay exposed to him, he traced her fingers.

She swallowed hard. No man had ever touched her like this. Who could have guessed it would be so ... so ...

Erotic. This seemed every bit as naughty as the pictures in that scandalous book—especially since it was happening to her.

Acclaim for Sabrina Jeffries!

"Sabrina Jeffries's wit, passion, and ardent characters will enthrall you."

—Christina Dodd

"Anyone who loves romance must read Sabrina Jeffries!"

—Lisa Kleypas

And praise for her previous works of romantic fiction

MARRIED TO THE VISCOUNT

"Jeffries's enticing tale will have readers rooting for the outgoing and upbeat Abby while she tames her dreadful viscount. It's an enjoyable and lusty read."

—*The Oakland Press*

DANCE OF SEDUCTION

"The biting, humorous repartee and slowly building sexual tension, along with a cast of utterly delightful characters, will have you captivated from the first page to the chilling climax. This delightful and passionate romance is guaranteed to win your heart and earn a space on your keeper shelf."

—*Romantic Times*

"A breezy, funny, sexy book . . ."

—All About Romance

"One will be wonderfully light of heart at its end, and pleasantly sated by Ms. Jeffries's wickedly nimble prose."

—Heartstrings

AFTER THE ABDUCTION

"Ms. Jeffries has created a delightful, light-hearted tale with winning characters and sparkling romance."

—*Romantic Times*

"I would recommend *After the Abduction* to anyone, but those who love Regency-type historicals definitely won't want to pass this one by."

—The Word on Romance

A NOTORIOUS LOVE

"A fabulous book . . . Satisfies on every level. Bravo!"

—Crescent Blues Book Views

"A charming and absorbing read, and very recommendable."

—The Romance Reader

A DANGEROUS LOVE

"An intriguing premise, a hefty dollop of deceit, nicely chosen literary quotations, and well-drawn . . . characters add interest to this . . . occasionally bawdy romp."

—*Library Journal*

"Ms. Jeffries has created a rousing, sexy romance with a heroine who is worthy of any Shakespearian heroine."

—*Romantic Times*

THE DANGEROUS LORD

"[A] luscious romance filled with sensuous moments that will make your heart beat a little faster."

—*The Oakland Press*

Sabrina Jeffries

In the Prince's Bed

POCKET STAR BOOKS

New York   London   Toronto   Sydney

The sale of this book without its cover is unauthorized. If you purchased
this book without a cover, you should be aware that it was reported to
the publisher as "unsold and destroyed." Neither the author nor the
publisher has received payment for the sale of this "stripped book."

This book is a work of fiction. Names, characters, places and
incidents are products of the author's imagination or are used
fictitiously. Any resemblance to actual events or locales or persons,
living or dead, is entirely coincidental.

An *Original* Publication of POCKET BOOKS

A Pocket Star Book published by
POCKET BOOKS, a division of Simon & Schuster, Inc.
1230 Avenue of the Americas, New York, NY 10020

Copyright © 2004 by Deborah Gonzales

All rights reserved, including the right to reproduce
this book or portions thereof in any form whatsoever.
For information address Pocket Books, 1230 Avenue
of the Americas, New York, NY 10020

ISBN: 0-7434-7770-7

First Pocket Books printing August 2004

10 9 8 7 6 5

POCKET STAR BOOKS and colophon are registered
trademarks of Simon & Schuster, Inc.

Cover and Stepback illustration by Alan Ayers
Handlettering by Dave Gatti

For information regarding special discounts for bulk purchases,
please contact Simon & Schuster Special Sales at 1-800-456-6798
or business@simonandschuster.com

Manufactured in the United States of America

To Micki Nuding, my wonderful editor, who has always believed in me.

And to all of the wonderful people at Bruegger's Bagels and Bushiban Coffeehouse, who've served me enough coffee to float a battleship during the writing of this book and others, and who never fail to put a smile on my face. This one's for you.

Acknowledgments

I am grateful for the help and encouragement of the following individuals:

Rexanne Becnel, Nora Armstrong, Debbie Bess, Caren Helms, and Liz Carlyle, whose input on the viability of this series and knowledge about the period was invaluable. And thanks for lending me all those books, Debbie!

Brenda Jernigan and Claudia Dain, who gave me much-needed moral support throughout the writing of the book. No writer could ask for a better support system.

Chapter One
London, 1813

❧

Take care not to sire any bastards; they will
haunt you long after the pleasure of
wenching has waned.
—Anonymous, *The Art of Seduction Reveal'd,*
or A Rake's Rhetorick

They were late.

By lamplight, Alexander Black consulted the pocket watch given him by Wellington. Damn. Twenty minutes late already. He'd used his meager funds on the proprietor's best French brandy, and now the men weren't coming.

At least the private dining room had cost him nothing. He strode to the window, cocking an ear toward the stables by force of habit. But no soothing sounds of horses settling in for the night reached him above the watchman's bell and the clacking of hackney wheels on cobblestone.

A knock at the door followed by a muffled "Lord Iversley?" made him start.

Right, *he* was Iversley. After he had lived for years as plain Mr. Black, returning to being a lord took some getting used to. "Come in."

A lad opened the door, his nervousness inexplicable until Alec spotted the man looming behind him. "L-Lord

D-Draker is here to see you." The cowering boy turned to the hulking figure, whose reputation as the Dragon Viscount had clearly preceded him. "W-Will that be all, m-my lord?"

Draker's fierce gaze swung to the servant. Even dressed in humble fustian, the shaggy-haired brute could crush stone to dust with a stare. "Begone," he growled. When the lad scampered for the stairs quicker than a skittish gelding, Draker rolled his eyes. "They think horns grow on my forehead."

"Then perhaps you shouldn't snarl at them," Alec said dryly.

The giant's dark brown eyes pinned him in place. "A wise man would keep his opinions to himself."

"A wise man would never invite you here. But I like taking risks."

"I don't." Hesitating on the threshold, the viscount examined the room warily. In keeping with a hotel popular with army officers, it boasted heavy oak chairs and a table borne on legs carved with lion heads in midroar.

Alec bit back a smile. Draker ought to feel right at home.

"So what's the reason for this meeting?" Draker demanded.

"I'll explain when my other guest arrives."

Draker snorted, but finally entered. "Did he also receive a ridiculous note inviting him to come here 'if you want to change your life'?"

"If you thought the note ridiculous, why did you come?"

"It's not every day that an earl I've never met is foolhardy enough to approach a man of my reputation."

Alec offered no explanation. Taking his seat, he gestured to another chair. "Make yourself comfortable. There's brandy if you wish to indulge."

Draker had settled himself into a chair with a glass when a tall auburn-haired gentleman sauntered in the open door. Flashing them an insolent glance, he tossed a folded sheet of foolscap onto the table with a white-gloved hand. "I assume one of you is the sender of this peculiar note?"

"Yes, I'm Iversley." Alec rose. "You must be the owner of the Blue Swan."

The man gave a dramatic bow. "Gavin Byrne at your service."

Noting how Draker stiffened, Alec gestured to the empty chairs. "Thanks for coming. Take a seat anywhere—"

"Take mine." Jerking to his feet, Draker headed for the door. "I'm leaving."

Alec tensed as he saw all his plans disintegrate before his very eyes.

"What's the matter, sir?" Byrne drawled. "Not brave enough to do business with me?"

Draker halted to frown at Byrne. "I don't think our host is interested in business. You've probably heard of me, as I've heard of you. I'm Draker."

He didn't have to say more. Shock suffused Byrne's angular features before he turned on Alec. "What is this, Iversley—some wager?" He crossed to the open window to glance out onto the ledge. "Where are your friends hiding to watch England's two most notorious half brothers meet for the first time?"

"There's no one here but us," Alec said evenly.

Byrne whirled from the window, eyes glittering from the shadows. "Ah. Then you're hoping for material reward, blackmail perhaps? I hate to disappoint you, but everyone in London already knows of my fine lineage."

"And mine." Draker dragged his finger down the scar barely showing above his beard. Draker's natural father hadn't been married to his mother, either. Fortunately for Draker, another man *had* been married to her, making him legitimate. "You've arranged this for nothing. Now if you'll excuse me—"

"So the fearsome Draker is actually a coward," Alec snapped, "afraid to spend a few minutes alone with his two brothers."

Draker whirled on him. "Now see here, you damned—" He broke off, eyes narrowing. "What do you mean, '*two* brothers'?"

"Despite my apparent legitimacy, I'm a by-blow like the two of you. More importantly, we share the same father." With an unsteady hand, Alec lifted his glass in the air. "Congratulations, gentlemen. You've just gained a half brother. And the Prince of Wales has gained another bastard son."

As he downed the liquor, a silence settled on the room as thick and deep as a London fog. For a moment the other two men only stared at him.

Then Draker stalked up to the table, scowling as fiercely as the carved lions supporting it. "Is this some sick joke, Iversley? No scandal of *that* sort has ever been whispered about your family."

"Perhaps no one knew," Byrne put in. "But I'm inclined to believe him."

Draker glared at Byrne. "Why?"

"Because what newly minted earl would lie about a thing like that?"

Alec released a breath. "Sit down, gentlemen, have some brandy, and hear me out. I swear you won't regret it."

Byrne shrugged. "Very well. I could use a stiff drink." He splashed a generous portion of brandy into a glass, dropped into a chair, and drank deeply. After a second's hesitation, Draker followed his lead.

So far, so good. Alec took his own seat and poured himself more brandy. The three of them drank in silence, looking each other over, searching for resemblances with furtive glances.

Hard to believe these were his brothers. Thick-chested and muscular, Draker had inherited the stocky build of the Hanovers, but without their sire's abundant flesh. Or concern for fashion. Draker's untrimmed chestnut hair, heavy beard, and suit of dull fustian bespoke a man who eschewed society and all its rules.

Then there was Byrne, who must have come straight from his highly successful gentlemen's club. His white marcella waistcoat and black Florentine silk breeches were finer than anything Alec could afford, yet except for the ruby pin winking in his cravat, Byrne's rig was surprisingly sober.

Especially considering the exalted circles Byrne moved in. His wry wit and clever hand at cards made him as popular with the Duke of Devonshire as with the lowliest waiter at White's, despite his illegitimacy.

"Your revelation does explain the odd gossip about you." Byrne ran his finger along the rim of his glass. "They say your father sent you on the Grand Tour, where you stayed for ten years pursuing pleasure, even after your mother died."

Alec fought down a surge of anger. Of course his "father" had spread lies about him. The old goat would hardly tell anyone the truth.

"Odd thing, though," Byrne went on. "Nobody ever

spoke of seeing you at entertainments abroad. And I met your . . . er . . . father once, who didn't seem the sort to tolerate his heir's defection for long. Not to mention the pesky matter of a war going on."

Alec drank deeply from his glass. He hated laying his life open before these half brothers he barely knew, but he had no choice. "There was no war when I left England. It was during the short-lived Peace of Amiens."

"Where exactly did you go?" Draker asked gruffly.

"To Portugal. The old earl sent me to live with his sister." Whose Portuguese husband believed in stiff punishments for wayward English boys. "I stayed only a few years. But I couldn't come home—my father had forbidden me to set foot on the family estate or speak to my mother." Bile rose in his throat. "He didn't even write me of her death until weeks after she was buried."

"He did all that because you were Prinny's by-blow?"

"Yes, though I didn't know it at the time." Alec swallowed some brandy. "Shortly after the old earl's death and my return to England, I found a letter Mother had hidden for me that revealed the truth." And transformed everything he'd thought about himself and his parents. "Apparently, when she conceived me my 'father' hadn't shared her bed in months. But he claimed me rather than let it be known Prinny had cuckolded him. He even tolerated my occasional presence at home until a prank at Harrow got me sent down. That's when he banished me from Edenmore for good."

"Bloody hell, what sort of prank was that?" Byrne asked.

Alec swirled his brandy, watching the play of lamplight on liquid. "I tried to obtain an expensive meal for me and my chuckleheaded friends by . . . er . . . impersonating a famous person. But despite my faint resemblance to the man and my padded clothes, I was a bit too young and thin to be convincing."

"You don't mean you pretended to be—" Byrne began.

"Oh, yes." Alec lifted a rueful gaze to them. "Unwittingly I picked the one fellow I should *not* have impersonated. The earl was not amused."

Both men blinked, then burst into laughter. After a second, Alec joined them. How odd to laugh over what had been the worst disaster of his young life.

"God, the irony . . ." Draker choked out. "Your father . . . I can only imagine—"

Their laughter erupted again, dissolving the earlier tension. By the time their laughs died, the warmth settling between them was almost . . . brotherly.

"Now that you mention it, there *is* a resemblance," Byrne managed as he brought his amusement under control. "You've got Prinny's eyes."

"But why are you telling us all this?" Draker asked. "Don't you care who knows?"

"Believe me, I've no desire to spawn more gossip about me and my family. But the truth is, I need your help."

Just that quickly, the tenuous connection between them was broken.

Byrne eyed him with cool cynicism. "Money. You think to turn to your wealthy 'brothers' for funds, is that it?"

Alec tensed. "I do need money, but I don't want any from either of you." At Draker's snort, he rose to face them. "When I discovered my connection to Prinny, I searched for information about his other by-blows. I learned that we're the only ones who haven't profited from the connection." He nodded to Draker. "You've been an outcast from society ever since you forcibly evicted the prince and your mother from your estate at Castlemaine."

Alec turned to Byrne. "And Prinny has callously refused to acknowledge your connection to him. You dine with dukes at your club, but though they call you Bonnie Byrne to your face, they call you Byblow Byrne, the Irish whore's son, behind your back."

"Only if they want their tongues cut out," Byrne snapped.

Alec shrugged off the threat. "And—as you've guessed—I'm penniless. The earl spent my mother's entire fortune."

In his last days, the old goat had invested in risky ventures that decimated what family monies hadn't been stolen by his corrupt steward. Thanks to that and the earl's obsessive—and expensive—pursuit of quack cures for some supposed illness, Alec had inherited an estate in shambles, but no blunt to save it.

"Each of us lacks something. I have no money." Alec glanced at Byrne. "You have no legitimate name." He nodded to Draker. "You have no acceptance in society."

"What does Draker care about society?" Byrne said. "He seems content enough moldering out there at Castlemaine."

"Ah, but I suspect he sometimes finds his outcast status inconvenient." Although Draker scowled, Alec noticed he didn't deny it. "Aren't you guardian to the daughter your mother bore the viscount? And isn't she approaching the age to marry? You may not care about your own situation, but I'll wager you care about hers."

"All right," Draker grumbled, "so my sister *has* been plaguing me with this maggoty idea about having a season. I've told her it won't work. Who would sponsor her?

Besides, after the lies my mother spread about me, Louisa will be treated like a leper for *my* sins."

"But if you don't give her a season," Alec pointed out, "how long before she runs off with the first footman or local idiot who shows her any affection?"

"Is there a point to this?" Draker asked tersely.

Alec cast Byrne a studied glance. "If all she needs is a sponsor and invitations, I'm sure Byrne knows several lords whose . . . er . . . indebtedness to him would persuade them and their wives to do as we ask."

"*We?*" Byrne queried.

"Yes, we. Thanks to our sire, we've been denied the advantages of most normal families—friendship, loyalty, unconditional aid. But that needn't stop us from success." Heartened by how intently they listened, he continued. "Each of us possesses something the others need, so I propose that we form an alliance. It would act as a family—we *are* half brothers, after all. Together, we could change our fortunes. We could help each other attain everything we desire."

Byrne lifted an eyebrow. "Which brings us back to what *you* desire. But if you think I'll lend you money because of our mutual connection to Prinny—"

"I don't want any loans," Alec retorted. "The earl left me sunk in debt up to my chin as it is."

"Yet you must want *something* from us. And since we're clearly not Prinny's favorites, you can't be hoping we'll get you money from him."

"Absolutely not," Alec said firmly. "I doubt he knows I'm his son, and I'd rather keep it that way. Besides, he doesn't have enough money for what I need."

Draker's eyes narrowed. "How much are you talking about?"

"To restore Edenmore to a working estate and the house to a livable condition—" He dragged in a heavy breath. "Roughly seventy-five thousand pounds. Perhaps more."

At Draker's low whistle, Byrne said, "You're damned right—nobody would loan you such a sum. I doubt you could even make it at the tables."

"If borrowing money will sink me further, gambling would bury me." Alec set his glass down. "No, I've thought about this, and I can find only one solution to my need for funds—marriage to an heiress."

"You're not getting Louisa, if that's what you're thinking," Draker growled.

Alec rolled his eyes. "For God's sake, I don't want a chit fresh out of the schoolroom. I'd prefer a mature woman who understands the rules of English society: Do as you please as long as you're discreet. Raise hell in private as long as you behave well in public. Pretend that marriage is about love, when we all know it's about money and position."

"Sounds rather cynical," Draker said.

"You of all people know it's accurate. Why else do you escape society at your estate in Hertfordshire?" When Draker scowled, Alec added, "Not that I blame you. I tried escaping by staying abroad instead of returning here to demand my due when I came of age. That's why I've nearly lost everything."

He smiled grimly. "I learned my lesson. You play by their rules—at least in public—to get what you want. And I want to restore Edenmore. If that means hunting a fortune like the other penniless lords, then, by God, I'll hunt a fortune."

Draker shook his head. "Any heiress with that kind of

money is armed to the teeth against fortune hunters. And if she isn't, her father will be."

"The man's an earl," Byrne told Draker. "Plenty of merchants would gladly pay to have their daughters made into countesses."

"For such a large sum?" Alec went to stoke up the fire. "What fool would hand over his precious daughter and seventy-five thousand pounds to a fortune-hunting lord with a reputation for abandoning his family in the pursuit of pleasure? I can't tell the truth about my time abroad without explaining the real reason for my estrangement from my father, which I don't want to do."

He stared into the flames. "But the rumors alone won't damage my chances, as long as I hide my penury while I'm courting. I plan to take my heiress in hand before she learns of my finances." He wouldn't make the old earl's mistake—letting his intended wife know he was marrying her for money. That only led to trouble.

Dusting his hands off on his trousers, he faced them again. "That's why I need your help. I have to secure my heiress before the truth about my situation reaches London. Trouble is, I don't know any. I was too young to be in society when I left, and I don't have the weeks it will take me to learn who's who."

He narrowed his gaze on Byrne. "You move in those circles and deal with financial matters every day. You could give me the information I need."

When Byrne looked stony, Draker cleared his throat. "Since I've been out of society half my life, I can't imagine what good *I* could do you."

Tearing his gaze from Byrne's, Alec said baldly, "You could loan me a carriage. Most things I can get on credit, but not something that large."

"You don't even own a carriage?" Byrne said in disbelief.

Alec stiffened. By God, he hated this begging. "My father sold both our carriages, along with the London town house, which is why I live here at the Stephens Hotel. I can keep my lodgings secret, but if I always show up in a hack, someone will get suspicious." He stared at Draker. "And I figured since you—"

"Don't go into society," Draker finished, "I could spare you a carriage."

Alec nodded tightly. "I promise to keep it in good working order."

Draker appeared more amused than insulted. "If you will also promise not to harness a lot of ill-matched nags to it—"

"You'll help me?" Alec broke in. "You'll join this alliance I propose?"

"I suppose it can't hurt. Especially if my pesky sister gets a decent husband out of it." Draker arched a shaggy brown brow. "And not a fortune hunter."

Alec smiled ruefully. "I hope my heiress's relations are not so particular."

"I know of one who might suit your needs," Byrne put in. When Alec turned to stare at him, he added with a shrug, "Gamblers do talk."

Alec's blood thundered in his ears. "So you'll join this alliance, too?"

"The Royal Brotherhood." A muscle ticked in Byrne's jaw. "It's all well and good for you and Draker—in the eyes of the law, you're legitimate. But you can't make me legitimate, or gain me the respect Prinny denied me and my mother."

"Surely we can help you obtain *something* you want.

I promise you'll gain as much as we do from this enterprise."

"I intend to," Byrne said tersely. "Besides, it might be amusing to watch you succeed under our good father's very nose."

For the first time in many weeks, hope swelled in Alec's chest. "Then it's agreed? We'll join hands as brothers to achieve all that we desire?"

"Agreed," Draker murmured.

"Agreed." Byrne poured more brandy for them all. "This calls for a toast." He rose and lifted his glass. "To the Royal Brotherhood of Bastards, and their future prosperity."

The other two stood and lifted their glasses to echo the toast.

They drank, and then Alec lifted his glass again with a grim smile. "And to Prinny, our royal sire. May he rot in hell."

Chapter Two

No woman can resist a man who undresses
her with his eyes.
—Anonymous, *A Rake's Rhetorick*

*K*atherine Merivale couldn't believe it. Apparently
Papa's scandalous chapbook had been right—a practiced
rakehell *could* tempt a woman to sin with just a look. Be-
cause only a nun could resist the power of the Earl of
Iversley's gaze from across Lady Jenner's ballroom.
Katherine had never been so unsettled by a man's stare.
But then, no man had ever looked at her quite like that,
either.

She tried to ignore him. Yet everywhere the waltz took
her and her dance partner, Sir Sydney Lovelace, she could
feel Lord Iversley's blue gaze following her, stripping her
bare, unveiling all her secrets.

And she didn't even *have* any secrets.

If she were to believe the gossip about him, however,
he certainly did—ten years of secrets from his wild and
reckless adventures in exotic ports. And every one of
those years showed in the darkly compelling eyes that
promised he could make any woman yearn for his caresses . . .

Lord preserve her, how her imagination ran away with her! And what right did the Earl of Iversley have to undress her with his eyes, anyway? She hadn't even been introduced to him, for goodness sake.

After another circuit around the ballroom, she sneaked a glance to where his lordship still stood by the gallery doors, holding a glass of champagne. Lady Jenner was with him now, leaning forward to give the man a generous view of her ample bosom.

Katherine rolled her eyes. Just because Lord Iversley was a handsome devil in that striped white-on-white waistcoat and suit of jet-black superfine was no reason for women to slobber over him.

Not that Katherine cared who slobbered over his lordship. She had Sydney, her betrothed. Her nearly betrothed, anyway, if he would ever get around to making their informal childhood "understanding" into a formal lifelong one.

All right, so Sydney's shoulders weren't quite that broad, and his hair fell in precise golden ringlets instead of that gloriously rumpled mass of smoky black waves—

She stifled a groan. There was no comparison. Sydney epitomized gentlemanly refinement. Lord Iversley looked downright dangerous, like that caged panther she and Mama had seen at the menagerie today. No true gentleman had such tanned skin, such large hands, such blatantly muscular thighs practically bursting from his tight knee breeches . . .

Goodness, what was wrong with her? And now both he and Lady Jenner were staring at her and murmuring together.

About her? Surely not. A man of his vast experience and taste for wild living would never pursue her. Not according to *The Rake's Rhetorick,* that horrible book she'd found hidden in her late father's study. It dictated that "since willing widows and wives abound, the pleasure-bent rake should avoid wellborn virgins. Seducing an in-nocent brings consequences that outweigh its delights."

She was certainly a wellborn virgin, and Lord Iversley was surely bent on the sort of pleasure only the Lady Jen-ners of this world could give.

"Kit?" Sydney said as he swept her into a turn.

She jerked her gaze from Lord Iversley. Wouldn't it be wonderful if Sydney had noticed the earl staring at her and was now insanely jealous? "Yes?"

"You're attending my reading tomorrow, aren't you?"

Suppressing a sigh, she gazed up into the sweet face she knew as well as her own. "Of course. I'm looking forward to it."

He beamed at her, then returned to his usual state of distraction, probably mulling over a difficult rhyme in his latest epic poem. No, Sydney would never notice the earl's glances.

And if Sydney didn't act soon, Mama might make good on her threats. Katherine set her shoulders. Perhaps it was time to force her suitor's hand. "I only wish I could also attend your reading at the Argyle Rooms next month."

He blinked. "Why can't you?"

"We lack the funds to stay in London much longer. Unless something changes in our situation, of course." How much broader a hint could she give?

With a frown, he glanced over at Katherine's mother. "You can't touch the funds your grandfather left you? You've spoken to the solicitor?"

"He says the will is inviolable. I can't access my fortune

until I marry." Which was why Mama was driving her mad about settling her future.

"Dashed inconsiderate of your grandfather to do that to you."

Katherine thought it rather clever. Between Papa's illicit pursuits and Mama's love of lavish spending, the money would have disappeared in a matter of weeks otherwise. Unfortunately, Grandfather hadn't expected Katherine to take so long to marry. Or his son-in-law to die young and leave them in debt to half of Heath's End.

Sydney whirled her beneath the crystal chandeliers threaded with sprigs of cherry blossoms. "Perhaps I should speak to Mother about inviting you to stay at our town house."

"No, we couldn't impose." And she cringed to think of Mama striding about his town house, calculating the cost of the furnishings. A week with Mama close by would make Sydney cry off for sure. "Besides, it might look improper."

"True." That seemed to settle the problem for Sydney. "What an unusual gown you're wearing tonight."

All right, so he was changing the subject, but at least he'd noticed her carefully chosen attire. "Do you like it?"

"It's an . . . interesting color."

She swallowed. "I figured red was appropriate for Lady Jenner's annual Cherry Blossom Ball."

"Cherry blossoms are white."

"Yes, but cherries are red."

"Well, your gown is certainly red. That particular shade is very . . . er . . ."

Fetching? Provocative?

"Bold," he finished. "But then, you always do wear bold gowns."

Bold was a bad thing in Sydney terms. "You don't like it," she murmured.

"I didn't say that. In fact, I was thinking that the color would be excellent for my character Serena in *La Belle Magnifique*."

Katherine stared at him. "The *courtesan*?" Her voice rose above the music. "The one who's so flashy she embarrasses the king?"

Sydney blinked. "Oh, no . . . I don't mean that you . . . I only meant—"

"Is that why Serena's hair is red like mine?" Her hurt deepened. "Is that how you see me, as flashy and—"

"No, not you—just your gown!" He paled. "Just the color . . . I mean— Dash it all, Kit, you know what I mean. It's rather scarlet, don't you think? And with that gold sash tied about it . . . well, it draws attention. Especially when you wear it with that cannetille and enamel jewelry."

"I can't afford real gems, Sydney. Not until we marry, at any rate."

He ignored that hint. "But young unmarried ladies don't usually dress so audaciously. They wear pearls and white gowns—"

"Which, with my hair and figure, would make me look like a candle. My hair is bold, whether I like it or not. But if I have to be conspicuous for it, I might as well give people something to look at."

"You could try a turban," he offered helpfully. "I hear they're fashionable."

She drew herself up with wounded dignity. "I am not wearing a turban, I am not giving up my jewelry, and I am not going to wear unflattering gowns."

Alarm spread over Sydney's face. He loathed arguments. "Or course not. I didn't mean you should." His voice turned placating. "You know I think you're delightful. You're my muse, always inspiring me to improve my verse."

And giving him ideas for his most shameless characters. So much for hoping that her gown would make Sydney notice her as a woman. Couldn't he see she was no longer the tomboyish Kit of their childhood? He never even tried to kiss her. He talked like a suitor but behaved like a friend. Although she wanted to marry the friend, it would be nice if for once he took her in his arms and—

"Come on, you can't stay mad at me." The waltz ended, and Sydney led her from the floor with his usual elegant grace. "You know I can't do without you."

"Because I'm the muse for your poetry," she grumbled.

"Because you *are* my poetry."

The tender statement dissolved all her anger. "Oh, Sydney, that's lovely."

He brightened. "It is, isn't it? What a good line—I must write that down." He began patting his pockets. "Dash it all, I have nothing to write on. I don't suppose you have any paper in your reticule?"

Numbly, she shook her head. She'd never get Sydney to the altar, never. Mama would plague her about their debts until she had to marry some fortune hunter just to access her fortune and keep her little sisters from becoming governesses and her five-year-old brother from inheriting a dilapidated manor.

Sydney was oblivious to her dejection. "That's all right. If I can only—" He stopped walking, forcing her to stop, too. When she glanced at him in surprise, he was scowling at something beyond her. "Don't look, but the Earl of Iversley is watching us."

She fought a smile. "Is he?" It had certainly taken Sydney long enough to notice. "He's probably staring at my shameless gown."

"I never said it was shameless," he snapped. "Besides, he's staring at us both."

"He is?" When Sydney's gaze shot to her, she added hastily, "Why would the Earl of Iversley be staring at *us*?"

"He probably recognizes me—I went to Harrow with the wicked devil. He and his friends were wild and reckless sorts, didn't study or do anything useful. Iversley was the worst—he never met a rule he didn't break. And he got away with it because he was heir to an earl." Sydney's resentment shone in his face. "We used to call him Alexander the Great. I suppose he's in London to burn through whatever fortune his late father left to him."

She stole another peek at Lord Iversley. Anyone who could rouse the amiable Sydney's ire must be a wicked devil indeed.

And he was staring at her again. Goodness, that frank gaze he skimmed down her gown was quite scandalous, a thrillingly slow appraisal that sucked the breath right out of her. By the time his eyes returned to her face, she was light-headed.

Then he lifted his glass of champagne in a toasting gesture, as if the two of them shared some secret. Like "two larks who alone know the words to their song," her favorite line from Sydney's poems.

With a blush, she jerked her gaze away. She was supposed to be coaxing Sydney into offering for her, not gaping at Lord Iversley.

"That dashed blackguard." Sydney tugged on her arm. "Let's go this way before he begs an introduction to you. I don't want you anywhere near him."

No, indeed. Because if the earl could make her breathless with only a look, imagine what he'd do up close. Probably stop her heart. Clearly, the man had a thorough knowledge of the secrets divulged in *The Rake's Rhetorick.*

"Besides," Sydney added, "I need to talk to you privately about something."

Katherine's heart lifted as Sydney pulled her toward the gallery doors. *Thank you, Lord Iversley.* Her own hints might not have penetrated Sydney's usual fog, but a little jealousy was apparently working beyond her wildest dreams.

It was about time.

With a scowl, Alec watched his fetching quarry disappear with the blond baronet. Had Lady Jenner been right? Was Miss Merivale nearly engaged to the man? Byrne hadn't mentioned it.

Alec had wanted to meet the flame-haired female even before he'd learned who she was. Her gown alone distinguished her from her insipid peers. None of that virginal white for Miss Merivale, oh no. She wore scarlet in a pattern with some life to it, like the richly hued costumes Alec used to see in Portugal and Spain.

And to think she was Byrne's little heiress—how could he be so lucky? Or cursed—the squire's daughter was now alone on the gallery with that damned Sir What's-His-Name. If Alec had to choose another heiress after all this, he was *not* going to be happy. Because this one already intrigued him. None of the others did.

Setting down his champagne glass, Alec strolled out the gallery doors, then edged down the marble walkway until he could see the couple. Sliding behind a pillar, he lit a cigar and tried to hear their conversation. He didn't have to try hard.

"Admit it, Kit," the man said peevishly, "you're upset because I haven't made any . . . well . . . formal offer for your hand."

"I'm not upset," Miss Merivale answered. "I'm sure you have your reasons."

Her voice, direct and capable yet still feminine, pleased Alec as much as her self-composed words. He couldn't stand simpering, vacuous women.

"Actually, I do," her companion said defensively. "For one thing, Mother's neuralgia has been acting up again, and she—"

"Forgive me, Sydney, but your mother's neuralgia seems to come and go at her whim. If you delay offering for me until she recovers, my funeral will come before my wedding." Miss Merivale's voice dropped so low, Alec had to strain to hear it. "Your mother doesn't seem to approve of me."

"It's not you; it's your family. She thinks they're a trifle . . . well—"

"Vulgar."

Her whispered word made Alec scowl. By God, how he loathed that term. He'd heard it far too often in his childhood.

"Not vulgar, exactly," Sydney corrected her. "But Mother never approved of my father's friendship with yours. Even you must admit that the squire was a coarse and immoral fellow. Not to mention that your mother is rather—"

"Crass. Yes, I'm perfectly aware of my family's faults." The woman's voice held such wounded dignity that Alec winced. "I know what you're trying to say, and I don't blame you for deciding we shouldn't marry."

"No! That's not it at all! You know you're the only woman for me."

Alec gritted his teeth. Blast. For a moment there, he'd thought—

"I merely need time to bring Mother round," Sydney went on.

"I don't have time," the woman said regretfully. "Mama has warned me that if you don't offer in the next two weeks, she'll tell everyone I'm free and take the best offer for my hand that presents itself before we return to Cornwall."

Alec pricked up his ears.

"She can't do that!" Sydney protested.

"Of course she can't. She knows I'd never comply with such a Gothic maneuver. But until I do, life at home will be horrible. And we do need money—"

"I know." Sydney gave a heavy sigh. "All right, give me the two weeks to bring Mother round. If I can't, I'll ask your mother for your hand anyway."

Alec rolled his eyes. *Offer for the woman and be done with it, or give her up and let someone else take the field.*

"What difference will two weeks make?" the woman asked quietly.

Smart wench.

"Dash it all, Kit, what do you want from me?" Sydney's voice turned bitter. "Unless you're the one changing your mind. Perhaps you've decided you want to marry a more exciting man than a quiet poet."

"Like who, pray tell?"

"Well, there's Iversley, for one, and all his staring at you."

Alec chomped down hard on his cigar to restrain his laugh. This was priceless. He ought to feel guilty for causing the poor blighter's misery, but any man who let his mother run his life brought that misery on himself.

"Just because he stared—" she began.

"You stared back. Why, you had that devil toasting you, of all things. Right in front of everyone."

"How do you know he wasn't toasting *you*? You're his school chum."

Alec frowned. Did he know a Sydney from Harrow?

"I was never his chum—he wouldn't have toasted me. And you know it, too, or you wouldn't have blushed so furiously."

"How else should I react when a man you called 'wild and reckless' stares at me?"

Alec's eyes narrowed. Wait a minute—wasn't there a versifying twit at Harrow who'd always eyed him with contempt? Ah yes, Sydney Lovelace, heir to a baronet and a mama's boy.

"You didn't have to encourage Iversley," Lovelace grumbled.

"I doubt a wicked fellow like that needs encouragement. Don't his sort consider it their mission to debauch everything in skirts? Lord knows Papa did."

By God, the woman was frank. But at least she understood society's hypocrisies, another point in her favor.

"Honestly, Kit," Lovelace said, "sometimes you know more than any respectable young lady should about . . . well . . . things like that."

"Now we reach the heart of the matter—how much my character resembles my immoral father's," she said bitterly. "Well, you may be right. Because I want to know even more about 'things like that.'"

Alec found this conversation more fascinating by the moment.

"Good Lord, what are you saying?"

That she wants you to show her those things, you clod-pate. Then you won't have to accuse her of flirting with complete strangers.

"I'm saying I want to know how you feel about me," the woman retorted.

"But you do. You're the only woman I want to marry. Why, I'm dedicating my poem to you at the reading tomorrow. How much more do you need?"

The man was thick as a post, for God's sake. If this was the competition, Alec would be married within the week.

"I need something more than a poem from you!" Her voice turned low and pleading. "For goodness sake, I'm twenty-two, and I've still never been kissed."

"Katherine!"

Sydney's unreasonable shock made Alec shake his head. Following propriety in public was one thing, but in private—

"We're as good as engaged," Miss Merivale pressed on, "and engaged people sometimes kiss. Even the proper ones."

"Yes . . . but . . . well . . . I would never show you such a lack of respect. And surely you wouldn't want me to."

"You might be surprised," she muttered.

Alec smothered a laugh. Seized by an urge to see as well as hear this fascinating discussion, he edged out from behind the pillar. Lovelace wore a look of sheer panic, but Miss Merivale stood resolute, her cheeks fetchingly flushed and her expression imploring.

The man was either stupid, blind, or mad. What sane man could resist a woman like that? Was there another woman, perhaps? Lovelace didn't seem the philandering type.

"I swear I don't know what's come over you." Lovelace scowled. "It's Iversley, isn't it? He's got you all confused, thinking about things you . . . shouldn't. Him, with his toasting and his flirting—"

"It has nothing to do with him!" the woman snapped. "I don't even know the man. But I'll bet *he* would kiss me if I asked him to."

As soon as she said it, she clapped her hand over her mouth in horror.

Too late for that, sweetheart, Alec thought smugly. *Now you've attacked the poor man's pride. Even a cock-robin like Lovelace won't stand for it.*

Lovelace drew himself up stiffly. "If that's the sort of reckless behavior you want, then perhaps I'm not what you need in a husband. But if you want a man who sees past the superficialities of the physical, and who adores you for your cleverness and your responsible character, you know where to find me." Turning on his heel, Lovelace stalked back into the ballroom.

Leaving Miss Merivale behind and the field clear.

Alec stepped out of the shadows. "As it happens, Miss Merivale, you're right. I would definitely kiss you if you asked me to."

Chapter Three

*Sometimes a proper female's public
behavior merely hides her thirst
for passion.*
—Anonymous, *A Rake's Rhetorick*

Katherine couldn't believe her eyes. Lord Iversley? Here on the gallery? Bad enough that she'd quarreled with Sydney so awfully, but to have a witness to her humiliation . . . Bother it all, had he heard the entire conversation?

"H-How long have you been there?" she stammered.

"Long enough." The moonlight glimmered over his handsome features as he fixed her with a decidedly predatory look.

What incredible eyes he had, direct and focused and unearthly blue. Although he couldn't be more than twenty-seven, his eyes said he knew secrets about life and the world beyond her ken. About her now, too, depending on how much he'd just heard.

Mortification seized her anew. "Why were you spying on us?"

Tossing down his cigar, he crushed it under his booted foot. "I merely came out for a smoke."

"It's rude to listen to other people's conversations."

"No more rude than talking about people behind their backs. Though I didn't realize I was such a wicked rascal."

Her face flamed. This was horrible. "We didn't mean . . . that is . . . My goodness, you must think us awful."

"I didn't really mind. Especially after hearing about your plight."

His low rumble of a voice and daring smile made her shiver deliciously. "My plight?"

"Twenty-two, and never been kissed. I stand ready to oblige you. As you said I would."

A thrill coursed through her, and she stamped it out. The last thing she needed was a man like him pursuing her. Especially when his only purpose was seduction. Perhaps Sydney was right about her gown—perhaps it had given his lordship erroneous ideas about her chastity. She'd lose both Sydney and her virtue if she weren't careful.

"Thank you for the offer, my lord, but I'm not yet sunk so low that I must beg a stranger for kisses."

"I'm not exactly a stranger." He stalked toward her with a tiger's lazy grace. "In the last ten minutes, I've learned quite a lot about you."

"Like what?" Edging back, she came up squarely against the marble rail.

He stopped only inches away. "You're straightforward and practical and—"

"Wanton? Isn't that why you're here—because I asked for Sir Sydney's kiss within your hearing?"

His eyes riveted her. "I'd call it brave. And honest. You go after what you want without apology. I admire that trait in anyone, but especially in a woman."

"Oh? Why 'especially in a woman'?"

A shadow eclipsed his rakish smile. "Because women are too often taught to do as they're told without question. That's never wise for anyone."

"Strange advice, coming from a man accosting a young woman alone."

The rakish smile reappeared. "I'm not accosting you. I'm only confirming what you already claimed—that I'd kiss you if you asked me to." His gaze trailed leisurely down her throat to her breasts, then her belly, then lower. Bold and seductive, it seared her wherever it touched. "Believe me, if I'd been in Lovelace's place, you wouldn't have had to ask."

Despite the thundering of her heart in her ears, she tried to sound light and sophisticated. "I've no doubt of that, judging from what I've heard about you."

His eyes narrowed. "Oh?"

"I'm sure you know the tale. Irresponsible young lord behaves badly, is sent off to foreign shores to keep him out of trouble, where he cavorts across the Continent until his father dies and the older—but probably not any wiser—lord comes home to see what havoc he can wreak there."

Amusement glinted in his eyes. "How clever of you to reduce my life to a cliché."

"How careless of you to turn it into one."

His amusement vanished. "So you believe what's said of me?"

"Your present behavior certainly confirms it."

He advanced on her until she was staring right up at the boldly carved cheeks and two slashes of eyebrows that gave him a roguish appearance. "And here I'd thought you might give a man the benefit of a doubt. You certainly gave Lovelace quite a lot of it."

She blushed. "I know that for all his faults, Sydney cares deeply for me."

"Just not enough to kiss you when you ask."

"You don't understand—"

"Ah, but I do. He's too much a coward to stand up to his mother, so he blames you and your family for his shortcomings." He bent close to add in a whisper, "But I'm no coward, and I, too, go after what I want, Katherine."

Exactly like the great Alexander himself, who'd conquered not only Asia, but several women, too. And why did his lordship's husky voice make her own perfectly ordinary name sound as exotic as Cleopatra? "How do you know my name?"

"Aside from the fact that Lovelace used it, I asked Lady Jenner about you."

Excitement shot through her. No man had ever asked about her before. Of course, she'd hardly been in society at all, but it was still flattering.

Which was probably why he'd said it. Her eyes narrowed. "You shouldn't call me Katherine. It's not proper."

"Would you prefer Kit? I don't think that suits you nearly as well."

Oh, he was very good at this—he'd probably memorized *The Rake's Rhetorick* by the age of twelve. His compliments muddled her thoughts when rational thinking was crucial.

She forced herself to sound cool and unaffected. "I prefer 'Miss Merivale.' In fact, until we're formally introduced, you shouldn't even speak to me."

He chuckled. "Aren't you rather strict about the proprieties for an unmarried woman who only moments ago was angling for a kiss in the moonlight?"

She lifted her chin. "Sydney and I are very nearly engaged."

"And he apparently intends to keep it that way forever."

Although she'd thought the same thing, she hated hearing it from this eavesdropping wastrel. "You don't know anything about him. He's an accomplished poet, well respected for his verse, and a better man than you are, for all your lofty title."

"No doubt. But he won't kiss you. And I will." Catching hold of the gold sash tied around her waist, he tugged her closer.

Her pulse jumped in a frenzied dance. "I don't want you to kiss me," she protested feebly.

He cast her a mocking smile. "No? Then why are you still here, instead of racing off inside to join your lackluster suitor?"

No wonder he'd formed the wrong impression. Taking him off guard, she yanked her sash free, then hurried toward the gallery door.

She made it only a few steps before he caught her by the elbow. "Come now, don't leave yet. There's no one to see if you break a rule or two."

A shiver went through her as he skimmed his gloved hand down her bare arm to capture her hand. It had to be fear she felt. So why didn't she resist when he tugged her back to stand between him and the railing?

Because sometimes she grew tired of being responsible. Ever since Grandfather's death, she'd been the one overseeing the servants, dealing with merchants, and teaching her siblings.

Still, she mustn't forget the lesson her parents' behavior had taught her daily—that recklessness led to ruin. "Sydney says you're very good at breaking rules."

"He also says you shouldn't want to be kissed. But you do." He braced his hands against the marble on either side of her to trap her between his arms. "So why not take advantage of a man who wants to satisfy your desire?"

How clever of him to make it sound as if *she'd* be taking advantage of *him.* "I don't want to impose," she said sarcastically. "I'm sure you're much too busy obliging the Lady Jenners of this world to bother with the likes of me."

"At least I'm not too busy catering to my mother."

That hurt, especially since it echoed her deepest fears. She swallowed. "Sydney will kiss me when the time is right."

The earl looked unconvinced. "Let's say he finally does unbend enough to do it." His warm breath wafted over her cheeks. "Perhaps on your wedding night, if that ever comes. That doesn't mean you can't kiss me tonight . . . to form a basis for comparison in the future."

"Why should I want that?"

"So when you're settled into your very dull marriage with your very dull Sydney, you'll know exactly what you're missing."

She eyed him askance. "And I suppose you can show me what that is."

"Most assuredly."

"Tell me, do most women find your arrogance appealing?"

He cast her a rueful grin. "I've never tried it on anyone but you."

"I seriously doubt that." When his eyes darkened, she added, "I hear you've had plenty of experience with women. You don't need me to add to your store."

"Ah, but you need me to add to yours. Because if you wait for Sydney, you might wait a lifetime."

The truth of that statement struck her mute. And it kept her mute when Lord Iversley lowered his head.

To be fair, he gave her plenty of time to protest. His lips lingered a breath away from hers for a long moment. When she did nothing, he took that for consent, which she supposed it was. She was curious, after all.

But the minute their lips met, she knew why curiosity was so dangerous. Because although her mind sputtered its outrage, her body gave in like the shameless wanton Sydney probably thought her to be.

Then the earl fit his mouth snugly over hers, and Sydney became irrelevant. *He* had never smelled of smoke and secrets. *He* had certainly never made her pulse race madly, except in her dreams at night.

Now her dreams would never be the same. But how could she have guessed kissing would be so . . . so delicious, even with the wrong man? And Lord Iversley was definitely the wrong man. Too bad he kissed like heaven, his lips gliding over hers softly . . . subtly—

She jerked her mouth away. How could she have let him go so far? "Enough, sir. You've shown me what kissing is. Now let me go."

Seizing her chin between his thumb and forefinger, he turned her face up to his. "Ah, but there's more to kissing than that. So much more."

"How can that be?" she blurted out, then cursed herself for the question.

His gaze smoldered as it played over her flushed cheeks and quivering chin. By the time it rested on her mouth, the fire was rising inside her, too. "I'll show you if you like."

If there *was* more, perhaps she ought to learn it, so she wouldn't seem completely inept when Sydney finally did kiss her. "You may show me, I suppose." She added quickly, "But only for a moment."

With a chuckle, he ran his thumb sensuously over her lower lip. "Such a sweet mouth you have. Let me inside it."

Inside it? Before she could question the curious demand, he bent to kiss her again, but this time his thumb pressed down on her chin, urging it open. And then his tongue slid right into her mouth.

Ohhhh. *Inside* it. So that's what he meant. How very . . . odd.

And hot. And bold and thrilling and . . .

His tongue withdrew, only to advance again. He repeated the intimate motion until she grew too flustered to think, too dizzy to stand. Grabbing at his shoulders, she held on for dear life.

With a low groan, he pressed against her. His arm gripped her about the waist, plastering her to him from breast to thigh, igniting fires wherever his body joined hers.

Lord preserve her, she'd had no idea kissing felt so . . . wonderful. And reckless. Anything this intensely pleasurable *had* to be reckless. She should stop him, really she should.

Instead she clung more tightly to his neck, savoring every bit of his kiss. It went on and on, a feast of sensation beyond her experience. She smelled the smoke on his breath, tasted the tart sweetness of champagne on his tongue, felt the muscles in his shoulders flex beneath her fingers as his kiss grew rougher, fiercer, faster, until her head swam and her body surged against his lean, hard frame, the way she'd always imagined it would do if Sydney ever—

Sydney! Oh, Lord!

Shoving the earl away, she broke the kiss. For a moment they merely stood staring, both panting too heavily for decorum.

Somehow she found her voice. "Thank you. That was a most enlightening . . . lesson. Now if you'll excuse me—" Her heart pounding, she started to escape before she lost complete control.

But that cursed hand of his shot out once more to stay her.

She glared at him. "You must let me go in, before my mother comes looking for me." Or worse, Sydney discovered them together.

Her commanding tone only made him smile. "Must I?"

Panic swirled in her chest. "Please?"

His smile faltered. He searched her face. "Afraid to continue the lesson, sweetheart?"

The rasped endearment gave her pause. She'd assumed this was merely some whim of his, but if he meant more by it . . .

No, that was absurd. The Earl of Iversley could have any woman he wanted—he didn't need to seduce a virgin. And if he really was as wild and reckless as everyone said, he certainly wasn't ready to settle down with a wife.

"The lesson is over," she said firmly.

"Surely it's a lesson that bears repeating."

"Definitely not, Lord Iversley."

For the first time that night, anger darkened his features. "Call me Alec, not Lord Iversley. I don't want you thinking of me as anything but Alec." He tugged her closer. "Who's already eager to repeat your lesson on kissing."

"No, we can't." Shaking her head, she struggled against his hold. "I have to go . . . Alec. Please."

Something dangerous flickered in his eyes. Then it vanished, replaced by a smooth smile she didn't entirely trust. "All right. For now." He dropped her arm. "But I warn you—this isn't the last you've seen of me."

"It has to be," she protested. "I'm marrying Sydney."

"Are you?"

The words hung in the air, their very existence questioning all her plans for her future. "I am. So I suggest that you leave me alone from now on."

As she turned and fled into the ballroom, she heard him murmur in that husky rasp of his, "There's little chance of that, sweet Katherine."

Chapter Four

&

*A woman is like a locked box. If you break
in, you risk destroying her. The wise fellow
finds the key.*
—Anonymous, *A Rake's Rhetorick*

*B*uoyed by his triumph, Alec watched her march off,
her shimmering silk gown highlighting every wiggle of
her tight little behind. The sight made his blood pound
in his temples.

Now he not only wanted to wed her, but to bed her. As
soon as possible.

He wanted to taste her again, to explore that mass of
fiery hair with his hands. To lay her down and strip her
bare. Find out if her flesh was as milky and flawless beneath her exotic gown as the creamy skin of her neck and
the upper swells of her breasts. Or if the impish freckles
scattered over her pert nose showed up on the slender
belly or the undoubtedly long legs—

*Careful, man, remember the rules—don't let your urges
run away with you. You'll have her soon enough.*

Oh, yes, he'd have her. Katherine didn't realize it, but
she'd handed him the secret to capturing her. Beneath
her propriety and uncommon good sense lay a wild pas-

sion barely held in check by Lovelace's admonitions and her upbringing.

He understood too well how it was to yearn for freedom from a choking tether. Unlike Lovelace, he was willing to release her from it, to run free with her when they were alone, and that would be her undoing. Alec had trained enough horses to know you couldn't keep a wild mare tethered for long. Katherine needed to kick up her heels, and he'd be the one to release her into the pasture.

But it would be *his* pasture, only his.

Smiling smugly, he returned to the ballroom. Perhaps he would ask her to dance. That would keep the pressure on.

Feeling someone come up beside him, Alec turned to find Gavin Byrne cradling a glass of champagne and surveying the milling crowd. Alec lifted an eyebrow at his half brother. "Checking up on me?"

"I'm making sure Eleanor invited our little heiress as promised."

"Lady Jenner has been very helpful." More helpful than he liked, actually.

Byrne chuckled. "Made advances, did she?" When Alec looked surprised, Byrne added, "I have no illusions about my present mistress. She has a lusty appetite, and I don't mind if she indulges it. I'm certainly not faithful to her."

"I suppose that shouldn't surprise me," Alec said tightly.

Byrne laughed. "Your life abroad wasn't as wild and reckless as people say, was it?"

Alec slanted him a glance. "Why do you think that?"

"I looked into it." Byrne swirled the champagne in his glass. "I discovered that my little brother is more interesting than I knew. Why didn't you tell us you were the Alexander Black who can stand atop a cantering horse and shoot a hole through a plum at a hundred paces?"

With a snort, Alec jerked his gaze away. "More like a cantaloupe. The thing shrinks with every retelling. Soon they'll have me shooting at a mustard seed."

"It's still impressive."

"A trick, nothing more."

"Yes, but not a usual skill for a lord. Something you learned abroad?"

"You could say that." After Alec's uncle had seen him perfecting a riding maneuver Alec had learned from local gypsies, he'd ordered Alec to perform regularly for all his friends. Alec had readily agreed, preferring the riding to his other chores.

Until the day at nineteen when he'd learned what his uncle had told his friends—that Alec was "a gypsy's bastard," which accounted for his skill with horses and his banishment to Portugal. Of all the lies his uncle could have told, how ironic he should choose one so painfully close to the truth.

Alec had left his uncle's house that day, and Alec's "father" had cut off his allowance to force him back into the cage he'd so carefully selected. But by then Alec had grown tired of cages.

"How do you know about my riding abilities, anyway?" Alec asked.

"I spoke to the proprietor of Stephens Hotel. He says you saved his life when he was a cavalry trooper. Says he would never have escaped a Frenchman's saber if you hadn't taught him how to ride 'fancy,' as he put it."

"He exaggerates."

"I doubt it, or he wouldn't have given you free lodging.

Besides, I'd already heard of the daring Alexander Black. You're a legend in horse circles."

"You're not in horse circles."

"Who do you think funds the bets on the Derby?" Byrne quaffed some champagne. "Is it true Wellesley hired you to teach the English cavalry after he saw you train the Portuguese recruits?"

Alec shrugged. "I enjoyed the work, and I had to fend for myself."

"You could have traded on your status as a lord."

"You mean, used my title to get credit? Or to gain invitations to the chateaus of people like my father? No, thank you. I much preferred working with horses. And it paid well enough to support me."

Byrne ran his gaze over Alec. "But not well enough for fine clothes like you're wearing now, I'll wager."

A grim smile crossed his face. "You'd be amazed how easily an earl can gain credit at the best tailors when no one knows he's broke."

"I thought you didn't want to add to your debt."

"I can't woo an heiress in rags, can I?"

"True." Byrne glanced away. "Send your tailor's bills to me."

Alec stiffened. "I told you I didn't want your money."

"I can wait for repayment until you marry. If you don't take too long."

A shiver ran down Alec's spine. He'd rather be in debt to a tailor than his Machiavellian half brother. On the other hand, he didn't need more strangers dunning him. "Very well," he bit out, "I accept your generous offer."

Byrne laughed. "You really hate this, don't you?"

"Begging? Taking charity? I loathe it."

But he also hated that Edenmore's tenants lived in cottages with leaking roofs and broken windows because his "father" had fallen behind on the upkeep. And that the stables, which once held the finest bloodstock in England, now contained two old jades and a cart horse. And even that the woods on the south end had been so plundered by poachers that a lonely but enterprising boy could no longer catch a rabbit with—

No, he mustn't get sentimental. That was where Mother had gone wrong, yearning for an affection her husband couldn't give her, which had made her ripe for the prince's plucking. Alec wouldn't be so foolish. He understood the rules as his mother had not, and he would play by them for now. But when he got his estate in order, by God, he would tell society to go to hell.

"This is no more than I deserve for turning my back on my duty for so long," he added. "Which reminds me, why didn't you tell me Miss Merivale is 'nearly engaged'?"

Byrne snorted. "It was hardly worth mentioning. Society has awaited the announcement of their betrothal for years—the man can't be seriously interested."

"You might be right." Alec's gaze swung to Katherine. She must have patched things up with her poet suitor, because they were now chatting amiably with Mrs. Merivale. "He doesn't seem to want her badly enough to settle matters, and I gather he doesn't need her money."

"Hardly. He's worth at least twenty thousand a year. Though I doubt any man would object to being handed a hundred thousand pounds outright."

Alec's eyes narrowed. "Are you sure it's so much? Miss Merivale doesn't act like an heiress, and Lady Jenner said the squire left them only a small estate."

"Not even Eleanor knows that Miss Merivale will inherit a fortune from her grandfather upon her marriage."

"You'd think Mrs. Merivale would shout that from the rooftops."

"She's pinning her hopes on Lovelace. Why solicit fortune hunters when she has a rich prospect already in hand?"

Alec scowled. "So the mother is partial to Lovelace."

"Only if he comes up to snuff. Believe me, she'll welcome any presentable gentleman. Though I believe she'd prefer a wealthy one who won't need her daughter's fortune for much beyond paying the late squire's debts."

"Especially the debt owed to you."

Byrne shrugged. "It's not my fault Merivale couldn't gamble worth a damn. Or that he died before he could tap his daughter's expected fortune to repay me."

"And since Lovelace is taking his sweet time proposing, you thought to hedge your bets by bringing me in."

A small smile touched Byrne's lips. "It can't hurt to have two of you on the field. Even if you don't win her, you might prod Sir Sydney into offering. The result is the same for me—Miss Merivale gets her fortune, her grasping mother pays off the five thousand owed to me, and everybody is happy."

"In other words," Alec bit out, "you don't much care if I'm the one to win her, as long as you get your money."

Byrne casually flicked a cherry blossom off his coat. "If you don't like the competition, say the word. I'll find you another heiress."

"No," Alec said, surprising himself with the swiftness of his response. "No, I want this one. But I don't like being manipulated. You intended all along to play Lovelace and me against each other, you devious bastard."

"Devious? I'm not the one marrying for money or hiding that fact from the lovely Miss Merivale, am I?"

Alec glared at him. "Why tell her now and ruin everything?"

"Because she'll find out eventually. And when she discovers she's been tricked into giving up her beloved poet for a penniless earl whose estate lies in a shambles, there will be hell to pay."

"Not if I can help it," Alec snapped. "She'll have no cause to complain about our marriage, fortune or no." He could certainly do better by her than the old earl had by Alec's mother. "I know how to keep a woman happy."

"Thanks to all that debauchery you engaged in abroad."

Alec ignored Byrne's sarcasm. "Granted, military camps provide few opportunities for that, but I've had my share of women." The occasional camp follower, a bored officer's wife, and, briefly, a Portuguese mistress.

"Do you intend to tell Miss Merivale what you were really doing abroad?"

"And explain why an earl's heir found it necessary to fend for himself? I don't think so. She'll have to accept me on my own merits."

"That's asking a lot." Byrne cast him a taunting glance. "Especially when you have Lovelace, the consummate gentleman, to compete against. And if she's in love with him—"

"She's not." *Or she would never have kissed me with such enthusiasm.* "Scoff at my chances, but you'll see—I'll steal the filly from Lovelace before he even knows what happened. I'll loop the halter about her pretty neck so loosely she won't realize she's caught until she's stepping blithely through her paces." Alec scanned the room. "Now excuse me, but I must find someone to introduce me formally to my future wife."

Time to follow the rules—at least until he could get her alone again.

Katherine ought to be relieved. Sydney had forgiven her "outburst," as he called it, and had easily fallen back into the way things were.

A pity she couldn't do the same. But her thoughts kept straying to Lord Iversley's kiss, so surprisingly tender, then hot, then—

Oh, why couldn't she forget it? It was an interesting experience, that's all. She'd had her taste of passion, and it was enough. It had to be; she was marrying Sydney.

"Shall we visit the card room, my dear?" Sydney asked, offering her his arm like the perfect gentleman that he was.

Nothing like a certain earl who backed her against a marble rail and took liberties with his mouth and his hands and his—

Curse him. "Yes, that would be lovely."

"No, indeed," Mama interrupted. "It's kind of you, Sir Sydney, to show Katherine so much attention, but you must allow her to converse with her other admirers. It's not as if you two are betrothed, you know."

When Sydney winced, Katherine wanted to sink through the floor. Mama was about as subtle as a sledgehammer. "You know very well, Mama, that I have no other admirers."

"Nonsense," Mama persisted. "That nice Mr. Jackson asked about you earlier. And I'm told that the new Earl of Iversley was watching you, though I'm not sure which man he is. Do point him out, so I can get you introduced—"

"Mama!" Katherine protested, as Sydney flushed a dull

red. "I have no desire to meet Lord Iversley. You know what they say about him."

"I know that Lady Jenner claims his income is—"

"Sydney," Katherine broke in, "would you be a dear and fetch me some punch? All this dancing has me parched."

Flicking his gaze between her and her mother, he released her arm and gave a gentlemanly bow. "I'll be happy to fetch whatever you wish." Then to her shock, he seized her hand and brushed a kiss to it. When he straightened, his smile was tremulous. "I'll count the minutes while we're apart."

As he hurried off to the refreshments room, Katherine gaped at him. Had Sydney actually kissed her hand? Was he finally realizing how he'd neglected her?

"Very nicely done." Mama's gaze followed the baronet as he disappeared beneath an arched doorway festooned with an entire tree's worth of cherry blossoms. "Shall I assume that Sir Sydney has finally—"

"Don't assume anything, Mama. Sydney isn't . . . quite ready to discuss marriage." She added brightly, "But as soon as his mother feels better—"

"His mother, bah! Time for you to relinquish your fancy for Sir Sydney and look elsewhere. You're too old to waste any more years waiting around for him."

"Yes, any minute now I shall fall off my rocking chair and break a hip. And then where will I be?"

Mama frowned at her. "You'd best watch that clever tongue of yours, missy. Men don't like impudent women, as my father should have told you when he was filling your head with all his nonsense about books and numbers."

Katherine tipped up her chin. "Some men like a clever

woman." Lord Iversley seemed to, anyway. Not that his opinion mattered in the least.

"You mean Sir Sydney, I suppose. But he hasn't offered for you, has he? So give some other man a chance. If you can't bring Sir Sydney to the point, he won't serve your purposes."

Katherine set her shoulders. "You mean *your* purposes."

Mama shrugged. "Yours. Mine. The family's. Same thing." She dropped her voice to the supplicating purr that had never worked on Papa, but still roused Katherine's guilt. "I only want what's best for all of us, dearest. Your brother simply *must* go to Eton, and your sisters must be able to spend every season here in town until they marry—"

"*I* never did," Katherine pointed out.

"Because you have Sydney. And we had no money for more than one season."

True. And Papa had never wanted his wife and daughter to be in town while he was behaving like a bachelor.

Not that she'd minded all that much. Her quiet life in Cornwall was good enough for her . . . really, it was. And whenever she tired of supervising her sisters and remaking her gowns to save funds, she had Sydney to discuss poetry with. When he wasn't dancing attendance on his mother, that is.

He's too much a coward to stand up to his mother.

A pox on that cursed Earl of Iversley, with his criticisms and sly remarks. Not to mention his inappropriate, unwise, and—dare she admit it—*thrilling* kisses, which had cast doubt on all her hopes for a future with Sydney. Even Mama's cynicism had never managed that.

"Stand up straight, Katherine," Mama hissed. "Our

hostess is headed this way. We're lucky she invited us. All the best people come to her affairs and . . ."

As Mama droned on, Katherine cast a longing glance in the direction Sydney had gone. If he would only hurry, she might escape the spectacle of Mama licking Lady Jenner's boots . . . er . . . dancing slippers.

". . . oh, dear, but she has that fellow with her, the rough-looking one."

"Who?" Katherine followed her mother's gaze to where their hostess was approaching with Lord Iversley himself on her arm. Oh no, not *him*.

"I don't know why she's so nice to that man," Mama went on. "He's probably her lover, some ill-bred army officer. But they usually wear uniforms—"

Katherine couldn't imagine Lord Iversley in any uniform but a dressing gown, a cigar, and a brandy glass. Like in one of those prints from Papa's scandalous book, where a man entertained a woman of questionable moral fiber.

The sort of woman who would let him kiss her—twice—on a gallery.

Her heart began to pound. Surely he wouldn't be so wicked as to reveal that, would he?

"You don't have to dance with him, you know, even if he asks," Mama went on in a low voice. "Really, I can't see why Lady Jenner is bringing him over here."

"Mama—"

"Hush, now, let me handle this." She smiled brightly as Lady Jenner and the earl reached them. "Good evening, my lady. I was just saying how lovely your ball is. Especially with all your pretty cherry blossoms everywhere. I have always found cherries to be hard on the constitution, but the blossoms—"

"Thank you," Lady Jenner interrupted coolly. "I'm so glad you like it."

"I've always said that the best place for dancing is at a London ball," Mama babbled on nervously, "the best music and the best dance floor and the most accomplished ladies and gentlemen. Haven't I always told you that, dear?" Her mother didn't pause for Katherine's answer because she didn't require one. "We get plenty of chances to dance in Heath's End, mind you, but it's not the same at those country balls, where the shopkeepers and farmers mingle with people of quality." She shot Lord Iversley a mildly contemptuous look. "Though I suppose that even in London one can't always avoid company of the wrong sort."

Mama paused for breath, and Lady Jenner leaped to halt the humiliating flow of words. "Lord Iversley has begged an introduction to you and your daughter, and of course I was happy to oblige him."

"L-Lord Iversley?" Mama's gaze met the earl's amused one. "*You're* the Earl of Iversley?"

"So I've been told," he said with an odd note of irony. Executing a perfect bow, he added, "And I'm most pleased to make your acquaintance, madam."

For once, Mama had the good sense to follow proper etiquette while introductions were performed. But when Katherine rose from a deep curtsy to meet the earl's gaze, she realized she wasn't safe yet. There was no mistaking the humor glinting in those unearthly blue eyes. Oh, no. Surely he wouldn't reveal—

"It's a pleasure to meet you at last, Miss Merivale."

Relief swept through her, followed swiftly by anger that he'd given her such a fright. She flashed him an arch smile. "I've heard so much about you that I feel as if I know you already, my lord."

Lord Iversley cocked one eyebrow. "It's not all bad, I hope."

"No more than usual for a young man returned to England after traveling abroad."

"Don't you mean 'cavorting' abroad?"

Katherine winced. Why had she been foolish enough to taunt him?

Mama gave a nervous titter. "Cavorting, is it? How clever you are, my lord, with your *bon mottes*."

"*Bon mots*, Mama," Katherine corrected under her breath. Mama thought any approximation of a French word was good enough.

"No, your mother's right," the earl said smoothly. "I *am* being a clod. It's wrong of me to assume you believe the gossip about me."

Not even his clever play on the French *motte* for "clod" could banish Katherine's mortification. She'd been the clod, mentioning his reputation when he'd been perfectly civil so far. "I don't know what gossip you mean, my lord."

"Don't you?" Mischief glittered in his eyes. "But you just said—"

"I only meant that everyone was talking about you. But I . . . er . . . did not listen to any gossip. Or at least I tried not to listen."

"Ah. So you're admirable enough to mind your own business. I'm afraid I'm not. If people are so indiscreet as to speak where I can hear, I tend to listen. And tonight I've overheard a number of interesting things."

She supposed she deserved that.

With a smirk at having won his point, he added, "Ah, but I'm forgetting what I came for. I was hoping to have the honor of your hand for the next dance."

A new voice entered the fray. "Sorry, old chum, but Miss Merivale promised it to me."

Katherine turned to find Sydney standing with two glasses of punch, his resentful gaze fixed on Lord Iversley. Goodness, this got worse by the moment.

"I beg your pardon, Sir Sydney," Mama put in, "but I believe you're confused. Katherine has already danced one set with you, and I know she agreed to let you have the last before supper." Her triumphant smile grated on Katherine's nerves. "It would be most improper for you two to dance more than that—what would people think? Why, you're not even betrothed."

Sydney looked positively apoplectic, while Lord Iversley looked as if he might burst into laughter. Katherine couldn't decide whom she wanted to strangle more— Lady Jenner for bringing Lord Iversley over in the first place, Sydney for lying, or Mama for catching him in the lie.

She settled her anger on the earl. "I'm sorry, my lord, but I don't much feel like dancing at the moment."

A lady was *never* supposed to refuse a gentleman's request to dance. Surely that would send him off insulted.

No such luck. If anything, he looked even more amused. "A pity. I wanted to tell you that interesting gossip I overheard. But if you'd rather we discuss it with your mother and Sir Sydney, we can sit this dance out."

Surely he was bluffing. If he said anything about what they'd done on the gallery, it would reflect as badly on him as it did on her.

Iversley never met a rule he didn't break.

She couldn't take the chance. Besides, from the dagger glances Mama was shooting at her, she'd never hear the end of it if she turned him down. "When you put it like that, how can I resist?"

Ignoring Sydney's wounded expression and Mama's suddenly sunny smile, Katherine took the arm the earl proffered and let him lead her to the floor.

Chapter Five

∽∾⬥∽∾

Plotting to seduce a woman is like planning
a military campaign. You must outflank
her at every turn until her only choice
is surrender.
—Anonymous, *A Rake's Rhetorick*

As Alec carried Katherine off to the floor, he reveled in the resentment festering on Lovelace's face. *Too bad, "old chum." You had your chance. She's mine now.* And for one of those new waltzes, too, which was even better.

Then Katherine faced him, her lovely eyes glinting mutinously. Uh-oh, perhaps his gloating was premature.

She tossed back her pretty head. "I hadn't realized you were so desperate for female companionship you'd resort to blackmail to gain a dance partner."

"I merely asked you to dance," he said, feigning innocence.

"And I asked you to leave me be." Despite her sharp words, a blush stained her cheeks.

The music started. Deliberately, he drew her into his arms far closer than propriety allowed for the waltz. "You didn't mean it."

As she fell into step, anger turned the amber glints in her brown eyes to flames. "You are the most pompous, arrogant man I've ever met."

"Ah, but I'm dancing with you, while your poet friend can only watch."

No doubt the baronet was getting an eyeful, too. Katherine danced surprisingly well for a country girl, with a natural grace that compensated for any uncertainty about the steps. As she matched his rhythm perfectly, he wondered if she'd do the same in bed. The thought of her rising eagerly to meet his every thrust made him tighten his grip on her hand.

She flashed him an annoyed glance. "Sydney was right about you."

"Was he? What else did my old school chum tell you about me?"

"That you got away with the most outrageous behavior simply because you were an earl's son."

God rot Lovelace's self-righteousness. Not to mention his selective memory. "Has it occurred to you that your friend Sydney might have his own reasons for not telling you the entire story?"

"Do you deny that your classmates at Harrow called you Alexander the Great because you were allowed to do as you pleased?"

"How do you know it wasn't because they admired my talents?"

"Sydney says you never studied, never applied yourself, and spent all your time getting into trouble with your friends."

"While Lovelace spent all *his* time crying for his mother."

A direct hit. She paled and dropped her gaze to his cravat. "There's nothing wrong with a boy . . . missing his mother."

"Perhaps not at first. But even in his third term, your

Sydney was writing his mother weekly. And receiving packages nearly as often."

Unerringly she homed in on his resentful tone. "Didn't your mother send you packages, too?"

He gritted his teeth. "I wouldn't let her," he lied, as he'd done so often at Harrow. "No boy with a spine wants his mother to coddle him."

The truth was, the old earl wouldn't allow it. While Lovelace had feasted on marzipan and fresh apples and the occasional saffron cake from home, Alec had pretended he didn't care about such nonsense.

"Is that why you dislike Sydney?" The sudden gentleness in her voice grated. "Because he got packages from his mother, and you didn't?"

"Don't be absurd. If I dislike Lovelace at all, it's because he doesn't appreciate life's finer things."

Her bristly expression returned. "Like wine, women, and song?"

"Like *you*. You deserve better than Lovelace, and we both know it."

The startled look she shot him, followed by her softly murmured "Oh," nearly unmanned him. He smoothed his hand from her waist to the tempting curve of her silk-sheathed back. A little lower and he could cup her fetching bottom. That would certainly shock all the matrons . . . and earn him a well-deserved slap.

He sighed. Wooing a woman had been a damned sight easier in Portugal. For one thing, there was no wooing with the sort of woman he'd known. A man could go straight to the swiving and forget all this dancing and chatter.

But if he wanted a wife, he must play by the rules. No dragging Miss Merivale off to the gallery, where he could lose himself in her honeyed lips again. Ladies preferred compliments. "I like your gown."

She looked skeptical. "It's not too red?"

Why would it be too red? "Of course not. It suits the theme of the ball."

A small smile touched her lips. "Cherry blossoms are white."

"Cherries are red." He lowered his voice. "Like your lips."

An inelegant snort erupted from her. "You must have found that one on page twenty-six." When he blinked, she added, "Of some . . . er . . . book of flatteries."

"Forgive me for not being as poetic as your precious suitor," he snapped. "I didn't think you'd want to hear my honest opinion of your gown."

"You're wrong—I much prefer sincerity to flattery." Eyeing him from beneath lowered lashes, she said, "So what do you *really* think of it?"

"That it's the most erotic gown I've ever seen." He swept his hand along the sash at her waist. "I love how it clings to your breasts and your—"

"That's enough." She blushed furiously. "You mustn't say such things."

"You told me to be honest."

"But not . . . I mean . . ." Sheer desperation shone in her eyes. "I'm sure this is all great fun to you, but it's my life. I can't have you mucking it up for your own entertainment."

Anger flared in his chest. "You think I'm toying with you?"

"I know you take a perverse pleasure in taunting Sydney, but you don't understand how difficult your mischief makes things for me."

"Your jealous poet friend may have told you about my boyhood exploits, but he knows nothing of me as a man except gossip. I don't get my 'entertainment' from toying with innocents."

"Then what reason *do* you have for continually thrusting yourself into my presence?"

"The same reason any man has for pursuing a woman. Courtship."

Her burst of laughter annoyed him. "You *must* be joking."

"Absolutely not." He bent close to her ear. "Perhaps I should take you back out on the gallery and remind you how sincere I am."

With a frown, she jerked back. "About kissing, yes. But that's not the same thing. Your sort is always sincere about kissing."

His eyes narrowed. "What sort is that?"

"You know—men of the world."

"Even men of the world have to get married sometime," he said irritably.

"Yes, but not to poor squires' daughters with country manners. Especially when you possess a title as old and venerable as England itself."

"What other reason could I have for pursuing you?"

"Don't assume that because I'm a country girl I'm naive. I know very well that men like you only find amusement in the chase. But once you catch the hare, you're done. While the hare is stewing in the pot."

Her determination to think badly of him aggravated him more by the moment. He tugged her closer in the turn. "Somehow I can't see you as a hare, Katherine."

With a deft maneuver, she slipped back to restore the

distance between them. "That's because I don't intend to be one. Ever."

Blast, she had her defenses up higher than Portugal's Mount Peneda. He should never have kissed her on the gallery—it had only added to her false impression of him. But how could he have resisted such an invitation?

Unfortunately, only the truth about how he'd lived abroad would change her mind about him, and that would also rouse questions he must avoid. It might even lead to questions about his current finances. *If* she even believed any explanation he gave her about what he'd done in Portugal.

No, better to let her get to know his character—then she'd discover that her impressions were wrong. But would that be enough? "Does your cynicism have anything to do with your father and his 'mission to debauch everything in skirts'?"

She blushed crimson. "My goodness, did you hear my entire conversation with Sydney out there?"

"Enough to know that you let your father influence your opinion of men too much. Just because your only example of a man happened to be a debaucher—"

"I had ample examples of good men growing up, I assure you. My grandfather lived with us until his death six years ago, and he was fine and moral."

"Like Sydney."

"Yes. And like Sydney's father. Whenever I visited the Lovelace estate, I saw how decent, upstanding people live—who respect each other and behave with courtesy and consideration instead of—" She broke off. "I decided then that I'd never let my . . . attraction to a man tempt me into doing anything I'd regret."

"Should I be flattered that you broke your rules for me on the gallery?"

She tipped up her chin. "It was an experiment, nothing more—to remind me that my decision about Sydney was wise. But I'm done with that particular experiment. For good."

Damn. She'd already tried and convicted him without a hearing. If he didn't do something quickly, she would avoid his company in future. And then how would he convince her of his true character?

Especially when she compared him to her precious Sir Perfect Poet, with his irreproachable manners. Alec glanced over to where Lovelace stood, ignoring Mrs. Merivale's incessant chatter to glare at him.

Time to switch courses. Lovelace had asked for two weeks—plenty of time for Alec to pursue an alternate plan for securing her. "You're missing a prime opportunity, you know."

She eyed him askance. "To let you catch me and stick me in your stewpot?"

"No, to force Lovelace into a position where he *has* to offer for you."

Her hand tightened convulsively on his. "What do you mean?"

"Jealousy is a powerful emotion, sweetheart. Perhaps if your Sydney thinks he's losing you, he'll finally come up to snuff."

"Or think I'm a shameless flirt not worth marrying."

"Playing the long-suffering friend hasn't worked, has it? You're still waiting for him to make a formal offer."

That sensual lower lip of hers trembled. "He says he'll do it soon."

"In two weeks. And only because you insisted. Do you

really believe he'll forget years of catering to his mother because of some arbitrary deadline? No, he won't act unless he thinks he has to. So you must convince him that he does."

"By making him jealous."

"Exactly."

"I can only guess how you propose to do that," she retorted.

"It's simple, really—I flirt with you publicly until Lovelace's jealousy drives him to offer for you."

Her pretty eyebrows quirked up. "What do you get out of this, I wonder?"

Marriage, I hope. "You said men like me enjoy the thrill of the chase. Well . . ." He caressed her waist. "I get to chase you."

A spark of fear leaped in her eyes. Good. At least she wasn't as immune to him as she pretended.

He gave an exaggerated shrug. "But if the idea of my chasing you worries you, then it probably wouldn't work. You'd fall madly in love with me and end up with a broken heart."

"Don't flatter yourself."

"Of course, I'm taking a risk, too." Like the possibility that Lovelace would crack under the pressure and offer for her before Alec could secure her. "I might fall madly for *you,* and then you'd run off with Lovelace and break *my* heart."

She sniffed. "Right. Directly after you give all your goods to the poor and become a lowly rector in the country."

His eyes narrowed. "Since you've got my 'sort' so neatly figured out, you shouldn't have any trouble resisting me. Knowledge is the best defense."

As they moved through the steps of the waltz, she frowned. Thank God he excelled at anything that required good balance, coordination, and sense of timing. Otherwise, he would have trod on her skirts a dozen times by now while trying to read her thoughts.

"There would have to be rules," she said at last.

He suppressed a triumphant smile. "Of course."

"You can't kiss me, for one thing."

Blast it. "What enjoyment can I find in that? I said I wanted to chase you, not trail behind you like your pet pony." He swept her close. "Besides, if you're wise to my 'sort,' what can a few kisses hurt?"

"No kissing," she repeated stubbornly. "Or no deal."

He considered refusing, but then she'd simply rebuff his attempts at courtship. Besides, she might protest his kisses in a well-lit, noisy ballroom, but when he had her alone in the dark . . .

He smothered a grin. He could work around her rules. And there were more ways to entice a woman than by kissing her. She had set the bar a little higher, but he could handle the jumps. "All right." When she smiled, he added, "But I have rules of my own."

Her smile faltered. "You don't get to have rules."

"I'm doing you a favor, remember? And I just agreed to take half the fun out of it by not kissing you."

She grimaced. "So what are your rules, my lord?"

Her formality made him stiffen. "The first is that you not call me 'my lord' when we're alone."

"You don't take any of the proprieties seriously, do you?"

"Not if I can help it." To prove it, he slipped his hand up beneath the gold sash around her waist and caressed the smooth silk beneath, delighting when she blushed prettily. He loved women who blushed. There seemed so few of them left. "I'd rather you called me Alec in private."

"All right . . . Alec."

Hearing her use his Christian name made him want to drag her out into the bushes and behave exactly like the "sort" of man she thought him to be.

Too bad he was a gentleman. "The second rule is that you inform me of all your plans. If you accept an invitation to a ball, then I should know about it, so I can show up to pursue you." He dragged his thumb over her silk-sheathed ribs.

"Th-that sounds fair," she said in a breathy little whisper that turned his blood to molten heat.

He pressed his advantage. "I expect complete honesty from you—no seeing Lovelace behind my back." When she scowled, he added, "You mustn't fall into old habits. If I'm not around, you might revert to the role of patient friend, and he'll return to his former complacency. Then you'll be back where you started."

"I begin to think I shouldn't have *left* where I started," she grumbled.

"Standing on a gallery unkissed and unbetrothed?"

She glared at him.

"And one more thing—when you're with me, you can't discuss Lovelace beyond planning our next encounter with him. I want no dreamy accounts of your first meeting and no whining about how he doesn't appreciate your undying love." He added dryly, "We both know there will be no gushing about your first kiss."

Color suffused her cheeks. "First of all, I do not whine or gush. Secondly, why do you care if I talk about Sydney?"

"Because I'm supposed to get some enjoyment from

this game, remember? And I won't get it from listening to a woman prattle on about another man."

She looked insulted. "I don't prattle, either."

"Excellent, then we'll deal together nicely. *If* you agree to my terms."

"I hardly see why I should refrain from talking about Sydney—"

"No talking about Sydney. Or no deal." He glanced over to where Katherine's mother was now regaling Lovelace with some tale that had the baronet looking frantic to escape. "Ah, look at your suitor and your mother. They get on so well, don't you think? Perhaps you won't need my help after all."

As Mrs. Merivale's grating laugh sounded clear across the ballroom, Katherine groaned. "Whoever dictated that young ladies need chaperones never knew Mama. She would drive even the most determined suitor away."

He'd feel sorry for her if her mother weren't playing so well into his plans. "So?" he pressed his point. "Do you agree to my terms or not?"

She cast him a grimly determined smile. "When do we start, my lord?"

An hour later, Katherine was already having second thoughts about Alec's plan. Especially since Sydney's response to Alec's attentions was to disappear into the card room. He hadn't even seen her accept Alec's second invitation to dance. And although that reel was ending and Alec was leading her from the floor, she still saw no sign of Sydney.

"Now we've run him off entirely," she muttered, as they squeezed past a clump of chattering girls and their chaperones.

Alec shot her an enigmatic glance. "You're not giving up already, are you? No race was ever won by a rider who accepted defeat fresh out of the gate. Stay the course and give him time. He'll come round."

"And if he doesn't?"

"Then he's an idiot, and you're better off without him."

"You don't understand—Sydney isn't like other men." She scanned the room, annoyed to find that neither Sydney nor her mother was anywhere in sight. "He's liable to see my flirtation with you either as a betrayal or as evidence of my vulgarity."

"You aren't vulgar," he snapped. "Don't ever let him say you are."

The edge to his tone took her by surprise. She glanced up to see him staring grimly ahead, his jaw taut with anger.

"Why do you care?" she asked softly.

His eyes met hers, vividly blue. "My father used to call my mother that. 'You're a vulgar little Cit,' he'd say, and she would bow her head and acknowledge the insult. As if she deserved it simply because she'd once—" He broke off, jerking his gaze away. "She didn't deserve it. And neither do you."

That glimpse into Alec's past intrigued her. "I thought perhaps you and your mother didn't get along. The gossips say you didn't even return to England when she fell ill. I understand she lingered for some time."

His face grew shuttered. "There was a war on, and the family had trouble . . . reaching me. I didn't receive word of her illness until long after her death. By then, there was no point."

"I see." But she didn't really. As much as she cringed at

her mother's raucous laugh or crass musings about what everything cost, she couldn't imagine losing touch with her so entirely that months of an illness could go by without her knowing. Or not coming to the family's aid even after her mother's death.

Then again, if Alec's father had been as awful as he sounded . . . Oh, why did she care? Alec was only a means to an end.

"Speaking of mothers," Alec remarked, "perhaps yours is in the refreshments room. We should look there."

She nodded and let him lead her under the cherry blossom arch into the other room. A blossom fell onto her gloved hand that lay on his arm. It clung there until he reached over and flicked it off. Then covered her hand with his.

She suddenly found it hard to breathe.

Painfully conscious of his warm hand atop hers, she searched the room, but Mama wasn't there, either. "Knowing my mother, she deliberately disappeared when she saw the dance ending. That way you couldn't bring me to her, and you'd be forced to spend more time in my company."

"What a sacrifice," he teased. "I see that your mother and I will be fast friends."

"You say that now because you don't know her. She's always doing things like this. I have half a mind to march off in search of her by myself."

"But you won't because . . ."

"It's not proper." She sighed. "Although that's a foolish rule if I ever heard one. What harm is there in a woman's traversing a ballroom alone?"

"Nice to know I'm not the only one who doesn't take the proprieties seriously."

"I *do* take them seriously. I merely wish I didn't have to."

He bent his head to whisper, "You don't. Not with me."

A frisson of anticipation shook her to her toes. Fighting to ignore it, she cast him a stern glance. "I can well imagine which proprieties you'd like me to ignore."

"I doubt that." His hand stroked hers with an intimacy that violated every rule of propriety. "But if you want to take a stroll in the garden, I'll show you."

She firmly removed his hand from hers before he melted her resolve entirely. "I've had quite enough lessons of that sort for one night, thank you." Sweeping her gaze about the room, she nearly collapsed with relief to see Mama and Sydney enter from the card room.

"Ah, look, there they both are," she said brightly.

"You see?" Alec rumbled. "You had nothing to worry about. Lovelace didn't abandon you after all."

"Actually, he'd already asked me to dance the last with him so he could take me in to supper. And Sydney is nothing if not conscious of his obligations."

"All except one." Alec slanted her a glance. "Would it matter so much if he didn't come up to snuff? If you ask me, you don't seem to suit."

"Why, because he won't kiss me? That will change once we're married."

Alec slowed his pace. "In my experience, marriage doesn't change a man. It merely throws his bad qualities into high relief."

"Really?" she said tartly. "So you've been married, have you?"

A reluctant smile touched his lips. "No. But I watched my father, who was not very . . . affectionate. His example has stayed with me."

"As my father's has with me. Believe me, indiscriminate affection can be every bit as damaging as none at all."

"So you've decided on a man who will give you the latter."

"I've decided on a man who can be my friend. Friendship will last long after the other is gone."

"Sounds dull to me," he retorted.

Sydney and Mama had spotted them, and Mama was waving in a most unladylike manner. Katherine winced. "That's because you're the one engaging in the wild revelries, not the one dealing with the aftermath. You're not the one living amidst the jealous rages and embarrassing village gossip about Squire Merivale's latest indiscretions. It's a good thing you never did marry. At least you've spared some hapless woman such a life."

Without warning, he tugged her out of sight behind a pillar and turned her to face him, his eyes glittering. "Let's settle one thing. No matter what you've heard about me, I did not spend my time abroad lurching from woman to woman in reckless abandon."

"Then how *did* you spend it?"

A muscle ticked in his jaw. "Keeping busy, that's all. There's plenty to do abroad when a man has all the time in the world to do it."

She snorted. "Oh yes, I'm sure you enjoy touring cathedrals and museums."

For a moment, he seemed at a loss for words. Then he sighed. "Actually, I spent much of it on horseback." He shot her an enigmatic glance. "Tell me, Katherine, do you ride?"

Chapter Six

The same methods for seducing women
often work equally well for allaying the
suspicions of overprotective mamas—
flattery, gifts, and those little courtesies
ladies so love.
—Anonymous, *A Rake's Rhetorick*

The next afternoon, Katherine sat at the desk in the tiny study of their rented town house dressed in her best violet riding habit. She'd just finished writing this morning's letters to Cornwall. What an exercise in futility *that* was. The one to the butcher offering him a prize spring lamb from Merivale Manor's new birthings to pay off their debt was offset by one to the tailor authorizing a new gown for her sprouting sister Bridget. The girl's gowns had grown so indecently short that the rector had actually complained to the Merivale housekeeper, who also served as their nanny, governess, and nursemaid.

Thank goodness for old family servants, or she and Mama could never have made this trip, which was *supposed* to end with her officially betrothed to Sydney and finally in possession of her fortune. Would that ever happen?

A glance at the clock made her sigh. Half an hour until she left to go riding with Alec instead of going to Sydney's poetry reading as she should. Oh, what had possessed her to agree to that last night?

Pure annoyance, that's what. Sydney had behaved abominably to her at the ball supper. If he'd even once mentioned the reading to her while he sulked on the journey home, she would have bowed out of her agreement to ride with Alec.

But no, he'd been too angry at her for consorting with his schoolboy nemesis to say a word about when or if he'd pick her up. And Alec was no help at all, gleefully stoking Sydney's anger by flirting with Katherine.

Her cheeks warmed, and she cursed under her breath. A pox on that man for kissing her and throwing everything into a muddle. Hadn't she learned *anything* from Papa's naughty book?

Clearly, she hadn't learned enough yet to hold her own with the quick-witted earl. It would behoove her to remind herself of what he was.

Opening the bottom desk drawer, she drew Papa's wicked chapbook from its hiding place. She read the cheap-looking pamphlet merely to gain knowledge about men, of course. How else could a young lady learn all the ways a rake tempted a woman to sin? As Alec had said last night, knowledge was the best defense.

Glancing around to be sure she was alone—not that Mama would ever venture in here to do any work—she flipped open the book. Then blushed as one of the naughty pictures in the back met her gaze.

The first time she'd seen the naked figures in contorted poses, she'd briefly thought them pictures of Greek sport. After all, the Greeks *had* performed their sports naked, and the captions—things like "A Wild Ride" and "The Sideward Thrust"—had sounded vaguely athletic.

Then she'd stumbled across "The Wheelbarrow," the very print she was looking for now. A man held a woman by her ankles as she held on to a wheel. It looked sportlike enough—as if he were pushing her along, perhaps in a race, with a big stick coming out from between his legs.

But a closer look revealed it wasn't a stick. And the couple clearly had no interest in athletics.

She probably should have thrown the book away when she'd realized what the pictures were, but they'd been too fascinating to ignore. Especially when her knowledge of that area of life had been limited to what she'd gleaned from watching horses and sheep on the estate.

Now she knew more—a *lot* more. But she wondered, why use such . . . well . . . odd positions for lovemaking? Some of them looked downright painful. Like the one where the woman put her ankles on a man's shoulders— how *did* a woman get her legs up so high, anyway?

Then there was this next one . . . but wait, it made more sense today. Perhaps a man would indeed want to put his tongue down *there*. Perhaps the woman would even enjoy it. Katherine had certainly enjoyed having Alec's tongue in her own mouth last night; it had made her feel hot all over. Apparently men liked putting their tongues in certain places, and women liked having them put there.

If she were to judge from these pictures, though, tongues weren't the only things men liked to stick into women. But she wasn't entirely convinced that the woman would like having that . . . that staff stuck into her.

Especially when it was as large as this one in the picture. She turned the book to the side and peered at it. Surely this was an exaggeration . . . like the woman's breasts, which were big as cantaloupes and not at all like Katherine's own decidedly modest ones.

But if the book wasn't meant to be realistic, then why

had Papa bought it in the first place? Or was it just another of his wicked curiosities, like the opera dancer Mama had accused him of toying with out of pure mischief?

Katherine winced, remembering that particular argument, after which she'd had to explain to her sisters what a *blowsy slut* was. Mama had never been very discreet, but after Grandfather died, any discretion she'd possessed had flown right out the window. Without the influence of her father, Mama felt free to be her natural self. Which unfortunately meant that no subject was too private to air before her children.

Realizing she was still staring at the picture of the man with his tongue in a naughty place, Katherine turned the pages swiftly back to the text. At least the book wasn't *all* wicked.

Like this chapter on gifts, about how a man should soften a woman's resistance with jewels and such. She read the line on flowers: *Costly hothouse blooms never fail to make a woman's heart beat faster, since women are primarily mercenary creatures.*

With a snort, she slammed the book shut and shoved it back in the drawer. How like a man to think he must spend money to make a woman's heart beat faster. But obviously Papa had slavishly followed that bit of advice, or she wouldn't be in her present fix, having to marry as soon as possible to access her fortune so she could pay the family debts.

The sound of a carriage stopping outside made her jump. Goodness, Alec had come for her early. Now, where had she put her gloves while she was working?

Moments later, she was debating whether the purple-spotted riding gloves she'd bought in that unusual shop in Bond Street were too odd to pair with her violet riding habit, or if she should go fetch sedate ones, when raised voices drifted up to her from the parlor.

Sydney. Lord have mercy.

Snatching up the gloves, she hurried down the stairs.

"What do you mean, Katherine's going riding with Iversley?" Sydney's voice sounded from below. "She was supposed to attend my poetry reading."

Katherine couldn't hear Mama's response, but doubted it would mollify him. Lifting the overlong skirts of her riding habit, Katherine flew down the last few steps. She hastened into the cramped parlor just in time to hear Mama say that poetry was a humbug she wished her daughter would give up entirely.

While Sydney turned apoplectic at such heresy, Katherine hastily interjected, "Good afternoon, Sydney. What are you doing here?"

He whirled around. "You know very well. The reading starts in an hour."

Katherine took a steadying breath. "You said nothing about it when you brought us home last night. I wasn't even sure what time it began."

Sydney winced. "I . . . er . . . forgot to . . . um . . ."

"I assumed you'd changed your mind about having me accompany you."

With a woeful expression, Sydney turned to her mother. "Mrs. Merivale, might I speak to Katherine alone?"

"I wouldn't dream of leaving you unchaperoned." A scheming expression crossed Mama's face. "Especially when the two of you aren't even *enceinte*."

Sydney blanched at the very mention of pregnancy. "I should say not!"

Katherine barely choked back a laugh. "Mama means 'engaged.'" Poor Sydney should know by now never to listen to her mother's tortured French.

"That's what I said," Mama protested.

"No, you said we were . . . oh, never mind. It doesn't matter." And Mama wouldn't remember anyway. "But please do give us a moment."

Her mother sniffed. "Very well. But don't forget that his lordship will be arriving shortly for your ride."

"His lordship can go to perdition," Sydney muttered under his breath, as Mama flounced from the room.

Katherine sighed. Sydney's jealousy should make him more attentive, not throw him into a sulk. And what right did he have to sulk anyway? He was the one taking her for granted. She'd had enough of it.

"See here," Sydney said, as soon as her mother was gone, "I don't want you anywhere near Iversley."

The high-handed statement sparked Katherine's temper. "You should have thought of that last night when you left here without a word."

He looked chagrined. "I'll admit that was rude, but I didn't expect—"

"That I would accept another man's invitation? Or make other plans? Or assume from your behavior at supper that you were washing your hands of me?"

"What? Did that devil Iversley put such ideas in your head? I've always intended to marry you, Kit. You know that."

"You have a funny way of showing it."

"Dash it all, I know I behaved horridly to you last night, but I was put out by your flirting with Iversley."

"I was *not* flirting—"

"I know you were upset with me, and rightly so." He

tugged nervously at his cravat. "I don't even blame you for dancing with the man—I see now that you were striking back at me for not . . . well . . . showing you what you mean to me." His sullen gaze met hers. "But I figured you'd be over your fit of temper by now."

How dare he dismiss her legitimate concerns as mere feminine pique! "I was not having a fit of temper last night, but I certainly am now. And if you think I'll go anywhere with you—"

A hard rap sounded on the front door. She lifted her head proudly. "That's probably Lord Iversley, come to take me riding. So if you'll excuse me . . ."

She started to brush past him, but Sydney stepped into her path. "Please, Kit, don't be cross with me. I can't bear it."

When she met his gaze, the hurt confusion on his face dissolved all her anger. The door opened in the hall, and her mother loudly welcomed the earl, but Katherine couldn't leave her dear friend. "I'm not cross at you. I'm merely frustrated. And you know why."

"I spoke to Mother about us this morning."

"What did she say?" Her hope was tempered by a healthy dose of cynicism.

A stubborn look crossed his face. "Mother didn't understand why we're in such a hurry to settle things. Why we can't wait until she's not ill."

Katherine ignored her roiling stomach. *Stay the course,* Alec had said. Clearly he'd been right—Sydney would never defy his mother without serious prodding. "Then you must explain it to her better. Because in two weeks—"

"All right, all right," he grumbled. "But why can't you . . . well . . . spend time with me while you're waiting? Instead of with that devil Iversley?"

"I don't know why you call him a devil." She drew on a

glove with studied nonchalance. "He seems perfectly nice to me."

He grabbed her arm as if to shake her. "The man's a blackguard if ever there was one. And if you think for one moment that he's interested in marriage—"

"Good afternoon, Miss Merivale," said a steely voice from the doorway.

Glancing up to find Alec watching them, she quickly withdrew her arm from Sydney's grip. Alec scowled at Sydney before his brooding gaze settled on her, hot and intense, drying the breath in her throat. As he swept it down her, she swallowed, suddenly conscious of how worn and out-of-fashion her favorite riding habit must seem to a man of his worldly sophistication.

But judging from the admiring gleam in his eye, he found nothing wanting. "You look very pretty this afternoon. That color suits you."

"Thank you, Lord Iversley. How nice of you to say so." She shot Sydney a cold glance. "*Some* men do not approve of my choice of colors."

Sydney flushed. "Or perhaps those men are simply too engrossed in more important matters to think up pretty flatteries for you."

From behind Alec, Mama scowled first at Katherine, then at Sydney. "Important matters? I hope you're not talking about poetry. Fashion is far more important than any silly old poem."

Sydney searched Katherine's face. "You don't think so, do you, Kit?"

"Of course not. But I'm afraid that doesn't change anything." She flashed Alec a brilliant smile. "I was just telling Sir Sydney that I can't attend his poetry reading at the Freeman Assembly Rooms this afternoon."

"I shall be quite lost without you there," Sydney said, ignoring Alec entirely. "And people will think it strange that I'm dedicating a poem to the most important woman in my life, yet she hasn't bothered to attend."

"You mean your mother won't be there, either?" Katherine said sweetly. The stricken look on Sydney's face made her instantly curse her quick tongue.

"I didn't tell Mother about it," he said. "I wanted to be with you instead."

She sucked in a breath. Sydney had actually chosen her over his mother?

No, more likely he'd thought he could better bring his mother round to his way of thinking if she weren't exposed to Katherine and her vulgar family too much.

"Miss Merivale," Alec interrupted from the doorway, "if we don't leave now, the park will be too crowded for riding."

Grateful for the earl's intervention, she said to Sydney, "I must go."

"Must you?" The mute appeal on his face made pain clench in her gut. Was she being too cruel, too demanding?

Mother didn't understand why we're in such a hurry.

She stiffened. Sometimes one had to demand what one deserved. Lord knew she deserved Sydney, after all the years she'd waited for him. "I'm afraid I must."

"Shall I stop by this evening to let you know how it went?" he asked hopefully.

On impulse, she reached out and squeezed his arm. "If you wish."

Mama chirped, "I'll see you out, Sir Sydney."

Sydney hesitated, but clearly recognized that he was outnumbered. With a bow, he murmured, "Good day, Katherine." Then, sweeping wordlessly past Alec, Sydney headed off down the hall with Mama.

Alec called after him, "Good day, Lovelace. Enjoy your poetry reading."

Katherine glared at Alec. "Must you rub it in?" She drew on her other glove. "The poor man is distraught enough as it is."

"And no wonder," Alec drawled as he strolled toward her. "He has to stay inside a moldy assembly room on this brilliant spring day while we're out riding."

She chewed on her lower lip, unable to shake her guilt at wounding Sydney.

Her mother reappeared in the doorway. "Katherine loves to ride. At home, I'm always having to send somebody out to the heath to find her."

Alec gazed warmly at Katherine. "Then you won't mind if we ride at St. James's Park instead of Rotten Row. I understand it's prettier and not so busy this time of year."

"Oh, Katherine loves all sorts of parks." Mama shot her a stern look. "Tell his lordship how you like parks, my dear."

After Mama's lecture this morning about how lucky Katherine was to have the attentions of a man as lofty as the Earl of Iversley, she was in no mood to start a row. "Yes, I do like parks. St. James's will be fine."

"You see?" her mother put in, mollified. "She won't care where you ride, my lord. You take her wherever you please."

An odd smile played over Alec's lips as he swept Katherine with a smoldering look. "Certainly, madam. I shall be pleased to take your daughter . . . anywhere."

Mama went on babbling about her daughter's excellent riding and other accomplishments, but Katherine paid no attention. Why had he given a perfectly ordinary word like "take" such a wicked intonation? How did he manage to imbue every word with a naughtier meaning? And that possessive way he stared at her, as if he couldn't wait to get his hands on her again . . .

A delicious shock of excitement trilled along her nerves, and she scowled. He said and did these things to provoke her. Or seduce her.

Goodness knew he looked handsome enough to tempt any woman, especially in that azure coat that made his eyes glitter lake blue in the sunny parlor. And those buckskin riding breeches and military long boots . . . must they fit him so well, lovingly outlining every wellwrought muscle in his—

Yanking her gaze back to his face, she found him watching her with thinly veiled satisfaction. When he had the audacity to wink at her as her mother chattered on, she couldn't prevent a blush.

This was a dangerous game she played, spending time with a rascal merely to entice the man she wanted. She'd always disapproved of girls who engaged in such antics, but she couldn't deny the effectiveness. Sydney had never before been so determined to have her company.

And she'd turned him down. He'd looked so stricken, poor thing, when she'd refused to go to his reading. A hollow fear settled in her belly. Had she gone too far? Might she lose Sydney entirely if she persisted?

She just couldn't.

"Mama," she broke in, "I left my pink shawl upstairs. Would you fetch it?"

"Of course, dear heart. Can't have you catching a chill, can we?"

Alec went on alert the instant Katherine banished her mother. He'd already guessed something was up with his wily wife-to-be, but now he suspected he knew what it was. So he wasn't surprised when she faced him as soon as her mother left, and said, "Instead of riding in St. James's Park, might we ride over to—"

"No."

She gaped at him. "You don't even know what I was going to say."

"You were going to ask if we could ride over to attend Lovelace's reading. And the answer is no."

With typical forthrightness, she didn't attempt to deny it. "But we could ride in the park afterward. And the Freeman Assembly Rooms are only a mile away."

"I don't care how close they are. We're not going there."

She glared at him. "Why not?"

Because he remembered how she'd looked a few moments ago—wearing her heart on her sleeve while that ass Lovelace begged her to go with him. And because the odd disquiet surging through Alec at the sight was as unwelcome as it was unfamiliar. "You agreed to spend the afternoon with me, not him. And I mean to have my afternoon."

His leashed temper must have shown in his face, for she swallowed. "We're supposed to make Sydney jealous, and he can only get jealous if he sees us together."

"He saw us here together, and he knows we're going riding together." He flashed her a taunting smile. "I'm sure his imagination will do the rest."

The willful wench set her shoulders stubbornly. "This scheme was meant to help me snag Sydney. But if you're going to turn it into some sort of competition, then I'll end it now."

He stepped closer. She was bluffing. Nothing had changed between her and Sydney last night, or she wouldn't have chosen Alec over her inattentive suitor today. Surely she realized that if she abandoned the scheme too early, her blasted Sydney would return to his old ways.

But did he dare risk that she wasn't bluffing? When he could just as easily turn this to his advantage?

A slow smile curved up his lips. "All right, we'll go to your precious poet's reading. But if I have to endure a drafty hall and bad verse, you have to promise me some reward for it."

She eyed him suspiciously. "What sort of reward?"

With a glance toward the open doorway, he lowered his voice. "A kiss."

Her breath quickened as she dropped her gaze. "We agreed to no kissing."

"We also agreed to no discussion of Sydney, yet you expect me to spend the afternoon watching you swoon over his verse."

"I do not swoon," she said with a petulant frown.

"That will make the afternoon only marginally better. So what's it to be? A kiss in exchange for the poetry reading? Or no kiss and a pleasant afternoon's ride through St. James's Park?"

He could see her weighing her options, but he suspected she would choose the kiss. This reading was clearly important to Lovelace—she wouldn't risk alienating him, thank God.

Ever since last night, Alec had burned to touch her again, to taste her luscious mouth and feel those trembling arms clinging to his neck as her rose water scent engulfed him. Now he'd have his chance.

"Very well." Approaching him with more boldness than sense, Katherine lifted her face. "Take your cursed 'reward' and let's go."

Foolish female. If she believed she could get around him that easily, she was in for a surprise. Alec wasn't about to let her play with him and escape unscathed.

With a chuckle he clasped her chin, taking a moment to relish the fine softness of her skin. Then he ran his thumb over her lower lip with a sensuous stroke. "You'd like that, wouldn't you? I start to kiss you, you hear your mother on the stairs, and it's over before it even begins." He dropped his hand. "Not a chance, sweetheart. I'll choose when, where, and how to take my kiss."

The flash of alarm in her face settled into annoyance quick enough. "As you wish, Alexander the Great. So when will that be?"

"I'll let you know." He grinned, then bent his head until his mouth hovered so close to her ear that he could smell the rose water in her hair. "But don't worry, my demanding Miss Merivale—I promise not to bring you home without one."

She jumped back so quickly that she nearly tripped over the tea table, and the becoming blush staining her cheeks told him all he needed to know. She wanted him to kiss her, whether she'd admit it or not.

Donning her I'm-a-proper-miss-and-don't-you-forget-it expression, she turned toward the door. "Then we might as well go. If we leave now, we'll have just enough time to make it."

"Make what?" her mother demanded from the doorway, the requested pink shawl trailing from her arm.

Panic leaped instantly in Katherine's face. Her eyes cast Alec a silent appeal he was sorely tempted to ignore. But that wouldn't gain him anything.

He flashed her mother a cordial smile. "Make a . . .

er . . . present. I was just telling your daughter about the gift I had made up for you at the Soho Bazaar."

"Really?" A girlish smile lit Mrs. Merivale's features.

Actually, he'd had it made up for Katherine, but under the circumstances . . .

Reaching into his coat pocket, he drew out a painted fan. "The man was painting scenes by request, so I thought of what you said last night about enjoying London balls and . . . *voilà*." With a little flourish, he offered it to her.

"Why, Lord Iversley, how thoughtful of you." She examined the sticks with a mercenary eye. "Carved ivory, very nice. It must have cost you a pretty penny."

Thank God the woman didn't know ivory from bone.

Mrs. Merivale opened the fan, then frowned. "But the couple is dancing alone on a balcony." She peered at it. "I *think* they're dancing. I can't quite—"

"There was no time to paint more than two figures," Alec put in hastily, hoping she wouldn't notice until later that the couple was kissing. "But I'm sure every fellow who dances with you wishes he had you all to himself."

Mrs. Merivale laughed her raucous laugh and told him he was a shameless flirt, but at least no more questions ensued about their destination.

The shawl was proffered and refused by Katherine, who said she'd decided against it. Moments later they headed down the steps with a maidservant to serve as a chaperone. Fortunately, he'd used some of his meager funds to hire an extra pony. By God, this courtship business got more expensive by the hour.

"That fan wasn't intended for my mother, was it?" Katherine whispered, as they descended the stairs.

Pleased that she'd figured it out, he cast her a look of mock outrage. "Are you accusing me of lying?"

"I'm accusing you of doing whatever suits your wicked purposes." But a small smile graced her lush lips, sending a hot rush of need straight to his loins.

"You were the only one to benefit from it."

"True." Her smile broadening, she squeezed his arm. "Thank you, not only for agreeing to take me to the reading, but for hiding it from Mama."

Pure mischief seized him. "Does that mean I get *two* rewards later?"

"Absolutely not!"

"Too bad. Now I'll have to make the one be worth all my trouble."

Chapter Seven

*One act of gallantry is worth any number
of compliments.*
—Anonymous, *A Rake's Rhetorick*

Now I'll have to make the one be worth all my trouble.

The words rang in Katherine's ears as they set off for the Freeman Assembly Rooms. Lord preserve her, how would she endure an entire afternoon wondering when Alec would claim his "reward"? Wondering if he would taste the same as before, if he'd do that strange thing with his tongue, if he . . .

With a curse, Katherine slanted a glance over at him. He rode his powerful mount with an ease that proved he hadn't lied about spending a lot of time on horseback.

What an intriguing scoundrel. He sat a horse better than any member of the Jockey Club. Just look at those leather-clad hips settled so perfectly into the saddle, those muscular thighs gripping the mare's flanks and controlling the animal with mere nudges, those gloved hands effortlessly manipulating the reins.

Even his choice of breed was unusual. "What sort of horse is that?" she ventured, as they trotted down the street with Molly lagging several lengths behind.

"A Lusitano. I obtained Beleza in Portugal." He reached forward to scratch behind the horse's ear, and she nickered softly. "We've been through thick and thin together, haven't we, girl?"

"Did she cavort her way through the Continent, too?" Katherine teased.

He shot her a sidelong glance. "You seem awfully interested in my cavorting. Do you wish you could do some yourself?"

She smiled. "Not the cavorting exactly, but the traveling. I should love to see Italy and Portugal and . . . oh, all of the Continent."

He shifted his gaze back to the road, his smile fading. "There's not much to see these days, I'm afraid."

Oh, yes, the war. Which reminded her . . .

"I've been wondering what a young man can possibly do for fun abroad if he has to avoid Napoleon's armies."

"Life goes on even in wartime," he said dismissively. "People still gamble, drink . . . cavort." As they approached an intersection, he slowed his horse to a walk. "Which way?"

"Left, I think."

He glanced behind them with a frown. "Perhaps we should wait for your maid."

Katherine looked back. For goodness sake, when had Molly fallen so far behind? And why was she letting the pony rattle her teeth right out of her head when all she had to do was post through the trot?

"Are you sure your maid knows how to ride?" he asked.

"She said she did," Katherine told him, "but she's a kitchen maid, and I'm afraid they don't ride much."

He eyed her closely. "Why didn't your mother send your lady's maid?"

Too mortified to admit the real reason, she shrugged. "We left most of our servants in Cornwall."

Though he looked skeptical, he merely shifted in the saddle to gaze back at Molly. "One of us should make sure she's all right."

"I'll go," Katherine said quickly. The last thing she wanted was Molly explaining why the dire financial situation of the Merivale family necessitated a kitchen maid filling in as lady's maid.

As he reined in, Katherine wheeled her horse round and cantered back to where Molly bounced atop the pony, her face frozen in fear. Katherine pulled up beside her, noting the girl's death grip on the pommel. "Are you all right?"

The maid gave a jerky nod. When that made her horse veer to the left and she grabbed for the edge of the sidesaddle, Katherine grew alarmed. Molly clearly had no idea how to control a horse. Right now he was blindly following the other two, but once they reached the busier streets . . .

"Molly, perhaps you should—"

The blare of a tin horn cut her off. Seemingly from out of nowhere, a coach thundered down the street behind them. Seeing the two of them half-blocking the road, the coachman blared his tin horn again, this time more loudly. Spooked by the horn and possessed of a fearful rider, Molly's pony bolted.

At Molly's shriek, Katherine spurred her horse into a gallop. As the pony barreled past Alec with a screaming Molly clinging to the saddle's far edge, he set his mare after it at a run.

The coach roared past Katherine with the coachman sawing on the reins and shouting a warning to the pair ahead, but it wasn't the coach that sent Katherine's heart plummeting into her stomach. She could see the pony's reins dragging the ground, and what was worse, Molly's right leg had slipped off the sidesaddle horn. Only her death grip on the saddle's edge was preventing her falling. With the coach hot on her heels and the intersection ahead, if she fell, she would surely be crushed beneath it or another approaching carriage.

Helplessly, Katherine watched as Alec's horse gained on the pony. In sheer astonishment, she saw him shift his body until he rode almost perpendicular to his mount. He came abreast of the pony just as Molly lost her grip on the sidesaddle.

Katherine wouldn't have believed what happened next if she hadn't seen it with her own eyes. Bending nearly to the ground, Alec snatched Molly before she hit, then flipped her up—up, mind you!—across his saddle as if she were no more than a blanket.

As Katherine watched in amazement, he shifted back up into the saddle from his seemingly impossible position at a right angle to the horse. Then he laid a hand on Molly's back to steady her while he reined in. Despite the girl slung over his saddle pommel and the coach thundering past with its cursing coachman, Alec easily controlled his mount, guiding it to the side of the road as it slowed to a trot.

With Molly safe, Katherine galloped after the riderless pony. Thankfully, the little fellow was slowing of his own steam now that the pesky screaming rider had been removed. By the time she'd caught up with him, snagged his reins, and wheeled him and her own mount back around, Alec had halted his horse and was leaping off with the ease of a panther on cat feet.

As she cantered back toward him with the pony in tow, Katherine's heart drummed madly in her ears, a delayed reaction to the near tragedy of a few seconds before. Yet Alec looked perfectly calm as he reached up to lift poor Molly off Beleza. Molly fell into his arms sobbing. When Katherine rode up, he was cradling her gently and murmuring soothing words while she cried into his shirt.

A crowd had formed around them, but it parted to allow Katherine through. While she guided her horse through the throng, all around her she heard offers of help and expressions of concern for the "poor miss" who'd had "quite a fright."

"Cor, did you see that gentry cove ride?" some lad close by told his friend.

"Aye. I only seen riding like that at Astley's Amphitheatre," his friend said.

Her heart still hammering, Katherine reined in and leaped from her horse. As she approached, Alec was setting Molly on her feet. When the poor maid continued to sob, he dug a handkerchief out of his pocket for her.

Katherine tried to imagine Sydney offering a kitchen maid his handkerchief. For all his gallantry to Katherine and his poetry about lords finding love with lowly shepherdesses and milkmaids, Sydney was a pure aristocrat at heart.

Whereas Alec seemed to be one only in name. How many aristocrats rode like *that*? If Alec hadn't acted so swiftly—and had the riding skills to manage it—Katherine shuddered to think what might have happened.

A member of the Foot Patrol pushed through the crowd to speak to Alec, and Katherine hastened to Molly's side.

"Oh, miss," Molly gasped between sniffles, "I'm so sorry I ruined your outing. I swear I didn't mean—"

"Hush now." Katherine looped her arm about the girl's trembling shoulders. "No more of that, dear. We're just glad you're unharmed."

"I nearly fell off that pony!" Molly's eyes were round as carriage wheels. "I might've been kilt if not for his lordship..."

When she trailed off with a worshipful look at Alec, who was still speaking to the officer, Katherine bit back a smile. Alec conquered hearts wherever he went, didn't he? No doubt poor Molly would relive the daring rescue for days to come. As would Katherine. She couldn't believe how close the girl had come to death.

The officer began to disperse the crowd, and Katherine squeezed the maid's shoulders. "Molly, why did you tell Mama you could ride?"

Dropping her gaze to the ground, Molly twisted the handkerchief about in her shaky fingers. "Somebody had to go with you, miss, and your mother's maid couldn't be spared and ... well ... she said it didn't matter if I could ride." With a glance over to where Alec seemed absorbed in tending his horse, she lowered her voice. "Mrs. Merivale said to come home once I lost sight of you, so you and his lordship could be alone. She said something was bound to happen and then he'd have to make you his countess."

Color flamed in Katherine's face. Nor did it help when she saw Alec go still, apparently having heard every word. But when his shoulders began to shake with laughter, she scowled at his back. Eavesdropping rogue.

She would deal with Mama and her tactics later. "We'd better get you home now," she told the maid.

"I'll take her back." Alec turned toward them. "She shouldn't go alone, and I know you don't want to miss the reading."

"We'll all go," Katherine said firmly.

"Please, miss, don't you do nothing like that!" Molly cried. "Your mother'll have my hide if she knows I ruined your outing with his lordship."

The officer walked up, having cleared the street of curious onlookers. "I can see the young miss home, if you like."

Katherine hesitated, but she didn't want Molly to get into trouble—unfairly or not, Mama *would* blame everything on her. Flashing the man a smile, she said, "We'd be most grateful."

She fished in her reticule for a coin, but Alec was already taking care of it. He even arranged for a passing hackney to carry Molly and the officer back. Within minutes, they were headed off with the pony tied to the back of the carriage.

Alec faced her, his eyes dark with concern. "Are you all right?"

"I'm fine," she said, managing a game smile.

"Do you still want to attend the reading? We'd be late, but if we go now, we should arrive in time for most of it. That is, if you're not too shaken."

"To be honest, I could use something to calm me, and the reading would be perfect since it's a less ... er ... adventurous sort of entertainment."

With a laugh, he strode over to retrieve his fallen hat, which had been trampled beneath the crowd's feet. He examined the flattened disc ruefully.

"Looks like you'll have to go without your poor hat," she said.

"Not a chance." He balanced it atop his head. "This and my mud-spattered breeches might convince them to ban me from the reading."

"Don't count on it. I doubt anyone there would even notice."

"Right, I forgot." Eyes twinkling, he tossed the ruined hat aside. "Poets consider poetry more important than fashion."

"I don't know how you can joke after what just happened," she said, as he strode back to her side. "My heart is still pounding."

He helped her mount. "If I'd realized that was all I had to do to make your heart pound, I would have arranged a whole day of horseback rescues."

"You could probably do it, too," she retorted, as he mounted his own horse, and they started off. This time, as if by mutual consent, they took it slower, walking the horses along the busy street instead of trotting. "You were amazing. I've never seen anyone ride so magnificently. And the way you caught her before she fell! Where on earth did you learn such a thing?"

Alec had to stifle his groan. The last thing he needed was Katherine probing into his past. "It was nothing. Something I picked up abroad."

"That's quite a something," she persisted. "When you said you spent your time in the saddle, I never dreamed—"

"You're not so bad a rider yourself." He had to distract her from *his* riding. Besides, she did ride well, even in that silly sidesaddle Englishwomen had to use. "You caught that pony in no time."

She blushed at his praise. "It was nothing, really. Anybody can catch a riderless pony. Whereas you—"

"—are grateful you made the effort." He had to get her off this subject. "I wouldn't have wanted to lose her." Especially since it would have cost him dearly.

They'd reached the intersection, and as he watched her guide her mount expertly through it, he imagined her riding across the Cornish heath, her flaming hair unfurling behind her, her firm little behind shifting in the saddle as she adjusted to the horse's motions. The same way she would adjust to Alec's motions when he had her beneath him in bed—

He stamped out that tempting image. Riding a horse with an erection was damned uncomfortable.

As soon as they'd maneuvered through the intersection, she asked, "I take it you had lots of time to ride abroad?"

Good God, were they back to that? It served him right for letting his imagination wander. "I rode quite a bit. But apparently you did, too, out there in the country. Or so your mother said."

Flushing, she ducked her head. "I am *so* sorry about Mama and her tactics. I had no idea she would do something so irresponsible in order to . . . well . . ."

"Get us alone?" Alec eagerly seized on the change of subject. "That's not the only reason she sent Molly, is it? Tell the truth—your family didn't leave all the servants in Cornwall, did they?" The best way to deflect unwanted questions was to ask your own.

She shifted her gaze to the road ahead. "It's just that . . . I mean . . ." She sighed. "I suppose you might as well know. Papa's death left us a bit pinched for funds. But that will change soon."

How far might this sudden honesty of hers extend? "You mean, when you marry your dull poet?"

"How did you . . . that is, what—"

"I understand that Sir Sydney is quite wealthy."

"Oh. Yes, he is." Then irritation flared in her face. "But that's not why I'm marrying him."

"Of course not, Miss Marry-well," he teased.

"Very funny," she snapped. "But I don't care about his money, because I—"

When she stopped short, he stared at her. Would she actually tell him of her inheritance? He probably shouldn't let her. If she admitted to expecting a fortune, his one advantage would be gone. "It's all right—I know you're not the mercenary sort."

She looked relieved. "Certainly not."

"So why *are* you marrying Sydney? Because he's one of those 'decent' men you so admire?"

"Not only that. We've been friends all our lives. And I care for him a great deal."

"But you're not in love with him."

Shifting her gaze to the road ahead, she stammered, "W-Well, I . . . yes, I suppose I love him. Of course I love him."

He seized on her discomfort. "You don't sound too certain."

A sigh escaped her lips. "To be honest, I don't know if I believe in love."

"Really? That surprises me."

"Why, because I'm a woman?" she said defensively.

"Because you enjoy romantic nonsense like poetry."

She shrugged. "Good poetry soothes me and takes my mind off my troubles. But I'm not foolish enough to think that life is like a poem."

"Good for you." Relief coursed through him. Matters would go much easier for him if she already understood and accepted life's realities. "All women should go into marriage with your attitude, realizing that it's an alliance made for practical reasons and not the romantic dream the poets make of it."

She eyed him thoughtfully. "I'd like to think it's some-where in the middle—not a dream, but not some practi-cal 'alliance' either. I should hope one would have a genuine liking for one's partner."

"And physical attraction, too." He shot her a searching glance. "Or doesn't that fit into your scheme?"

She averted her gaze. "Physical attraction can lead one astray. My mother married my father because of it. Her parents wanted her to marry Sydney's wealthy father, but she eloped with his scapegrace best friend instead. Which turned out to be disastrous." Her hands tightened on her reins. "A sensible woman should rely only on her . . . ra-tional parts when choosing a husband."

Certainly a sensible woman should marry for more than the prestige of a title, which was all Alec could offer. Good thing she didn't know that. "So Sydney's money and re-spectable position are enough for you, Miss Marry-well."

"Stop calling me that." A tiny frown knit her freckled brow. "I told you, Sydney and I are friends. He'll make me a good companion. I understand him, and he under-stands me."

"Does he? Is that why you had to ask him to kiss you? Why he sat and sulked last night while another man flirted with you?"

She glared at him. "I thought you didn't want to talk about Sydney when you and I were together."

True. But the way she held him in such high esteem needled Alec. He couldn't figure out why. It certainly wasn't jealousy. So why did he bring up the subject at every turn, like a child picking at a scab until it bled?

Her eyes narrowed. "I don't want to talk about Sydney, anyway. I want to talk about you. How did you learn to ride so magnificently?"

By God, she was like a dog with a bone. Wondering how to put her off, he jerked his gaze back to the road. Then he spotted a sign swinging on a building up ahead and relaxed.

"Discussion of my riding will have to wait, sweetheart." He gestured to the sign that read FREEMAN ASSEMBLY ROOMS. "We're here."

Chapter Eight

*Pave the way for your seduction with
illicit touches.*
—Anonymous, *A Rake's Rhetorick*

Katherine followed Alec's gaze. They had indeed arrived.

But how strange that he would not discuss his riding. Most men loved to boast of their superior skills. By now, they would have thrice retold the story of how they'd rescued the fair damsel.

Either Alec was inordinately modest . . . or he was hiding something. But what? And why? He was amazingly reticent about his years abroad—surely that wasn't typical of world travelers.

Unless, of course, most of his time abroad had been spent doing things no decent Englishwoman should know about. She colored. That was probably it.

Alec leaped easily from his mare and tied it off before helping her dismount. But when her feet touched the ground, and he didn't immediately release her, all her curiosity about his years abroad vanished. His warm hands on her waist stopped her breath in her throat, especially when he then fixed his gaze on her mouth with dark intent.

Lord preserve her. Did he mean to claim his kiss here, in the street?

She held her breath. Then his hands dropped away, and he offered her his arm. She took it, her heart thundering in her ears. She was glad he hadn't kissed her—yes, glad. What wanton would allow a man to kiss her in public? And someone might see and tell Sydney, incensing him enough to break with her. No, it wouldn't have been wise.

As they entered, a smartly dressed young woman thrust programs at them that read "A Gathering of New Poets" and directed them to a large room adjoining the foyer. When they slipped inside and every eye turned their way, Katherine smiled weakly. Alec ignored them as he led her along the back of the crowded room, his hand resting intimately on the small of her back.

At least Sydney hadn't looked up to see them enter so rudely. He was reading over his poems, oblivious to the voice that droned from the podium.

As soon as they settled into the back row, the only one still empty, Alec bent his head to whisper, "Do these things usually draw so many people?"

"If Sydney is reading, they do." She added with a little burst of pride, "*Gentleman's Magazine* recently lauded him as 'the new Wordsworth,' you know."

"I must have missed that astounding news."

A bookish young man in front of them turned around to glare at Alec. With a roll of his eyes, Alec leaned back against the hard bench and removed his riding gloves. Then he busied himself with looking through the program, shifting position on the uncomfortable oak every few seconds.

She bit back a smile. Poor man, he would never make it

through the whole reading. This must be awfully dull for a man of action. She expected to find most of it dull herself. The other poets paled next to Sydney, and he'd only agreed to participate because one of them was his closest friend. In fact, Julian Wainscot, the Baron Napier, sat next to Sydney looking unusually cheery. Generally he was a peevish sort, at least whenever she was around. But now he seemed to bask in the glow of the audience's attention.

Then the slender fellow caught sight of her, and his face fell. She smiled at him anyway, but Alec leaned over to complain that her "precious Sydney" was last on the program, and she was forced to answer.

When she returned her gaze to Lord Napier, he was nudging Sydney. As Sydney spotted her, a sunny smile broke over his face . . . until he saw who was with her. Though she smiled back, his pleasure rapidly turned into a sullen frown.

Meanwhile, Lord Napier looked smug. Curse that wretch. He probably agreed with Lady Lovelace that Katherine wasn't good enough for his best friend. Too bad. No matter what Lord Napier or Lady Lovelace thought of her, she meant to marry Sydney.

Alec's rumbling voice broke through her thoughts. "A gathering of poets," he murmured as he brandished the program before her. "Is that like a herd of horses? Or better yet, a gaggle of geese?"

"Shh," Katherine whispered.

The doe-eyed Lord Napier was coming to the podium, and she wanted to hear him. With a self-important air, he cleared his throat. "The title of my poem is 'The Discus Match.' "

As he began to read, she bit the inside of her cheek to keep from smiling. All this gushing over an athletic event—how silly. But what else could one expect from a man who oiled his whiskers and dithered over the starch in his cravats? He ought to learn from Sydney, who wrote about important things like love and history and tragedy. But Lord Napier had never been deep.

He intoned:

His sinewed arm draws back to throw.
The discus gleams, a moon on high,
And when it flies forth to slice the air,
The crowd doth give a matchless sigh.

From beside her, Alec asked, "Exactly what constitutes a matchless sigh? How quickly the breath leaves the lips? How loud it sounds? Or is it a certain musical quality in the exhalation—"

"Hush," she whispered, struggling not to smile. "People are staring."

Actually, no one was staring but Sydney. Chastened by his frown, she sat up straight and tried to look impressed. Thankfully, Lord Napier's poem was as brief as his mind was frivolous. Even better, Alec stayed quiet through the rest of it and the next two poems.

Then the worst poet of the lot took the podium. In a quavering voice that Katherine knew was meant to signify deep emotion, he launched into a poem so gushingly awful that even Sydney winced.

Alec bent close to whisper, "Didn't 'thee' and 'thine' go out of fashion with the Renaissance?"

"You forget that poets pay no attention to fashion," she whispered back. When Alec's eyes gleamed at her, she regretted encouraging his nonsense. Forcing her gaze back to the stage, she added, "But he's really not so bad."

Alec snorted, but at least he said nothing more. Until the fifteenth verse, when the poet read:

Thou lovely temptress, beautiful and wise,
Thou turneth my reluctance into ashes
I gaze into the embers of your eyes . . .

"And pray they don't ignite your pretty lashes," Alec finished under his breath.

She couldn't help it—she laughed. Out loud, drawing every eye her way. With a blush, she shrank into her seat and hissed at Alec, "Do be quiet, for goodness sake."

But it was too late to close that Pandora's box. Now that he'd discovered how much his witticisms amused her, Alec lobbed them at her with appalling regularity. Soon she was weak from holding back her laughter, sure that she would perish of repressed hilarity.

"Remind me never to let that man near my horse," Alec whispered as a particularly dreadful poet finished. "If he orders 'my noble steed' Beleza to 'peregrinate along the Elysian plain' with her 'fortuitous fetlocks shimmering' and her 'mane aglow,' she might just trample him underfoot. She hates it when her mane glows and her fetlocks shimmer—all the other horses poke fun. And exactly what pace *is* 'peregrinate'? Something between a trot and a canter, I suppose—"

"Stop it, I beg you," she hissed, futilely trying to restrain her giggles. "When this is over, I'm going to kill you."

Alec shot her a devilish grin. "Would that be with the 'trenchant sword of Damocles' or the 'impenitent smoke of Vesuvius's wrath'?"

"The linen handkerchief of Merivale. I shall strangle

you with it." She glanced at the dais. "Now hush—they're introducing Sydney. Try not to be rude when he reads, will you?"

"Me, rude?" Alec retorted. "What's 'rude' is the arrant nonsense these idiots call poetry. And if your Sydney—"

She reached over and pinched his bare hand as hard as she could.

"Ow!" He scowled at her.

"Don't say another word, or I swear I'll turn your hand black-and-blue before this is over."

When she started to draw her hand back, he caught it in his. "I'll be quiet . . . but only if you let me hold on to this." His gaze hot on her, he enfolded her gloved hand in his large naked one, then drew it to rest scandalously on his thigh. His well-hewn, buckskin-clad, and exceedingly warm thigh.

Her breath caught somewhere in the vicinity of her lungs. Lord preserve her . . . he should not . . . she should not . . .

She cast a furtive glance around, but no one paid attention to them. Since they were alone in their row, their hands were hidden from anyone's view. The very idea stopped her heart.

Private. Secret. Forbidden. Why must that hold such an allure? Guiltily, she glanced to the podium, where Sydney was arranging his sheets of paper.

Never mind. She didn't want anything to ruin Sydney's presentation, and if that meant letting Alec hold her hand, she would sacrifice. It had nothing to do with this cursed fluttering in her chest. Or the breathless anticipation of wondering what Alec would do with her hand.

Sydney cleared his throat at the podium, and only then did she realize she'd been watching Alec's hand, caught up in the wildly exciting sensation of having her flesh sandwiched between the hard muscle of his thigh and his heated fingers. She forced herself to turn her attention to Sydney, to smile at him, to *pay attention*.

Sydney was to read two poems, one about the Fall of Troy and one listed only as "title to be announced." He began the Troy poem by explaining which version of the tale he'd relied on.

That's when Alec's hand moved on hers. At first he contented himself with skimming his bare thumb along the contours of her gloved one, but that didn't satisfy him for long. Shifting their joined hands so that hers lay atop his, he began to drag her glove off with his other hand.

"No!" she hissed under her breath.

"Yes." He smiled, the way Boney must have smiled when he chose the first prime bit of Prussia to conquer.

She tried to jerk her hand free, but he held on to it.

When she glared at him, he added in a whisper, "It's only fair, sweetheart. You took away my other source of entertainment." He tipped his head toward the dais. "Of course, if you want me to return to commenting on the verse . . ."

Gritting her teeth, she let her hand go limp in his.

"That's better," he murmured, then reached for her glove once more. He stripped it off each finger inch by inch, the way Alexander the Great himself had probably stripped the female captives he'd made his wives.

Heat rose in her cheeks as she stared at the dais, vainly trying to absorb Sydney's words. Unfortunately, Sydney had read this poem to her before, so her mind readily drifted to the thrill of Alec baring her hand.

He tossed her limp glove into her lap. Then began the real distraction. Turning her hand up so that the back rested on his thigh and the soft palm lay exposed to him, Alec traced her fingers.

She swallowed hard. No man had ever touched her like this. Who could have guessed it would be so . . . so . . .

Erotic. This seemed every bit as naughty as the pictures in Papa's book; especially since it was actually happening to her.

She could hardly breathe as he burrowed lightly in the crevices between her fingers, drew circles in her palm, then dragged his thumbnail up until he reached the pulse beating frantically in her inner wrist. Pressing his thumb against it as if to relish the throbbing of her blood, he stretched his other fingers wide over her open hand to multiply his caresses fourfold.

Lord preserve her, she might just faint. No, that was silly—what ninny would faint simply because a man stroked her hand . . . caressed her flesh . . . made love to each of her bare fingers . . .

"Did Helen grow to hate Paris's touch / As she observed the smoking ruin?" Sydney read from the podium.

Not for one minute, she answered. Not if Paris's touch had been anything like Alec's.

Katherine wanted to hate it. She wanted to hate him for doing it. But how could she? It wasn't all that improper. And *The Rake's Rhetorick* had never mentioned hand fondling as a tactic for seduction—though clearly it was.

Each sweep of his fingers was a whisper, each press of his thumb an endearment that inflamed her senses. She might actually burn a hole in the bench before the reading was over.

The longer it went on, the more she ached to explore *him*. Casting him a furtive glance, she stilled his hand, then began her own discovery.

His gaze locked with hers. If there'd been even a trace of arrogance on his face, she would have tossed his hand aside. But his eyes shone with need and heat as her fingers moved tentatively over his rough masculine flesh.

He sucked in a harsh breath as her touch grew bolder. His hands were certainly not those of a gentleman. His skin bore hard calluses, and a scar split the knuckle of his thumb. When she stroked the raised ridge with her forefinger, Alec curled his fingers into hers, stroking, seeking.

By the time Sydney finished his Troy poem, her blood was thrumming wildly. She'd never been so aware of a man as a *man* in all her life. What would it be like to have Alec's strong hands on her shoulders, her ribs, her breasts—

The applause began, and the blood flamed in her cheeks. Quickly, she tugged her hand free of Alec's so she could clap.

And break his spell, before he turned her completely into mush. Because if she wasn't careful, she'd soon be begging for his kiss—and that would not do at all.

Chapter Nine

Women are particularly susceptible to romantic verse. Never underestimate the power of a flowery sonnet.

—Anonymous, *A Rake's Rhetorick*

*A*lec hated releasing her hand. The exquisite play of fingers had only whetted his desire. It had taken every ounce of his will not to flatten her hand on his inner thigh, then drag it to the embarrassing fullness growing in his trousers. He'd never been so aroused by something so innocent in his life.

By God, the woman would drive him mad before he got her to the altar. She had the curiosity of an innocent, but the passionate impulses of an experienced woman. If she were like this here, imagine what she'd be like in bed. He hardened instantly at the thought.

As soon as the applause ended, he recaptured her hand, intending to renew their reckless intimacies. Then Lovelace's voice forced its way into his awareness.

"This next poem is dedicated to the most important woman in my life," the man said.

Alec glanced to the podium, scowling when he saw Lovelace's gaze fix on Katherine.

"The title is 'The Muse,' " the poet added.

Alec rolled his eyes. If that idiot thought Katherine would fall for such a blatant ploy . . .

Then her fingers slipped from his. Alec shifted his gaze to her, wincing to see the mixture of pleasure and guilt on her face. With grim determination, he grabbed for her hand, but she held it back.

"Please, Alec . . ." she whispered.

God rot Sydney Lovelace. So the poet knew the way to her affections after all. She might respond to Alec's caresses, but that blasted baronet all too easily made her feel guilty for it.

He relented and released Katherine's hand, relishing the audible sigh that escaped her lips as she hastily dragged her glove back on.

But he felt bereft without her fingers entwined with his. Nor did the sound of Sydney's voice, sure and strong, make him feel any better.

Sydney read with quiet authority:

When all my visions creep away
When verse eludes my fevered brain.
I seek my comfort in her voice,
That cadence is my cure for pain.

God rot Sydney Lovelace. It was simple, elegant, and most importantly, not silly. Instead—

She's my poetry, my song
My sighs of woe she turns to grace
And in her smiles I find my will,
For hope lies in her lovely face.

Why must the man be a halfway-decent poet? Even Alec, who only enjoyed the kind of verse sung by drunk cavalrymen in taverns, could tell that Sydney's talent exceeded that of most amateurs.

Annoyed, Alec glanced over to find that hope did indeed lie in "her lovely face." She hoped that Sydney, not Alec, might care for her, might marry her . . . might love her. As Alec watched, a tear rolled unheeded down her cheek.

Jealousy struck him then, so powerfully he could no longer deny it. Finally, Alec understood what she saw in Lovelace. The man's facility with words drew her as surely as an army officer's masculine skill with a sword drew other women. She might let Alec caress her hand, but it was Lovelace she listened to and Lovelace she admired. God rot the man, it was Lovelace she wanted.

Lovelace finished the poem, and for a second silence hung in the air, rich with the wonder of a crowd enraptured. Then enthusiastic applause broke over them. Several leaped to their feet—Katherine among them—and as Alec rose grudgingly beside her, he watched Lovelace's reaction to the thundering applause, hoping for an arrogant glance to tarnish the man's character.

All he got was Lovelace's hesitant smile, as if he were pleasantly surprised by the effect of his words on his listeners. Scanning the crowd until he found Katherine, Lovelace beamed at her like a boy basking in the approval of his tutor.

That's when it hit Alec.

The poem's title was "The Muse," not "The Lover" or even "The Betrothed." Sydney wanted someone who would inspire his creations and praise his talent, someone who "understood the delicate dance/Between the pen and the poet's trance," as one of his lines read.

Alec's mood lightened. Lovelace didn't want the

warm-blooded Katherine who yearned to be kissed and touched and desired. He wanted to keep her frozen on his pedestal, and that could never suit her.

She's my poetry, my song.

Ruthlessly, Alec thrust the blasted line from his head. She would *not* be Lovelace's "poetry." She wanted something better than that—excitement and passion, as well as companionship. And only Alec could give *that* to her, thank God.

The applause faded into chatter now that the reading was over. Ladies gathered their shawls and reticules, and men stuffed their programs into coat pockets. A few people converged on the dais to speak to the poets milling there.

Katherine rose without looking at him. "I'll be right back. I want to congratulate Sydney. It won't take me long." She hurried to the end of the row. But instead of going to the front, she swept through the doors bordering the auditorium, clearly headed for wherever the poets congregated after the reading.

Alec stood there flummoxed. Should he let her have her few minutes alone with Lovelace?

She's my poetry, my song.

Alec's eyes narrowed. Not a chance.

Stuffing his gloves in his coat pocket, he pushed through the crowds until he emerged into the less choked hall adjoining the other assembly rooms. Within moments, he spotted her. Since she moved against the flow, she hadn't gone far in her steady press toward the upper end of the hall. Toward Sydney, blast her.

"Miss Merivale, wait!" he called out.

By some miracle, she heard him and halted. As he approached, color rose in her cheeks, but at least she didn't run. She even waited for him, eyes flashing.

"What is it, Lord Iversley?" she asked primly, as he reached her.

Only then did he realize he'd come after her with no plan whatsoever. A thousand comments rose to his lips. *Sydney is an ass . . . You deserve better . . . I want you, and he only admires you.*

But he wasn't skilled at pretty words like her poet suitor. His skills lay elsewhere. He glanced over at the open doorways leading to empty assembly rooms. "This way," he said, taking her arm and tugging her across the now-thinning flow of traffic into the nearest room.

Thank God she went willingly. But as soon as he closed the door, she set her shoulders. "What do you want? I told you I'd only be a moment."

"I've held up my end of the bargain. Now you owe me my reward."

As awareness dawned, she swallowed visibly. "Why here? Why now?"

Because I want to banish Sydney from your thoughts. "Why *not* here and now?" he countered, striding up to haul her into his arms.

She shot him her best imploring look. "Please, Alec—"

"No," he snapped. "I've heeded your 'please, Alec' too many times already today. So before you trot off to Sydney, I'm getting what I came for." Giving her no more time to protest, he kissed her.

He'd expected some resistance, but what she did was worse. She stood still, not fighting him but not responding, either. It was like kissing a statue.

Temper flaring, he jerked back to glower at her. "Kiss me back, blast you."

Her expression was eerily composed after the heated confusion she'd shown when their hands were caressing.

"You didn't mention anything about my having to kiss you back. You wanted a kiss, that's all. And now you've had it."

"I said a reward. And this is no reward."

Though her blush acknowledged the truth of that, she wriggled free of his hold and headed for the door. "It's all the reward you're getting from me."

He reached her just as she laid her hand on the doorknob. Catching her by the arm, he dragged her as far from the door's inset window as the small room allowed. Then he lifted her onto a nearby table, ignoring her shriek of protest as he trapped her between the hands he braced against its surface.

"I let you talk me into sitting through two hours of damned awful poetry, so by God, you'll give me my rightful reward if I have to keep you here all day."

Challenge shone in her face. "Kiss me again if you wish, but I can't help my response. I don't feel that way about you."

"The hell you don't," he bit out, then grabbed her by the shoulders and covered her mouth once more with his.

The anger that rode him made him kiss her too hard, too fiercely, so this time she did fight him, fisting her hands against his chest and nipping his lip like some wild thing.

As her resistance registered in the midst of his anger, he fought to bring his volatile emotions under control. He forced himself to be more gentle, to kiss her with the consideration she deserved. She wasn't going to accuse him later of assaulting her when he had merely wanted her to fulfill her promise.

He rubbed his lips over hers, measuring their softness. He tugged playfully at her lower lip with his teeth. And the longer he worshiped her mouth with his, relishing the tender lips and drinking in her hot little breaths, the more she yielded, until soon she was kissing him back.

Only then did he deepen the kiss. Exulting in her response, he delved over and over into the sweet heat of her silken mouth. She flattened her hands on his chest, then clung to him, her fingers grabbing fistfuls of coat as she strained higher against his mouth.

By God, she was soft everywhere—not just her lips, but her hands and her waist and her hips . . . He would never get enough of this heady enjoyment, never be able to drink his fill of her delicious mouth.

Only when she stiffened and tore her lips from his did he realize he was cupping her breast. Her achingly soft breast. The one he wanted to take in his mouth and suck—

"Touching me isn't . . . part of your reward," she gasped.

But she didn't push his hand away or slap him, which told him plenty. "I know." He branded her neck with kisses, his hand still kneading her breast.

"You shouldn't . . . do it."

"Why not? Because you don't feel 'that way' about me?" he growled against her ear. He rubbed his thumb over the tip of her breast, fiercely pleased when her nipple hardened.

"Please . . . Alec . . ."

The breathy little sigh fired his need to greater heights. "Tell me again how you hate having my hands on you, my mouth on yours—"

"You don't play fair," she grumbled.

"The man who plays fair loses, sweetheart, and I hate losing." He pressed an openmouthed kiss to her blush-warmed cheek. "Tell me you hate this." He caught her ear-lobe in his teeth, her delicate little earlobe he could nibble on all day. "And this." He kneaded her breast. "And this."

"I hate . . . I . . . don't want . . ."

"Tell me what you *do* want." *So I can drive that blasted Lovelace from your mind once and for all.*

But Katherine's mind was miles away from Sydney. Alec's hand, that hot, questing hand that had driven her mad during the reading, was all she could think of, caressing her breast, fondling it, searing her with this wild excitement.

She should protest the outrage. She should push him away.

But no wonder all those ladies in the Rhetorick looked rapturous when men touched them so intimately. It was the most deliciously naughty feeling. Only think what it would be like if he touched her bare flesh . . .

As if he'd read her thoughts, Alec began to unbutton the bodice of her riding habit.

"Alec, what are you doing?" she tore her mouth from his to whisper, scandalized. Fascinated. Dying to see how far he'd go and what it would feel like.

When had she become so very wicked?

He nipped at her earlobe again, sparking an electric sensation along her every nerve. "Tell me what you want."

She couldn't catch her breath. Another button came free. And another, while she waited in shameless anticipation. "Not this," she said feebly.

"No?" Her bodice gaped open, and Alec slid his hand inside, then beneath the low neck of her chemise to cup her naked breast.

She sucked in a breath and curled her fingers into his coat.

"You don't like this?" he asked, his voice low, guttural.

"Oh, my word," she choked out. Sin should not feel so sweet and amazing . . . and incredibly erotic. His hot hand warmed her flesh, turned it molten. He thumbed her bare nipple, and she nearly shot off the table. Heaven, pure heaven. When it ought to be anything but.

He nuzzled her cheek, his breath ragged against her skin. "I wanted to touch you like this last night, sweetheart. But I didn't dare."

"Yet you dare to do it now?" she whispered, then shivered delightfully when he moved his hand to fondle her other breast.

"If that's what it takes to convince you that you want me as much as I want you, then I'm eager to oblige."

Before she could answer, he kissed her again, so deeply and thoroughly that she hardly noticed him settling his body between her thighs until her skirts inched up to accommodate him. Then catching her behind her hips, he pulled her flush up against him, so tightly she could feel the bulge in his trousers even through her bunched-up riding habit and petticoat.

"Alec, you have to stop this." She sighed against his lips.

"Not yet." He rubbed his thickening flesh against her, rousing a strange new ache between her legs. "Not until you admit you like having my hands and my mouth on you, that you like having me touch you."

He caressed her naked breast so temptingly that she groaned aloud.

"Tell me," he urged. "Tell me you want me, Katherine."

"I . . . I . . ."

"Tell me!" he demanded as he pressed between her legs so firmly that pleasure bolted through her, making her cry out.

"Yes, you devil, yes—I want you!" she practically screamed.

His eyes shone with triumph, as if he'd won a battle. Which he had, of course.

Ashamed, she hid her face in his coat. "There, you got what you wanted."

"Hardly," he murmured. "I want much more than that from you."

That statement brought her fully to her senses. "Well, you can't have it." She grabbed his hand and tried to pull it out of her gown. "Stop touching me."

"Katherine—"

"Now, Alec! Before someone sees us in here, and my reputation is ruined forever."

He hesitated, the fierce hunger in his face feeding her sudden panic. Then he stiffened, as if fighting for control over himself.

When at last he drew his hand from her bodice, she could have wept with relief. "Thank you," she whispered. Swiftly she fastened her buttons, but when she tried to get off the table, his body still held her pinned there. "Please let me down."

Clasping her about the waist, he pulled her off the table until she slid slowly down his body, every inch of his rigid flesh branding her even through her skirts.

His eyes darkened. "One more kiss," he whispered, "then we'll leave." And before she could even protest, he took her mouth again.

Chapter Ten

Jealousy has no place in a rake's arsenal,
for it makes a man foolish and liable to err.
—Anonymous, *A Rake's Rhetorick*

*S*ydney glanced at the clock in the back room where all the poets were gathered. He'd seen Katherine leave Iversley and head into the hall. So where was she? Hadn't she been coming to offer him her congratulations?

She hadn't been waiting when Sydney entered, and the thinning crowd had revealed no sign of Iversley inside the assembly room, either. Sydney scowled. That dashed scoundrel had probably talked her out of coming back here, the way he had tried to keep her from attending the reading.

Unsuccessfully, of course. Satisfaction spread through Sydney as he remembered Katherine's smiles. *Take that, Iversley. She came anyway, didn't she? Came to see me.* And perhaps she was waiting for him even now in the hall . . .

He headed for the door, but Julian stepped into his path, blocking his exit. "For God's sake, don't make a fool of yourself over some silly chit."

"Stay out of it, Napier. This does not concern you."

Jules flushed. "So it's 'Napier' now? What happened to 'my dearest Jules'?"

"Shut up!" Sydney hissed. "We're not alone."

"I know that." Glancing around the room to make sure no one noticed, Jules stepped closer and lowered his voice. "The same way you know, even if you won't admit it, that anything concerning you concerns me."

A delicious shiver swept Sydney. Jules's hints about the nature of their friendship became bolder by the day, and—what was worse—more accurate.

No, what was he thinking? He didn't feel like *that* about Jules. It was unspeakable, intolerable. Sydney loved Kit. He always had and always would. Jules—*Napier*—didn't understand the pure and holy love that could exist between a woman and a man, purer than the . . . the wicked sort of friendship Jules wanted.

"Leave me be." Sydney pushed past his longtime friend. "You're wrong about me and Kit. Utterly wrong."

Pain slashed over Jules's face. "You only wish I were, because that would mean that you are not a—"

"Don't you even say it!" Sydney snapped. "I've told you time and again—all I want is to marry Kit and have a family. But you won't listen."

"Because that's not what you want. That's what you've been told to want. But I know better."

Sydney swallowed. He should never have responded to Jules's surprising kiss a few weeks ago. Though they hadn't spoken of it since, it had changed everything between them. Worse yet, it had crystallized all that had been wrong his entire life, and made him want—

No, he didn't want *that*. He couldn't. But Jules refused to see their one kiss for the mistake it had been.

"I can't be what you want, Jules," Sydney whispered. "Can't you see that?"

"No, I can't." Jealousy turned Jules's tone bitter. "I care

more about you than she ever could. For God's sake, man, she came here with Iversley!"

When Sydney glared at him, Jules added cruelly, "Or is that the real reason you're trying to keep her? Because you can't bear to lose even her to *him*. And all because of some silly schoolboy rivalry—"

"Don't be absurd." But Julian's words rang in his ears as he headed out the door into the hall. It was true—until Iversley had started sniffing around Kit, Sydney had actually toyed with the idea of *not* marrying her.

But the earl was infuriating, with his title and easy manner and reckless disregard for rules. Sydney always followed the rules, was terrified not to.

Except when it came to Jules.

Heat flooded his face so powerfully that he scanned the hall to see if anybody had noticed. But it was empty. No remaining audience members and no Iversley and Kit.

Dash it all if he didn't feel relieved. Relieved, of all things! What kind of man was he?

He sagged onto a bench that sat against one wall and buried his face in his hands. When had everything become so muddled? Kit was pressing him for marriage, Mother was against it, and Jules—

He sucked in a breath. Jules wanted him to *really* break the rules, to leave England and go to Greece with him on an extended trip. Sydney laughed madly. Mother was actually enthusiastic about *that* idea. She thought it would separate him from Kit so he could find some "better" woman.

If Mother only knew what Jules intended for them . . .

A thrill shot through him that he squelched ruthlessly. He mustn't think of Jules like that. He *mustn't*. It was wrong. The man's plans were simply impossible. A life outside of England engaged in— No, he couldn't.

Besides, how would Mother manage all alone? And there was Kit to consider, too—Sydney could never leave her to Iversley. That scoundrel would ruin Kit's life. He could never make her happy.

Yes, but can you?

He wanted to. He really did. It was just that Kit had grown into such a . . . a woman. Suddenly, the amiable playmate who'd joined him in all manner of innocent boyish activities—boating and fishing and climbing trees—had become this creature of blatant femininity who scared the devil out of him. He still enjoyed their talks and admired her clever mind. But the thought of sharing a bed with Kit—Katherine—made him break out in a sweat.

It's only because you've never been with a woman. Jules confused you, that's all. Just kiss her as she asked, and that will break the ice and then everything will be fine.

But what if it wasn't? What if, God forbid, he hated it?

No, Jules was wrong about him. Sydney stood up and strode down the hall. He'd prove it, too. He'd find Kit, and he'd demand that she stop spending time with Iversley. Then he'd take her in his arms and—

A muffled noise from one of the nearby rooms broke into his thoughts. Curious, he approached the door—the only closed one in the hall—and peered through the little window to the inside.

His heart stopped. Iversley was kissing Kit. Anger surged through Sydney. How dared that blackguard touch *his* Kit?

Sydney opened the door. He would put a stop to the man's insolent attentions.

Then he caught sight of Kit's arms, looped about Iversley's shoulders, clinging to his neck. She was kissing the man back. And when Iversley moved to kiss her neck and her ear, her face showed pure rapture—her eyes were closed and her lips were parted and she looked as if she'd finally found heaven.

And Sydney felt . . . nothing. No surge of jealousy, no outrage . . . nothing.

Well, that wasn't entirely true. The sight of such passionate fervor made him wish he were the object of it. He was envious.

And to his horror, it wasn't Iversley he envied.

"Unhand the lady, you blackguard!"

As the words penetrated the sensual spell Alec wove around her, Katherine shoved him away. Dreading what she would see, she turned her gaze slowly to the door.

Lord preserve her, it was Sydney! How much had he witnessed? Had he been here when Alec removed his hand from her bodice a few moments ago? Judging from his furious expression, he might have been.

Except that his fury seemed directed more at Alec than at her.

Alec turned, too, his expression carefully controlled. "Good afternoon, Lovelace." Not "This isn't what you think," or "Sorry, Lovelace, didn't mean to steal your woman." Then again, Alec was always honest about his desires.

What was she going to do? Sydney would never forgive her for this, never.

Like an avenging angel, her friend stalked up to them. "Dash it all, Iversley, you have no right to kiss her!"

Relief coursed through Katherine. Sydney had only seen their kiss, thank goodness.

"I've as much right as you, *old chum*," Alec shot back.

"As long as the lady doesn't protest my kisses, our activities don't concern you."

"Kisses?" Sydney's gaze shot to her. "You let this scoundrel kiss you more than once?"

This was her chance to proclaim Alec a liar, to say she had been forced.

But she couldn't. Even though Alec's grim expression showed he half expected her to, she couldn't speak such a lie. It might save her pride, but it would compel Sydney to defend her honor, which was unthinkable. Men of action like Alec were inevitably good shots.

"Lord Iversley," she whispered, "would you give me a moment alone with Sir Sydney?"

Alec searched her face, surprise flickering in his eyes. Then he nodded grimly. "I'll go see to the horses." He strode out past Sydney, who glared at him every step of the way.

As Alec's footsteps receded down the hall, Sydney approached her. "Dash it all, have you lost your mind? What are you thinking, to let that man kiss you?"

An odd speech for a man who should be jealous. He sounded more like an overprotective brother than a lover.

"I wasn't thinking at all, Sydney. It . . . it just happened." She wasn't about to tell him of her bargain with Alec—Sydney would certainly find *that* appalling.

"The only man you should kiss is *me*," Sydney said with uncommon fierceness.

She gaped at him. So Alec's scheme was working? "You're absolutely right," she said stoutly. "And I would much prefer that you be the one to kiss me."

Liar, her conscience whispered.

Be quiet, she told it. She meant it—she only wanted Sydney. Really, she did. Even if she *had* just been behaving like a shameless wanton with Alec.

She blushed. "My kissing Al— Lord Iversley was a mistake. I promise it will never happen again." Or at least she fervently prayed it wouldn't.

A flush spread over Sydney's cheeks. "Glad to hear it." He stepped toward her with clear intent.

"If you can forgive me—"

"I can forgive you. I *do* forgive you." Sydney stared at her uncertainly, then reached up to caress her cheek. "As long as you can forgive me for neglecting you these past few weeks."

Months, more like, but she wasn't about to point that out now. She'd been waiting half her life for this moment. "It's already forgiven."

He set his jaw, as if preparing for a hard task, then bent his head to press his lips to hers. His kiss was careful, respectful . . . and totally lacking in passion.

But shouldn't she expect that of a considerate gentleman like him? His kisses would never be indecently thorough like Alec's, and he would certainly never touch her so scandalously. That must be why her pulse wasn't quickening and her heart flipping over in her chest.

So why did she wish they were? When Sydney drew back, she frowned at him. *This* was Sydney's idea of a kiss? Couldn't he even take her in his arms or hold her close?

Apparently not. He was already backing away, as if relieved it was over. Oh no, he would not get away with this.

Grabbing his hands, she pulled him back and placed his arms about her waist. Then she twined her own arms about his neck. "Let's try that again, Sydney," she whispered to his shocked face.

And before he could even react, she kissed him. Hard. Thoroughly. She parted her lips against his and mimicked the motions Alec had taught her. But when she tentatively touched her tongue to his mouth, Sydney recoiled, thrusting her away as if she'd bitten him.

Flushing from his cravat to his forelock, he whispered, "That . . . sort of thing should wait until we're married, my dear."

It was her turn to blush. Served her right for taking kissing lessons from a proclaimed scoundrel. She'd blundered again, making Sydney think she was fast and coarse. "I'm sorry, Sydney—"

"No, don't be sorry," he said quickly. "You were fine. It was me. I don't . . . that is . . ." He ran his fingers through his hair, clearly discomposed. "I-I think I'm not very good at . . . these sorts of things."

That was certainly true.

No, she wouldn't think that—it was too disloyal. Though she could use a *bit* more enthusiasm from him. "We only need practice, that's all," she said gamely.

"I suppose." The flush deepened in his cheeks. "The thing is, I'm not sure we should rush into . . . That is—"

"What my surprisingly inarticulate friend is trying to tell you," said a voice from the doorway, "is that he and I are planning a trip to Greece this summer. And a wedding doesn't exactly fit into those plans."

The change that came over Sydney's face was frightening. Anger mingled with mortification as he whirled toward the door. "Dash it all, Napier, go away!"

But Katherine was still trying to absorb Lord Napier's claims. Surely Sydney wouldn't— He didn't mean to— "Is that true, Sydney?"

His alarmed gaze shot back to her. "No!"

"Don't lie to her, for God's sake," Napier snapped.

Sydney looked positively frantic. "All right, perhaps

Napier and I did talk about it, but nothing has been decided—"

"If you even talked about it," she said, feeling as if the floor fell from beneath her very feet, "clearly you weren't considering marriage anytime soon."

"It's just that . . . until the other night, I didn't realize your mother was pressing you so." Sydney tugged nervously at his cravat. "If I'd known you were in such haste to marry—"

"You would have informed your mother you were marrying me no matter what, right?" She snorted. "You didn't even do that after I told you. And your friend there clearly thinks your trip to Greece is still taking place."

"Ignore Napier. He just—"

"Hates me? Like your mother hates me?" She choked down the tears swelling in her throat. "You know what, Sydney? I'm tired of fighting to prove myself to your friend and your mother and . . . and even to you. It's your turn to prove yourself to me. If you want to marry me, you'll have to make an offer. Until you do, I'm assuming there is nothing between us, do you understand? Nothing."

"You don't mean that," Sydney said hoarsely.

"Oh yes, I do." She simply couldn't take this torture anymore. Tears flooded her eyes, but she refused to let him see them. "Good afternoon, Sydney." She hurried toward the door.

"Wait, Kit—" Sydney called out behind her.

"Let her go," Napier put in irritably. "You can't give her what she wants."

He could, if the rest of you would let him, she thought bitterly as she approached the room's exit.

Was she always to have witnesses to her humiliation?

First Alec, then Sydney's horrible friend? She hurried past Napier, praying she could at least keep from crying in front of him.

"You're better off without him, you know, Miss Merivale," Lord Napier said in a low voice.

She stopped, then turned, determined to face down his gloating. "Don't you mean *he's* better off without *me*, Lord Napier?"

But he wasn't gloating. He looked oddly sympathetic. "No. You and I might both be better off without Sydney. But you have another choice. I have none."

That statement was so peculiar, she couldn't even begin to respond. Gathering the remnants of her dignity, she turned and stalked off down the hall.

What a preposterous man. Of course he had other choices for friends. And whom did he consider her other choice to be?

Alec, of course. But Napier was mad if he thought Alec was any choice. Sydney might not be right for her, but neither was Alec. Unless she *wanted* to end up ruined and alone. He might sit a horse like a conqueror and make her laugh, but that was no reason to run into his arms. Papa had cut just such a dashing figure in his day—and look what that had done to Mama.

Besides, Alec's interest in her wasn't the sort to lead to marriage anyway. He wanted to "chase" her, remember?

A hollow pain settled in the pit of her stomach. Alec wanted to chase her, and Sydney wanted to run from her. Neither was seriously interested in marrying her, no matter what nonsense Alec blathered about courting her.

A pox on them both. She paused inside the entrance door to brush the tears from her eyes and straighten her bonnet. Bad enough that Sydney had apparently planned to put off marrying her indefinitely—she wasn't about to let Alec know he was right about that. She still had some pride, thank goodness.

She marched outside to where Alec stood holding the horses. He looked irritable. Fine. She *felt* irritable. They'd make a wonderful pair on the ride home.

"You were in there a long time," he snapped as he helped her mount. "That must have been some discussion."

"It was." If he thought she'd talk about any of this with him, he was in for a surprise.

He scowled up at her. "So what did your precious Sydney do? Chastise you for your immoral character? Regale you with more tales of my wild and reckless school days?"

Her temper flared. "If you really must know, he kissed me." When Alec's eyes darkened, she added, "Apparently your little plan worked brilliantly. Thank you, my lord. I'm most indebted to you."

Chapter Eleven

∽∾∾∞∾∾∾

Most women are fickle creatures, easily led.
And those who are not should be avoided,
for they will let you chase them right into
a marriage shackle.
—Anonymous, *A Rake's Rhetorick*

Alec gaped at Katherine. That idiot Lovelace had actually kissed her? And she'd *let* him? After Alec had kissed and caressed her like a lover?

Anger exploded through him. If he had thought for one second that Lovelace had it in him, he would never have left her alone with the man. Just the thought of Lovelace's mouth on hers drove him insane.

Having dropped that surprise in his lap, Katherine nudged her horse into a walk. Alec cursed as he hurried to mount his own horse. Catching up to her moments later, he searched her face for a sign of how she felt. Her grim expression mollified him a bit.

"You don't seem very happy about Lovelace's kiss," he said coolly.

She colored. "Of course I'm happy. Why wouldn't I be?"

"Because it didn't live up to your expectations?"

Her back went ramrod straight. "I thought we agreed not to discuss Sydney when we were together."

Nice try, sweetheart, but you're not escaping this. "That was *my* rule, not yours. I can break it if I want."

"You're very good at breaking rules, aren't you? After all, you don't have to face the consequences afterward. Whereas the rest of us—"

"Blast it, I've had enough of this. Tell me what Lovelace said to you."

Now he could see the tears glittering in her eyes. It made him want to ride right back to the assembly rooms and put his fist through Sydney's jaw. How dared the man hurt her? How dared he?

Katherine shot him a game smile. "I'm not in any mood to talk right now, my lord. I'd much prefer a good hard ride. So if you'll excuse me . . ."

She prodded her mount into a gallop, leaving him in the dust.

After a second of surprise, he followed her, swearing as he drove Beleza to catch up to her. God rot the woman; she knew they couldn't talk at this speed. She was lucky this part of town had little traffic, or her headlong ride would be dangerously reckless as well as annoying.

At least he could keep her from getting into trouble. He matched her pace, scanning the road ahead to prepare for any obstacles, making sure she maneuvered the intersection without incident. By the time he saw her town house up ahead, both their mounts were blowing hard.

When she finally reined in, she didn't even wait for Alec to help her dismount, but leaped from her horse and handed the reins to the waiting groom, then hurried up the steps. Alec scowled, then did the same. If the blasted female thought to go hide under the protective eye of her mother without answering his questions, she was mad.

Taking the steps two at a time behind her, he caught up

to her at the door. He snagged her hand as she reached for the knocker. "For God's sake, what's all the hurry?"

"You wanted to chase me, didn't you?" she said shakily.

"Not like this."

"What's wrong, Alec?" Her tone was laced with bitterness. "Is our game not living up to your expectations?"

"It's not a game to me, sweetheart, no matter what you think. And I don't like seeing you so upset."

"I'm not upset," she said, but her trembling voice belied her. "The man I intend to marry kissed me. How could I be upset?"

Alec tightened his grip on her hand. "Tell me one thing. Did you enjoy Sydney's kiss?"

She swallowed and looked away. "You've got what you wanted out of this. Why do you care how I feel about his kiss?"

"Because if you enjoyed it," he said with deadly quiet, "I might just have to kill him."

Her gaze swung back to him, wide and disbelieving. Then the doors swung open behind her, and Mrs. Merivale appeared in the entrance, her face wreathed in smiles. "There you are at last. I can't imagine where you two could have gone to be out riding so long."

Turning Katherine toward the door, Alec tucked her hand in the crook of his elbow. As he led her up the last few steps, he cast her mother a smooth smile. "Your daughter took a notion to hear a poetry reading, so I went along."

Katherine stiffened at his betrayal, then tried to snatch her hand free, but he grabbed it with his, holding it pressed to his arm.

Her mother scowled. "Indeed? I hope your lordship didn't find it too dull."

"Not at all," Alec answered. "I believe it's best for a man to learn a woman's tastes as early in the courtship as possible."

"C-Courtship?" her mother sputtered.

"Indeed. My intentions toward your daughter are perfectly honorable, Mrs. Merivale." He smiled broadly at his future mother-in-law. "In fact, I'm asking your permission to court her."

Katherine dug her fingers into his arm, but he ignored her. No way in hell would he continue watching her moon over Sydney Lovelace. The baronet wasn't right for her, and she knew it. All Alec had to do was convince her he could be a good husband.

That might take some doing, judging from the killer grip she had on his arm as they followed her happily babbling mother into the house. God only knew how Katherine would react if she ever found out he had no money.

A chill swept over him. She mustn't find that out until he'd secured her.

"Sit down, sit down, Lord Iversley," her mother gushed as she welcomed them into the tiny parlor. "This calls for a celebration."

"Mama!" Katherine said, color suffusing her too-pale cheeks at her mother's inappropriate response to Alec's announcement. "He has not . . . that is . . ."

"Your mother's right," Alec said smoothly. "This is definitely cause to celebrate."

"You see, Katherine? His lordship knows the way of things. Now, you two lovebirds sit down, and I'll see to having some tea and cakes brought." Her mother headed out the door, still talking. "Oh, and I shall have to send round to Pollock's for champagne . . ."

As her voice receded down the hall, Katherine snatched

her hand free and whirled on him. "What on earth are you doing? Did you decide to make the chase more exciting?"

"Hardly. Falsely asking for permission to court you would brand me a scoundrel in society."

"Society already brands you a scoundrel."

"No, only your friend Sydney does that."

"He's not my friend; he's my . . . my—"

"Intended? Did he ask you to marry him while I was waiting outside with the horses?" When she paled but said nothing, he added, "I didn't think so. If he'd proposed, you wouldn't have ridden like a madwoman all the way home."

With a scowl, she removed her bonnet and tossed it onto the nearby sofa. "Why are you doing this? You can't be in earnest."

"I showed how earnest I was when I kissed you. Several times, I might add."

"Yes, but that's just . . . well . . ."

"Physical desire?" He advanced on her. "That's more than many married couples have."

"But less than I want," she whispered.

"It's more than you'll get from Sydney."

She pressed her fingertips to her temples, rubbing circles on them. "I can't marry you, Alec."

By God, she would turn him down before he even asked. He couldn't let her. "I haven't asked you to marry me."

She tipped up her chin. "You asked permission to court me, which is practically the same thing. And there's no point. I won't marry you."

Think, man. Give her a reason for continuing this that she'll accept. "You don't have to. I only spoke of courtship to your mother because I saw you weakening in your determination to continue this scheme with Sydney. So I took steps to make sure we continue."

A strange mix of emotions crossed her face. "If that's your plan, I can relieve you on that score. The truth is, I suspect Sydney and I are done anyway."

"Really?"

"I told him it was over between us. Unless he makes an offer, I want nothing to do with him, and since he seems in no hurry to do that . . ." She gave him a shaky smile. "So you see, there's no reason for you to take such a high-handed measure. I've given up on making him jealous."

When her bitter tone showed she meant it, triumph surged through Alec. Until he realized she was trying to tell him his "services" were no longer needed.

Like hell they weren't. "Ah, but you still want to marry him, don't you?"

"I . . . I . . . it's hopeless. He'll never marry me."

"Last night you would have said he'd never kiss you, but he did. Who knows how he'll react if he learns I'm courting you? I'm sure your mother will spread that news quickly, so he's bound to hear. And then . . ." He shrugged.

She stared at him with suspicion. "I don't understand why you care."

Dragging her into his arms, he nuzzled her hair. "I'm not ready to give up the chase, sweetheart. Why, we've hardly even become acquainted." Something he fully intended to remedy, now that he'd made his intentions clear.

"We're far too acquainted, if you ask me," she hissed, and cast a furtive glance at the door. "Let go of me, Alec. Mama might see."

He hoped she did; then Katherine would have to marry him. "Do you think she'd care? She's so eager for a marriage between us that she'd dance for joy."

Katherine stiffened. "She'd insist that you marry me right away." Her voice was a breathy whisper that fired his blood. "Doesn't that worry you?"

"I enjoy taking risks," he murmured, then pressed his lips to her heated cheek.

She drew her head back to glare at him. "But I don't."

"Don't you? You like riding headlong through London—that's a risk." He traced her mouth with his thumb. "You like kissing me—that's a risk. So why not take the ultimate risk? Let me court you. It will drive your Sydney insane." He smiled, devilishly.

Her breath quickened. "But will it make him offer for me?"

"If not, at least you will have done everything you could to win him." He heard her mother's step in the hall. "Think of it this way, sweetheart—it will keep your mother from plaguing you for a while. Whereas if you tell her that Sydney is no longer interested, she'll expect you to entertain offers from men you don't know. At least with me, you know what you're getting."

She lifted one eyebrow.

"You know I won't hurt you. And if it doesn't work, what have you lost?"

Katherine sighed. "All right. I suppose it's worth a try." Then she slipped from his arms. "But no more of this . . . reckless behavior, do you hear? Or you'll find yourself married to me whether you want it or not."

He bit back a grin. He damned well hoped so.

For the next hour, Katherine smiled and endured her mother's unsubtle probing into the earl's affairs, but her mind was awhirl.

And if it doesn't work, what have you lost?

Her heart? No, she wouldn't lose her heart to such a rogue—she wouldn't allow it. But she might lose her freedom to choose her own husband.

He'd already proved she wasn't immune to his advances. Every time he kissed her . . . Well, she'd simply have to hold firm on her no-kissing rule.

If only he didn't make it so difficult. Especially when he showed his charming side. Look at how kindly he'd treated Molly earlier, too. From the tenets in *The Rake's Rhetorick,* she'd assumed all rakes were selfish boors. Papa had always ranked his own needs above anyone else's.

But Alec had endured a poetry reading to be with her. All right, so he'd poked fun at the poets and demanded a kiss for his trouble . . .

She scowled. Yes, he had, hadn't he? A kiss and much more. That was the trouble with men like him—they would do anything to seduce a woman. Idly, she rubbed the hand he'd caressed earlier. Given how easily he could breach her defenses, she must be out of her mind to go along with his scheme.

And yet . . . she *did* enjoy his company. He made her laugh, something she sorely needed these days. And if he did hope to seduce her in the end—which was clearly his aim—she could withstand that. She knew Alec for what he was, and as he had said, knowledge was the best defense.

Or was that one more tactic to seduce her?

"You are very quiet, my angel," Mama said from her seat on the sofa beside Alec. "You haven't asked Lord Iversley one question about his estate in Suffolk."

"That's because you were handling it quite nicely, Mama."

Besides, she would never get to see his estate. But she

wished she could. From his fervent descriptions, Edenmore sounded as idyllic as its name, and for a man pleasure-bent, he seemed inordinately proud of it.

"Surely you're curious," Mama persisted. "I know how interested you are in household management—always questioning Cook about this or that."

Katherine gave her mother a tight smile. "Somebody has to."

"Nonsense. These things take care of themselves if you have a good housekeeper." She turned to Alec. "I'm always telling her she doesn't have enough fun. She's so serious all the time, worrying about the price of our coal and such."

Alec's gaze fell warmly on her. "Not a frivolous woman, I take it?"

"No, indeed. That one could use some frivolity. She's too dull by half."

Katherine stuck out her chin. "That's not true. I ride and I read."

Mama shook her head. "I don't call that exciting, going off for hours on your gelding so you can brood over our little troubles . . . or in bad weather sitting in the window seat to brood over poems."

"I don't brood; I think." More important, she escaped the mad whirlwind that was life with Mama—and Papa, the few times he'd been home. "There's nothing wrong with thinking."

Her mother waved her hand dismissively. "It's not healthy, I tell you. Young ladies should be dancing and going on picnics with young gentlemen and what all, not 'thinking.' "

Alec shot Katherine a sympathetic glance. "A little thinking never hurt anyone."

"But she broods for *hours*. Why, she hardly ever attends the assemblies in Heath's End, as I always urge her to do."

These days, they couldn't afford more than one frivolous person in the family. "I simply enjoy different activities than you, Mama."

"Poetry, hmmph. Too depressing by half, if you ask me."

"Now there I must agree with you," Alec put in.

"You didn't seem to find it depressing today," Katherine snapped. "Indeed, you found it quite entertaining."

"It wasn't the poetry I found entertaining." He grinned rakishly. "It was the company."

She smiled in spite of herself.

"All the same, you mustn't let her drag you to any more poetry readings, my lord," Mama went on, "or she'll turn you into a dull and serious creature."

"There's little chance of that," Katherine said dryly. "Lord Iversley couldn't be dull if his life depended on it. And goodness knows he's never serious."

"Not true. Certain matters I'm *very* serious about." He raked his gaze down her body, lowering his voice to a rumble. "Very serious indeed."

He might as well have touched her, and she had to dig her fingernails into her palms to keep from blushing.

Eyes twinkling, he went on in that lazy drawl of his, "But I'd hoped you might join me for less serious entertainment this week."

"Oh?" Mama asked.

"If you haven't seen the mechanical museum yet, we should go there. And Madame Tussaud's exhibit is in the Strand—we might even look in on the infamous Separate Room. Then there's Vauxhall Gardens—"

"Or Astley's Amphitheatre?" Katherine blurted out.

He smiled. "Why not?"

Mama slanted Katherine a knowing glance. "You see how obliging *some* gentlemen can be compared to *other* gentlemen?"

"Mama, please . . ." Katherine protested.

Alec cast Katherine a teasing smile. "Don't tell me somebody was fool enough to disoblige Miss Merivale."

"Oh, yes," Mama said, to Katherine's chagrin. "She tried to convince Sir Sydney to accompany us to the Royal Amphitheatre when we first came to London, but he refused, and most sourly, too. He said it was much too rough a place for young ladies."

Which had roused Katherine's interest even more, though she'd never admit it to Alec. "You can't fault him for that. Sydney thinks women should be——"

"Coddled and cosseted," Alec finished.

"Protected," Katherine corrected him.

"From excitement and adventure and anything remotely interesting in life."

She could hardly disagree, since Alec had hit it exactly.

"Fortunately," Alec went on, "I think ladies with a taste for adventure should be obliged."

"Of course you do," she teased. "It keeps you from having to take them to poetry readings and the like."

"Trust me, Miss Merivale," Alec said, "you'll enjoy Astley's much better."

That's precisely what she was afraid of.

Nor did it help that Alec stayed at the town house longer that evening than she'd expected. He accepted Mama's invitation to dinner and had her laughing so hard that she forgot to keep interrogating him about his financial affairs. By the time Alec left, he had Mama completely in his thrall.

As she dressed for bed, Katherine realized how strange that was. Not that Mama was captivated; Alec could certainly captivate any woman if he set his mind to it. But why do so if seduction were his aim? Why humor Mama's rude prying or laugh at her silly jokes? He acted almost as if he were really . . .

Courting her.

No, how could that be? She had nothing to commend her but her fortune, and nobody knew of that. Did they?

Her door swung open, and Mama came in. Before she could launch into one of her rambling discussions, Katherine asked, "Mama, you haven't told anyone about the money left to me by Grandfather, have you?"

"No, indeed. You asked me to wait until Sir Sydney offered for you."

"Yes, but might you have mentioned it to someone anyway? You know, to impress them? Someone like Lady Jenner or—"

"I think I have sense enough to know when to keep my mouth closed," her mother said with a sniff. "With two gentlemen interested in you, there's no reason to attract fortune hunters, is there?"

Of course not. In this, Mama's wishes matched Katherine's perfectly. Even if the money was technically going to Katherine, Mama looked on it as hers, to be wheedled out of her daughter after she married a wealthy man like Sydney.

Or Alec. Although come to think of it, Katherine had no idea if he was wealthy. "You didn't mention it to Alec today, did you?"

"No. But now that his lordship is courting you, I suppose we should have your father's solicitor speak to him."

"Not yet. Not until we know more about him."

Her mother snorted. "Surely you aren't worried that Lord Iversley wants your fortune. If you'd listened to the man at all this evening, you would have heard about his grand estate in Suffolk. Twelve thousand acres, he has! That's ten times the size of our little place. Only think of how much the land must bring him."

"If it's well managed. He might have no funds to maintain it."

"That's highly unlikely. Look at the fine clothing he wears."

"Anyone can get fine clothing on credit."

"Yes, but I asked Lady Jenner about him last night— she said his mother had been a huge heiress, some merchant's daughter or another." Mama sighed. "I suppose there will be talk about his mother's family being in trade and such—"

"I don't care about that. What else did Lady Jenner say about his estate?"

"I confess I didn't pay much attention. I never dreamed that his lordship—" She smiled apologetically. "You're a perfectly lovely girl, of course, but ... well ... it's not as if you're a raving beauty, with that unfortunate hair of yours and those freckles. You do dress well, I'll grant you, but you don't even play the pianoforte or sing! And all young ladies do that."

Impatiently, Katherine waved off her mother's usual criticisms. "You know I have the singing voice of a frog. That's exactly my point—why should the earl want me, when he could have any accomplished woman of rank he might choose?"

Her mother rolled her eyes. "Who knows what attracts a man, dear? You do have nice features, and you dance prettily. And he seems to like your pert comments, though Lord only knows why. In my day, a woman wanting to snag a husband didn't speak so impertinently—"

"Mama! Just tell me this—are you sure he's not interested in my fortune?"

"Yes, my angel. Absolutely sure. Before we even met the man, Lady Jenner said he was worth fifteen thousand a year."

Katherine would believe it, if the woman hadn't seemed so friendly with Alec. What if he'd asked her to lie to Mama about his fortune?

No, he would only have done that if he'd known of Katherine's expectations and was pursuing her from the beginning. If Mama could be believed, he couldn't know. And when he'd met her on the balcony, he certainly hadn't seemed to know anything about her except her name and what Sydney and she had—

Oh, no, might Alec have heard her say something to Sydney while he'd been eavesdropping? Frantically, she replayed last night's conversation in her head. But she was nearly certain they hadn't discussed her fortune in his hearing. And since she'd balked at mentioning it herself today, Alec couldn't possibly know the truth about it. Which meant he had no reason to court her.

Except that he desired her. But he wasn't the kind of man who'd marry just for that—when he spoke of chasing her, he meant chasing her into his bed.

A heavy disappointment settled upon her chest. She shouldn't care that he wanted only to seduce her, but she did. It was utterly foolish of her, for she wouldn't marry him even if he earnestly asked her to. Yet she wanted him to ask.

Pride, that's all it was. It pricked her pride that he didn't want her for a wife, even though she didn't want him for a husband.

"Now that your curiosity about Lord Iversley's intentions is satisfied," Mama said, "I do hope you'll conduct yourself better with him."

Goodness, had Mama somehow found out about those scandalous kisses and caresses she'd shared with Alec? "I-I don't know what you mean."

"Oh, yes, you do." Her mother planted her hands on her hips. "Taking his lordship to a poetry reading—what were you thinking?"

Relief coursed through Katherine. "I promised Sydney I'd go."

"Yes, and he has certainly fulfilled all of *his* promises, hasn't he?" When Katherine sighed, she added, "If you know what's good for you, you'll forget about Sir Sydney now that his lordship is courting you. Don't you want to be a wealthy countess?"

"Not really." Nervous about raising expectations for a nonexistent marriage, Katherine added, "I wouldn't take the earl's attentions too seriously, Mama. He may just be toying with me. You've heard what they say about him."

"You mean that he's a *rouille?*"

"*Roué*, Mama. *Rouille* means 'blight.'" Katherine paused. "Come to think of it, you're right. He *is* a *rouille*."

"*Roué, rouille*—it's all just gossip. And even if he was one, what does that matter? Every man sows his wild oats, but once they set their minds to marrying, that's different."

"Oh?" Katherine sat on her bed to brush her hair. "Some men continue sowing long after they marry. I have no desire for such a husband."

"Don't be silly. That's how men are. Women learn to look the other way."

Katherine's gaze shot to her mother. "Like you did?"

A flush darkened Mama's cheeks. "Is that what you think? That your father and I argued because I was jealous of him and his . . . his little whores? I assure you, I didn't care one whit about that. It was the money that bothered me, all that money he spent on them when he wouldn't even bring me to town during the season." She sniffed. "And his gambling, too."

Katherine blushed. She never knew whether to be grateful for Mama's candor about Papa's indiscretions, which served as a warning to her, or appalled by Mama's lack of shame, which simply mortified her. "Still, given your experience with Papa, you should understand my reluctance about Lord Iversley."

"It's not the same thing. With your father and me, there was never enough money to go around, but you won't have to worry about that. Why, with Lord Iversley's income and the fortune he surely got from his mother, you might not even need that money from my father, God rest his soul."

Katherine sighed. Mama was so transparent. "We still have to pay Papa's debts. Not to mention that we owe that gaming fellow five thousand pounds. We'll have to pay that at once."

Mama scowled. "How could your father get into debt to that awful man?"

"Actually, Mr. Byrne has been very decent. At least he hasn't pressed us for payment too strenuously."

"I suppose. But I still say he should have forgiven a widow's debt entirely."

"Five thousand pounds? He'd have to be mad. Besides, a gentleman is expected to pay his debts even after he dies."

"Perhaps if they're owed to another gentleman, but to

a creature like Mr. Byrne? You know what they say about his parentage—"

"Yes, Mama. He's a walking illustration of why I shouldn't marry the earl."

"Nonsense." Settling onto Katherine's bed, she laid a motherly hand on her daughter's leg. "If even the prince has his fancy women, you can't escape it. What you want is a man who's discreet. Not like your father." Her lips tightened into a thin line. "He couldn't even die discreetly, the wretch."

He had died choking on a fishbone while dining with his mistress, the final mortification for their family.

Mama squeezed Katherine's knee. "But your Lord Iversley will be discreet. I can tell these things, you know. He's a very private man, not given to boasting about his conquests like your father."

The very thought of such discretion sickened her. "I don't want discretion in a husband. I want fidelity."

"We all want that, my angel. But men can't give it."

She eyed her mother mutinously. "Sydney can."

"Even if that were true, his fidelity would hardly compensate for his other disadvantages. For one thing, there's his awful mother."

Katherine choked down a laugh. That was like Genghis Khan calling Attila the Hun cruel. "She was your friend once."

"Yes, but that was before I eloped with your father. She never approved of him. And she positively hates that her husband chose to marry her only after I'd thrown him over. What she saw in Lovelace, I'll never know. He was as dull as dishwater." She shot Katherine an arch glance. "Just like his son."

Katherine bristled. "I thought you liked Sydney."

"Until I saw the other choices. After we came to town

and he dragged us to salons and lectures, I viewed your union differently. What sort of life will you have with him? He has some cachet in society, I'll grant you, because his family is so old and respected, but it's nothing to what Lord Iversley will have."

"I don't care about society, Mama."

"You'll care when you're trapped out in Cornwall at Sir Sydney's estate, with his mother guiding your every activity." Mama's face took on a glow as she recited the holy mantra of every society matron scheming for her child. "But if you marry his lordship, only think of the parties and balls and routs you'll be invited to—why, you might even rub elbows with the prince himself."

"Yes, wouldn't that be grand?" Katherine snapped.

"You can come to town every year for the season and give your sisters a real coming out—"

"Which would mean your coming to town with them."

Her mother blinked, then dropped her gaze to her lap. "Of course." She smoothed her skirts nervously. "That goes without saying. Besides, you'd want your mother here to help you with all your own balls and parties, wouldn't you?"

"I don't intend to have any balls and parties."

"Oh, but you must! It will be expected of the new Countess of Iversley." Mama took up the mantra once more. "You'll be called Lady Iversley."

"If I marry Sydney, I'll be called Lady Lovelace."

Mama flipped her hand. "It's not the same—that's merely being a baronet's wife. But a countess—" She gave a longing sigh. "And your sons will all be called 'Lord,' and your eldest will be the heir—"

"And I'll be lonely because my husband spends all his time at his club, and brokenhearted because he keeps a mistress."

"Lonely! In London? Don't be absurd. Who could be lonely in London? As for being brokenhearted, there's nothing to say you can't . . . well . . . have friends of your own. After you bear the heir and a spare, of course."

"Mama!" Katherine blushed to the roots of her hair. "I would never—"

"Oh, don't be a ninny. You'll be a fashionable woman then—you can do as you please."

"If that's being fashionable, I want none of it." The picture her mother painted of her future life with Alec made her ill—it contrasted so sharply with the life she thought to have with Sydney. But if Sydney didn't react to the news of Alec's courtship by offering for her, what was she going to do?

Her mother rose stiffly, her face drawn in anger. "I see there's no use talking to you—you don't know a good thing when it's dropped into your lap."

Tossing back her head, she marched off to jerk the door open, then turned to glare at Katherine. "Go on and choose your baronet, then, and have a dull life. But I warn you: If you don't accept an offer from either Sir Sydney or Lord Iversley in the next two weeks, the whole world will hear of the fortune you expect. Then you'll have quite a choice of husbands, won't you? Fortune hunters and schemers, for the most part. And I'll turn a deaf ear to your protests, too. Because one way or the other, missy, you're going to marry *someone* before the season is over."

Chapter Twelve

Use gifts to soften the woman's defenses.
—Anonymous, *A Rake's Rhetorick*

A week later, as the well-sprung coach Alec had borrowed from Draker swept down the crowded London streets toward the Merivale town house, Alec admitted he'd made a serious tactical error. In letting Katherine continue to believe his interest in her was merely wicked, he'd put her further on her guard.

For some reason, the hothouse flowers he'd spent a pretty penny on only angered her. Weren't women supposed to like flowers? The book of poetry he'd brought had been better received, until she noticed it was by some fellow named Byron, who apparently had a scandalous reputation. By God, who would have thought a book of poetry could be a problem?

At least she'd enjoyed the entertainments he took her and her mother to, but she'd spent them glued to Mrs. Merivale's side. And she absolutely refused to go riding with him, saying there was no one to chaperone.

He snorted. She merely wanted to avoid being alone with him again. And neither Mrs. Merivale's determined efforts to leave them alone together nor Alec's similar attempts had worked—Katherine held tight to the strictest proprieties. He hadn't even managed to hold her hand, much less sneak a kiss.

It drove him insane. He'd give anything for one stolen kiss from her sweet, artless mouth. And he would have it, too, if tonight went according to plan. He had to secure her soon. Matters at Edenmore were desperate—he couldn't afford to remain in London much longer.

At least Sir Sydney was keeping away. But that could be bad, too—if Katherine decided the courtship ploy wasn't working, she would refuse Alec and he'd have wasted days of effort.

Perhaps he should have chosen one of those simpering misses who would have welcomed his attention, accepted his guidance . . . and bored him to tears, in bed and out.

Blast it, that shouldn't matter. Saving Edenmore should be his prime concern. But he craved Katherine like he craved wild rides across Edenmore's clay hills. Being with her pleased him, talking to her stimulated him . . . touching her aroused him.

That mustn't matter. His tenants and servants depended on him to set Edenmore to rights. So if his plan failed, if Katherine didn't soften toward him tonight at Astley's Royal Amphitheatre, he would make himself give her up and tell Byrne it hadn't worked.

His plan *had* to work. She was only suspicious because of his evasions about why he'd remained abroad. As long as she believed it was a wastrel's lack of interest in his estate, she'd never give him a chance. So he had to tell her some of the truth, even if it were threaded with a bit of . . . fabrication.

When he arrived at the Merivale's rented town house,

their manservant, Thomas, let him in. "Good evening, my lord. Mrs. Merivale is indisposed, and Miss Merivale is in the parlor with another gentleman. Would you prefer to wait here, or shall I announce you?"

A gentleman, eh? Only one gentleman would come here so late in the day—that blasted Lovelace. "I'll announce myself, thank you. I know the way."

Alec paused only long enough to relinquish his coat and hat before stalking off to the parlor, his temper rising with every step. Competing with that damned poet for her affections had really begun to pall. He couldn't wait to make his real intentions clear tonight and put an end to Lovelace's hold on her once and for all.

But the gentleman in the room wasn't Lovelace. It was Gavin Byrne.

Katherine broke off midsentence. "Alec! I-I mean, Lord Iversley. You're here."

His gaze bored into Byrne. "Sorry to disturb you and your guest," he said without contrition.

"No need to be concerned." Byrne rose and bowed. "Miss Merivale and I have finished our business, so I'll take my leave."

"Business?" Alec said.

"This is Mr. Byrne," Katherine said quickly. "He was a . . . er . . . associate of my father's. He came to speak to Mama, but she was feeling unwell, so—"

"Miss Merivale was kind enough to meet with me," Byrne finished.

"I see." His eyes narrowed. What was his devious half brother up to? "I'm Iversley, a close friend of the family. And one who hopes to be closer still, if I can talk Miss Merivale into accepting my suit."

Byrne smiled broadly. "Well then, I see my visit was

unnecessary. Good luck to you, my lord." He bowed to Katherine. "Thank you for the tea, madam."

As Byrne passed him, Alec told Katherine, "I'll just make sure Mr. Byrne can find his way out." Then he followed his half brother into the hall.

As soon as they were out of earshot of the parlor, Alec drew Byrne aside. "What in God's name are you doing?"

Byrne shrugged. "Helping you. Before I go off to Bath for a week, I figured I'd visit Mrs. Merivale to remind her how urgent the situation is."

"I don't need your help," Alec snapped, his pride pricked. "I can win Katherine on my own."

"I have yet to see any announcement of an engagement in the paper, even though Sydney Lovelace seems to be relinquishing the field."

Alec's eyes narrowed. "What do you mean?"

"I hear he's been a visitor at Napier's estate in Kent all this week."

A heady triumph swamped Alec. So Lovelace had retreated, had he? That settled everything. Alec would make Katherine marry him, no matter what it took. Though surely she wouldn't fight him anymore when she realized he was her only chance for marriage.

"It's up to you to marry the chit and get me my money." Byrne rubbed his chin. "A pity she and her mother are so set on a respectable marriage, or I could marry her myself. I must admit that Miss Merivale is much lovelier than I'd realized."

"Stay away from her," Alec warned. "*I'm* the only man she's marrying."

Byrne's laugh showed that he'd only wanted to annoy Alec. "I don't know, Iversley—she didn't talk like a woman on the verge of marriage."

"She will after tonight."

"Good luck. Miss Merivale strikes me as a woman not easily swayed."

Alec gritted his teeth as his presumptuous ass of a half brother walked off with his self-assured gait. When he reentered the parlor, Katherine was pacing and frowning.

"Byrne wouldn't say why he was here," Alec lied, "so I trust that you will."

She halted, her cheeks flushing. "It's nothing to concern you."

"The man isn't respectable, so if he's causing trouble for you—"

"You know him?"

He hesitated. He'd avoided outright lies until now. But matters were desperate. "I know of him. From what I've heard, your father would never have considered him an associate."

Would she confide in him? Did she trust him even that much?

She sighed. "Mr. Byrne is one of Papa's creditors."

"One of?" His heart sank. If they married, would any of her fortune be left for Edenmore after he had paid her father's debts?

She stiffened. "There are a few others, but we owe him the most by far."

He relaxed. "How often does he come to demand his money?"

"This is only the second time that I know of."

"Too often to suit me," he growled.

"You mustn't worry; he was a perfect gentleman. People only say awful things about him because of the circumstances of his birth."

He went still. "You know about that?"

"That he's the unacknowledged natural child of His Highness? I've heard the rumors, yes."

He sucked in a breath. "Having such a man in your parlor doesn't make you nervous?"

"Of course it does. The Prince of Wales is the most debauched man in England. If Mr. Byrne's anything like him, he probably spends his time chasing after every woman he meets."

He fought to contain his temper. "Then why did you meet with such a man alone? If your mother was too ill to talk to him, you should have told him to return another day."

Katherine gave a bitter laugh. "Mama isn't ill. She only said that so she wouldn't have to deal with him."

His temper exploded. "And instead, you would?"

"No!" She sighed. "But Mama thinks if she keeps refusing to see him, he'll get tired and go away. Unfortunately, that only delays the inevitable. He'll come again and again until he gets his money."

"So you thought to talk him out of it? Convince him to forgive the debt?"

She tipped up her chin defensively. "Something like that."

"Did it work?"

Her chin trembled. "Well . . . no, but he did agree to give us more time."

"Time for you to get a wealthy husband," he snapped.

She glanced away. "My marrying is the only solution to the problem."

His temper flared once more. "It's your mother's problem, not yours. Why do you take the responsibility for your parents' mistakes on your own shoulders?"

When she lifted her gaze to his, it was bright with tears. "Someone must."

Blast it, how could Mrs. Merivale allow her daughter to meet with a man like Byrne, rather than deal with matters herself? "So you're willing to sacrifice your own happiness to pay off debts you never asked for. To keep a frivolous woman like your mother from being bothered by the likes of Byrne."

"I don't do it for Mama—I do it for the rest of my family. If we can't resolve our financial situation, my sisters will have to make advantageous marriages, which is unlikely, and my brother will inherit a ravaged estate. Besides, it's no sacrifice to marry Sydney. I care about him, and he cares about me."

He would end her little delusion once and for all. "I see how much he cares about you," he said coolly. "You're here dealing with your late father's legacy, while he's abandoned you to run off to his friend's estate."

"What do you mean?" she asked. "What have you heard about Sydney?"

Though her stricken expression gave him pause, he pressed on. "Rumor has it he's been at Napier's estate in Kent for the past week."

The tears shimmering in her eyes belied her overly brilliant smile. "You see? I told you this wouldn't work. He doesn't even care that we're courting. "We're wasting our time with this *faux* courtship, Alec."

"It's not a *faux* courtship to me."

A sad smile touched her lips. "It's nice of you to say so, but we both know it is. And I'm all right, truly I am." She squared her shoulders. "Let's not discuss this anymore tonight. We'll just enjoy ourselves for the last time. I'll fetch Mama—"

"Not yet." He snagged her arm as she started to walk past him. Time for another gift. If she didn't like this one . . . "I brought you something."

She faced him with an indulgent look. "More poetry by known rakehells?"

"No, not poetry." Removing the velvet box from his pocket, he handed it to her.

"I see." She still wore that cursed indulgent smile. "Jewels. How original."

"Open it."

"You know, my lord," she said as she opened the box, "you're wasting your money on me. I'm not some silly chit easily tempted by—" She broke off when she saw the contents. "Ohh . . . that's so . . ."

"Original?" he prodded smugly.

Two spots of color stained her cheeks. "Now that you mention it . . . yes. It's lovely. I've never seen anything like it."

Taking it from her, he removed the black-and-gold brooch and set the box aside. "It's damascene. I noticed that you prefer unusual jewelry." He unclasped the pin, a horse of blackened steel galloping through an intricate forest worked in gold. "I bought it during a trip to Spain some years ago."

She stiffened. "For some other woman. Did your paramour not like it or—"

"I bought it for my mother."

"Oh," she said in a small voice.

"I watched it being made in Toledo." He slid his hand beneath the edge of her gown so he could affix the pin. "They lay gold wire in a grooved steel design. Then they fire the whole thing to blacken the exposed steel before embossing the gold to enhance the design. When I saw the finished piece, I had to buy it."

"What did your mother say when you gave it to her?"

"I never did. I didn't want to send it through the post."

Especially since the old earl would have confiscated it. "After I learned of her death sometime later, I kept it."

She stayed his hand on her bodice. "I can't accept this."

"You don't like it?"

"No . . . I-I mean, yes, I adore it, but something with such sentimental value should be kept for your wife."

"I want you to have it, all right?" he growled, feeling helpless in the face of her determination to disbelieve him. "It suits you." That much was certainly true.

When she looked as if she wavered, he added, "Besides, I doubt anyone else would show it the appreciation it deserves."

With a hesitant smile, she dropped her hand. "It really is beautiful."

"Especially on you." He finished fastening it, then swept his hand up along the smooth, silky skin of her collarbone. "You're like damascene, you know—steel and gold entwined, strength softened by beauty."

"I-I'm no beauty," she said in a breathless whisper as he caressed the skin of her lovely neck, pressing his finger to the pulse that beat so frantically there.

"If I were a poet, I could tell you in pretty words how much I want you for my wife, and you might believe me." He curved his fingers behind her neck. "But I can only show you." Then he pulled her close for the kiss he'd craved for days.

For a moment, her mouth was pliant and responsive beneath his. Then she stiffened and pushed him away, a fiery blush staining her cheeks. "You aren't supposed to kiss me."

"I can't help what I want, Katherine. It has nothing to do with my breaking rules, or your blasted Sydney, or your fears about my character. I want to marry you, and you can't change that."

He kissed her fiercely this time, demanding her response. And after a second's hesitation she gave it, parting her lips to let him in.

By God, her mouth was everything he remembered and more, soft and eager and warm. He kissed her deeply, seeking proof that she still wanted him, too.

Then he heard footsteps in the hall and groaned.

Katherine wriggled from his arms. "Someone is coming." She shifted her gaze to the door. "Why, hello, Mama."

"Oh, Lord Iversley," her mother exclaimed. "I didn't realize you'd arrived. Um . . . you did arrive just now, didn't you?"

"He saw Mr. Byrne out," Katherine said flatly.

Her mother paled. Clearly, she hadn't wanted Katherine's suitor to know about the family debts. "I see."

"He won't bother you anymore," Alec asserted. "I'll make sure of that."

Katherine's shocked gaze swung to him, but he ignored it. Let her think he meant to pay the debt with his own funds. In a way, he did. Once they married.

And they *would* be married. With Lovelace out of the picture, he finally had his chance. So no matter how thorny she got or how long it took to win her, he'd keep at it until she accepted his suit.

Chapter Thirteen

◆◆◆◆

The soberest women are often the ones
secretly longing for adventure.
—Anonymous, *A Rake's Rhetorick*

Katherine didn't know what to think of Alec's astonishing insistence that he really was courting her. Could he be sincere? But if not, why had he made that lofty pronouncement about taking care of their debt to Mr. Byrne?

Then there was his gift. She couldn't believe he'd noticed her taste in jewelry. And to give her something originally intended for his mother . . . Oh, what was she to think?

She slanted a glance across the carriage to where he lounged against the lavishly upholstered cushions that bespoke his wealth. His gaze locked with hers, smoldering with the same heat she'd felt in the parlor. When he dropped it to fix on her mouth, a delicious shiver swept along her spine. Goodness, but the man knew how to tempt a woman.

It wasn't just his kisses and caresses, either—every day they spent together, she liked him more. Yet she still knew so little about him. He was so cursedly secretive.

"You said you went to Spain. Wasn't it dangerous for an Englishman to be there?"

"Not in 1805. Napoleon hadn't yet set his brother on the Spanish throne."

Katherine did some quick figuring. If Alec were about Sydney's age . . . "So when you went there, you must have been about—"

"Eighteen, yes."

The thought of a young Alec buying his mother a brooch, only to learn later that she was dead, tightened a knot in Katherine's chest.

Then he added, "I went there with my uncle to buy horses."

"You have an uncle?" Katherine said in surprise.

"By marriage. The husband of my father's sister is a Portuguese count." His gaze met hers. "Portugal was my home for my ten years abroad."

More surprises. "But I thought . . . that is . . . everyone says . . ."

"That I was cavorting across the Continent?" His eyes twinkled. "I've heard that rumor myself."

"So it's not true?"

"It depends on what you call 'cavorting.' I was on the Continent, after all."

"You went there on the Grand Tour," she prodded. He'd never revealed so much before, and she intended to take advantage of it.

"Actually, no. But my father was too proud to tell people the truth."

"Which was . . ."

"He took exception to my rule-breaking ways when I was sent down from school for a petty offense, so he packed me off to live with my aunt and uncle."

The pain latent in those words was too palpable to be feigned, yet she could hardly believe his claim. "And you stayed for ten years?"

He shrugged. "I preferred it to the insanity of London society. My uncle bred racehorses as a hobby, and I like to ride, so I stayed on."

"During a war."

"We lived in a part of Portugal largely unaffected by Napoleon's armies."

She eyed him suspiciously. Had there been any such place? She should have paid more attention to the accounts of the war in the newspapers. "Why didn't you tell anyone this before?"

"It didn't come up," he said smoothly.

"It *did* come up," she persisted. "Several times."

"You were determined to believe in my cavorting, no matter what I said."

"Only because you gave no other reason for your absence from England."

"Pshaw, Katherine," Mama put in. "The poor man explained himself. Must you plague him so? I don't care what he did in Portugal. I only want to know if he ever got to France and what *le beau mont* were wearing there."

Katherine nearly snapped that she didn't care what "the beautiful hill" of France was wearing, but Alec responded first, smoothly ignoring her mother's fractured French. After apologizing for not having been to France, he quickly launched into a discussion of Portuguese bonnets to placate her.

Giving Katherine no choice but to mull over his revelations. She knew he was still hiding something. His tale seemed too contrived to be true—the estranged heir to an earl sent abroad, where he found joy living the simpler life of a Portuguese noble? Hard to believe this sophisticated man had gained his knowledge of the world by breeding horses.

Although it explained why he rode so well and how he'd acquired his Lusitano, why not tell her the truth in the first place? Why not tell *everyone* the truth? There was nothing ignoble in it. Eccentric perhaps, but not ignoble.

The man was pure enigma. Sometimes he was a perfect gentleman, giving her a brooch meant for his mother and promising to pay her family's debts. Sometimes he was suspiciously smooth, like when he handled Mama as expertly as he handled his mare. And sometimes . . .

Sometimes he was a bold conqueror who dragged her into his arms to demand kisses. Unfortunately, she liked the conqueror as much as the gentleman . . . possibly even more.

Truth be told, her craving for the conqueror's kisses had become insatiable. She often lay awake at night for hours, trying to remember how he'd tasted and felt, reliving the wicked caresses of a scoundrel.

If Alec really was a scoundrel. She hardly knew anymore.

The surprises continued when they reached the Royal Amphitheatre. He'd reserved a private box, which was never done here. Tickets were issued by the person, and boxes weren't rented. If he was trying to impress them, he was certainly succeeding.

They had excellent seats—close enough to see the exaggerated expressions of the clowning "tailor" who was dragged about by one horse, pinned beneath another, and chased through an open window by a third. Then came the hippodrama, "The Blood Red Knight," about the beautiful Isabella, whose evil brother-in-law carried her off to a set of a castle.

Mama was bored, of course—she would prefer Vaux-hall Gardens—but Katherine couldn't tear her eyes from the action in the sawdust ring, or the romantic tale being played out on the huge stage behind it. Cornwall had nothing like this. And though she missed her quiet country life, she also enjoyed these London entertainments.

Glancing at Mama, who was dozing now, Alec draped his arm over the back of Katherine's chair and leaned close. "Well?" he asked in a low rumble. "Is it what you imagined?"

"Even better. How do they get so many horses to behave?"

"Lots of carrots," he quipped.

"Very funny. But really, do you know how?"

He smiled. "Training a horse merely requires patience and plenty of rewards. For example, if you want to accustom a horse to the jingling of armor—or a soldier's gear—you tie a metal flask containing a coin to his saddle. You put the horse through his paces, moving the flask around. Once he's used to one coin rattling, you add more coins, then more flasks, until the horse ignores any metallic sound coming from his rider. And to accustom him to pistol shots—"

"You certainly know a great deal about training horses."

Alec blinked. "Sorry, I . . . get carried away on the subject."

"It's all right. I find it fascinating. I didn't realize you knew so much."

He fixed his gaze on the stage. "I helped my uncle."

She said quickly, "I suspect that training horses isn't as difficult as training humans. Take that fellow on the stage there—" She gestured to a rider whose horse kept shying from crossing the stage bridge other horses were stepping blithely over. "He doesn't seem to know what he's doing."

Alec nodded. "He's giving the horse mixed signals—pressing too hard with his heels while reining him in too much. He's clearly not experienced with this sort of riding. I wonder why Astley would use him at all. Astley is very particular about his employees."

"Do you know Mr. Astley?"

"I . . . er . . . met him once." He slid his hand to cup her shoulder. "But what do you think of the famous Miss Woolford? She's good, isn't she?"

Sneaky devil, trying to distract her from all her questions. "Indeed she is. I'd love to learn how to ride like her."

He shot her a heated look as he caressed her shoulder. "I could teach you."

Her mouth went dry. The very thought of Alec and her alone, his large hands moving over her legs to correct her seat on the horse, one of them resting on her thigh while he gave some instruction—

"I can't imagine why I'd need such lessons," she said, fighting back a blush.

"Why not do it for fun?" As if he'd read her thoughts, he bent close to whisper, "I promise I would make it fun." When he punctuated that promise with a kiss to her ear, a shiver of anticipation ran through her.

"Stop that, Alec." She cast Mama a furtive glance. "You really shouldn't—"

The door to their box suddenly swung open with great force, and a swarthy man with his arm in a sling strode in. "Senhor Black!" the man exclaimed as he hurried to Alec's side. "Thank God Senhor Astley was right, and you are really here."

Alec rose to face the stranger. "França? What are you doing in England?"

"Did the senhor not tell you I work for him now? No matter, he sent me to find you because—" The man broke off as he caught sight of Katherine. He gave a quick bow. "Forgive me, senhorita, but we are in urgent need of Senhor Black."

Alec scowled, and Katherine waited for him to demand that he be addressed by his title. Instead he said, "I already told Astley—"

"That you would ride for him another time, yes. But surely you can oblige him tonight. I broke my arm in a foolish stunt last night, and we are desperate."

The noise had awakened Mama, and she came up out of her chair sputtering, "What is . . . who . . . young man, what do you think you're doing in our box?"

Alec's jaw tightened. "Mrs. Merivale, Miss Katherine Merivale, this is Mr. Miguel França, a friend of mine from Portugal. He has come to . . . er . . ."

"Beg Senhor Black to help us." Mr. França flashed Mama a courtly smile.

But she was having none of it. "If you want his lordship's help, you should address him properly."

"Pardon?" Then the man's confusion turned to surprised pleasure. "So Senhor Astley was not joking? You truly are a lord, my friend? *Magnifico!* I suppose that I must now call you Lord Something-or-Other—"

"That isn't necessary, França," Alec said.

"You should call him Lord Iversley," Mama put in helpfully.

"Thank you, senhora. Now if you will excuse me, I must steal your Lord Iversley away. The cavalry officer Senhor Astley hired to replace me tonight has not appeared. Since he only demonstrates cavalry cuts and does a few tricks on horseback, we thought perhaps Senhor Black—that is, Lord Iversley—"

"It's out of the question, França," Alec snapped. "I'm not dressed for it, and I won't abandon my guests."

"Don't worry about us." Katherine rose, thoroughly intrigued. "I'd love to see you ride in the arena." And that would keep her from falling prey to his amorous attentions yet again.

Alec's gaze narrowed on her. Had he guessed why she was so eager to send him off?

"Yes, yes, Lord Iversley," her mother put in, "you should do it, most assuredly. What a lark!"

"It would be rude of me to leave you here alone." Alec turned to França. "Give Astley my sincerest regrets, but I cannot oblige him tonight."

França began to fiddle nervously with his sling. "Ah, but Mr. Astley said that if you refuse, I am to remind you that he was kind enough to offer—"

"Right." Alec bowed stiffly. "Very well, I suppose I can manage it."

Relief spread over Mr. França's face. "You can wear my uniform. And if you do not want to leave the lovely senhorita and her mother alone, bring them with us. They can watch from behind the scenes."

Alec shot Katherine a considering glance. "I have a better idea. What if Miss Merivale were to participate in the interlude, too?"

Mr. França's face lit up. "*Magnifico,* senhor! That flaming red hair and that smile . . . she would charm the audience."

Alec nodded. "And keep them from noticing my mistakes."

França waved his hand dismissively. "Then we can perform 'The Angry Wife'—it is simple enough for her, don't you think?"

"Are you both insane?" Katherine broke in. "I couldn't possibly ride well enough to do tricks."

"You need not ride at all, senhorita," Mr. França said. " 'The Angry Wife' is more like—"

"Theater," Alec put in. "You only have to stand still while I ride past and steal your hat and such with my sword. It's mostly acting—you just pretend to be angry with me." He grinned. "Surely you can manage that with no trouble."

"But—"

"Do you have a costume that will fit her?" Alec asked Mr. França.

"Most certainly. But her hair will have to be dressed differently."

"Now see here," Katherine broke in. "I haven't agreed to this. I can't—"

"You can." Alec caught her gaze. "What's more, you know you want to."

She sucked in a breath. He was right. She did want to. This was quite possibly the most exciting thing ever to happen to her. But still . . . "It isn't proper, and you know it. If anyone recognizes me, I'll be considered fast, or worse."

"Don't be such a prude," Mama said. "It sounds like jolly good fun to me."

Katherine whirled on her. "You can hardly find this acceptable, Mama—"

"We can put a mask on you," Mr. França broke in. Clearly, he would do anything to gain Alec's compliance, and if Alec wanted her along, then he would oblige. "Senhor Black can wear a mask, too, if he wishes."

Mama scowled at him. "As long as *his lordship* promises to look out for my daughter, I'm sure it will be fine."

"Of course I'll look out for her." Alec gazed warmly into Katherine's eyes. "I promise not to let anything hurt or embarrass you." He lowered his voice. "Take a risk, sweetheart. You might enjoy it."

She simply couldn't resist the intriguing idea. "All right. But you must put a mask on me. And the dress mustn't be too . . . well . . ."

"It will be beautiful, do not worry," Mr. França put in, oblivious to her real source of concern. "Now come, we must hurry." He glanced to the stage, where the fair maiden was being rescued from the burning castle by a dashing fellow on horseback. "We have little time to prepare for the interlude."

As they hurried out the door, Mama took her seat again.

Katherine stopped. "Aren't you coming, Mama?"

"No, indeed. How can I see everything from back there behind the stage? I shall stay right here and watch your adventure. Go on, my angel. I'll be fine."

Katherine hesitated. But arguing with Mama was pointless, so she left with Alec and Mr. França.

As they hurried down the stairs, Mr. França began explaining which maneuvers Alec would perform.

"Wait a minute," Katherine broke in. "You expect him to know these cavalry maneuvers?"

"Of course," Mr. França answered. "Senhor Black invented two of them."

"Really?" She glanced at Alec, who was avoiding her gaze all of a sudden. Her eyes narrowed. "Was he in the cavalry?"

"No, although Wellington tried many times to con-

vince him to join. But Senhor Black is stubborn and
would only agree to teach riding to the recruits." Mr.
França smiled. "That is how we met. I was in the Portuguese cavalry, and he was my teacher. I owe everything I
know about good riding to him."

"Nonsense," Alec put in firmly as they reached the bottom floor. "Now about this interlude—"

"But I thought he helped his uncle breed horses?"
Katherine said, refusing to let him change the subject.

"He did—when he first went to Portugal. But not after
the army hired him." Mr. França laughed. "Not unless he
flew to south Portugal on a winged Pegasus each night.
The cavalry training camp was in Lisbon, in the west. And
he lodged at . . . what was the name of that little hotel,
Alec?"

"St. John's," Alec bit out behind her. Then he launched
into a flow of what had to be Portuguese.

Mr. França certainly understood it. And judging from
the tone of his reply, he offered an apology. When they
spoke English after that, every word concerned the cavalry maneuvers Alec was to demonstrate.

But Katherine had found out quite enough. She'd been
right to think Alec was hiding something—but it wasn't
what she'd assumed. Why hadn't he said he'd been in the
thick of the war?

Because earls' sons weren't supposed to work for
money. Ironically, he could serve as an officer without reproach, but teaching for pay was beneath him.

Surely he realized she wouldn't care about that. Then
again, she *had* been awfully conscious of propriety
around him. Otherwise, why would he prefer she think
him a wastrel rather than a man hired by the army?

Well, she would set him straight after this was over. She

would tell him how proud she was that he'd served his country, no matter how. Because the truth was, she was tired of fighting him, tired of staying on her guard, tired of assuming the worst, when he clearly wasn't what she'd thought.

Suddenly, her attention was arrested by something Mr. França said. "What do you mean, 'as long as the senhorita can stay still for the final cut'?"

Alec grinned as he led her out the arena's back door. "That's the last part of the 'Angry Wife,' sweetheart. You lift up an object that I slice pieces off of as I gallop past."

Her breath caught in her throat. "You can do that?"

"Without a second thought."

Then it must be a very large object. "What is it? Because if it's too heavy for me to lift—"

Alec and Mr. França burst into laughter. "It won't be," Alec said, as they headed toward some outbuildings. "It's a pear."

Chapter Fourteen

∽⟡∼

*Nothing impresses a female more than a
display of manly strength, and if you can
make such a display while well-seated
upon a fine thoroughbred, so much
the better.*
—Anonymous, *A Rake's Rhetorick*

*A*lec was still grinning when he and França left Katherine a little while later. Her voice echoed from the outbuilding behind Astley's where the maid was helping to dress her.

"Just remember, Alec," Katherine called after them, "that had better be the largest pear in Christendom! And if you so much as scratch my fingers, I'll skewer you with the sword myself!"

He laughed. "You see what you've entangled me in, França?" he told his friend, as they headed across the yard toward the stables.

França glanced back at the outbuilding with a worried frown. "The senhorita seems very angry—are you sure she wants to do this?"

"She agreed to her part of the routine when you explained it, didn't she? Don't let her fool you—she protests, but she'll do fine. She has a hidden wild streak." One he was determined to plumb.

"So you are not angry with me for . . . er . . . persuading you to ride."

"Not anymore." Little Miss Marry-Well needed shaking up, and this was the perfect way to do it. "Besides, you know I had no choice."

"I am most sorry før that. Senhor Astley did not like to press the matter, but he was desperate."

Astley had a right to demand Alec's services—he'd provided the private box and the free admissions in exchange for Alec's agreeing to ride in one show. But Alec had meant a future show; Astley apparently was fuzzy on that condition.

França opened the doors to the stables. "So the senhorita did not know of your skill with the horses?"

"She knew most of it." But not all, and later, he'd have to deal with her questions about why an earl's son had chosen to work for hire.

Perhaps it wouldn't be so bad. It might even weigh in his favor. She preferred eccentric men—like that damned poet Lovelace. As long as she didn't probe too deeply into his family situation, he might get through this all right.

As they entered the stables, Alec relaxed. Here he felt at home, among the snuffling of horses, the shifting of hooves, the smell of straw and horse sweat and manure. The first thing he would do after he married was get Edenmore's stables in order.

But for now he had only to pick which of Astley's well-trained horses to ride, and listen while França went over what was expected of him.

By the time Alec was mounted and waiting for the back doors to the amphitheatre to open, he felt ready. The doors opened, and Alec nudged his mount into a gallop. Might as well make a dramatic entrance.

As Alec rode into the sawdust ring, the crowd cheered wildly. He cantered for one circuit, flourishing his sword while França began his patter from the side of the ring.

He missed this. It was what he did best, not all that nonsense with balls and poetry readings. He never felt comfortable there. *This* was his home. He could perform cavalry maneuvers in his sleep.

He had refused the mask because it would hamper his vision, but no one would connect "Captain Black" in his plumed shako and blue dolman jacket with the Earl of Iversley, especially from a distance.

He halted at the edge of the ring for dramatic effect, then launched right into the demonstration. *Prepare to guard. Guard. Assault. Left protect.* Each maneuver was instinctive to a man who'd taught them day after day, year after year.

Bridle arm protect. Sword arm protect. Saint George. To the rear cut. Guard. Slope swords. By the time he'd reached the Cut V and VI in the fifth division, the crowd was primed for more adventurous riding.

Now came the tricks. These weren't as familiar to him as cavalry maneuvers, but he'd performed them often enough to entertain the men he'd trained. Riding in a circle made it easier—Philip Astley had discovered years ago that centrifugal force allowed a man to do amazing feats on horseback. Alec easily stood atop the saddle while brandishing his sword, dismounted and mounted while the horse was at a gallop, and even rode with his head inches from the ground, a trick that gained him wild applause.

By the time he halted his horse upstage of the ring to take a bow, França was announcing a masked Katherine: "For our next diversion, the lovely Senhora Encantador has agreed to play Captain Black's wife."

Alec smiled. With any luck, she'd soon be playing it outside the ring, too.

"The Angry Wife" was a diversion meant to provide comic relief between the patriotic military maneuvers and the sheer drama of the upcoming finale. It also allowed the stage manager's staff to prepare for the ambitious staging of the Battle of Salamanca, which included fifty horses and a set of two hills to be mounted behind the curtains.

As França began his patter—explaining that Mrs. Black had grown tired of waiting at home for her cavalry officer husband, and had come to fetch him— Katherine took her place slightly off center of the ring, wearing a voluminous cloak and a comical bonnet.

She pretended to chide Alec for being late, shaking a parasol at him while França stated that Mrs. Black had a hot temper. Alec galloped past to slice the parasol in half, and the crowd laughed.

Katherine, however, mimed outrage as França cried, "Mrs. Black is most annoyed—that was her favorite parasol." On cue, Katherine tossed the other half of it after Alec and continued her mimed harangue.

He made his second circuit, this time catching her bonnet on the point of his sword, and tossing it over to land on França's head. Katherine's hair tumbled down as it was supposed to, eliciting more laughter from the crowd.

But it had an entirely different effect on Alec. He'd never seen her hair down. God help him, there was so much of it. And the lights made the brilliantly hued mass appear to engulf her cloaked shoulders in dancing flames. What he wouldn't give to drag his fingers through that lush—

No, he mustn't think about that right now. He had to concentrate.

Katherine patted her head, then stamped her feet and pointed over at her bonnet. He couldn't hold back a laugh. Who would have expected Miss Marry-Well to be such a showman?

As she continued her antics, he cantered toward her and aimed his sword for a billow of her cloak far below her arm. Normally the swordsman would cut the purposely large bow so that the cloak fell to the ground, but Katherine had balked at letting Alec near her neck with the tip of his sword.

Praying she'd remembered to unfasten the ties, he caught the cloak on the end of his sword as he passed. She *had* remembered, thank God, and the cloak fluttered free so easily he had no trouble tossing it into França's open arms.

As Alec made the next circuit, França continued his recitation. "I fear that Captain Black is in deep trouble now for ruining his wife's best cloak."

Damned right he was. Because now Alec could see the costume *beneath* the cloak—God help him.

Hardly aware of what he did, he slowed his mount to a trot as he looked Katherine over. The shocking orange gown would break any man's concentration. Sparkling with paste jewels of green and gold, it sheathed her body so eloquently he could see every curve. Especially the two curves spilling out of the low-cut bodice. Katherine filled the gown out far too well for his peace of mind.

It took a supreme effort of will—and an extra circuit of the ring—for him to beat his feverish lust into submission. How was he supposed to think when all he wanted was to strip her bare and take her right here in the ring? That was *not* the sort of show the crowd had come to see.

Oblivious to his agitation, Katherine brandished the pear she'd been hiding under the cloak. França's loud voice called out to the crowd, "Mrs. Black tells the captain that she kept the last of the winter pears for him, but now he will get none. She will eat it herself."

That was Alec's cue. But as he rode toward her, he noticed the trembling of Katherine's arm as she swung the pear in the air. She held the fruit with the tips of her fingers. The pear was plenty big enough for his purposes, but judging from how her eyes nervously followed his approach, she didn't believe that.

Just trust me, sweetheart, he admonished silently as he cantered toward her.

Within seconds, he'd made his first pass, cutting the top half of the pear right off. The crowd applauded loudly.

Katherine was supposed to pantomime outrage, but she only stood frozen as he circled the ring again. Thankfully, the audience thought that was part of the routine and laughed.

But Alec worried about the next part, where she was to lift the other half of the pear to her mouth while he rode up to skewer it with his sword, then canter from the ring with her racing after him on foot.

Though she awaited his second approach gamely, every bit the trouper, her eyes showed her apprehension. Blast. What if she moved as he thrust? At best, she would ruin the routine. At worst, she might move into danger.

He couldn't risk it. Time for a change of plan.

Chapter Fifteen

~~~

*Don't wait until conditions for a seduction
are ideal. Seize your chance whenever
you can.*
—Anonymous, *A Rake's Rhetorick*

He knows what he's doing, Katherine repeated to herself as Alec circled back toward her. *He won't hurt you, he won't.*

Now, if she could just convince her hand. She couldn't keep it still. The half a pear looked *so* small. But if she gripped it any closer to the edge, she'd drop it. Probably just as he went to skewer it, and then he'd skewer her hand instead.

She was supposed to lift the pear to her mouth, right? *Lift the pear,* she ordered her hand.

It ignored her. Apparently, her fingers balked at being chopped off.

Too late—he was here, sword in hand . . . rising up in the stirrups . . . coming nearer . . . nearer . . . Wait, why was he leaning out like that?

Before she could react, he bent his head to snatch the pear with his mouth.

The crowd clapped, but she just stood there bewildered as he continued the circuit. She watched as he thrust his sword into the sawdust. What should she do? Run after him as they'd originally planned? But he wasn't leaving the arena, so that would look silly. Of course, this was supposed to be funny . . .

Then he was approaching her again with the pear half still gripped in his mouth, and next thing she knew, she was soaring aloft, being hoisted into the air onto the front of the extra-deep trick saddle.

She threw her arms about his neck to keep from falling, which sent the crowd into wild applause until Mr. França's quickly improvised patter broke in. "Will Mrs. Black forgive her wayward husband?" he called out as the audience fell silent to hear him. "Or will she send him packing?"

She and Alec were making another slow circuit of the ring. Eyes alight with mischief, Alec offered her the pear half with his mouth. Compelled forward by the invitation in his hot blue gaze, she bit into the fruit, bringing their lips together in a kiss.

The crowd roared, loving a good romance. She heard them cheering even after Alec exited through the back doors with her in his arms and his mouth pressed to hers around the pear half.

Behind the amphitheatre was a hive of activity as horses lined up and riders put the finishing touches to their costumes, preparing for the big finale, but Katherine hardly noticed as Alec reined in with her still clinging to his neck.

He bit down, breaking the pear in half again, then drew back and chewed his quarter, his eyes smoldering at her as she chewed hers, too, and swallowed. His gaze followed the motion of her throat, then darkened, and before she could even think, his mouth was on hers, kissing her deeply, hotly . . . thoroughly.

She didn't care. Her blood still thrummed from the excitement of the ring and the thrill of performing with him. Straining against him, she returned his kiss eagerly, nearly knocking off her mask. She tasted pear juice on his tongue, sweetening their kiss even more as she twined her tongue with his to seek the deepest sweetness.

Heedless of the performers around them, he kissed her as blatantly as a lover, lingering over her mouth, tangling his tongue with hers, making her so dizzy that she—

"Sorry, sir, but we need the horse."

They broke apart, with Alec looking as dazed as she felt. Then they both glanced down to find a groom tugging on the reins of Alec's mount.

The groom smirked up at them. "For the finale. We need the horse."

As Katherine blushed furiously, Alec dismounted, then reached up to lift her down beside him.

Even after the groom led the horse away, Alec kept his hands firmly on her waist. "Are you all right? I didn't hurt you back there in the ring when I—"

"No," she whispered, still breathless from their kiss.

A faint smile played over his lips. "I could tell you were nervous about letting me skewer the pear, so I improvised."

She arched an eyebrow. "You broke my rules about kissing."

His eyes glittered in the light of the field lamps. "That's what happens when you give me rules." With a grin, he tugged her closer and lowered his head. "I have to go out of my way to break them."

With a laugh, she wriggled out of his arms and headed toward the outbuilding where she'd changed clothes earlier. "Rather publicly, don't you think?"

Catching up to her, he laid his hand possessively on the small of her back. "Were there other people there? I didn't notice."

Another laugh bubbled up inside her. "You really are incorrigible."

"And you're magnificent."

Her breath caught in her throat. "Am I?" she asked coyly.

What was wrong with her? She was never coy. It must be the cursed costume—it made her feel like someone else, someone free to answer the invitation in his eyes. She reached up to remove her mask, then thought better of it. People still milled around who might connect her with the lady who'd come out here with Lord Iversley.

"I can't think of any other woman who would adapt so quickly to performing," Alec said. "You were wonderful. And the audience loved you—I wasn't the only one eating out of your hand."

She eyed him askance. "I hardly think my little pantomiming compared to your spectacular riding. No wonder Wellington wanted you to train his cavalry." She straightened her mask. "I do wish I could ride like that."

His hand swept up her back. "I meant what I said about teaching you. You're a good rider. You could master the easier tricks without any trouble."

"If I had the horse for it." She sighed. "Even if I did, Mama would never allow it. It's one thing for me to do something like this on a whim—it's quite another to make a practice of it."

"But you won't always be under your mother's control. If you marry me, you can do as you please."

Her head shot around, her gaze locking with his. With a dark smile, he slid his arm to encircle her waist, but before he could do more, the maid who'd dressed Katherine earlier came running up to them from the nearby outbuilding. "Sorry, miss, but I can't help you dress just now. I have to help the others with the finale."

"It's all right," Katherine said. "I can manage on my own."

The maid turned to Alec. "And forgive me, sir, but we need your uniform. We can make do without the breeches and Hessians, but—"

"No problem." Alec removed the plumed hat thing, then stripped off the blue jacket, black stock, and red-and-gold sash of a dragoon officer. "Senhora Encantador is used to theatrical necessity, aren't you, sweetheart?" He handed the uniform to the maid.

"Of course," Katherine choked out, the sight of him in shirtsleeves making it hard for her to breathe. "But you do look dashing in it."

"Any man looks dashing in a uniform," he retorted.

But no other man could look like Alec, in a uniform or out. Even after the maid scurried off, Katherine couldn't stop staring at him in his thin linen shirt and form-fitting white breeches, his collar hanging open to reveal a few dark chest hairs.

Goodness, but he was one fine figure of a man. There'd certainly been no padding beneath *his* coat, nor did his shirt appear to hide stays like the ones Papa had worn to hold in his thick belly. It was all pure Alec.

Pure, handsome, tempting Alec.

He knew what he did to her, too, the rascal. As she stared at him, desire leaped in his face. Opening the door to the outbuilding, he pulled her inside and closed the door. The light of the single low-burning lamp revealed a completely deserted dressing room.

Everyone was in the finale except them. She and Alec were alone.

Her heart skipped a beat as he drew her into his arms, then reached for her mask.

"No," she whispered, staying his hand. "Let me be Senhora Encantador a while longer." Senhora Encantador could kiss him without reproach, whereas Miss Merivale could not. "Who chose my stage name, anyway?"

"I did." He cupped her head in his hands. "It's Portuguese."

As he lowered his mouth, her breath quickened. "What does it mean?"

"Enchanter," he said in a husky whisper. "It means 'enchanter.'"

Then he sealed her lips with his.

She rose to his kiss without protest. He was a cavalry officer, and she was the reckless Senhora Encantador, who wore daringly cut costumes and kissed a man in front of everybody.

Besides, who could resist a man who called her "the enchanter" even though he professed to hate poetry? Especially when he commanded her mouth as if the kiss were his due. Over and over he plundered her lips, first tenderly, then ardently, fiercely, until she couldn't think, couldn't breathe, couldn't do anything but slide her arms about his waist to pull him closer.

The taste of pears mingled with the scent of horses and leather to fill her senses. Not even the muted sounds of the performers milling beyond the door could dampen her excitement.

When at last Alec drew back, she was too dazed to notice him reaching for her mask again. "I want to see your face, sweetheart," he murmured as he tossed the mask onto a nearby table heaped high with bonnets, combs, and other feminine paraphernalia. "Though I must admit I like you as Senhora Encantador. And even better as Mrs. Black."

"Don't let Mama hear you say that," she said, trying for nonchalance. "It's Lady Iversley or nothing."

The intensity of his gaze made her heart flip over. "Then Lady Iversley it is."

When he bent his head toward her once more, she pressed him back, determined to get some answers. "Do you mean that?"

"Why won't you believe me?"

Her pulse thundered in time to the horses' hooves outside as the company rode into the arena. "Why did you say a week ago that this courtship was only for Sydney's benefit?"

"You were ready to toss me out on my ear again, and I couldn't figure out any other way to stay close to you." His eyes shone like blue flames. "Why do you think I came to London in the first place? To find a wife. Believe me, from the night we met, it was marriage I wanted."

"You wanted to seduce me," she breathed, though she grew less certain of that by the moment.

He smiled. "I wanted both. Because I can't keep my hands off you." To prove it, he slid his hands back to tangle them in her scandalously undone hair.

A wanton heat settled low in her belly. "Y-You should go. I have to dress. Mama will wonder what is taking us so long back here."

He bent his head to kiss a path down her neck. "We'll tell her we decided to watch the finale from behind the scenes." He nipped her earlobe. "Come now, where's Senhora Encantador, the shameless woman with the beautiful hair?"

She shot him a skeptical look. "Mama calls it my 'unfortunate hair.' And Sydney thinks it's so bold I should cover it up with a turban."

"Don't you dare." As he stroked her unruly locks, the raw need burning in his eyes was unmistakable. "I've wanted to see it down like this ever since we first met. I've wanted to touch it, to run my fingers through it . . ."

When he did just that, a shiver of pleasure coursed through her. Wrapping a hank of it around his hand, he kissed it, then tugged it to draw her close so he could press a slow, sweet kiss to her mouth.

Then he shifted his lips to her cheek and entangled both his hands in her hair to hold her fast. "The only unfortunate thing about your hair is that you have to keep it pinned up." He trailed warm, openmouthed kisses over her cheek to her ear. "Once we're married, you can wear it down as much as you please."

"I haven't agreed to marry you yet, you know," she whispered.

"Why not?"

"Because I don't really . . . know you."

"You know me well enough." He laved her ear with his tongue.

She shivered deliciously. "Until tonight, I didn't know you at all." She drew back to stare at him. "Why did you let me think you were so wicked?"

His hungry gaze bored into her. "As I recall, I tried to tell you otherwise. You refused to believe me." A rakish grin crossed his lips. "Besides, I *am* wicked. At least when it comes to you."

He slid his hand beneath the edge of her bodice and chemise to caress her bare shoulder, then added in a whisper, "And you're wicked, too, when it comes to me . . .

Senhora Encantador." Her pulse went positively mad as he trailed kisses over her neck.

"Senhora Encantador . . . disappeared when you removed . . . her mask," she choked out.

"Are you sure?" Still kissing her neck, he pushed her gown off her shoulder. "Or is she just hiding behind the proper Miss Merivale?"

He was kissing her shoulder, fogging her brain, making her dizzy from the sensation of his mouth caressing her bare skin in a place no man would dare to touch. "I suppose you've been with many . . . senhoras?"

"Not as many as most gentlemen. There aren't many senhoras in a cavalry camp." He dragged one finger down her throat, into the valley between her breasts. "And certainly none so intriguing as Senhora Encantador."

When his finger lodged beneath her bodice, she caught her breath. "Is that who you really want—the senhora?"

"I want Miss Merivale, but she refuses to be reckless and wicked with me. Perhaps the senhora could show her how?"

The idea intrigued and excited her. Now he was kissing his way down her collarbone toward her bodice . . . and her breasts. Would he kiss her there? Like in the pictures from the *Rhetorick?* Would it be even better than his caresses there the day of the reading?

A wild fever flashed over her at the thought. "Suppose you happened to be alone . . . with the senhora. What would you do with that wicked creature? Hypothetically, of course."

He lifted his head, eyes gleaming in the dim lamplight. "Hypothetically?"

She nodded, unable to speak.

Taking her by surprise, he lifted her in his arms.

"What on earth are you doing?" Katherine grabbed at his neck to hold on as he carried her off between the open bureaus, past a scarf-draped dressmaker's dummy, toward the back of the outbuilding.

He cast her a smile rampant with mischief. "I'm taking the senhora to where we can be more comfortable."

A laugh escaped her. "This isn't hypothetical."

"I need the right setting for . . . speculating." He laid her on a pile of discarded costumes and cloaks, then stretched out beside her. "Now, where were we? Ah, yes, determining what I would do to Senhora Encantador, that reckless female." He grinned as he propped his head up on one arm, then laid the other over her waist. "Hypothetically, of course."

"Of course," she whispered.

One shoulder of her gown still hung down her arm, and now he snagged the shoulder of her chemise and tugged it down, too. "First, I'd do this," he murmured, as her breast scandalously sprang free. "And then this . . ." He molded her naked breast in his hot palm.

Lord preserve her, it was every bit as wonderful as she remembered, every bit as naughty and thrilling. Which was why she ought to stop him. "Wouldn't the senhora . . . protest such . . . liberties?"

"Not at all. She would expect it from her latest lover."

"What if you were her first lover?"

A fierce desire leaped in his face. "Then I'd have to be more careful with her . . . make sure I taught her how to find her pleasure. Hypothetically, of course."

"Of course," she whispered, then gasped when he thumbed her nipple, sending a delicious excitement pulsing along her heightened nerves. She dug her fingers into his shirt. "The senhora is very wicked, isn't she?"

"Curious," he corrected her. "Adventurous. The sort of woman who will participate in an equestrian exhibition without a qualm."

Which had whetted her appetite for more adventures. With him. And he knew it, too. Why else was he lowering his head and taking her breast in his mouth to . . . *ohhhh, yes . . . like that . . . goodness, what a feeling . . .*

His tongue swirled over her nipple, tightening it into a knot of aching need. She fisted her hands in the night-dark waves of his hair to hold him there, and his mouth grew ravenous, sucking hard, making her squirm and yearn to feel it in other, more outrageous places—like in that naughty picture . . .

Oh, she was as bad as him . . . and she didn't even care. This was the most thrilling thing that had ever happened to her.

The naive country girl can provide a nice change for the jaded rake's palate.

When those horrible words from the *Rake's Rhetorick* spilled into her mind, she thrust them out determinedly. Alec wasn't a rake—he wanted to marry her. He'd made that very clear.

"You taste so damned good," he murmured as he lifted his head. "And I've wanted to taste and touch you like this for so long."

The words were out of her mouth before she could stop them. "And when do I get to taste and touch you?" She was *not* a naive country girl he wanted for his "jaded palate." She was *not*.

Alec reacted instantly to her bold words; heat leaped in his face as he sat up. "Whenever you please, senhora." He dragged his shirt off so quickly that his cuff buttons popped off. "*Now*, if you want."

Katherine's mouth went dry. Lord preserve her, he was every bit as handsome as those strutting men in the pictures—thickly muscled, leanly built, and hairy.

She was still drinking in the astonishing sight of him bare-chested when he lay back down, grabbed her hand, and flattened it on his chest. "I would give a king's ransom to have you touch me."

The yearning in his face convinced her as nothing else could have.

Leaning forward, she pressed a kiss to his chest, reveling in his sharp intake of breath. Remembering how good his mouth on her breast had felt, she swirled her tongue around his flat male nipple. "And what will you give me for tasting you, Captain Black?" she teased.

With a growl, he pressed her head to his chest and closed his eyes. "Anything you want, sweetheart. Anything you want."

Further emboldened, Katherine took her time exploring his chest, marveling at how the rough velvet of his flesh leaped and flexed when she flicked her tongue or stroked her fingers over it.

The senhora had taken her over, and she had no will to fight her. The whole night already seemed like one long dream, and the unfamiliar scents of sawdust and leather on his skin added to her feeling of unreality. Not even the muffled drumbeats coming from the amphitheatre could drag her from the heady spell.

Until his hand caught the hem of her gown and dragged it up to bare her thighs. Coming to her senses in a rush of panic, she jerked her head from his chest.

"Alec, you mustn't—"

"I only want to touch you." His hot blue gaze seared her. "A little touching, that's all." He skimmed his hand up the inside of her thighs, making her gasp. "Don't you want to see what I'd do next to Senhora Encantador? Hypothetically?"

Frantically, she tried to hang on to her objections. It wasn't easy when her skin felt too tight for her body, every inch alive and alert to his amazing caresses. "This goes . . . beyond hypothetical."

His hand slid inexorably higher. "Then call it a sample. Of what I would do." He smiled impishly when his fingers brushed the slit in her drawers. "Put yourself in the senhora's place and tell me how she'd like my sample."

A laugh bubbled up inside her throat that she firmly squelched, not wanting to encourage his naughty behavior. "Sample, hah. That's just rhetoric."

"If you say so." He slid his hand inside her drawers. "You're the one who knows such things. I'm but a simple man with simple pleasures."

"There's nothing simple about—" His hand cupped the warm, throbbing place between her thighs as if he'd guessed exactly where she craved his touch. "Ohh . . . that's . . . truly . . . outrageous . . ."

"Would the senhora like that, do you think?" His fingers fondled her shamelessly, sweeping through her tangled curls to find the hidden tender flesh.

She gasped when he pressed against some delicate spot that sent the blood beating in her veins in time to the drums sounding more loudly from the amphitheatre. "The senhora would . . . certainly like . . . that."

With a devilish smile, he bent his head to brush a kiss to her breast. "Are you sure? You seem very agitated by it."

"Because . . . ohh, what . . . are you . . . doing to me?"

"Showing you how I would touch the senhora." His

finger slid along the slick flesh of her most intimate place, then delved deep between the folds.

She grabbed for his arm in shock. "Alec!"

"Yes, senhora? Do you like my sample?" Ignoring her grip on his arm, he repeated that devilish driving motion with his finger. When she moaned, he cast her a knowing smile. "Those sounds you're making say you do." He stroked her deftly. "Does this please you?"

"Yes." It made her ache and yearn . . . and want him never to stop touching her in the shameless and exhilarating way he touched her now.

"Do you . . . would the senhora . . . want more?" he asked hoarsely as he thrust his finger inside her over and over, his thumb caressing that tender spot higher up.

"Please, Alec . . . please . . ." she choked out, scarcely noticing that her hand had fallen away from his arm.

"Please what?" His strokes grew bolder, hotter, melting her resistance away with their sheer heat. "Please stop? Or please give you more?"

Please stop. "Please . . . more," she whispered.

With a growl of satisfaction, he took her mouth in a long, searching kiss, all the while stroking between her legs so adroitly that he soon had her gasping and undulating wantonly against his clever hand.

"That's it, sweetheart," he tore his lips free to whisper against her hot cheek. "Reach for your pleasure. It's there for you. Relax and let it come."

She barely heard the words, too caught up in the incredible tension coiling right where his fingers rubbed and fondled. It tightened as his strokes quickened, until she was writhing beneath him and wanting . . . needing . . . longing . . .

The explosion of heat took her off guard, wringing a

hoarse cry from her lips. As the burst of flames devoured her, then slowly died to smoldering embers, she melted into the nest of costumes. Her eyes closed in rapt contentment as she held on to the last bit of wanton warmth.

A mock battle still raged inside the amphitheatre, but out here, a comfortable peace stole over her. "What . . . what did you . . . do to me?" she whispered.

"Pleasured you, that's all."

If the woman resists, pleasure her well to bring her willingly to your bed.

Wincing, she cursed *The Rake's Rhetorick* for poisoning her enjoyment. She opened her eyes to search Alec's face. His expression was strained, his jaw taut as he hovered over her.

"And is that all . . . you intend to do to me?" she couldn't help asking.

Deliberately, he drew his hand from between her thighs and tugged her skirts down. "For now. I don't deflower innocents." He bent to kiss her breast so tenderly, it made her heart leap. "But once we're married . . ."

He left the promise dangling in the air between them, rousing a feverish anticipation. The very idea of the liberties he might take with her as a husband sent heat washing over her, starting at her cheeks, flashing to the breasts he'd caressed so wildly, then moving lower to the still-throbbing place between her legs.

She tamped down her excitement firmly. This was no time to get carried away. These were serious matters they were discussing, no matter how eager her body was to throw caution to the wind.

Sitting up, she tugged her chemise over her breasts. "I still haven't agreed to marry you. You haven't really even asked me."

He sat up, too, looking earnest and infinitely dear. "All right, I'm asking you now. Will you marry me, Katherine?"

Her foolish heart leaped to hear the actual words, but she forced herself to respond rationally. "Why do you want me to?"

That seemed to flummox him, but his gaze steadied on hers. "Because you're the only woman I can ever imagine marrying."

She swallowed. He hadn't spoken of love, but neither had she. Given the choice between Sydney, who said he loved her but acted otherwise, and Alec, who treated her as if he did without saying the words, she might be better off with Alec.

You barely know him, her good sense cautioned. *You can't even be sure of his character.*

But all of that faded to nothing when he was with her, when he kissed and fondled her, when he rode up on a Thoroughbred to snatch a piece of pear out of her hand rather than risk hurting her, or halted his seductions because he didn't deflower innocents.

"Yes," she whispered before she could regret it. "Yes, I'll marry you."

"Good," was all he said, but he leaned forward to punctuate the word with a long, searing kiss that roused her blood yet again.

When she wrapped her hands about his waist, he groaned and drew back. "We have to stop this." He jerked his head toward the door. "Listen."

When she did as he bade, she heard a rising hubbub in the field beyond the outbuilding that signaled the end of the final performance.

"They'll be trying to get in here any minute," he said.

"You don't want them to find us together like this, do you?"

Her face flamed, both at the possibility and at the fact that only he had thought of it. "Of course not."

The sounds in the field increased, and he rose swiftly. "Thank God I latched the front door." He snagged his shirt and drew it over his head, then held out his hand to help her up. "I'll take the back way out, while you stay in your chemise. They'll assume that you took off your costume unassisted, but couldn't put on your gown without help."

Feeling useless and bereft, she watched him stride about the room, making sure nothing was amiss and no evidence of their scandalous encounter remained.

"Tonight I'll speak to your mother," he went on. "Tomorrow I'll send the announcement to the papers. I can procure a special license—"

"Alec," she broke in. "Don't speak to Mama tonight about our marrying."

He froze, then faced her warily. "Why not?"

"I'd like to tell Sydney first."

His eyes glittered dangerously as he strode up to her. "Send him a letter. Better yet, let him read it in the paper. He's a poet—I'm told they read a *lot*."

She bit back a smile. "I've been half-betrothed to him most of my life. He at least deserves the courtesy of hearing about my engagement in person."

"I see." A muscle worked in his jaw as he glanced away. "So how long will you make me wait? He's in the country, and you don't know when he'll return."

"Lord Napier's estate is only a short ride from London. I'll call on Sydney's mother tomorrow to find out the direction, then send a message saying I want to see him. If he doesn't come in a few days, then we can assume we're free to announce the marriage."

He scowled at her. "We *are* free. You're the only one saying otherwise."

He looked so delightfully grumpy about the whole thing, she couldn't help smiling. "You're adorable when you're jealous, you know."

His rigid features slowly relaxed, though he grumbled, "Adorable, am I? Next you'll tell me I'm sweet."

"You *are* sweet." She laid her hand on his arm. "Most of the time."

Drawing her close, he kissed her roughly, brazenly, his hands roaming her body as if to mark his claim. When he pulled back, her heart was racing.

"And the rest of the time?" he rasped. "What am I then?"

"The only man I can ever imagine marrying."

Relief showed in his eyes as he rubbed his thumb over her lower lip. "How in God's name will I wait until after we marry to make you mine? I can hardly bear to leave you now."

The sincerity of his tone warmed her heart, making her smile and lean into him. With a sigh, he lowered his head toward her lips again, but the sound of the door rattling, followed by a loud knock, made him release her.

"Blast. I have to go. If they can't get in the front, they'll come to the back and I'll be trapped."

The door rattled again. "Miss?" came a worried voice. "Are you in there?"

"I'm here!" Katherine turned to the door to call out. "I'm coming."

When she turned back to tell Alec she would see him outside, he was gone.

Chapter Sixteen

*The rake should never let duty come in the
way of pleasure—unless he wants lectures
on crop planting to be his only
entertainment.*
—Anonymous, *A Rake's Rhetorick*

As the carriage trundled back to the town house, Alec
ignored Mrs. Merivale's nonstop gushing about his "feats
of daring." All he thought of was Katherine, all he saw
was Katherine, sitting across from him in her demure
gown.

Which now hid nothing from him. Because he knew
what her pert breasts looked like under the layers of fabric, how fine her skin was to the touch . . . how reckless
the nature that lay coiled beneath her controlled de-
meanor.

His wife-to-be might possess the practical instincts of
a woman used to taking care of everybody and everything . . . but they were tempered with a healthy dose of
pure animal lust.

And when do I get to taste and touch you? He broke out
in a sweat just thinking of her lips pressed to his chest,
her teeth tugging on his nipple, her tongue licking over
his—

By God, how would he make it until their wedding

night? Especially with her no longer resisting his physical advances. Just to see what she'd do, he stroked his boot up the side of her leg farthest from her mother, using the darkness and her skirts to cover his actions.

Her eyes widened, then grew sultry. Casting a furtive glance at her mother, she echoed his caress with her slipper.

Every muscle in his body went instantly hard. Which wasn't wise when he wore glove-tight breeches and sat across from his future mother-in-law.

Ruthlessly he wrestled his lust into submission. Had he ever desired a woman this intensely? If so, he didn't re-member it. But Katherine was no ordinary woman. Who else could take in stride his impulsive inclusion of her in an equestrian performance?

Not to mention his revelation of secrets any other woman of rank would have found appalling. But not Katherine; oh no. She merely found them intriguing.

Thank God she didn't know the worst of them. He must go to any length to keep her from finding out until after the wedding.

But what then? After they were married and back at his estate, she would have to learn how poor he was. Given her clever little mind, she would probably realize that her fortune had provoked his initial interest.

She wouldn't like that one bit. And when he revealed that he was really the by-blow of a debauchee whom she regarded with contempt . . .

He shook off his niggling unease. It didn't matter what she thought. By the time she discovered all his secrets, it would be too late for her to do anything but resign herself to the marriage.

The thought of a resigned Katherine going through

the motions as his wife chilled his blood, but he refused to let it bother him. She wouldn't sulk for long—he'd make sure of that. He'd simply use Katherine's wanton nature against her, pleasure her so often and so well in bed that she'd eventually forgive his deception.

A smile touched his lips. That certainly gave him something to look forward to.

But he had to get there first. That meant he'd have to keep her too busy to look closely into his finances.

When Mrs. Merivale paused for breath, he seized the opportunity to speak to Katherine. "We never did have that ride in the park. Perhaps we should attempt it again tomorrow."

Her smile faded. "I can't. I have a prior engagement, remember?"

Ah, yes, Lovelace. She was going to see Lovelace's mother. Damn that poet and his hold on her. "Sorry, I forgot. What about tomorrow evening, the fete at Holland House?"

Katherine sighed. "We weren't invited. Mama and I don't exactly move in the same circles as you do."

Mrs. Merivale scowled at her daughter. "We *were* invited. You don't see all the invitations we receive, you know." When Katherine raised an eyebrow, her mother grew suddenly absorbed in straightening her skirts. "I turned it down, is all. That Lady Holland is too scandalous a woman for my daughter to associate with. A divorcée, imagine!"

"That divorcée is the toast of London except among the high sticklers, Mama. You would never have turned down her invitation." Katherine shot Alec a rueful smile. "Mama simply doesn't want you to know that we are so low on the social ladder that even a 'scandalous' woman like Lady Holland wouldn't invite us to a party."

"Katherine, really!"

"It's all right, Mrs. Merivale," Alec said, suppressing a chuckle. "I'm not courting your daughter for her connections, I assure you."

Katherine rewarded him for that truthful statement with a warm smile that sent the blood rushing right to his head.

"If you aren't invited," he continued, "I won't go, either." He winked at Katherine. "It sounds like too shocking a party for a respectable man like me."

Her mother's face lit up. "Do you hear that, my angel? Isn't his lordship the very model of propriety?"

Katherine's lips twitched. "Yes, Mama. We should all follow his sterling example."

"And here you were worried that he was a wild sort," her mother said.

"Surely not," Alec retorted in mock outrage. "Miss Merivale, have you been thinking unjustly of me?"

"I don't believe so, my lord," Katherine said sweetly. "But then, I'm still trying to determine your true character."

That worried him. She'd agreed to marry him . . . but she didn't quite trust him even now. He would have to stay on his guard.

"If you have no other engagement for tomorrow night," her mother said, "you must dine with us."

"It would be an honor," he replied. "The night after, I'd like to accompany you to Lady Purefoy's birthday supper. And if you have no invitation—"

"We *were* invited to that," Katherine said with a relieved smile. "Lady Purefoy and Mama came out together—they've been friends ever since."

"Oh, yes," Mrs. Merivale gushed. "We were like three peas in a pod before we married, me and Lady Purefoy and Lady Lovelace—" She broke off. "Of course, Lady Lovelace and I no longer see each other. I don't even know if she will attend, and—"

"It's all right, Mama," Katherine interjected. "His lordship is a gentleman. He understands these things."

Alec grimaced. In other words, her former suitor might be there and she would expect them both to behave like gentlemen. What a damned annoying prospect. "Then it's settled. Evening after next, I'll come for you at eight o'clock."

"And you'll come for dinner tomorrow night," Mrs. Merivale prodded.

"Yes. Tomorrow night."

But even the prospect of two evenings in Katherine's company couldn't revive his lowered spirits. The very thought of her anywhere near Sydney Lovelace dampened all his pleasure.

What if the pompous ass tried to change her mind? Or worse yet, tried to kiss her again? The possibility sickened him.

By God, what was wrong with him? This jealousy nonsense—even his former mistress had never roused it in him. Why must it appear with Katherine, the one person he should be calm and reasonable and blasted gentlemanly around?

But the mad possessiveness she brought out in him did shed new light on his parents' marriage. He'd never understood how a man who ignored his wife could treat her badly when she found pleasure elsewhere.

Now he understood. Not the bad treatment; there was no excuse for that. But the power of jealousy was stronger than he'd realized. Acting on a bitter man of no character, like the old earl, it was bound to wreak havoc.

He mustn't let it wreak havoc on him. He had Katherine now—he mustn't jeopardize that. *Follow the rules. Don't let passion deter you from your objective.*

So after they arrived, and he accompanied the ladies into the town house, he was surprised to hear himself say, "Mrs. Merivale, may I speak to your daughter privately?"

The woman's gaze grew speculative as she glanced from him to Katherine. "I daresay you've been private enough with my daughter this evening." She smiled. "But I suppose a few minutes more can't hurt."

She strode off down the hall as Alec led Katherine to the parlor. As soon as they entered, he hauled Katherine into his arms and kissed her thoroughly, seeking reassurance in the sweet warmth of her mouth.

When he drew back, she gaped at him. "Alec? What—"

"That's to remind you of me when you meet with Lovelace. In case he resorts to my own tactics to tempt you back to his side."

Her eyes gleamed with mischief. "What happened to the man who urged me to try other men's kisses? And said I needed more of a basis for comparison? Perhaps you're right—if Sydney will kiss me again, I can make a proper—"

He cut her off with a kiss so long and deep that she melted completely in his arms. When he pulled away to see her eyes closed, her breath coming in urgent gasps, and her body swaying, the hard knot in his gut finally loosened.

As she opened her eyes in a daze, he growled, "And that, you impertinent minx, is for having so much fun tormenting me."

"Just wait until we're married," she teased, undeterred by his gruff manner.

"I'm not sure I can last until then if we're always seeing Lovelace in society," he grumbled.

She eyed him askance. "Promise you'll be civil to him at Lady Purefoy's supper."

He scowled. "I'll be very civil. If he attempts to kiss you, I'll use great civility in knocking him into the next county."

A shadow fell over her features. "Now, Alec, you would never—"

"No." With an effort, he reined in his powerful feelings. "I'm only joking." When both her eyebrows arched high, he added ruefully, "Half-joking anyway. But I promise not to embarrass you."

"And after we're married? Will you refrain from embarrassing me then?"

"I'll try not to be too jealous a husband, if that's what you mean."

She chewed her lower lip. "And will you . . . um . . . give *me* cause to be jealous? I know most gentlemen have their dalliances, but—"

He pressed a finger to her lips. "I'm not like most gentlemen. And I intend to share my bed with only one woman once I marry." As the product of a household shattered by a single unfaithful act, he had no intention of repeating history. "Some of us gentlemen do believe in fidelity, you know."

"I hope so. Because I won't stand by and meekly accept infidelity—I'm not like most ladies, either."

He bit back a smile. "I came to that conclusion the first time I met you, sweetheart. It's what I like about you."

Her features softened. "As long as we understand each other."

A throat being cleared in the hall made him groan. "Your mother is signaling that it's time for my retreat."

Katherine sighed. "Mama is nothing if not subtle." He turned away, but she stayed him with one hand. "Just so you'll know, you were right about Sydney's kiss that day at the reading—it didn't live up to my expectations."

"I figured that out, too."

She stiffened. "Rather sure of yourself, aren't you?"

"If you'd enjoyed kissing Sydney, you would never have let me court you," he said simply. "You wouldn't have toyed with either of our affections like that."

"Then why did I agree to your scheme?"

"Because deep down you *wanted* to marry me, and it gave you an excuse to be with me." With a grin, he glanced down to where her hand lay on his arm. "And because you can't keep your hands off me, any more than I can keep mine off you."

With a sniff, she withdrew her hand, but he caught it and lifted it to his lips, pressing kisses against her gloved palm and each fingertip until her eyes softened, and she smiled. Only then did he release it.

"Sleep well, sweetheart. Because we won't get much sleep *after* we're married."

She was still blushing as he left. It took all his will to order the coachman to "go on," when all he wanted was to toss her in the carriage and carry her off with him to Gretna Green.

That wouldn't be wise, considering what was at stake. Men were hanged for kidnapping heiresses. So he'd have to resign himself to a few more restless nights while he imagined their future wedding night.

His pleasant thoughts of such delights only lasted until he reached the hotel, where he was accosted by a surprise visitor awaiting him in the lobby.

"Emson!" he exclaimed as his aging butler approached. "What are you doing in London?"

Emson had stayed at Edenmore when many of the other servants left. They'd feared Alec might not turn the place around after it had been neglected for so long. "Mr. Dawes sent me to fetch you home."

Dawes was the new steward. Alec's blood chilled. "What's wrong?"

With a glance at the other men milling in the lobby, Emson drew him outside. "It's that dreadful Mr. Harris in Ipswich. He's returned early from his trip to Scotland to see his sister. Mr. Dawes rode over there yesterday to fetch the new tillers and plows you ordered for the barley sowing, but Harris says he wants his money in cash, or he'll not release them."

"But his son agreed to let me have them on credit."

"As it happens, Mr. Harris had left strict instructions not to allow anyone from the estate to purchase on credit anymore, but young Master Harris says—"

"That I talked him into it, which is exactly what I did. Harris's son appreciates the difficulties a man might find himself in." He sighed. "Very well, I'll write a note explaining that I'm now engaged to marry an heiress. If he can only wait a while longer for his money—"

"A note won't convince him, my lord. You must come

yourself. 'Tis the only way. Mr. Dawes says if you don't get the new plows—"

"I know—I can't plant that new strain of barley in my untenanted fields. And the tenants won't try it in their own fields until they see me succeed with it. If I'm to expand the farms and increase all our incomes, I must improve their yields."

"Mr. Dawes says that the seed must go in the ground now, or it will be another year before he can try it."

"Without those tillers, they'll never get that soil turned. Blast, blast, and double-blast." Perhaps he shouldn't have been so eager to hire a new steward with modern ideas.

But what else could he do? His "father's" old steward had been stealing him blind, something Alec had figured out within two days of taking over the estate. And the tenants, burdened by increasing rents and low yields, were too beaten down to try anything new—they considered themselves lucky if they eked out a living.

The new steward was trying to change all that, but though the tenants had hated the old steward, they hadn't yet come to trust the new one. Or Alec himself, for that matter. And they weren't alone, judging from Harris's behavior.

Alec dragged his fingers through his hair. Damn, what to do now? If he could order the equipment in the village of Fenbridge near the estate, he could use his lordly influence to intimidate the merchant into doing as he wished, but the village was too small to provide such things.

Unfortunately, the owner of Harris's Fine Agricultural Implements in Ipswich was immune to influence. He supplied half the landowners in Suffolk—so he would hardly squawk if an impoverished earl withdrew his business.

"How can I improve an estate when no one will even give me the chance?" Alec bit out. "Harris doesn't trust me, my own tenants don't trust me—"

"That is not entirely true, my lord. But you must realize that with your being off in town, some of the tenants think—"

"I'm my 'father's' son. But I have no choice. I have to marry—it's the only answer. Which means I have to be in London right now."

"Not if you want your tillers, my lord." Old Emson always spoke his mind with impunity, and for good reason. He'd left service years ago, after marrying. But when his replacement had left, too, the old earl had begged Emson to return until matters improved at Edenmore. He was still there, and since he worked for a mere promise of pay, he felt free to say exactly what he thought.

Alec sighed. "Very well, I'll come."

"It should not take more than a day. Then you can return to London. If we post through the night, we can be there by late morning."

"Yes." And after Alec finished dealing with Harris, he could be back here day after tomorrow in plenty of time to take Katherine to the Purefoy ball. But he'd miss dinner with her tomorrow night, blast it. "We'll take the carriage. It'll be faster, and I can get some sleep before I face Harris tomorrow."

"Buying carriages now, are we?" Emson said dryly. "My, my, how we've come up in the world."

Alec raised an eyebrow. "For your information, I *borrowed* a carriage from my ... er ... business associate."

Emson still saw him as a sixteen-year-old rough-and-tumble ne'er-do-well. It would take time to change the old servant's opinion, and Alec had only been master for a few weeks.

"I needed the carriage to court my heiress," Alec went on. "I only hope Lord Draker doesn't hear how far I took it from town."

That shook even Emson's composure. "You borrowed a carriage from the Dragon Viscount? Oh, dear."

Alec cast Emson a rueful smile. "These are desperate times." He gestured toward the stables. "Give me a minute to throw some clothes in a bag and leave a note for my betrothed. Then I'll be ready."

Emson nodded. "I shall see to the horses."

As soon as Alec reentered the lobby, he called for paper. He scribbled an explanation for Katherine, then handed it to one of the footboys. "Make sure you take this directly to the address marked on the front, all right?"

"Yes, milord."

"Hand it to the manservant who answers the door, say it's for Miss Merivale, and then leave. Don't tarry." He paused. "Better yet, go in the afternoon, when ladies pay their social calls. She won't even be home then."

"Yes, milord," the boy answered, though he seemed perplexed by Alec's conditions.

"You mustn't tell anyone in the household where you came from. Just leave the note with the servant and go. The man won't think to ask about me at the door, and if by some chance Miss Merivale or Mrs. Merivale *is* at home, they can't question you if you're gone. Is that clear?"

"Yes, milord, I understand."

"Good." The last thing Alec needed was Katherine—or worse yet, Mrs. Merivale—learning he was forced to live in a hotel. That would certainly rouse their suspicions.

And he must avoid that at all cost now that success finally lay within his reach.

Chapter Seventeen

⚬≋⚬

*If you wish to be a successful rake, you
must learn the art of deception. 'Tis better
to be the deceiver than the deceived.*
—Anonymous, *A Rake's Rhetorick*

Katherine's visit to Lady Lovelace the next morning went as well as could be expected. At first, her ladyship insisted upon being the one to send any message from Katherine to Sydney. But Katherine remained steadfast in her determination to send it herself, and finally the woman revealed that Sydney was indeed at Lord Napier's estate. It took more coaxing to gain the address from her, but Katherine finally came away from the Lovelace town house successful.

After she returned home and sent her message to Sydney, however, she found herself at loose ends. She started half a dozen volumes of poetry before tossing them aside to pace the parlor restlessly.

What on earth was wrong with her? Poetry generally took her mind off her troubles, but not today. Any overly flowery passage reminded her of Alec's witty comments and made her laugh. And the love poems, with their talk of ruby lips and sweet kisses, sent her imagination into wild fancies about touching Alec—

She cursed under her breath. This was all his fault. The things he'd done last night, the things he'd made her hope for, had thrown all her emotions into confusion. Her feelings had never vacillated so wildly, and it frightened her. This was the whirlwind she'd sought to avoid, this heady excitement one minute and fearful anxiety the next.

Yet she couldn't regret her agreement to marry him. By altering all her perceptions of him, he'd made her believe that a life of passion might not be so terrible. Perhaps a woman really *could* have a husband who was both passionate and responsible, exciting and reliable.

The idea of marrying him grew more appealing by the moment. She couldn't wait for his next kiss, for their next encounter, for the day when they would say their vows and the night when he would—

"Let go of me—I told you, he don't need me to stay for no answer!" squeaked an unfamiliar voice from the hall.

She hurried out to find Thomas dragging a liveried footboy toward her, lecturing him all the way. "Now see here, you little whelp, you'll do this proper-like, the way your master would want, and not be shirking your duties so you can stroll through the park on your way back—"

"I ain't shirking nothin'! His lordship told me . . ." He trailed off as he caught sight of Katherine watching the curious byplay.

"What's going on here?" she asked.

Thomas yanked the boy to a halt. "This lad has brought a letter for you from his lordship." As her foolish heart began to pound, Thomas cast the boy a stern glance. "But he's *trying* to scurry off without delivering it proper-like."

Katherine bit back a smile. Being an older man from

the country, Thomas had often expressed his disapproval of the lax ways of city servants.

The boy gave a quick bow. "Begging your pardon, miss, but I promised his lordship I'd give the note to your servant, so as not to . . . er . . . disturb you." He scowled up at Thomas.

"I see," she said, though she did not see at all. "And this note is—"

"I got it right here." The boy handed her a folded sheet of paper. "Now you have it." He turned toward the door. "If you please, miss, I'll just be going—"

"Not so fast, boy." Thomas jerked the lad back. "Wait until the miss reads it. *Then* you can go."

The boy's eyes widened. "A-All right."

Something about the footboy's persistent attempts to leave struck warning bells. "You came from his lordship's town house?" she asked.

"No, miss."

When he didn't elaborate, she raised an eyebrow, but he just stood there, eyes fixed ahead and back ramrod straight. Growing more curious by the moment, she opened the note and read:

Dearest Katherine,

    Forgive me, but urgent estate business has called me to Suffolk, so I will be unable to join you and your mother for dinner. I will, however, be back by tomorrow night to take you to the Purefoy affair. Give your mother my sincerest regrets and assure her that I would much prefer to be dining in your excellent company than taking care of emergencies at Edenmore.

               Fondly,
               Alec

She folded the note, swallowing her disappointment. She should be pleased that Alec had so responsible a character. Not many lords would dash off to their estates to deal with such matters. They would rely on their stewards to handle it.

Yes, they would, wouldn't they?

Her eyes narrowed on the footboy. "What do you mean, you didn't come from his lordship's town house? Aren't you his servant?"

"No, miss."

Ignoring the unease settling into her belly, she waited for him to say more, and when he didn't, she asked, "Then whose servant are you?"

The boy shifted nervously from foot to foot. "I . . . um . . . would prefer not to say, miss."

Her unease swelled to a roiling in her stomach. "Whyever not?"

"I'm not supposed to say, is all."

"And who gave you that particular instruction?"

When the boy didn't answer, Thomas shook him. "Answer the lady!"

The boy sighed. "His lordship asked me not to say, miss."

She swallowed. "I see. Well, I wouldn't want to get you into any trouble. You may go, and you may tell your master—or rather, his lordship—that you followed his instructions to the letter."

The boy's face cleared. "Thank you, miss, very kind of you, miss," he babbled as he bowed a couple of times.

When he scurried off to the front door, Katherine turned to Thomas and said in a low voice, "Follow him. Find out who he works for and how he knows Lord Iversley. But don't let him see you."

Thomas nodded. "I won't fail you, miss."

As Thomas headed after the boy, she returned to the parlor. Was she being too hasty in suspecting Alec of deception? Sending Thomas off like a spy—that was absurd, really. What did it matter if Alec didn't want her to know where he spent his time? Some men were private like that.

Like Papa, with all his "private meetings in town." The ones that had generally involved some merchant's wife or a fetching taproom maid or—

She shook her head, trying to ignore the sudden churning in her stomach. Alec would never be so callous as to send her a note from another woman's house. But then, why had he tried to hide where he was when he sent the note?

For the next hour she tortured herself with such thoughts, alternately calling herself a fool for making so much of it, then a fool for ever trusting a man as smooth-tongued as Alec.

By the time Thomas entered the parlor, her stomach was a bundle of knots. "Well?" she asked him. "Who employed the lad?"

"Stephens Hotel, miss."

That wasn't an answer she'd expected. She frowned. "I've never heard of it."

"It's in Mayfair, not a top hotel, but fashionable enough with men from the military. I'm told that a great many cavalry officers and the like dine there."

Relief swamped her. Of course. She'd been silly to worry. Where else would a man like Alec go to have a bite to eat?

But then, why hide it if his reason were so innocuous?

She swallowed. "And did you ask about Lord Iversley?"

Thomas looked stonily ahead. "Yes, miss. Spoke to the owner himself. He said he never met his lordship and knew nothing of him."

Her heart raced. "But you didn't believe him."

Thomas's expression grew pained. "The question made the man a mite nervous. All the other servants were close-mouthed, too. They seemed—"

"To be hiding something?" she whispered through a throat raw with hurt.

"Perhaps." He forced a smile. "Or perhaps they were just too busy to talk to me. There's lots of gentlemen going in and out of that hotel—I daresay they'd have a time of it remembering them all."

That still didn't explain why Alec had asked the boy to keep it secret. "And ladies? Were there ladies coming in and out, too?"

Thomas's eyes went wide. "Oh, no, miss, it wasn't *that* sort of hotel. I mean, yes, there were ladies—there's ladies in every hotel—but—"

"So he could have been meeting a woman there. Which is why the owner wouldn't discuss it."

Thomas's face went carefully blank. "I wouldn't know, miss."

She gritted her teeth. That had always been Thomas's standard answer for questions about Papa, too. Why did men invariably stick together when it came to infidelity? They hid each other's indiscretions with a loyalty that would be admirable if it weren't also disgusting.

Thomas took one look at her face, and added hastily, "I expect his lordship went there for supper just the one time, and they didn't remember him."

She bit back a hot retort. Thomas was right—she had nothing to base her suspicions on but some footboy's words. He could have misunderstood Alec's instructions. Or Alec might not have wanted her to know he'd been carousing with his friends. She mustn't jump to conclusions until she spoke to him.

Could Alec really have left here after proposing marriage and gone directly to spend the night with a doxy in a hotel?

She didn't want to believe it. Oh, men could lie through their teeth when it suited them, but surely he couldn't have stared her in the face and promised fidelity, then turned right around and betrayed her. Could he?

"Thank you, Thomas. I do appreciate your help in this. And if you would be so good as not to tell Mama, I would be most grateful."

"Certainly, miss."

All the servants had learned long ago that Katherine ran the house, not her mother. So if they wanted to be paid, they did as Katherine said. Unfortunately, while she could keep the footboy incident secret from Mama, she couldn't keep the contents of Alec's note from her. Best to get that over with.

She found her mother in her bedchamber, where she sat atop the bed surrounded by her many fans. Mama explained that she was sorting them according to use—one pile for "paying calls," one for "important social occasions," and one for "parties to be given by my daughter when she's a countess." The fan Alec had given her was on the top of the last pile. Would it be demoted when Mama heard he wasn't coming for dinner?

Unsurprisingly, Mama took the news badly. "What do you mean, he's gone to Suffolk on estate business?" Mama fluttered a lower-ranked fan in extreme agitation.

"That's just silly. Nobody runs off to their estate in the middle of the season unless they're having a house party."

"I gather it was an emergency. But he promised to return for tomorrow night."

Mama scowled at her. "He's not at his estate, I tell you. He's gone off to Lady Holland's—that's what it is."

Katherine blinked. "I doubt that seriously, Mama."

"I tell you—that's where he's off to tonight. And it's all your fault, too. You just had to tell him we weren't invited, didn't you?" She shook her head. "You never listen to me, but I do know some things. One of them is that you don't let an earl think you're not welcome somewhere. Either you want to marry the man or you don't. If you do, you're certainly going about it the wrong way."

Katherine gritted her teeth, sorely tempted to reveal that Alec had already proposed marriage, and she'd already accepted. But something held her back.

Part of it was the fact that Mama would trumpet the news throughout London before Katherine could even get to talk to Sydney. And part of it was . . .

Fear, pure and simple. Fear that she'd been wrong to trust Alec. Fear that she'd been wrong to accept his suit. Fear that she'd find out something so horrible about him that she'd have to refuse to marry him in the end. And then Mama would never let her hear the end of it.

"He's not going to Lady Holland's," Katherine said firmly. "Really, do you think he's stupid? Why would he lie about such a thing when he knows it would get back to us? Half of society would see him there—the fete will probably be mentioned in the papers tomorrow. So I seriously doubt he'll be anywhere near Lady Holland's fete tonight."

But would he be anywhere near any other lady's fete? That was what she couldn't answer.

That evening, Alec was in his borrowed carriage again, barreling toward Hertfordshire after a frustrating afternoon futilely trying to convince Harris in Ipswich to extend him credit for his tillers and plows.

The man had held firm—he wanted his five hundred pounds, and nothing else would do. But Alec didn't have five hundred pounds, not until he married Katherine.

Unfortunately, he needed the money immediately. Harris was threatening to sell the implements to another customer. If he did, it would be weeks before Alec could get more, and then it would be too late to do the planting.

Somehow he'd convinced Harris to give him two more days to raise the funds, leaving Alec with only one choice: He'd have to borrow it. Worse, he'd have to borrow it from Draker. Byrne was in Bath, and no bank would lend Alec money fast enough. Draker was his only hope.

That was how Alec found himself at Castlemaine early the next morning, restlessly pacing the floor of Draker's study. His eyes itched and burned from lack of sleep, his stomach rumbled, and every muscle felt taxed to the breaking point.

Yet he couldn't sit still while he waited for the viscount to appear. His headlong trip to Hertfordshire could very well have been for naught. What if Draker refused to see him? What if the man had second thoughts about helping a half brother he'd only recently discovered existed?

What if he simply laughed in Alec's face?

Alec balled his hands into fists. He hated that he was here doing the very thing he'd sworn never to do.

The door opened, and Draker strode in, looking as harried as Alec felt. "This had better be good, Iversley. I was out in the north pasture—got in a new flock of sheep, you see—when the servant found me."

Alec gazed at the man in surprise. "It's rather early to be out, isn't it?"

"Not for me. I'm not like you city folk, out all night dancing, then sleeping until noon the next day. I come by my wealth honestly. Early bird catches the worm and all that." He ran his gaze over Alec's tired face and rumpled attire. "And frankly, you're not the sort of worm I'd hoped to catch this morning."

"I know." Alec fought down his resentment at being called a worm. Right now, he felt like one.

Draker walked purposefully to take a seat behind his desk. If not for his scruffy clothing and his wild man's beard, Draker would look the very picture of the wealthy landowner receiving a supplicant. He certainly had the superior manner down pat.

Planting his elbows on the desk, Draker steepled his fingers and eyed Alec with lordly contempt. "Well? Why have you come?"

Alec dragged in a deep breath. "I need to borrow five hundred pounds."

Draker's face betrayed no reaction. "Things not going well with the fortune hunting?"

"Actually, I've convinced Miss Merivale to marry me. And according to Byrne, she'll inherit a hundred thousand pounds upon her marriage."

Draker scowled. "I wouldn't trust Byrne, if I were you."

"I don't have any choice." Alec flashed Draker a rueful smile. "And since the Merivales are in debt to him, he knows what he's talking about."

"Ah. So why do you need five hundred pounds?"

Swallowing his resentment at having to explain himself, Alec related the entirety of the situation between him and his tenant farmers and Harris.

When he finished, Draker's lordly manner had softened. "I see. Sounds like you've got a good steward there in Mr. Dawes. That strain of barley is high-yielding indeed. If the man is suggesting you plant that, he's got a good head on his shoulders." When Alec raised an eyebrow, Draker shrugged. "Half of my own tenants have been planting it for three years now, with excellent results."

"I've read the literature Dawes gave me about it, and it sounds like a viable crop, especially in Suffolk's soil. But the clay gets so hard that we need those heavy tillers, and I'll soon have to buy some Suffolk punch horses—"

"I've heard of those. A kind of draft horse, isn't it? Only bred in Suffolk. I wonder if they'd be useful around here."

"I'll send you the first foal I get from them," Alec offered, "if you can see your way clear to loaning me that five hundred pounds."

Draker's face went carefully blank. "Why didn't you borrow it from Byrne? You're doing him a favor by marrying this heiress."

"Byrne is in Bath right now, and I need the money by tomorrow night."

"So I'm just supposed to hand over five hundred pounds to you, is that it?"

"I have something to offer as collateral." He'd pondered the problem all the way here and had come up with one enticement, though not one he relished offering.

Draker raised an eyebrow. "Oh?"

He steeled himself. "My horse."

Interest flickered in Draker's eyes. "Your horse?"

"It's a Lusitano of excellent bloodlines, worth over a thousand pounds."

"Then how did *you* come by it?"

"General Beresford acquired it in battle and gave it to me for my service to the cavalry."

Draker's eyes narrowed. "Yes, Byrne told me how you'd actually spent the past ten years."

That surprised Alec. He hadn't realized his brothers had spoken again since that night at his hotel.

"He says," Draker continued, "that you can do amazing tricks on a horse. Not a particularly useful skill for a man trying to get an estate running again."

Alec gritted his teeth. "I'm willing to learn the right skills. I just need help."

"Five hundred pounds of help."

"For which I'm offering my horse as collateral, and it's worth twice that. If you know of my work in Portugal, then you know I can assess a horse's value. And that I'm not exaggerating Beleza's attributes."

"You could be. Horse merchants do it all the time."

Alec bit back an oath. "But I'm a gentleman and a man of good character, not a horse merchant."

"That remains to be seen." Draker settled back in his chair. "If it's so fine a horse, why didn't you offer it to your Mr. Harris as collateral?"

"I tried. Having been taken in by my father one too

many times, he's beyond accepting anything but money from my family—he made that very clear."

"Did you bring this horse with you?"

"No. I came straight here from Suffolk."

"In my carriage," Draker said dryly.

Alec glared at him. "Yes. I needed speed." He tamped down his temper. "But if you want to see Beleza, meet me at my hotel in the morning, and I'll let you look her over. Then you can decide whether to loan me the money."

For several long moments, Draker seemed to consider Alec's offer. "So why don't you sell the horse?"

"I want to keep her if I can," Alec growled. "And since all I need is a loan for a few weeks until I marry—"

"*If* you marry. What if it doesn't work out with your heiress? Will you still give me the horse in lieu of payment?"

Feeling as if someone had reached inside to rip out his heart, Alec said, "Yes."

"And what would you ride?"

"A nag," Alec snapped. "Now, will you loan me the money or not?"

Draker gave him a speculative glance. "I tell you what. Let me show you *my* estate while I'm thinking it over. You can talk to my tenants about the barley. You can even speak to my steward about husbandry. Then I'll give you my answer."

Alec held back his hot retort. This was a test. Draker wanted to determine if Alec had what it took to make a go of an estate, or if he was just playing at it.

Although Alec didn't blame the man for doubting him, time grew short. He glanced at the clock on Draker's desk. He had ten hours before he had to pick up Katherine and Mrs. Merivale for the Purefoy party, including an hour to drive back to London and an hour to dress. He couldn't miss the party—he was hoping Katherine would finally have spoken to Sydney so Alec could make their betrothal official.

But there was still time left. And he had no choice but to play Draker's game if he wanted his money. "All right," Alec told his half brother. "Let's go."

Chapter Eighteen

∽◈∾

*The true rake has no heart. A desire for
pleasure is the only thing beating inside
his chest.*
—Anonymous, *A Rake's Rhetorick*

It was happening all over again. How many times had
Katherine sat with Mama, waiting for Papa to show up
to take them to an assembly in town as he'd promised,
only to have him stagger in with his cravat askew, reeking of ale?

How many times had she listened to his lies that he'd
been delayed by a broken carriage axle or a lamed horse,
watching Mama's temper rise until it erupted into
shouts? All the while her own anger simmered deep inside where she always thrust it, because *somebody* in the
family had to keep a clear head.

Tonight, however, she was the one ready to erupt
while Mama sat and watched warily, having long ago
fallen into an uncharacteristic silence.

Katherine refused to endure this any longer. Gathering up her reticule, she rose and headed for the parlor
door.

"Katherine Merivale, where do you think you're
going?" Mama asked.

"Upstairs." Katherine gestured to the clock. "He's an hour and a half late. You might as well accept that he's not coming. And since we have no carriage and we turned down the one Lady Purefoy offered to send for us, we have no way of going by ourselves. Thomas will never find a hackney at this hour, not with all the parties going on."

She gathered in a steadying breath, fighting not to show her anger. "So I'm going upstairs to change clothes and read. At least it will keep my mind off . . . everything."

"Now, Katherine, perhaps he was held up on his estate—"

"You said you didn't believe he'd gone to his estate." Her mother's troubled frown only heightened Katherine's temper. "Even if he did, and even if he found upon his arrival that he wouldn't be able to get back for the party, he's had plenty of time to send us a message from Suffolk. The mails are quick these days."

"He might have had an accident on the roads, you know. It does happen. And there are highwaymen, too."

That brought her up short. Oh, God, what if something horrible *had* happened to him? The idea of Alec lying in some ditch—

No, she couldn't believe it. Alec, of all people, would keep his team and carriage in perfect shape and hire the best coachman. And any highwayman confronting a man who could slice a pear in half at a dead gallop would surely find himself bested.

His evasions concerning the Stephens Hotel told her Alec was deceiving her about something, and his absence was part of it. She just knew it.

"I seriously doubt his lordship has had an accident. He is simply exercising his right to behave like a cad, now that I've agreed—" She broke off, hoping Mama hadn't caught her slip.

But her mother could be very clever when it came to certain matters. "Now that you've agreed to what, Katherine?"

Katherine sighed. "To his proposal of marriage. That night at Astley's, he asked me to marry him, and I agreed."

Mama's face lit up. "My dear girl, that's wonderful!" She pressed her hands to her heart. "My daughter, the countess . . . oh, I knew it would happen, I knew it! The way his lordship looks at you, and his kind courtesies—"

"Like not showing up to take me to a party when he promised?"

"Pshaw, these things happen." Mama waved her hand dismissively. "You'll see what I mean when you're married."

Which was precisely what worried Katherine.

Her mother frowned. "But why didn't you tell me this before? And why didn't he speak to me about it?"

"He wanted to, but I . . . um . . . asked him to wait until I could tell Sydney."

"*What?*" Mama leaped to her feet and began to pace, gesticulating wildly. "For a clever girl, you are sometimes exceedingly foolish. When a man proposes marriage, a girl in your position does not keep him dangling on a string. It would be one thing if men were clamoring for introductions, but they aren't. Even Sir Sydney Lovelace has dropped you. And you put off the earl? Are you mad? It's no wonder the man has abandoned you."

"I hardly think—"

"Exactly—you don't think at all! You've been so cool to him that Lord Iversley probably thought you meant to toy with his affections. Then you told him we weren't invited to Lady Holland's. Now he has second thoughts, no doubt, which is why he's dallying at his estate or . . . wherever."

"If you're right, then we're well rid of him." Kathleen swallowed down the tears threatening to well up. "I don't want to marry a man who'd be scared off by our low connections or by my wanting to do right by a friend."

But if he was the sort of man she'd come to believe he was, he would be here. Or at the very least, would have sent a message. Instead of taking for granted that she would wait on his whim. Instead of hiding things from her and pretending to be other than he really was—whatever *that* happened to be.

She squared her shoulders. "I'm going upstairs, Mama. Come fetch me if he should happen to appear." Then she would give him a piece of her mind, and this time, no amount of kissing would distract her.

She'd actually let him persuade her that all his evasions were reasonable. That he'd kept his unorthodox past hidden for a legitimate reason, even though there'd been holes the size of caverns in his stories. But the past two days had given her plenty of time to ponder them.

Why had one childhood incident estranged him from his father? Why had his father allowed his only heir to work for a living in a country wracked by war, instead of coming home to do his duty? That was a rather profound estrangement, it seemed to her—Alec must have done something truly awful to warrant it.

And what did the uncle have to do with anything? Surely as Alec's guardian *he* would not have approved of Alec's work with the cavalry. She would question Alec's entire tale, except that she'd seen him ride and perform cavalry maneuvers. One didn't learn that sort of thing overnight. But he was keeping something from her; she was sure of it. Aside from his mysterious evasions about the Stephens Hotel.

Entering her room, she tossed her reticule on the bed, and as she passed the mirror she caught sight of her reflection and the damascene brooch she'd worn especially for Alec.

A lump settled in her throat. What if he'd lied about the pin and had bought it for a woman other than his mother? That might explain his determination not to return to England—some Portuguese beauty might have captured his heart.

He might even have left his uncle's house to be with her. That would explain why he'd had to make money. Though he was conscious enough of his obligations not to marry such a woman, he *could* make her his mistress . . . and keep her at a place like the Stephens Hotel, while he looked for an acceptable English wife to bear his heir.

Katherine groaned. Yes, that would be more in keeping with the Alec she'd come to know. She couldn't see him cavorting with some doxy as Papa had, but Alec in love with an unacceptable woman . . . that fit his character.

And was much more painful to contemplate. Alec loving another woman while he'd kissed and caressed Katherine . . . the very thought made her ill.

She rubbed her aching temples. This was ridiculous—she was letting her imagination run away with her. He would hardly have given Katherine a pin he'd bought for a Portuguese mistress he was still seeing. Besides, if he were leading such a duplicitous life, wouldn't it behoove him to try even harder to allay Katherine's suspicions, instead of not showing up when he was supposed to?

He'd probably just been delayed at his estate. But the fact remained that whatever the reason for his absence, it was tying her into knots, which was *precisely* what she'd wanted to avoid by marrying Sydney. Did she really want a lifetime of emotional tumult with Alec?

Then again, what choice did she have? Sydney had disappeared and might never be coming back. And could she even find another husband to suit her?

She dropped onto her bed, then felt something dig into her bottom. *The Rake's Rhetorick.* She'd been reading it earlier, during a bout of worry about the Stephens Hotel.

Tugging it out, she opened it to the chapter entitled "The Married Rakehell." She couldn't bring herself to read it before, but now one sentence leaped out at her: "If a rake knows he must eventually marry to fulfill his duty, he should hide his pursuit of pleasure from the world. The more discreet the rake, the better his chances of continuing his activities after his nuptials."

A shudder wracked her. Was Alec trying to be discreet? Lulling her into believing he would be faithful? But then, why choose to court *her?* Why not fix on a less suspicious sort of female?

The sound of a carriage halting in front brought her to her feet. He was here after all! He would explain everything, and it would be all right. *If* she could believe his explanations.

Grabbing her reticule, she hurried out so quickly that she was halfway down the stairs before she realized she still held *The Rake's Rhetorick.* As she debated whether to return it to her room, a man appeared at the bottom of the stairs.

Sydney.

She froze. He must have received her note. But why

come now? Cramming the chapbook into her reticule, she went warily down to meet him.

"When you didn't show up, Lady Purefoy asked me to fetch you and your mother," he said in a low voice as she approached. "I readily agreed, hoping I could speak with you. If you'll allow it."

"Why wouldn't I? Didn't you get my note?"

He frowned. "What note?"

"I sent a message to Lord Napier's estate, asking you to come here. When I paid your mother a visit, she told me that's where you'd gone."

He flushed a deep scarlet, then glanced away. "Yes, I needed to think. And Ju— . . . Napier . . . said I could do so at his house." His gaze swung back to her, dark and troubled. "But I left yesterday and returned to London. Mother didn't mention your visit, and Napier . . . well . . . I left after we argued, so I suppose he was too petty to send your note on."

Mama burst into the hall. "I thought I heard—" She stopped short, confusion flooding her face. "Oh, hello, Sir Sydney. What are you doing here?"

Sydney gave his usual gentlemanly bow. "I've come to take you to Lady Purefoy's party. Apparently there was a misunderstanding. She said you'd told her not to send a carriage."

"We did," Katherine said tightly. "Lord Iversley promised to take us, but he's not here."

"He was detained at his estate," Mama said hastily. "I'm sure he'll be here any moment, however."

Katherine squared her shoulders, then descended the last few steps. "I'm not waiting to find out. Neither should you, Mama. If Lady Purefoy was kind enough to send someone for us, the least we can do is go."

In the end, Mama couldn't stand the possibility of missing her friend's birthday party, so she allowed Sydney to take them off.

Katherine hardly knew what to think of Sydney's strange behavior toward her on the way there. He shot her earnest glances, toyed nervously with his cravat, and in general seemed very disturbed. What did he want to talk to her about? Why had he quarreled with Lord Napier? Could he be reconsidering his rude behavior toward her of late?

And how on earth would she break the news to him about her engagement to Alec? Or should she even do so, when she was so uncertain of Alec herself?

By the time they disembarked at Lady Purefoy's, Katherine was so agitated that she didn't know whether to be relieved or alarmed when Lady Purefoy commandeered her mother after they entered, leaving her alone with Sydney.

A waltz was struck, and Sydney held out his hand. "Will you honor me with this dance, Kit?"

She nodded. Right now she needed the steady comfort of being with Sydney, who'd always been her lifeline in the storm that was her family.

But as they danced, that steady comfort evaded her. Being with him felt . . . unfamiliar. Awkward. And she'd never felt awkward with Sydney in her life.

"Have I lost all chance with you then, Kit?" Sydney asked in a low voice.

With a start, she gazed up into his worried face. Had he read her mind, for goodness sake? "What do you mean?"

"I hear Iversley is courting you. And if I were to judge from that kiss you gave him at the reading, you are not . . . averse to the courtship."

"Sydney—"

"No, let me say this first. I know you're unhappy with me, but I can make it up to you. If you'll consent to marry me, I'll go to Mother now and tell her. I'll announce it at this very party, before I even tell her, if that is what you wish."

She gaped at him. Alec's little scheme, false as it had been, had worked. Sydney was actually proposing.

"Why?" she asked. "What has made you suddenly eager to marry, when you haven't spoken to me for a week?"

"I've finally realized what's good for me. And you're good for me."

She arched one eyebrow. "Like eating well and taking exercise?"

"No . . . that is . . . you'll keep me from doing anything foolish or reckless."

She managed a smile. "You couldn't do anything foolish or reckless if you tried."

He swallowed and looked away. "You never know. Temptation lies everywhere." His gaze swung back to her. "So will you do it? Marry me, I mean?"

She stared at him, temporarily at a loss for words. Sydney was the same man she'd always known, the same man she'd imagined marrying for years—kind, attentive, a brilliant poet. He was still her friend, with the same handsome, aristocratic features, the same close-shaven chin and artfully arranged curls.

But when she tried to imagine him kissing her as passionately as Alec, or making her heart race with a word, she couldn't. She simply couldn't.

Still, that was a good thing, wasn't it? With Sydney she would never feel the hollow pain of the past two days, the cruel uncertainty, the fierce desires that came to her unexpectedly in the night. Everything would be courteous and quiet and peaceful.

Sounds boring to me.

Alec's words pounded in her ears. Cursed arrogant scoundrel—it was so like him to invade her thoughts! Look what he'd done to her. He'd ruined Sydney for her. He'd made her as bad as *he* was—eager for excitement and dissatisfied with the quiet life.

And a breaker of rules.

Sydney watched her with pain in his face. "Does your silence mean 'no'?"

"You wouldn't be happy with me now." As angry as she was at Alec, as confused as he made her feel, she did know that Sydney wasn't the right man for her.

He tensed. "It's *him*, isn't it? He's turned you against me."

"Not exactly—"

"Even if you don't wish to have *me* anymore," Sydney said tightly, "at least choose someone better than Iversley to replace me."

"He's not as bad as you think."

"He didn't arrive to take you to the party, did he?"

"Mama told you—he was held up at his estate."

Sydney snorted. "A likely tale. I doubt he would care enough about his estate to get held up there."

She thought of the fervor with which Alec had described Edenmore and shook her head. "I think you're wrong."

"Why are you defending him?"

She blinked. "I don't know."

"He's off somewhere doing God knows what and breaking his promise, yet you put up with it—"

"Oh, no, I shan't put up with it, believe me." There

would be no more evasions, no more inconsiderate behavior, or she would send him packing. "But I believe there's good in him."

Until she said it, she hadn't realized it. But it was true. It might be buried rather deep, but there *was* good in him.

"You're wrong about him, Kit. At best, he's a prankster who makes fun of bad poets for entertainment." When she gaped at him, Sydney added, "Yes, I noticed all his antics at the reading. It was exactly the sort of thing he did at Harrow. He never takes anything seriously."

Whereas Sydney took everything so seriously that he couldn't even make up his mind about marriage.

"At worst," Sydney continued, "he's a duplicitous defiler of women."

"And how do you know that about him?"

"Surely you recognize the type—charming, quick-witted, skilled at seduction, and completely without moral fiber."

"In other words, you know it because you assume it. Not because you have any evidence that he defiles or deceives women."

Sydney grew sullen. "He used to flatter the maids at Harrow so he could kiss them."

A giggle floated up inside her. She could easily imagine a sixteen-year-old Alec feeling his oats, flirting with some chambermaid so he could steal a kiss. It would be just like him. "If he did, he probably kissed a great many. I doubt few maids could resist Alec's charm."

"You're not listening—"

"Why should I? It would be one thing if you could show me how dastardly he's been since he's arrived in England, but all this nonsense from his days at Harrow . . . goodness, every boy does those things."

"*I* didn't."

"I'll bet your friend Lord Napier did. He seems the sort."

Sydney gave a strangely harsh laugh. "One thing I can promise you—Napier has never tried to kiss a chambermaid in his life."

"If you say so. But all boys act foolishly sometimes. You can't judge a man's character by the pranks he played as a lad." Especially a man who'd been estranged from his father and sent abroad in the middle of a war.

A thought suddenly occurred to her. "Tell me something, Sydney—what exactly did Alec do to get sent down from school?" That was one subject Alec had been tight-lipped about.

Sydney frowned. "His stupid friends had some notion that they could pass themselves off as a royal entourage if Iversley would pretend to be the Prince of Wales. They strolled into an inn they'd never gone to in a neighboring town and demanded an expensive meal. When the innkeeper challenged them, they ran off, but the man reported it to Harrow and picked every one of them out."

She gaped at him. "That's it? *That's* the horrible act that got him banished to Portugal?"

"I don't know about Portugal, but it got him kicked out of Harrow."

She laughed. She couldn't *stop* laughing. Considering all the awful crimes she'd imagined, she'd never guessed it could be something so silly.

Sydney was scowling. "It's not funny, you know. There was a terrible furor over it. All the boys got in trouble, and Iversley's father hauled him off, swearing he would thrash him when he got him home."

She sobered. His father had done far worse than thrash

him, judging from the wistfulness in Alec's voice whenever he spoke of his mother.

The waltz was ending, so Sydney took her arm to lead her from the floor. "Promise me you won't make any hasty decisions about Iversley, Kit."

She sighed. It was time to tell him that she'd agreed to marry the man. And she didn't relish his reaction.

The voice of Lady Purefoy's butler suddenly sounded over the crowd, announcing a new arrival. "The Right Honorable The Earl of Iversley."

She started and turned as the crowd murmured around her.

And no wonder. The man descending the steps didn't look like an earl or even a lord. Instead of evening attire, Alec wore a rumpled frock coat of olive green, buckskin trousers, and top boots caked with mud. His raven hair was mussed, and his chin looked as if it hadn't seen a razor in days.

Such an ungentlemanly appearance would have roused comment anywhere, but at a party as elegant as Lady Purefoy's, it sparked loudly voiced disapproval.

Alec paid it no heed, striding into the ballroom with a dark gaze that warned everyone off. When at last his gaze settled on her, Katherine felt a sudden thrill of fear. Because while no one else in the ballroom might realize it, Alec was furious.

And judging from the direction of his glare, his anger was all for her.

Chapter Nineteen

❧

Sometimes a rake should simply act
on instinct.
—Anonymous, *A Rake's Rhetorick*

*W*hen Alec spotted Katherine on Lovelace's arm he saw red, and no amount of rational thought could rein in his thundering temper.

Never mind that *he'd* been the one to let the time get away from him while touring his half brother's fascinating estate. Never mind that she had every right to dance with whomever she pleased.

According to Katherine's manservant, she'd let *Lovelace* bring her and her mother here. She was letting Lovelace squire her about now, as if Alec had never existed . . . as if she hadn't agreed to marry him a mere two days ago.

He wouldn't stand for it.

As he approached, Lovelace stepped between them, surveying Alec with clear contempt. "So you've finally dragged yourself out of whatever hole you were wallowing in? You ought to be ashamed, embarrassing Miss Merivale like this."

Katherine stepped out from behind Lovelace, looking distinctly uncomfortable. "That's enough, Sydney."

"Yes, 'Sydney,' " Alec echoed snidely. "Why don't you stay out of it? This is between me and my betrothed."

"B-Betrothed?" Lovelace stammered.

Alec's gaze narrowed on Katherine, whose blush confirmed why Lovelace looked confused. Alec's temper went into full stampede. "Yes. Miss Merivale has agreed to marry me, a little fact she apparently forgot to tell you."

Katherine glared at him. "I was about to do that, my lord."

"Aren't you glad I spared you the trouble?" With a scowl, he held out his arm. "And now, madam, I'd like a word with you."

"See here—" Lovelace began.

"It's all right, Sydney." With a little lift of her chin, Katherine took Alec's arm. "I'd like a word with his lordship, myself."

They marched across the ballroom as people stared and whispered around them. Damn. He and Katherine would get no privacy here. And he wanted privacy for this little talk.

"Alec—" she began.

"Not yet," he murmured. "Let's go into the garden, where we can be alone."

She started to pull her hand from his arm. "I don't think I want to be alone with you just now."

He gripped her hand as he steered her toward the doors leading outside. "You have no choice . . . unless you want me to go back and knock Lovelace into the next county after all."

She shot him a nervous glance. "You wouldn't."

"Right now, I just might."

She headed out the doors without a murmur. But as soon as they'd entered the garden, she wrenched free of his grip to whirl on him. "You are unconscionable. You don't show up, you don't send word, and then you get angry with *me* because I danced with Sydney?"

He stalked forward. "It wasn't your dancing with him that sparked my temper, sweetheart. It was the fact that you hadn't told him we're marrying."

Backing away, she shook her head. "You were angry before you even knew that."

"How would *you* react if you'd raced here after two frantic days dealing with an emergency, only to find your intended on another man's arm?"

Her eyes narrowed. "Probably the same way *you'd* react if you heard that your intended had gone to some hotel the very night he offered marriage. And that he didn't want you to know about it."

That knocked the wind right out of him. Only now did he notice the tears shining in her eyes and the trembling of her chin. Blast, blast, and double-blast.

A sound beyond her made him look up to see several people watching them from the balcony. Katherine followed his gaze and cursed under her breath.

He leveled a black look on their audience, who one by one disappeared back into the ballroom. Spotting an orangery at the end of the walk, he grabbed her arm and towed her toward it.

"What are you doing?" she snapped, trying to wriggle free.

"Do you really want to have this argument in front of half the world?"

"They're gone now."

"They'll return, I assure you. No one can resist a public quarrel."

That seemed to decide her, for she let him lead her inside the orangery. Despite the windows on the opposite end, the place was as black as gunpowder on the moonless night. He removed his gloves, then felt along the ledge near the door until he found a lamp and the flint box beside it.

Once lit, the lamp illuminated a very annoyed Katherine, who watched him with thinly disguised impatience. "Well? I had good reason to dance with Sydney. What is your reason for going to the Stephens Hotel and keeping it from me?"

He should have known Katherine would wheedle the truth out of that damned footboy. But how much had she learned? It would be just like his clever wife-to-be to pretend ignorance in order to catch him in a lie.

Better to stick to the facts. "I live there."

Judging from the shock on her face, she hadn't learned *that.* "Y-You what?"

In for a penny, in for a pound. "I live at the Stephens Hotel when I'm in town. My father sold our town house when he grew too ill to come into society, and I haven't had time to buy a new one." Or the money to rent one.

Confusion knit her brow. "But why didn't you want me to know that?"

"The Stephens Hotel isn't exactly the grand lodgings an earl should have. I could have gone to the Clarendon, but the owner of Stephens is a friend of mine." And the Clarendon was beyond his means.

She eyed him suspiciously. "Then why did your 'friend' say he'd never heard of you?"

Alarm swamped him. "What did you do—have a runner interrogate him?"

She had the good grace to blush. "No, but . . . well, when the footboy you sent wouldn't say where he worked, I . . . had Thomas follow him. Thomas talked to the owner, who denied knowing you."

Alec shrugged. "I requested that Jack not mention it to anyone. I didn't want to deal with people's questions about why I had no town house."

"You know I wouldn't care about something like that."

"But your mother would. I didn't think she'd be impressed to hear I was living at the Stephens Hotel."

He took a step toward Katherine, but she stepped back quickly, still wary. "Do you care so much what Mama thinks of you?"

"You want her approval for our marriage, don't you?"

"You know very well she'll approve." Her eyebrow cocked up. "She's terribly pleased that you're an earl."

"But *you're* not. You'd prefer Sir Sydney, the poet," he said acidly, unable to squelch his jealousy.

"I'd prefer a man I can trust. I'm not entirely sure that's you."

Unfortunately, Katherine was too intelligent to be fooled by his flimsy excuses, so rational argument was futile. Only one tactic worked on her.

He headed purposefully for her. "You do trust me." His gaze flicked down to her brooch. "Or you wouldn't wear my gift. You trusted me to ride at you with a sword and not hurt you. You trusted me not to deflower you at Astley's—"

"That was different," she said, backing away. "You weren't waltzing in from two days out of town without explaining or apologizing—"

"I'm apologizing now," he said as he stalked her.

"Trying to kiss me is not apologizing."

"It could be." He reached for her.

She slapped his hand with her reticule, which was surprisingly heavy for such a flimsy-looking thing.

"Ow! What was that for?"

"For thinking you can get around me with kisses." She put some distance between them. "Now stay back. I want to know why you're here so late and why you couldn't send a message."

He rubbed his stinging hand in annoyance. "Because by the time I realized it would take me longer than expected to deal with things, it was too late to send a message."

"What things?" she persisted.

"Estate matters—I told you."

"Be specific, Alec. What estate matters?"

He scowled at her. "If you think I'll be the sort of husband who reports to his wife every time he sneezes, think again."

"You won't be any sort of husband at all if you don't give me some answers."

He sucked in a lungful of orange-scented air. Blast her. She was too curious by half. And he was on very shaky ground. "I had to return to my estate to ensure the delivery of some plows and tillers we need for the spring planting. There, are you happy?"

"Why couldn't your steward do it?"

"Because I fired my father's thieving steward, and neither my tenants nor the local merchants know the new one well enough yet to trust him." He cocked his head. "Forgive me for not explaining all this earlier, but I didn't realize estate management is your hobby."

Crossing her arms over her chest, she ignored his sarcasm. " 'To ensure the delivery' took you two days?"

He gritted his teeth. "When the merchant refuses to honor his son's word, it does. He wouldn't deliver, so I had to make other arrangements, and that meant a stop in Hertfordshire at a friend's estate."

He was congratulating himself for telling her everything without lying when she said, "What other arrangements?"

"I'm in no mood to discuss all the workings of my estate," he growled as he headed for her again. "After two days of dealing with stubborn merchants, suspicious tenants, and a worried steward, I'm in the mood for only one thing—reminding my intended which man she agreed to marry. Something she seems to have conveniently forgotten."

Her eyes went wide as she started backing away again. "I didn't forget. I-I was working up to telling him . . ."

"While you danced with him. And promenaded on his arm."

She stepped back, only to come up against an orange tree so hard that it dropped leaves onto her gown and into her hair. Wielding her reticule like a weapon, she glared at him. "Stay back, or I'll hit you again."

"Go ahead." He reached for her. "I dare you."

When she tried to swat him with her reticule, he easily snatched it out of her hand. He started to toss it aside, but its weight gave him pause. "What do you carry in this thing—cannonballs?"

Alarm spread over her features. "Give it back!"

With a shake of his head, he opened it. When he saw the book inside, curiosity turned to anger. "Poetry from your friend, I suppose."

He drew the book out, then walked over to the lamp. When he read the title, he couldn't believe it. Scowling, he waved the book at her. "Lovelace gave you *this*?"

She shook her head. "I . . . um . . . it . . . belonged to my father."

That shocked him even more. "And *he* gave it to you?"

"No!" Even in the lamplight, he could see her blush. "I-I found it hidden in his study after he died."

Eyes narrowing, he flipped through the flimsy thing, noting the chapter headings: "The Best Gifts for Seduction," "Discretion for the Rake," "Finding a Woman's Weakness" . . .

His anger burst into full flame. He shook it at her. "*This* is why you won't trust me, why you fight my suit at every turn? Because you've been reading some claptrap—"

"It's not claptrap, unfortunately," she said bitterly. "Papa seems to have followed every instruction."

"Then he was an idiot."

She folded her arms over her chest. "True. But I wanted to understand what made him an idiot. And why *some* men like to seduce women for fun."

"I suppose you include *me* in that group. How dare you compare me to your blasted father? I've given you no reason to think I'm like him."

"Haven't you?"

The light suddenly dawned. "That's what you thought I was doing at Stephens Hotel—seeing some woman."

"You did go to a lot of trouble to make sure I didn't find out."

"Blast it, Katherine. How could you think I'd do that to you? Do you still trust me that little?"

Her gaze met his, wide and wary. "I don't know what to make of you. I never have."

He brandished the book. "So you've filled your head with this nonsense and decided I'm a rakehell, based on a few rumors and Lovelace's resentment."

She stuck out her chin. "And the way you behave."

"You mean, by kissing you?" He lowered his voice. "By pleasuring you?"

"By lying—"

"I've never lied to you." But of course he had. Small lies, evasions, minor deceptions . . . and the one great deception still going on.

All the same, she had no right to attribute to him worse crimes than he deserved. "Your distrust has nothing to do with what I've actually done. No matter what I do or say, you'll still think me the epitome of wickedness and debauchery."

"You have to admit—"

"I don't have to admit anything." He marched toward her. "I'm a rakehell, a liar, and a cheat, a man who deceives women for entertainment. I'm . . . let's see . . ." He flipped open the book and read at random, "A master seducer."

He narrowed his gaze on her. "Yes, I like that. A master seducer. And all this time, I thought I was merely a man courting a woman he wanted to marry." He tossed the book aside and stripped off his coat, then began unfastening the buttons of his waistcoat. "Little did I know."

Her eyes went wide. "Now, Alec, you aren't going to—"

"Shh, sweetheart." Shucking his waistcoat, he caught her to him. "Let the master work."

His temper spurring him on, he took her mouth with grim determination. Time to show his wife-to-be that he meant to master her, one way or the other. And if he had to do it by seducing her, then so be it.

Chapter Twenty

Some women are too clever to be seduced.
—Anonymous, *A Rake's Rhetorick*

*T*he man was infuriating! He always thought to get round her by kissing her . . . turning her knees to mush . . . sparking a low heat inside her belly that—

No! She jerked back from him. "What do you think you're doing?"

Anger still rode him; she could see it in his glittering eyes as he removed his cravat. "What I should have done two nights ago—making sure we get married."

His words sent a thrill coursing through her. "By seducing me."

"That's what I'm supposed to do, isn't it?" His words were clipped. Flicking open the buttons of his shirt with one hand, he glared at her. "That's what we rakehells live for—seducing young innocents."

He yanked his shirt over his head, and her mouth went dry. For a moment, she forgot about their argument and his anger. She could only stare at his bare chest—the sculpted muscles, lean waist, the strands of black hair caught in the glow of the lamp, reminding her of that wonderful night at Astley's . . .

She shook herself. "I know you're not a rakehell."

"Really?" He dragged her into his arms. "Is that why you carry that blasted book around in your reticule like a talisman?"

"It's not . . . I just—"

He cut off her feeble protest with a hot, furious kiss. For a moment, she let him kiss her. She shouldn't blame him for his fury; his explanations had been totally plausible. And she *had* overreacted to his lateness. Nor had she told Sydney of their betrothal as she'd promised.

But she still didn't quite trust him, either. He was hiding something; she could sense it in the way he avoided certain questions.

She wriggled out of his embrace to slip from between him and the orange tree and back farther down the path. "You can't seduce me."

He prowled after her as relentlessly as a conqueror marching over a vulnerable land. "I can do as I please. I'm a rakehell, remember?"

"Would you stop saying that?" She nearly stumbled over a watering pot before catching her balance and backing farther away. "You don't mean it. You're just annoyed by my book."

"I'm far beyond mere annoyance, I assure you."

The determined way he stalked her sent a shiver down her spine. Unfortunately, it wasn't a shiver of fear. "You can't do this. People might see."

"Not back here, away from the windows."

Goodness, he was serious. "But everyone will guess what we're doing." She thrust a chair in his path.

He knocked it aside. "*If* they even guess we're in here.

Anyone who has returned to the balcony will find the garden empty and assume that we've returned to the house. And if they don't, that's fine, too. Then you'll *have* to marry me."

He cornered her in a little alcove with a wide, cushioned bench at her back. But when he pounced, it wasn't to haul her into his arms. Instead, he turned her so he could unfasten her buttons.

The mere brush of his fingers down her gown uncoiled a reckless excitement in her belly that she struggled to ignore. "We cannot do this."

"We can." He raked kisses along her neck, in her hair, on the parts of her upper back he bared inch by inch.

It was all she could do to keep her mind unfogged by his seductions. "We're not married yet."

"We will be." He pushed her gown off her shoulders, and it fell to her waist, baring her corset and chemise. He unlaced her corset so easily that it annoyed her.

"You certainly know very well how to undress a woman."

"I've undressed a few," he admitted as he tossed the corset aside. "Though not as many as you seem to think. And not for some time." From behind her, he brought his hands up to cup her thinly clad breasts. "Is that what's worrying you—that I'm wicked enough to seduce you and not marry you?"

"I never said you were wic—"

"What does your book say about rakes marrying, anyway? Or are they not supposed to?"

It was hard to think with him fondling her breasts so deliciously, but she roused herself to answer. "It says . . . married rakes should be . . . discreet."

"God rot it. I'll have to burn that blasted thing."

"Or stop following it."

He tugged her around to face him, his face ablaze. "I've *never*—"

"I know." She pressed her hand to his lips. "I do know." Only when his fury abated did she drop her hand. "But apparently rakehells and respectable men on the prowl think alike."

He eyed her warily. "In what way?"

"You're trying to seduce me, aren't you?"

He hesitated, then gave a tight shake of his head. "I'm trying to make love to you. It's not the same thing."

"Isn't it?"

"Seduction is when a man coerces a woman into saying yes to sharing his bed." He drew her close, then bent his head to whisper, "Making love is when she says yes because she wants to be there."

That was certainly not in *The Rake's Rhetorick*. She'd read enough to know that the anonymous author didn't believe in giving the woman much choice.

"And why should I say yes?" As soon as the words left her mouth, she realized she was doomed. Because she was already thinking about it, already wanting it, already—

"Because you need me as much as I need you." He kissed her again, the slow-burning kiss of a man who knew what he wanted, who knew what *she* wanted, better than she knew herself. "Show me you trust me, sweetheart." He nibbled her lip. "Show me you won't go running to Lovelace the minute I disappoint you. Show me you want to marry me."

Now that his anger seemed to have ebbed, he was far more dangerous to her self-control. "I do want to marry you, but . . . there will have to be rules."

"No rules." His face shone hard as steel.

"But—"

"No," he growled, dragging her chemise over her head and tossing it aside.

She wore no drawers, and his eyes widened, raking her naked body with obvious desire. Self-conscious, she started to cover herself with her hands, but he caught them in his as he drank his fill.

He lifted a fiery gaze to her face. "You have too many rules, sweetheart. Demand anything of me you wish when we're in society, but when we're alone, there will be only one rule."

Her bared nipples puckered beneath his hot glance. "Wh-what rule is that?"

"The rule of lovers: All that matters is pleasing each other."

"And if I want more? If I want . . ." What? Love? She'd told him she didn't believe in love. "Mutual affection? Consideration for my feelings?"

"You'll have that, too," he said, though a strangely haunted look shadowed his features as he drew her close. "You will, I swear."

For some insane reason, she believed him. "All right. Then, yes."

His hands tightened on her waist. "Yes, what?"

"You said making love is when a woman says—"

He brought his mouth fiercely down on hers, taking command of her. Soon she was drowning in sensations . . . his tongue stabbing deep . . . his thumb teasing her nipple into a fine, hard point . . . his other hand cupping her hips and tugging her flush against his pelvis.

As hard male flesh dug into soft feminine curves, she suddenly remembered the shocking prints from *The*

Rake's Rhetorick, where the men's "staffs" were so ridiculously large.

Lord preserve her—could that have been . . . could a man really be . . . Curious, she slid her hand between them to explore the bulge in his trousers. When it jumped in her hand, she jerked back with a squeak. "My word, it moves!"

Alec gave a strained laugh. "Nothing to be afraid of, sweetheart. Here, try it again." He brought her hand back to the heavy rod trapped inside his buckskins. His eyes slid shut as she stroked him tentatively. Then he rasped, "Wait—" and stepped back to undo the buttons.

In the dim light, his eyes looked almost black as he shoved his trousers off his hips. His drawers quickly followed, and she could only stare at the thick flesh that jutted out from between his well-hewn thighs. Except for its nest of sable hair, his member was the very image of the ones in the book. My goodness! So men really could increase in size until they—

"Touch me again," he said, grabbing her hand and drawing it back. "I promise to stay still . . . just touch it . . . please . . ."

The hoarse need in his voice delighted her. Alec had never begged her for anything; he was always too self-assured for that. Feeling terribly wicked—and terribly excited—she let him close her hand around his "staff."

Well! He was certainly as big as any of those men in the pictures. And stiff—how did flesh get so stiff? Or feel so warm, and be so responsive when she stroked it?

At his groan, she hesitated. "Am I doing it right?"

"Yes . . ." His breathing was weighted, thick.

"Show me how to please you. What do I do?"

His eyes shot open to scour her with raw hunger. Then

he gripped her fingers and molded them to his rigid length. "Just . . . hold it."

"Like this?"

"Tighter." When she did as he said, he moaned and thrust into her hand. "My God, sweetheart . . . that feels so good."

"Does it?" She exulted to see his rapt face, to hear his rough sounds of pleasure. He'd always been the one to make her react. Having the shoe on the other foot was exhilarating—and deliriously freeing.

The way his flesh leaped beneath her touch, the way it felt in her hand, was more thrilling than she'd imagined. The only thing more thrilling would be to have him touch her the way he'd done before.

As if he'd read her mind, he reached down between her legs, found the damp aching flesh there, and fondled her as boldly as she was fondling him.

When his finger delved inside her, she gasped and thrust her hips against his maddening palm. He rubbed her hard, making her insane, blotting out everything but the glorious thrill of his hand caressing her so intimately. Her knees faltered, and she swayed against him.

"Does that please you?" he growled.

"You know . . . that it does," she gasped.

She tugged hard on his staff, and he shuddered. "Does this please *you*?" she countered, his response making her stroke more boldly.

"Too much," he said thickly. Suddenly, he was brushing her hand away and lowering her onto the cushions. As he followed her down, spreading her thighs so he could kneel between them, he growled, "You're mine now, Katherine Merivale. Not Lovelace's—*mine*."

"Yes," she breathed as she flung her arms about his neck.

He parted the flesh between her legs with wicked, knowing fingers. "You'll marry me," he commanded. "As soon as possible."

"Yes." She squirmed beneath him, wanting to feel his fingers driving deep inside her again. "Whatever you say."

He stared down at her with a heavy-lidded gaze. "You do know how this works, don't you?"

His solemn expression, coupled with the amazing intimacy of him lying between her legs with his fingers teasing her in the most shameless manner, made her giggle. "If I don't, then I'm about to have quite a surprise."

"Katherine—"

"Yes, I know how it works." She arched against his hand, instinctively craving more. "I'm a country girl, remember?" Not to mention that she'd been looking at pictures of it for months.

"I don't want to hurt you," he said as he continued to hover over her.

"You can't avoid it." She turned her head to kiss his muscular left arm, the one straining to hold him off her. "So unless you're thinking of stopping—"

"No," he growled. "No stopping now." Then it was no longer his fingers, but something bigger and firmer forging its way up her slick passage.

Her eyes slid shut. How very . . . interesting. It was tight . . . hot . . . thrilling even, as it stretched her in a place she'd never imagined being stretched, heated her in a place she'd never imagined being heated.

Suddenly he stopped moving to press his lips to her ear. "All right, country girl, here it comes. Try to relax, and it will go easier for you."

She nodded, but braced herself anyway. Relaxing was impossible. Every inch of her lower body felt alive to his flesh within her, as if she'd waited for him a hundred years, waited to become his woman, pain or no.

But when he thrust, she felt nothing but a little pinch, so fleeting that she laughed aloud. *That* was the virtue she'd been protecting so fiercely? That barrier so easily disposed of?

Planted to the hilt inside her, he whispered, "What's so funny?"

She opened her eyes to stare up at him. He looked concerned. "It's not . . . what I expected, that's all."

He raised an eyebrow. "What did you expect?"

"The sky to fall, and the earth to shake." And all because she'd shamelessly given her virtue to a man outside of marriage.

He smiled rakishly, then brushed his lips over hers. "Just wait," he said in a tone of promise.

"For what?"

Then he moved. And moved again. And again and again, driving deep, thrusting hard, sweeping all thoughts from her mind, banishing all protests.

"Oh . . . my . . . goodness . . ." she whispered, as he rode her as masterfully as he'd ridden his horses. "That's . . . oh . . ."

"Yes," he rasped against her ear. "By God, sweetheart . . . you feel incredible . . . you have no idea . . ."

"I do, I do," she chanted as he thundered inside her, around her, with her. And when he slipped his hand between them to flick his finger over the tender nub he'd touched before, she went positively wild, thrashing beneath him, nearly throwing him off the bench with her writhing.

Satisfaction blazed in his face as he drew back far enough to look into her eyes, his breath harsh and ragged. "Remember this . . . remember you find it . . . with me . . . not Lovelace . . . me."

She could only nod, because the sensations he created made it too hard to speak . . . to think . . . to do anything but wrap her legs about his hips so she could press into him higher, harder . . .

"Mine," he said in a guttural voice against her ear as he gave a sudden mighty thrust, driving into her so deeply that she felt him in the very heart of her. "Mine now. Only mine."

Then the earth did shake, and the sky did fall . . . and she was lost to anything but him straining against her, spilling himself inside her as a cry of pleasure tore from her lips.

He muffled it with his mouth, so it didn't betray their presence in the orangery.

But in her mind she repeated his vow—*Mine. Mine now. Only mine.*

Chapter Twenty-one

If a woman becomes more possessive after
seduction, nip her expectations in the bud
at once if you want any peace.
—Anonymous, *A Rake's Rhetorick*

Alec was in no hurry to return to the ballroom. It was cozy out here in the orangery, with a naked Katherine cradled in his lap as he sprawled on the bench, also naked, with his back against the cold wall.

It was the only cold thing here. The orangery kept out the faint chill of spring, cocooning them in warm, humid air. With the night shielding them from prying eyes, it felt like their private haven.

Out here, there was no Edenmore to worry about, no deceptions to hide, no guilt. Out here, it was just he and Katherine.

And the way she'd been when they'd made love . . . His throat constricted just to think of it. What a wild, sweet lover—so eager and so entirely his. He tightened his arms around her possessively. He would never let anything come between them now.

She snuggled into his chest, her breath tickling his skin. "I like it here."

With a chuckle, he brushed a kiss to her tangled hair.

"I like it here, too, sweetheart. I'll have to build an orangery at Edenmore."

She nuzzled his nipple, and it tightened instantly to a hard nub. "It's a pity we have to go back inside."

"Must we?" His blood—and something else—was already rising again.

"You know we must. Mama will come looking for me soon."

"Good, we'll stay here until she finds us. Then you'll be thoroughly compromised." He tipped her face up to his. "You know you have to marry me now, sweetheart."

When delight sparked in her eyes, he realized a tiny part of her had still feared he wanted only seduction. Trying not to let it bother him, he added, "In fact, we'll be marrying as soon as possible."

"Will we?" she teased.

"Yes, we will," he said firmly.

With a minxish smile, she slid off his lap and stood, stretching like a cat. When she caught him staring at her pert breasts, she blushed and jerked up the chemise to cover her. But not before he'd glimpsed her smooth white belly and the patch of fiery red hair between her thighs . . . the thighs she'd wrapped around him with an instinctive knowledge of lovemaking as old as Eve.

His cock stirred once more, especially when she swept her own glance down his body to fix on the growing erection he couldn't hide.

Still clutching the chemise to her chest, she approached and bent to touch her finger to the swollen tip of his cock. He tugged the chemise out of her grip so he could seize her breast in his mouth to tongue the rapidly tightening tip.

Just as he wondered if he could toss her back down on

the bench and make love to her again, she stepped back, forcing him to relinquish his hold on her breast. His breath coming heavily, he watched her shimmy into her chemise.

Then she smiled. "You know, *The Rake's Rhetorick* has pictures, too."

He went painfully hard. "What kind of pictures?"

"Naughty ones. Of rakes with women." She gestured to his rock-hard cock. "A couple of the pictures even show a man's ... er ... staff."

He could only imagine what a book like that would show as an "average" male member. "I really will have to burn that thing," he grumbled as he rose and reached for her.

Laughing, she brushed his hands away. "I thought the pictures were exaggerations, but apparently men really do look like that."

"Like what?"

"Like you, all long and hard and ..." Her gaze grew sultry as she closed her hand around his erection. "Firm."

He dragged in a breath. He'd known she had a reckless streak, but who would have guessed that loosing it would turn her into such a delightful wanton?

A wanton he couldn't wait to bed again.

With a growl, he caught her to him. "That does it— now I'll have to remind you what my 'staff' is for." He bent his head to suck her neck, and she arched her back, pressing her soft, thinly clad breasts against him.

Before thrusting him away and marching off to look for her gown.

He scowled after her. "Not so fast, senhora." He walked up and tried to snatch it from her hand. "Now that you've got my staff firm—"

"—you aren't apt to forget whom you're marrying." Eyes twinkling, she danced away, taking her gown with her.

Blast the woman for using his own words against him. He didn't know whether to laugh or to throw her over his shoulder and carry her back to the bench. "As if I can forget that when all I think about is you naked," he grumbled.

Her musical laugh only annoyed him further. "Good. Keep that thought in your mind until we're married."

"To hell with waiting until we're married. I want to make love to you now."

When he headed for her once more, she smiled and tossed his drawers at him. "You can't, and you know it. So get dressed, before we're discovered."

Which would put a quick end to this torture. With a sly smile, he sidled toward her, his drawers in his hand. "One kiss, that's all I want. To hold me until our wedding night."

She eyed him askance. "Do you think you can stop with a kiss?"

Of course he couldn't. Neither could she. That was the point. "Why don't we find out?"

"Oh, no, you don't." She darted around behind the short wall separating the orange trees from the sitting area. "I do *not* intend to be found naked in your arms, no matter how appealing you find the idea at the moment."

He groaned. "Blast you for your sense of propriety. I thought I'd coaxed it out of you."

"Not yet." She slipped into her gown with another teasing smile. "But you're welcome to keep trying. *After* we're married."

He opened his mouth to tell her that he intended to

keep her in bed for a week after they married, but loud noises coming from the garden kept him silent.

"Are you sure you saw her out here?" came the unmistakably loud voice of Mrs. Merivale.

He couldn't hear the answer, but he didn't need to. Though it sounded as if the intruders were still far off, they'd soon reach the orangery. And judging from Katherine's panicked expression, she wasn't eager to be caught like this.

Very well, he would preserve her proprieties. For now.

They dressed swiftly, their hands moving in a silent frenzy. He laced up her corset and fastened her gown; she helped him tie his cravat. Thank God he'd already looked rumpled when he'd arrived, so his disordered attire wouldn't rouse more comment.

Her appearance was more likely to do so, but between the two of them, they managed to get her looking presentable. Thankfully, by the time the voices neared them, he was already helping her with her hair.

She'd just put the last pin in place when the orangery door opened and a brace of candles was thrust inside, followed by their hostess and Mrs. Merivale.

As Lady Purefoy swept the candles in an arc over the room, Alec spotted *The Rake's Rhetorick* lying on the floor. He stepped in front of it just before the light hit it. Seconds later, he and Katherine were fully illuminated.

Mrs. Merivale looked disappointed to find them fully clothed and standing respectably apart, but that didn't halt her purpose. "My lord! How dare you—"

"Good evening, ladies," Alec put in swiftly. "You're just in time. Miss Merivale has finally agreed to be my bride."

The two women blinked. Then everything changed. Smiling broadly, Mrs. Merivale hurried forward to hug her daughter. "Oh, my angel, I'm so happy for you. How wonderful to have it settled at last!"

Lady Purefoy's shock turned to smug self-congratulation. "Didn't I tell you, Totty?" the baroness said to Mrs. Merivale. "I knew his lordship would never enter my house dressed so shamefully without good purpose. And to have the match assured at my party! What a coup!"

As if she'd had a blasted thing to do with it, Alec thought wryly. "Forgive me, Lady Purefoy, for bursting in with such a lack of ceremony, but I couldn't wait another minute to ask Miss Merivale to marry me." Taking Katherine's hand, Alec gazed down into her smiling face.

"No apology needed." Lady Purefoy winked at Mrs. Merivale. "We matrons aren't so old as to forget how impetuous young gentlemen in love can be."

The two women laughed, but Katherine went still and her smile faltered.

Alec bit back a curse. He'd asked her—*commanded* her to marry him—without once saying the words of love any young woman wanted to hear from her intended.

Then again, hadn't she said she didn't believe in love? This was a marriage between two people who desired each other, nothing more. Surely she must realize that, and if she didn't, it was better to make it clear before she began nurturing such feelings for him.

Before he started to *want* her nurturing them. No, he wouldn't spend his life like his mother, yearning for what he couldn't have. He could desire Katherine, yes. Enjoy her company, certainly. But crave her love?

That way lay disaster.

"I'm afraid we must all return to the ballroom," Lady Purefoy said, "before people start to talk about what's going on out here."

"Of course," Alec said. "Besides, I want to dance with my betrothed."

The two women exchanged knowing glances, then headed for the door. As soon as their backs were turned, Katherine bent to retrieve that blasted book. He'd hoped she hadn't seen it, but no such luck.

When she started to shove it into her reticule, he grabbed it. "I'll hold on to this," he murmured as he slid it into his frock coat pocket.

She raised both eyebrows. "Why?"

"You said it has naughty pictures, didn't you?"

"Alec—" she began in a warning tone.

"Relax, sweetheart." Taking her arm, he led her toward the door. "I'll give it back to you as soon as we're married. Until then, I don't want anything reminding you of your previous objections to my suit."

"Now see here, my arrogant Lord Iversley, I will not—"

"Are you two coming?" Mrs. Merivale poked her head back into the orangery to ask. "We have a betrothal to announce."

"Yes, sweetheart," he teased, "why do you dawdle?" He laughed when Katherine scowled first at him, then her mother.

And when Mrs. Merivale stood there and watched until they followed her out, he decided he might like having a pushy mother-in-law. Especially when she was so clearly on *his* side.

Katherine had never been the belle of the ball or even known how one rose to that lofty status. Now she knew. A woman need only have an attractive and highly desirable earl propose marriage. Because once the news swept through Lady Purefoy's guests, Katherine suddenly became the most popular person there.

How ridiculous. She'd been in London for weeks—weeks, mind you! But until she'd met Alec, the only men other than Sydney asking her to dance had been Sydney's poet friends and the occasional squinty-eyed old gentleman. Between her "unfortunate hair," Mama's gushing, and Papa's reputation as a wild-living squire, she hadn't stood a chance.

She was her same old self, but now she couldn't beat the men off. Although judging from how Alec frowned at her present partner—a handsome, if somewhat dull-witted viscount—Alec wished *he* could.

She smothered a laugh. He was trapped in an extended conversation with Mama, while Katherine danced with yet another respectable gentleman. Hah! That's what he got for stealing the *Rhetorick*.

He exacted his own revenge soon enough, however, when the viscount brought her back. As they approached, Alec skimmed his smoldering gaze down her body, resting it briefly on her breasts, then her belly, and finally the place between her thighs that he'd conquered so shamelessly earlier.

Thank goodness the viscount was too busy chattering to notice. Alec's look was so blatantly sensual, she could hardly manage a response to the viscount's commentary on the dance. Undressing her with his eyes, indeed—he was *seducing* her with his eyes, curse him.

Most effectively, too. By the time she and the viscount reached Alec and her mother, Katherine wanted to throw herself at her future husband and beg him to take her again right there.

She didn't even notice when the viscount left.

With a pantherish smile, Alec stepped close. "Shall I fetch you some punch, Miss Merivale? You look a bit . . . warm."

She just had time to raise an eyebrow before Mama answered. "Oh, yes, do fetch us both some punch. I swear I'm going quite hoarse from discussing your impending *mésalliance*."

Alec covered his laugh with a cough, but Katherine could only sigh. One of these days her mother would be the death of her. "Mama, please say you haven't been telling all and sundry that ours is a 'bad match.'"

"What? Indeed not! A perfect *mésalliance*—that's what I was just saying to Lady Winthrop. Though I confess she looked oddly startled to hear it."

Katherine wanted to drop through the floor in mortification, but Alec's eyes twinkled madly. "Never mind Lady Winthrop, madam. On my way to get the punch, I'll be sure to . . . er . . . explain the matter more thoroughly to her."

As he strode off, his shoulders shaking with laughter, Mama said, "He's such a nice man, don't you think?"

"Tolerant, too," Katherine said, suppressing a smile.

"You've made me so happy, dear. I knew when he walked in tonight that he'd forgiven you."

She frowned. "For what, pray tell?"

"For all that business of delaying the announcement so you could talk to Sir Sydney first." Her mother scowled at something past her. "And speaking of Sir Sydney, he's headed this way."

That was all the warning Katherine got before Sydney was upon them, looking dignified and vulnerable and a little sad.

He bowed to them both. "I came to give you my felicitations. I hope you and Iversley will be very happy together, Kit."

Katherine recognized the olive branch for what it was. "Thank you."

"I'm certain Mother would give you her felicitations, too, if she were here."

Mama scowled at him. "Do be sure to tell your mother exactly whom my girl is marrying. Katherine may be beneath a baronet, but apparently she's quite high enough for an earl."

Sydney flushed a dark red.

"Mama, please—" Katherine began.

"No, my dear," her mother interrupted, "it needs to be said. Lady Lovelace is too high in the instep, if you ask me. And it's time she knew it. Furthermore—"

"Excuse me, Mama, but I need a word with Sydney alone." Ignoring propriety, Katherine tugged Sydney off with her.

As soon as they were out of earshot, she murmured, "I'm sorry about that. You know Mama—she speaks any thought that comes into her head."

"And yet Iversley doesn't seem to mind it."

Oddly enough, that was true. "I think Lord Iversley finds Mama amusing."

"Ah. He seems to find a great many things amusing, doesn't he?"

She smiled, ignoring the insult implicit in his words. "Perhaps it's time I had some amusement in my life."

Sydney cast her an earnest glance. "I meant what I said about wanting you to be happy. I hope you'll still consider me your friend."

"Of course." But the nature of their friendship would change. Even if she weren't moving halfway across England, a respectable woman couldn't spend hours with a male friend discussing poetry. Not if she wanted to avoid gossip.

She sighed. She would miss their talks. Still, there would be other compensations—her own home, a husband who made her laugh, children.

Children! She hadn't even thought about that. Oh, wouldn't it be wonderful to have Alec's children?

Sydney was watching her with a frown. "You love him, don't you?"

"What? No! I-I mean . . . I don't know . . . I—"

"I know you, Kit—you'd never marry a man you didn't love."

"Right," she mumbled. She *wasn't* marrying Alec for love. She'd never be that foolish. It was a simple matter of enjoying his company and seeing the advantages to such a match.

And of desiring him beyond all endurance.

She blushed. If love was a foolish reason for marrying, desire was an idiotic one. This was merely the sensible way to deal with her need for a husband. And it was purely coincidental that it was also the most appealing.

"Promise me one thing." Sydney gazed down at her tenderly. "If you ever need me, if Iversley ever mistreats you, either before or after you marry, promise you'll come to me."

After she married? She eyed him closely. "I mean to be faithful to my husband."

His look of outrage set her straight. "I should hope so! I didn't mean . . . why, I'd never come between a man and his wife, even if the man *is* a . . . a—"

"A scoundrel?" She laughed. This Sydney she wouldn't miss at all, the one who disapproved of people who didn't share his serious outlook or his love of poetry. "I'll be all right with him, you know. You needn't worry. Besides, you won't even be around. You're headed to Greece with Lord Napier."

He stared off across the ballroom. "Actually, I'm not. I . . . we argued. I told him I wouldn't go."

"Oh, but you *should* go." Now that she was happy, she wanted to see Sydney happy, too, and surely a trip to an exotic place with his close friend would accomplish that. "You would enjoy yourself."

"That's precisely why I mustn't go." Before she could question that enigmatic statement, he changed the subject. "So when is the wedding?" he asked a bit too cheerily, as if trying to put a good face on things.

"As soon as possible, I hope," Alec answered from behind them.

Startled, she whirled around so fast she nearly overset the glass of punch he held. Mama stood beside him, scowling her disapproval, but Alec's expression betrayed nothing.

His eyes, however, glittered a brilliant blue in the candlelight, alive with some emotion she couldn't read. Anger? Jealousy? Perhaps a little. But there was something else there, too. It looked oddly like fear.

"Good evening, Iversley," Sydney said. "I was just giving your . . . intended wife my felicitations on the announcement of your betrothal."

"How kind of you." Alec handed Katherine her punch. "I'm sorry we can't invite you to the wedding. It's going to be a private affair, just Katherine's family. We're marrying by special license within the week."

Katherine nearly dropped her glass of punch. "We . . . we are?"

Alec's gaze settled on her. "I assumed you'd want to marry soon. There is Mr. Byrne to consider, after all."

"Who's Mr. Byrne?" Sydney asked.

"Nobody of consequence." Katherine certainly didn't want Sydney to know how deeply Papa had sunk them into debt. She shot Alec a cool glance. "So we're marrying by special license? I suppose you've chosen a gown for me as well?"

Her acerbic tone made Alec arch one brow. "Forgive me, sweetheart—I thought you'd be pleased. But if you'd rather we post the banns and marry from your home in Heath's End, just say so."

"Don't be silly," Mama protested. "What would people think if you married like common day laborers?" She clapped her hands to her chest with a dreamy sigh. "To marry by special license—how romantic that will be! All the ladies will envy you, my angel!"

With a glance at Katherine, Sydney asked, "What's your hurry?"

"I see no reason to wait." Alec cast Katherine a warm smile. "I came to London to find a wife, and now that I have, I want to go home with her to Suffolk and begin our life together."

Katherine melted. So Mama had been wrong about that, too—Alec didn't want a "fashionable marriage." He only wanted *her*.

That didn't sit well with Mama. "What? Go home? But it's the middle of the season! We'll have to arrange a ball at your town house, at the very least."

"There's no need for all that," Katherine put in to cover Alec's grimace.

"Of course there is! There should be parties to celebrate the marriage and breakfasts and a soiree . . . what can you mean, to be scampering off to the country now, my lord? People will think something is amiss."

"We don't care what people think." Katherine moved to Alec's side to lay her free hand on his arm. He covered it with his own and squeezed.

Any lingering objections to a hasty wedding went right out the window. This, after all, was what she wanted from marriage—two people joined against the world, ready to stand firm against the frivolous Mamas and the naysaying Sydneys. Two people who understood each other.

Sydney stared down at their joined hands, and his lips tightened. "Well, then, I shan't intrude on this cozy family scene any longer." He cast Alec a resentful glance. "I assume that you'll accompany the ladies home tonight?"

Alec nodded tersely.

Sydney turned to Katherine. "Remember, if you ever need anything—"

"Yes, thank you," she broke in, feeling Alec's hand stiffen on hers.

As the baronet walked off, Alec glared daggers into his back. Fortunately, Alec had no time to ask what Sydney's last words had meant before Mama commanded his attention again. "Now see here, my lord, you simply cannot drag my daughter off to the country without so much as a warning."

Which meant, *you can't remove my only excuse for being in London.*

A perverse mischief seized Katherine. "I believe he can do as he pleases once he marries me, Mama."

Alec raised an eyebrow at Katherine, but merely added, "I'm sorry, I can't stay in London just now. My father neglected Edenmore for years, and I must be there to turn things around. But of course if Katherine prefers to remain here—"

"I don't," she said. "I'm looking forward to seeing your country estate."

Alec smiled at her, then her mother. "You're welcome to stay with us whenever you like, Mrs. Merivale, if you don't mind the workmen and interruptions of tenants."

"No, indeed," Mama said hastily. "I shall stay right here in London, if you please."

That same urge for mischief pressed Katherine on. "Someone will need to oversee Merivale Manor now that I won't be doing it, Mama. Unless you intend to take over my letter-writing duties?"

The pained look on her mother's face nearly made her laugh aloud. Mama loathed writing letters as much as she loathed being packed away to the country.

Katherine could almost feel sorry for her. Almost.

But really, it served Mama right to have this happen. By promoting the earl's suit, Mama had probably not realized she would lose Katherine's management skills. Whereas if Katherine had married Sydney, she might have been able to continue her activities from the nearby Lovelace estate.

Thank goodness she was marrying Alec.

Chapter Twenty-two

*Even the cleverest rake cannot ensure the
smooth running of his plans. Learn
to be flexible.*
—Anonymous, *A Rake's Rhetorick*

You've nearly made it, Alec told himself later in the
evening as he and the Merivale ladies waited for his carriage. *Another week at most, and you're safe.*

Unless they found out about his finances in that time,
but that was unlikely.

Of course, once he got Katherine back to Edenmore,
there'd be hell to pay. But by then it would be too late for
her to escape the marriage—and he sincerely hoped he
could eventually make her not want to escape.

Lady Purefoy's footman approached them with a
frown. "My lord, I cannot seem to rouse your coachman.
If you can suggest—"

"It's all right." Alec pressed a few coins into the man's
hand, hoping his companions didn't notice how few they
were. "I'll take care of it myself."

Mrs. Merivale gazed at him in horror. "Didn't you
bring your own footman, my lord? Can't he rouse the
coachman?"

"I left my footman at your town house," Alec explained, "in case you returned before I caught up to you. But it's nothing to worry about. I'll rouse him."

"*We'll* rouse him," Katherine put in.

Though Mrs. Merivale grumbled at the indignity of having to don her pattens to keep from soiling her dancing slippers, she went along with them to where the carriage was parked a short distance from the Purefoy town house.

"John, wake up," Alec said sharply as they approached.

The coachman's loud snore was his only answer.

"John!" Alec said more loudly, punctuating the command by jiggling the coachman's leg.

John shifted his position on the perch and resumed his snoring. Not that Alec blamed the man, after the day they'd had.

"Blast it, John," Alec grumbled as he shoved the coachman hard.

Too hard, apparently, for John fell off the other side, hitting the ground like a sack of barley. At least that woke him up. "Thieves! Robbers! Watchman, ho!" John cried as he scrambled to his feet.

Then he spotted his master. Turning a sickly pale, he hurried around the coach. "Oh, m'lord, beggin' your pardon, I didn't mean to doze off . . . It won't happen again, I swear."

"It's all right, John," Alec said.

"Truly, m'lord—" He caught sight of Katherine and Mrs. Merivale. "'Odsfish, you've got the ladies with you, too. Please forgive me, madam, miss. It's just that we been on the road for days, seems like, and this last trip from Lord Draker's in Hertfordshire was such a mad rush."

"Lord Draker's?" Katherine looked at Alec. "Isn't he the one they call—"

"The Dragon Viscount, yes," Alec said irritably. "Doesn't anybody ever use the man's name, for God's sake?"

She blinked. "I'm sorry, I didn't realize he was a friend of yours."

"Well, he is. Come on, let's get in." Alec glanced to John. "Can you get us home without falling asleep on the perch again?"

"Yes, m'lord." John bobbed his head even more furiously because of the ladies watching him.

As soon as they set off in the carriage, Katherine shot Alec a curious glance. "How do you know Lord Draker? I understand he doesn't go into society."

"He's an old family friend," Alec muttered. What would she say if she knew the truth? Would it bother her? "If you like, I can introduce you to him."

"Heavens, no!" Mrs. Merivale retorted. "He's not the sort of man we'd want to be associated with."

"A man with a well-ordered estate, happy tenants, and contented servants?" he snapped. "*That* is the sort of man you would avoid?"

Mrs. Merivale gaped at him, but Katherine merely said in a soft voice, "Mama, you're speaking of his lordship's friend. We know nothing about the man but gossip, so perhaps we shouldn't be so quick to judge." She cast him a sweet smile that reminded him why he preferred her to any other woman he'd met in London.

"Thank you," he answered.

At least Katherine could appreciate Draker's admirable qualities, buried deeply though they were. Mrs. Merivale and her ilk could never appreciate them; those fools looked only at appearances. A fortune hunter pretending to be rich was accepted in an instant, but God forbid a respectable, responsible gentleman like Draker, who'd made a few mistakes years ago, should darken society's doors.

Alec couldn't wait to be away from such hypocrisy and out in the country with his beautiful new wife, who shared his opinion of society.

"You know, my lord," Katherine remarked, "this is the first I've heard of any of your friends, other than Mr. França. And you haven't said much about your family either. I don't even know what your parents looked like. Was your mother dark-haired, too? Or do you get your coloring from your father?"

"I resemble my father to a marked degree, actually," he said, trying to keep the irony from his voice. Thank God she wouldn't see a portrait of the old earl until after they were married. "Except for my hair. That I did indeed get from my mother."

She looked wistful. "I wish I could have met them."

"Mother would have liked you. As a timid woman, she envied women who could speak their minds."

Perhaps if she'd spoken her mind to Prinny, she wouldn't have succumbed to his seductions and carried his bastard. But then Alec wouldn't have been born.

A loud snore sounded in the carriage. Glancing over at her dozing mother, Katherine flashed him a wry smile. "I would have loved your mother for being timid. Lord knows I've endured the opposite long enough."

"That reminds me—earlier you mentioned your letter-writing duties. What exactly did you mean?"

She shrugged. "I'm the one who corresponds with the housekeeper at Merivale Manor about the children. I choose where our meager funds should be allotted, authorize all expenditures, and approve any requests by the servants for time off or leave to visit family or whatever."

"In other words, you run the household."

"Such as it is, yes."

"When your mother said you always worried about such things, I didn't realize you were the *only* one to do so."

She arched an eyebrow. "Did you think Mama would do it? Not likely."

"But surely in your childhood, *someone* must have done such things."

She nodded. "My grandfather. Until he died six years ago."

"The two of you must have been very close."

She stared out at the street that was damp from spring rains. "He was the only one in my family who understood me."

Which explained why the man had left her a fortune. But it would be Edenmore benefiting from the fruits of her labor, Edenmore profiting from the fortune intended for her own family. "You must enjoy household management, or surely you wouldn't keep doing it."

"Actually, I look forward to leaving it all behind." When she caught him frowning, she added, "Not that I don't mean to fulfill my wifely duties at your estate—"

"*Our* estate," he corrected her.

She smiled. "Yes, of course. But managing a staff is a far cry from having to perform half the servants' duties because there's too much work to go round. Then there's the incessant concerns about our debts . . . I'll be very happy not to have to worry about *that* anymore."

"Will you?" he said uneasily. She wouldn't be leaving her worries and hard work behind. If anything, until he set Edenmore to rights, she'd have more. Because even with her fortune, it would take careful management to do all that must be done.

"Why do you think I read so much poetry? To take my mind off the realities of my life." She cast him a teasing smile. "But you'll be happy to know that since I won't have to worry about such things now, I won't have to read nearly so much of that stuff you detest."

Uh-oh. He'd better lay in a large supply of books in verse. He'd need it to soothe her temper when she found out how he'd tricked her.

Blast, blast, blast. He'd assumed that she'd be grateful to be free of her flighty mother and that too-serious idiot Sydney. When she discovered that marrying him had merely forced her to exchange one prison for another, she might not be so grateful. She might even resent having lost Sydney's wealth and servants and easy life.

He squelched the burst of unfamiliar guilt. All right, so her days might not go quite as she hoped, but at least the nights would be better than anything Sydney could give her. Of that, he was sure.

The carriage shuddered to a halt in front of the Merivale town house, jolting her mother awake. Mrs. Merivale blinked and looked around. "Katherine . . . where . . . Oh. Forgive me, I must have dozed." She cast him a bright smile. "You will come in and have some supper, won't you, Lord Iversley? I daresay Lady Purefoy's wretched fare was scarcely enough to keep a man's body and soul together, especially after he spent the day racing about the countryside."

"Tempting as that sounds, I can only come in for a few minutes," he said, as his footman hurried down the stairs to open the carriage door.

"Nonsense, I won't hear of it. Katherine told Cook to prepare some cold viands for our return, and it will take Thomas only a moment to set it out and uncork the wine."

Alec climbed down from the carriage, then handed the two ladies out. No point in waiting any longer to break the bad news to them. "Actually, I have to be up before dawn's light. I must return to Suffolk by nightfall tomorrow."

"Tomorrow!" Katherine exclaimed. With a frown, she took the arm he offered her. "But you just returned!"

After her mother took his other arm, he led them both up the stairs. "You forget that I still have my problem with the tillers—I must finish dealing with that. Not to mention that I must prepare my staff and make sure that Edenmore is in a condition suitable for your arrival."

"You needn't make a fuss for me," Katherine protested.

"It's no fuss, believe me. After we're married, I want to be able to take you right home and have you be comfortable."

"Won't you take a honeymoon trip first?" Mrs. Merivale asked, as they entered the house.

"Perhaps after the spring planting is done, but not right now. As it is, I can barely spare the time to return to London for our wedding later in the week."

"A week is not enough time to plan a wedding, my lord," Mrs. Merivale snapped, as Alec handed his hat and great coat to Thomas. "When you said a small ceremony, I didn't think you meant it. Why, you're an earl, for heaven's sake. We should at the very least—"

"I would prefer just ourselves. Fortunately, I've already acquired the special license, so as soon as I return from Suffolk we can marry." Thank God the archbishop happened to have a son in the cavalry who sang Alec's praises. He glanced down at Katherine. "Is that all right with you?"

He held his breath. If Katherine preferred a big wedding some weeks hence in Heath's End, he wasn't sure he could keep up appearances or hide his true financial state from his skittish intended that long.

"I don't much care whether we have a large wedding." Katherine lifted her troubled gaze to him as Thomas took her coat. "But a week really is a short time, especially if you spend part of it in the country. You and Mama still have to speak with Papa's solicitor and arrange the marriage settlement—"

"Just a formality, my lord," her mother put in quickly. "But it must be done. And you'll be delighted to find that Katherine—"

"—has a small dowry," Katherine finished, casting her mother a dark look.

He stiffened. So she didn't trust him enough yet to tell him of her fortune. Meanwhile, he still had to evade questions about his own finances.

Mrs. Merivale and the solicitor wouldn't much care about his situation, however, as long as he promised Katherine a certain amount of pin money and a sufficient jointure in case he died first and left her a widow. He could promise the latter easily. By the time he died, he intended to have a substantial income.

As for pin money, he fully intended to give Katherine a nice portion of the fortune she would inherit. He'd even be willing to offer her mother some of it in exchange for her cooperation. So he could probably manage the meeting with the solicitor without revealing too much of his current state of affairs.

"Of course I'll meet with your father's solicitor, and that can be done upon my return. It shouldn't take more than a few hours. Then we can have a small ceremony here, and afterward—"

"No, no, my lord, how can you think of such a thing?" Mrs. Merivale let out an exasperated sigh. "But there is no use talking to a man about these things when he's hungry." She turned to Thomas. "Is the food laid out in the dining room?"

"Yes, madam. I set it out as soon as I heard you drive up."

She waved her beringed hand toward the dining room. "Katherine, take his lordship off and feed him while I fetch the wine. And do tell your intended how impossible his plan is. Why, the wedding might not even appear in the papers if we do it his way."

Mrs. Merivale marched off, leaving them no choice but to follow Thomas into the dining room. But as soon as they entered, Katherine turned to the manservant. "That will be all for now, Thomas. I'll ring if I need you."

"Very good, miss," he murmured.

After he left, Katherine faced Alec. "Must you return to Suffolk so soon?"

That caught him off guard. He'd expected complaints about the small wedding. "Believe me, I'd rather stay with you until we marry, but duty calls." Not wanting to discuss it further, he scanned the room. "Perhaps I *should* eat something before I go." He shot her a wicked smile as he headed for the sideboard. "I suddenly have an enormous appetite, thanks to our . . . er . . . vigorous activity earlier."

Though she blushed, she ignored his insinuation as she came up beside him. "What if Mama and I were to go with you to Suffolk?"

He froze as he was picking up a plate. Blast. "That wouldn't be wise."

"Why not? You and I could simply marry at your estate. You want a small wedding, and Mama and I need a quick one, no matter what she thinks. There is Mr. Byrne to consider, after all. If we marry at Edenmore, that would all be settled. And we wouldn't have to be parted."

No, the parting would come when she saw the condition of his estate, and they wouldn't even make it to the wedding.

Not good, not good at all. He served himself some cold roast beef, though he'd suddenly lost his appetite. "It's not practical for us to marry in Suffolk. We'd have to return to London anyway to pay off your debt to Mr. Byrne, and there's the solicitor to talk to—"

"Surely you could do that tomorrow morning, before you leave. And you said you already got the special license. So why not have the wedding at *your* home?"

"I'm sorry, sweetheart, but Edenmore is in no condition right now for a wedding. And I don't have time to meet with the solicitor before I leave."

"All right then, let us go with you for a visit. Then we'll return to London for the wedding when you've finished your business. Mama and I could see your estate and meet your servants—"

"No," he said quickly. Too quickly, judging from the suspicion flaring in her face.

He gritted his teeth. Her request was perfectly logical, so he must give her an irreproachable answer. "I won't be able to spend any time entertaining you—"

"You needn't worry about us—we'll fend for ourselves."

He averted his gaze, unsettled by the disappointment in her face. Mechanically, he heaped food on his plate, hardly noticing what he put there. It got harder by the moment to deceive her.

Yet deceive her he must. "I'm sorry, but it would be too

much a distraction for me. *You* can take care of yourself, but your mother would be bored. And I must focus on dealing with the spring planting. I can't manage guests right now."

A heavy silence fell. After a few moments, he could stand it no longer. Setting down his plate, he faced her. "You do understand, don't you?"

Her eyes were unnaturally bright. "Alec, I know you said there should be no rules between us, but I wish you'd agree to at least one rule."

The abrupt change of subject set off alarm bells. "And what might that be?"

"That we are always honest with each other."

Blast. "I *am* being honest with you."

With an arch of one brow, she searched his face, and he forced himself to meet her gaze boldly. He *was* being honest, at least about this. She and her mother would be a distraction, and he wouldn't be able to entertain them.

And they'd find out that you have no money.

Perhaps he should tell her the truth. He grew tired of the lies and evasions, of trying to think one step ahead of her clever mind. Perhaps if he laid the situation out for her, she'd accept he had no choice, and the deception would all be over.

Or she would refuse to marry him.

He dared not take that chance. "You'll see Edenmore soon enough, you know. There's no need to rush."

A stubborn look spread over her face. "Alec, I need your promise. Can you swear to be honest with me and never hide anything from me after we're married?"

That he could promise. Because after they married, there'd be no reason to hide anything—although he wasn't looking forward to the storm that would follow all his revelations.

"Yes, I promise," he said solemnly. "I swear on my mother's grave that once we're married, I'll always be honest with you and not hide anything."

Some of the stiffness left her posture. "Thank you."

"You're welcome." Why did he suspect that his answer hadn't completely satisfied her? "Any other rules you wish to foist on me? An agreement not to wear fustian at dinner, a promise never to smoke in bed, that sort of thing?"

A smile tugged at her lips. "No, I think the honesty thing will be quite enough." She glanced away. "And as long as we're being honest, I suppose I should tell you that Sydney proposed marriage to me this evening. He promised to tell his mother and everything if I would only agree to marry him."

His gut twisted into a knot. "Did he?"

"Yes. Before you arrived at the party."

He chose his words carefully. "And what answer did you give him?"

She shifted her gaze to his. "I'm here with you, aren't I?"

Why was she telling him this? To remind him that she had other choices? Or show him how much she'd given up to be with him?

He chose to believe the latter. Drawing her close, he stared at her country-girl face with its sunny freckles and trembling mouth and vulnerable eyes. "Listen to me, Katherine, and listen well. I will do my best to keep you from regretting your choice. I promise to be a good husband to you. You needn't fear on that score."

She searched his face. "And I promise to be a good wife. I only hope that you and I agree on what that is."

"I'm sure we do," he said as he enfolded her in his arms.

Though she let him hold her, he wasn't certain he'd

convinced her. Never mind. He only had to keep her content until he got her to the altar, and that would come within the week.

He was in the final stretch of the race. Nothing short of an act of God could stop him from reaching the finish line now.

Chapter Twenty-three

Remember that women are unpredictable.
Just when you think you have them under
your thumb, they will appear where you
least expect, wagging their tongues.
—Anonymous, *A Rake's Rhetorick*

"You know that you've lost your mind, don't you?" Katherine's mother said two days later from across the hired carriage.

"I know."

She really did. The closer they traveled to a tiny village called Fenbridge, the more insane this trip seemed. Yet she had to make it. She had to find out what Alec was hiding.

Because she *knew* he was hiding something. Otherwise, why not let them go with him to Suffolk?

Her stomach tightening with every mile, she stared out at the forest they passed. His reluctance simply made no sense. If he was so eager to bring her home with him to begin their life together, why not do it at once?

Unless his trip to Suffolk had nothing to do with the spring planting.

She shook off the thought that plagued her constantly. She'd made the mistake of leaping to conclusions before—she wouldn't do it again. But neither would she head blithely into marriage to a man she couldn't trust. Until she was sure she knew all his secrets, she couldn't marry him. And the only way to do that was to go to his home and see what he seemed determined to keep hidden.

"Really, my angel," Mama said as she bounced on the uncomfortable seat, "I don't understand why you're doing this. First you insist upon our visiting some fellow at the Stephens Hotel yesterday. Then you spend our meager funds to hire a coach, rouse me before dawn, and drag me on this trip across two counties . . . and all to appear at an estate where you're clearly not expected. Faith, you'd think you didn't *want* to marry his lordship."

"Of course I want to marry him," she said mechanically. "I just want to be certain whom I'm marrying."

"The Earl of Iversley, of course. Surely you're not confused about *that*."

"It's not his title I'm confused about, Mama." Katherine had grown tired of going round and round on the same subject. "It's his character."

"Character, character . . . you're obsessed with character. Most girls would be happy to marry an earl with an estate of twelve thousand acres. But not you, oh no. You must run him down at his home, whether he wants you there or not. You'll ruin all your chances with him yet," her mother predicted.

"That's a risk I'll have to take."

Ever since the night he'd left her at the town house with a kiss and a promise to return within the week, she'd fretted over his odd behavior. Especially after she'd gone to speak to the owner of the Stephens Hotel the next day. She'd told him that she wanted to retrieve *The Rake's Rhetorick* while Alec was off in Suffolk.

"Jack" had been more than happy to sing Alec's praises

once she'd made it clear that she knew Alec had been living in his establishment. But though he'd professed to know she was Alec's betrothed, he'd politely refused to let her into Alec's room to look for "the book she'd lent him that he'd forgotten to return." And when she'd asked for Alec's direction so she could send him a note, he'd flatly refused to give it to her.

That had only deepened her suspicions. Alec hadn't given her his direction, either—what if she needed to reach him? Clearly, he'd intended to keep her in the dark.

Combined with Alec's peculiar reaction to her request to go with him—and his strange insistence on taking care of estate matters in person—it had been enough to send her on this quest.

It had taken her half the afternoon yesterday to coax someone at the hotel into telling her exactly where Alec was headed. Even then, she'd only managed to get the name of the nearby town. But if he was as well-known a landowner as her mother thought, then someone could direct them from there.

One way or the other, however, she intended to surprise him at his estate.

"What exactly do you expect to find out?" Mama asked her peevishly.

"I don't know." And that was the God's honest truth.

"If you surprise a man in his own home, you'd best be prepared for what you find. Men often dismiss their mistresses just before they marry, you know."

She did know. And it shouldn't bother her if he was getting rid of a mistress. It was certainly better than keeping the mistress after they married. But it did bother her, and it boded ill for their life to come. She refused to marry a man with Papa's morals.

Of course, he might be hiding something else entirely. Or perhaps she was being unduly cautious again. No, she didn't think so. She only prayed she didn't get more than she'd bargained for by surprising him like this.

They traveled in silence a while as thick forests of ash and elm turned to clay hills, and the sun slid toward the horizon. It was nearly dusk when Katherine saw a sign-post that said, FENBRIDGE—2 MILES.

Her heart began to pound. "We can't be far," she told her mother.

"It's not too late to return to London," Mama retorted. "Why risk it when you have so much to lose?"

"Because I must."

She spotted a farm laborer driving a cart ahead of them. As they came alongside, she ordered the hired coachman to stop.

The laborer, a weathered man with an unusually tall brow and long-fingered hands, reined in as well, turning a pair of suspicious eyes on her. "Lost, are ye?"

Katherine flashed him a smile out the open window. "Indeed we are. We're looking for Lord Iversley's estate. Edenmore."

The man jerked his head to the field that ran by the road. "You been driving by it for a good bit. You can see the house from the road up ahead—it's a big 'un."

"Thank you," she said, and offered him a coin.

With a derisive snort, he ignored it and clicked his tongue to send his odd-looking horse clopping on down the road.

As they passed him, Katherine gazed at the cleared fields he'd indicated and felt a moment's unease. Three men toiled in them with horses much like the odd one she'd just seen—short, barrel-bodied, and devoid of the thick hair usual to the legs of draft horses. They were turning the earth in nice, neat rows . . . with shiny new tillers.

What if Alec *had* been telling the truth? Might he get angry enough at her distrust to toss her aside, as Mama feared?

Then where would she be? She couldn't go back to Sydney—not unchaste as she was. And even if Sydney would have her, she'd already realized he wasn't the man for her. Indeed, she greatly feared that no man could make her feel what she felt for Alec.

But what *did* she feel for Alec? Did she dare give a name to the dizzy pleasure she felt when he entered a room? The way his teasing always brightened her day? She could say anything to him, and he understood. Even around Sydney she'd always had to censor her more . . . reckless thoughts.

So why couldn't she trust Alec? Why did she still hold a piece of her heart back from him?

Just as she wondered if she should turn back to London after all, she caught sight of the house the laborer had described, and her heart leaped into her throat.

This was to be her home, this huge house of red brick and a hundred glass windows, with an elm-lined drive they now entered, and a fishpond and flower gardens and long lawns . . .

But they were overgrown flower gardens, choked with weeds. And the fishpond was covered with a thick green scum. And of the hundred windows, a good third of them were boarded up, turning what had once been a beauty of a house into a pockmarked crone.

"He wasn't lying when he said the place was in no condition for a wedding," Mama remarked.

Katherine glanced over to see her mother scrutinizing the place with a frown. "Don't you remember, Mama? He said his father neglected the place for years. That's why he wanted to be here rather than in London."

No wonder Alec had spoken so fiercely of his poor home. What sort of unconscionable creature had his father been, to let this beautiful old building fall into such disrepair?

"This is more than neglect, girl," her mother said. "This doesn't look good to me, not good at all."

Katherine ignored her mother as they drove up before the front entrance. Of course it didn't look good; that's what happened when a man didn't do his duty. And it wasn't as if there'd been much time for Alec to turn things around.

It was odd, though—Alec had mentioned workmen, yet there were none around. No one repaired the sagging eaves, no one pulled the weeds in the beds of rosebushes gone wild, and no groom ran out to greet them as they approached.

Indeed, even after they disembarked, it took several moments to get any response to their knock at the front door. When at last it opened, the aging fellow who greeted them seemed confused by their appearance. "May I help you?"

Katherine forced a smile, though her unease increased by the moment. "I'm Lord Iversley's intended, Miss Katherine Merivale. My mother and I have come to see him."

There was no mistaking the poor man's alarm. "All the way from London?"

"Yes. If you could just announce us—"

"Forgive me, miss, but his lordship isn't here at present."

Her eyes narrowed. "Where is he?"

"He's . . . er . . . in town. So you'll have to come back later." He actually started to close the door, but she was too quick for him and thrust her foot in the opening to block it.

"Then let us in, and we'll wait for him to return," she said.

"Oh, no, miss," the man said, so violently she feared he might keel over in shock right there. "You mustn't come in. But if you'd be so good as to wait outside with your carriage—"

"We will do no such thing." She pushed past him into the house. She'd been right all along—Alec *was* hiding something. Scarcely noticing the frayed carpets and sparse furnishings, she turned a dark scowl on the man. "Now where exactly has he gone?"

"Wait here, and I shall send for him at once."

That was the *last* thing she wanted—for this fellow to warn Alec. "Never mind. I'll find someone else to tell me."

Hearing voices upstairs, she headed for the main staircase. Mama followed right behind her.

So did the annoying servant. "I beg you, miss," he said as he struggled to keep pace with her, breathing hard, "do not go up there. I know that his lordship would prefer that you wait while I fetch him—"

"Oh, I'm sure he would," she retorted, her steps more resolute the farther she marched up the stairs.

If she hadn't been so upset, she might have noticed the lack of other servants coming to the man's aid or the shaky banister that clearly needed repair. But her entire focus was on the laughter coming from upstairs. Because she recognized it. Alec was up there, along with some female. The masculine laughter was interspersed with decidedly feminine giggles.

As she reached the next floor she caught sight of beds through open doors. This was where the bedchambers were, and the laughter was coming from the one at the end of the hall, probably the master bedroom.

She stalked toward the sound of laughter, growing sicker by the moment. How many times had she gone to fetch Papa, only to find him with some tart he tried to pass off as a servant? How often had she had to turn away while he fumbled with his breeches even as he lied to her?

Now she could make out the voices, and they only spurred her on.

"What do you think?" said the voice she definitely recognized as Alec's. "Is it too wicked?"

There came that feminine giggle again. "Not for a bedchamber, master."

Some grunting ensued. "Is that all right?"

"It's fine."

"I don't think it belongs there."

"It'll be fine if you put it more to the back."

"A naked woman should never go to the back."

That sent the female into peals of laughter. "Oh, go on with you, now. You ought to be ashamed of yourself, my lord." Then the only sound was more grunting and groaning.

Katherine rushed the last few steps to the end of the hall. She would make the wretch ashamed of himself, only see if she didn't.

He was cursing now, but that didn't stop her from bursting through the open door to cry, "What is going on here?"

A fully dressed Alec jumped and lost his grip on the

three-foot-high marble sculpture he was taking down from atop a massive mahogany tallboy. It plummeted from his raised hands, glanced off his skull, and went crashing to the floor . . . with Alec close behind.

"Alec!" she screamed, racing over to where he lay prone.

She was quickly joined by a portly woman at least twice his age. "Oh my word, master . . . master, are you all right?"

Katherine knelt to cradle his head in her hands, cursing herself for being ten kinds of a fool. "Lord preserve me, he's dead. I've killed him!"

"He's not dead," the older woman said in a soothing voice. She took his hand and pressed a finger to his wrist. "He's got a good strong pulse."

"But look, he's bleeding!" Katherine's heart twisted painfully to see the thin trickle of blood running down the side of his face. "He's hurt badly."

"I don't think so, miss," the other woman said. "He's just knocked senseless is all. Give him a minute. His lordship has a hard head—he'll be all right."

But the older woman's voice held an edge, and Katherine knew she wasn't as sanguine as she tried to sound. "You must be his intended," the woman added. "I'm Mrs. Brown, the housekeeper."

"I'm Katherine Merivale," she choked out. *The ninny who nearly killed your master.* Tears welled in her eyes. "This is a fine way to meet, isn't it?" Brushing the hair from his forehead, she examined the gash while the housekeeper chafed his limp fingers.

Katherine glanced up, suddenly remembering Mama, who stood in the doorway, eyeing everything with suspicion. "That's my mother over there." She cast Mrs. Brown an imploring glance. "Can't we make him more comfortable than here on the floor?"

"Best not to move him just yet," the woman said. "He's breathing right, and the color is coming back into his cheeks. I think he'll come round."

"This is all my fault. I should never have burst in like that." Katherine glanced over at the sculpture of a woman on horseback draped only in her own hair. Lady Godiva . . . the naked woman.

Her tears burned her eyes. "What was he doing, anyway?"

Mrs. Brown shrugged. "He wanted to make the room nice for you, and there weren't too many things left in the attic to do it with but this old sculpture of his father's and a few paintings nobody would buy. I told him he shouldn't try to put that up so high himself, but he wouldn't go fetch the ladder."

"One of the footmen should have helped him, or—"

"We have no footmen, miss." The woman caught herself, then said, "That is, they're . . . er . . . all out . . . um . . . in town."

Mrs. Brown was as bad a liar as the butler. And suddenly it hit her. The lack of servants, faded carpet, dilapidated stairs, and overgrown gardens . . . As Mama said, it was more than just neglect. Katherine recognized a lack of money when she saw it. She'd certainly lived with it enough since Papa had died.

She stared at Mrs. Brown. "He has no money, does he? His lordship has no money."

The old woman blanched, then shook her head.

That was why Alec stayed in a hotel. Because he needed money. And all his other secrets and evasions simply came down to that.

A weight lifted from her heart, leaving it to soar. Alec was poor! Never had she thought such a thing would make her so happy. His refusal to bring her here hadn't stemmed from a desire to consort with a mistress, or have one last wild orgy, or hide a passel of illegitimate children from her, or any of the insane possibilities that had plagued her over the past few sleepless nights.

No, he'd hidden it from her because he was ashamed.

Yet despite his own poverty, he'd chosen to marry her even after she'd told him she had no money, either. He could have found an heiress, but instead he'd pursued her, not knowing that she expected a fortune. How much more proof did she need that he really cared for her?

And now she'd killed him. With a little sob, she pulled his head against her breast. He groaned.

"Alec!" she cried. "Speak to me, darling. Can you hear me?"

With his eyes still closed, he frowned against her breast and mumbled, "Katherine . . . must be . . . dreaming . . ."

"You're not dreaming," she whispered.

"Mmm," he murmured as he turned his face into her breasts. "Nice. Soft."

She choked back a hysterical laugh. "Wake up, you silly fool, or I'll never forgive myself." She cupped his face in her hands. "Oh, please, Alec, wake up."

His eyes fluttered open, and he frowned at her. "Katherine? What are you doing here?" He shook his head as if to clear it, then glanced around. "And why in God's name am I on the floor?"

With a little cry, she clutched his head to her chest. "You're all right," she whispered. "Thank goodness you're all right."

"My head hurts," he muttered into her breasts.

"I know, my darling." Guilt assailed her again. "But I'm here, and everything will be fine now."

"You're here . . ." He stiffened and tried to sit up, alarm on his face. "You're here! What the hell are you doing here?"

"It's all right," she said quickly, guessing the reason for his alarm. "I know everything now. I know that you're poor."

He scowled. "Add insult to injury, why don't you?"

She gave a relieved laugh. "It doesn't matter, not to me. Not now that you're all right."

"I don't feel all right," he complained, rubbing his head. "I have a devil of a headache."

"I suspect that will last for a while," Mrs. Brown said.

He sat up, then struggled to stand. Katherine leaped up beside him. "No, you must rest!"

"I'm not going to lie on the blasted floor." But he swayed on his feet.

She looped his arm quickly about her shoulders. "Come on then, we'll get you to the bed." She called back to Mrs. Brown, "Fetch some warm water, will you? And a cloth to clean his wound with."

"At once, miss," the housekeeper said cheerily, clearly happy to be of use.

"Katherine, I need to speak to you," her mother put in.

"Not now, Mama," she answered as she helped Alec to the bed.

"But, my angel—"

"Mrs. Brown," Katherine called to the woman as she was leaving the room. "Take my mother with you, will you? We've had a long trip, and she could use some tea and something to eat."

"Yes, miss," the old servant chirped, "and I'll bring something for you and his lordship, too."

"Nothing too heavy for him!" Katherine cried, as the old housekeeper rather firmly led her mother off.

She caught Alec staring down at her with a bemused expression. "You take charge right away, don't you?" he said.

"Somebody has to." She helped him sit on the bed. "Since I'm the one responsible—"

"It was an accident." He pulled her down to sit beside him. "Though I still can't figure out why you're here." There was definite tension in his voice.

"It doesn't matter," she said quickly. "All that matters is we're together, and I know the truth about you."

He went still. "But you aren't . . . angry."

"That you're poor?" When his lips tightened at that bald phrase, she hastened to add, "It's nothing to be ashamed of, my darling. You can't help what your father did."

He only stared at her as if she'd gone mad. "You could have married Sydney, and instead I convinced you to marry me."

"Yes, and I'm glad you did! *Glad,* do you hear?" She was giddy with relief, aware of nothing but the joy of knowing he was all right. And that he was a man of character, for clearly he cared about his estate and was trying to turn things round. "But you should have told me, Alec. If anyone would understand, you should have known it would be me, for goodness sake."

He still looked confused. "I thought you'd refuse to marry me if you knew."

"No, indeed! How could you think it? Have I ever cared about such things?" Memories came flooding back. "Oh, that's why you asked me if I were marrying Sydney for money—because you thought it mattered to me. But it doesn't. Indeed, it means that I can at last give you something. You see, I have a fortune myself, left to me by my grandfather! What do you think of that? Now we can restore Edenmore exactly how we want. Isn't that marvelous?"

Chapter Twenty-four

❦

A rake is always in the mood for seduction.
—Anonymous, *A Rake's Rhetorick*

The thundering in Alec's head intensified as his muddled brain put two and two together and came up with a hundred thousand. Pounds, to be precise. A fortune that Katherine thought he didn't know about.

Blast it all. No wonder she wasn't angry—she hadn't yet figured out that he'd courted her precisely because of that fortune.

He should tell her the truth while she was still feeling guilty for causing his little accident. He should lay his case before her, beg her to forgive him for all his deceptions, and convince her that they should still marry despite his wretched behavior. Because later, when she wasn't in this state of relief, she might figure it all out. And then it would be worse for him.

But she might not figure it out. Or at least not until after the wedding.

"Alec? Did you hear me?" she asked. "I have a fortune."

"I'm sorry, sweetheart," he stalled, "my head is still spinning and . . ."

"Oh, yes, of course!" She leaped up from the bed. "Where is Mrs. Brown with that water?" She hurried to the door just as Emson walked in carrying a pan, towels draped over his arm.

After his butler set the pan down, she dipped a cloth in the warm water and came back to Alec's side to dab at the drying blood. "At least the bleeding has stopped."

"Has it?" he said hoarsely. What in God's name was he going to do? He didn't want this to end, and it would certainly end if he told her the truth. He liked having her fuss over him. No woman had fussed over him in years, unless he could count Mrs. Brown's constant attempts to get him to eat more of her awful cooking.

Katherine touched the cloth to the gash, and he cursed as fire streaked through his head.

Remorse flooded her face. "I'm so sorry. I didn't mean to hurt you—"

He choked back more curses. "It's all right, sweetheart."

Emson watched them warily.

"We'll get a doctor to look at it," she said. When he started to protest, she added, "You mustn't worry about the cost, do you hear? I told you, I can afford it. Or I'll be able to once we marry."

The moment of truth had arrived. He hesitated, loathing the idea of letting her continue in her mistaken assumption.

But he had no choice. His servants and tenants were depending on him. Emson was watching him even now, waiting for what he would do, hoping that he wouldn't ruin Edenmore's chance for a future. Their chance for a future.

Damn. "Yes, you said something about . . . a fortune. But you told me before that you had no money."

Every lying word filled him with self-disgust. It had been one thing to avoid telling her the truth before, but this was a more deliberate deception. How could he lie to her so egregiously when she trusted him and even accepted his situation?

Because she would never marry him if she knew the truth. He was sure of that.

"Appearances to the contrary," she said brightly as she threw the soiled rag aside and got a fresh one, "I have a fortune of a hundred thousand pounds that will come to me upon my marriage. My grandfather left it to me."

"Really?" He glanced to Emson, whose face showed relief that Alec was pretending not to know of her fortune. "You may go now, Emson," he snapped, unable to bear having the man watch him lie.

Emson nodded, then left, obviously satisfied that all was well.

All was not well. The man didn't know Katherine, so he didn't care if Alec lied to her. But Alec knew that every lie drove a wedge between them that he'd have to push past after they married. Every evasion was one more eventual stake in her heart.

Would it be worth it? God, he hoped so. Because he was now committed to that path.

"It's true." She wiped away the rest of the dried blood. "Aren't you pleased? You look as if you aren't."

"Of course I'm pleased. It's just my . . . head, that's all. I'm still a little shaky." When her face clouded over, he added quickly, "But I feel much better now that you're taking care of me." *Forgive me, sweetheart, if you can.*

"It's the least I can do after causing this," she said sorrowfully.

"It was merely an accident. Besides, it's well worth it to have you here."

Watching me lie like a fiend. How could he continue this deception until the wedding? He could hardly speak the lies now without gagging on them.

He forced himself to continue. "But you never did explain why you decided to come here. I thought we'd agreed that you would stay in London."

Ducking her head, she busied herself with unknotting his cravat. "Here, let's make you more comfortable."

"I'm fine," he bit out. "Really, it's all right."

"Your said your head was still spinning." She dropped to her knees and tugged off one shoe, then the other.

By God, she was already catching him in his lies. He allowed her to finish removing his shoes and made no quarrel when she took off his coat. But when she went to work on his waistcoat buttons, he stayed her hand. "Thanks, that's much better. But I still want to know why you came here."

A blush turned her cheeks a pretty pink. "I-I knew you were hiding something, that's all. It made no sense that you wouldn't want us to visit."

"So you rushed here from London?"

She shrugged. "I might have stayed there, if your friend at the Stephens Hotel hadn't behaved so suspiciously, evading all my questions the same way you did."

That's because Jack knew the whole of Alec's financial situation and his need to marry an heiress.

"You said you don't care about my . . . er . . . lack of money. But I seem to remember you bursting in here demanding to know what was going on."

"I . . . um . . . may have said something to that effect."
She stood. "Now you really should lie down—"

"I want to know what you thought was going on when
you rushed in here," he persisted.

She uttered a long sigh. "It's just that . . . well, I heard
female giggling and talk of wickedness and a naked
woman and . . ."

When she trailed off, the light dawned. "You thought I
was 'cavorting,'" he said irritably. "I was trying to
arrange—"

"I know, I know." She pressed her fingers to his mouth,
then glanced over to the sculpture of Lady Godiva.
"Though your taste in . . . er . . . art is rather—"

"Wicked, yes. Like your taste in books. But you don't
find me bursting into rooms to surprise *you*." Given the
circumstances, her distrust shouldn't annoy him, yet it
did.

"I'm sorry. You must think me horrible. I've misjudged
you over and over, with no good reason."

Just that quickly, his annoyance turned to guilt. "It's all
right. Your suspicions were understandable."

She shook her head. "I let my fears about your character run away with me, and I shouldn't have. I know better.
You've shown me time and again that you're a good man,
and yet—"

"That's enough, sweetheart, no apology necessary," he
said hoarsely. "It's forgotten."

"Not by me. But I'll make it up to you. With my fortune we can turn Edenmore into the most beautiful home
you've ever seen."

His guilt nearly choked him. "You said you would be
glad to put all the responsibility of estate management
behind you. I hate to think of burdening you."

"It's no burden when you have money," she said brightly. She turned to roam his bedchamber. "Only think of what we can do to this. If you repair the crumbling moldings, replace the wallpaper and the carpet and perhaps the drapes . . . why, it would be stunning." She faced him, her eyes sparkling as she swept her hand to encompass the room. "Though the furniture needs some refurbishing, it's really quite fine, and that marvelous fireplace is perfect as it is."

"So you . . . like it."

"The house? Oh, yes, what I've seen of it. Even in my brief walk through, I could tell it was solidly constructed."

"The fifth earl, the one who built it, used top-quality oak timbers and the best red brick. And every room has a mantelpiece of Italian marble exactly like that one. My . . . er . . . father never got desperate enough to tear those out and sell them, thank God."

Her face clouded over. "How did your lovely house come to such a pass?"

"It's a long story," he said, unwilling to tell it when he'd have to mix the truth with so many lies.

"I like long stories." Coming back to sit beside him, she laid her hand tenderly on his thigh.

What else could he do? With a sigh, he explained about his "father's" bad management, the corrupt steward, the worthless investments . . . everything he dared to tell her. He'd just begun to describe how the estate looked in his youth when Mrs. Brown hurried in with the tea and a plate of brown lumps obviously meant to be food.

"Sorry it took me so long," the housekeeper said cheerily. "Your mother had all sorts of questions about the house, miss."

"I can only imagine," Katherine said dryly, as Alec stiffened.

"I put her in the front parlor while I was making the tea." Mrs. Brown set the tray by the bed. "But when I returned, she'd gone off to sleep, poor thing. Right there in the chair."

"We did have a long trip." Katherine poured the tea and handed Alec a cup. "And we rose very early."

Mrs. Brown wiped her hands on her apron. "I put a shawl over her, so she wouldn't catch cold." She looked them both over. "I see you're feeling better, my lord. But I could make a poultice for your head—"

"No need. Miss Merivale is taking good care of me."

"You'd best eat something."

Not if he wanted to *keep* feeling better. "That will be all, Mrs. Brown."

Pursing her lips, she said primly, "Very well. Then I'll go see about supper."

After she left, Katherine cast him a chastening glance. "I know you don't feel well, but you didn't need to be rude."

"It was either that or eat those." He gestured to the lumps. "I'd rather die."

She eyed him askance. "Don't be silly—how bad can they be?"

"Mrs. Brown has been our housekeeper for years, but she didn't do the cooking until we lost our cook right before I came home. She's not very good."

"She can't be *that* awful," she said as she picked a lump up and took a bite. Or rather, attempted to take a bite. It was more like a tearing with the teeth, the way a dog tears meat off the bone. As she chewed, she carefully laid the lump back down on the platter. "I . . . um . . . see what you mean. What on earth is that supposed to be?"

"Does it taste like spiced mud? And have the consistency of leather?"

She nodded, eyes round.

"Gingerbread cakes. Those are actually tolerable compared to her apple tarts. She takes the 'tart' part very seriously."

"My goodness, we'll have to hire a cook at once."

"If you want me to live here, you will."

She laughed. "Are Mrs. Brown and Mr. Emson your only servants?"

"Almost. There's John, the coachman you met, and Mrs. Brown's two daughters, who are housemaids. Her husband is the gamekeeper. He makes sure the larder stays stocked with fresh meat for his wife to cook badly. I need more staff."

Her eyes twinkled. "I should say so. We have nearly that many servants at Merivale Manor, and this place is four times its size." She glanced around. "Oh, dear, will it be too much a hardship for Mama and me to stay here tonight?"

"Blast." He rose, wincing when his head pounded. "I forgot to tell Mrs. Brown to prepare a couple of rooms for you—"

"Don't!" She tugged him back onto the bed. "I'll go tell her. You lie back and rest."

"I don't want to rest." He reached for the shoes she'd removed earlier.

She whisked them away, along with his coat. "Now, now, none of that. Lie down. I'll be back in just a minute."

Watching as she left, carrying his clothing with her, he couldn't decide whether to feel irritated or heartened by her overprotectiveness.

Or just plain guilty. But telling the truth would devastate her. She seemed so happy to be of use to him, so delighted by the prospect of using her money to restore Edenmore. How could he deprive her of that pleasure?

All right, so he was making excuses. The truth was, he didn't want to lose her. If he could only keep her happy until they married—

Damn, had he brought the special license with him from London? If he hadn't, that would delay everything more.

He left the bed, swayed a bit, then was able to steady himself. Now, where had Emson put those papers? Ah, yes, in his study downstairs. He looked for his shoes, remembered Katherine had taken them, then went looking for another pair in his closet. As he rummaged around, he heard her come up behind him.

"What are you doing, you stubborn man? Get back in that bed at once!"

He picked up a pair of shoes and faced her. "I'm fine, I told you."

"You are *not* fine." She took his arm. "Now come back to the bed—"

"No." Shrugging off her hand, he put on the shoes. "I have to check something in my study. I'll just be a moment." He had to find that license, had to make sure he could marry her before she figured out the truth.

Purposefully he headed out the door. He heard her following after him and quickened his pace toward the stairs.

"Wait!" she called out.

He halted with his hand on the banister. "What is it, Katherine?"

Her voice lowered to a throaty murmur. "I know one way to keep you in bed."

His blood roared in his ears. He turned to find her standing in the doorway, wearing a seductive smile. She couldn't mean what he thought. Could she?

As he watched, she removed the pins from her hair, then shook it out with the mischievous look of a woman who knew she was being naughty. "Come back to bed, Alec. I promise to make it worth your while."

His mouth went dry. Damn her. It had been two long days since he'd touched her, two long nights since he'd felt her sweet softness beneath him.

"No, you come here," he ordered, before he lost what was left of his control.

Wordlessly, she shook her head and disappeared inside the room.

"Blast it all." He couldn't do as she wanted—and not because of his throbbing skull, either. Making love to her with this lie between them would poison everything. Once they were married and he could tell her the truth, it would be different, but he couldn't compound the deception by making love to her now.

Perhaps he should go downstairs and stay there until supper. But she'd left the bedchamber door open, and the thought of Emson or one of the housemaids finding her in some state of dishevelment . . .

Just imagining that state of dishevelment sent his cock into instant attention. He walked back to the bedchamber in a trance. His mind might balk, but his body knew exactly what it wanted.

Even if he couldn't have it. He approached the open door, bracing himself for anything, yet he still wasn't prepared for what he saw through the doorway—Katherine wearing only her chemise and stockings. Katherine with her hair spilling freely over her barely clad shoulders.

Katherine leaning against a bedpost, her eyes a smoldering chocolate brown as she stepped out of her shoes. "Come in and close the door, Alec," she said in a throaty voice that nearly undid him.

He couldn't move. He could only stand there staring, his eyes scouring the translucent muslin for whatever glimpses of her flesh he could get. And there were plenty, blast it. Her nut brown nipples showed dark and pouty through the fabric, and he could even see the flaming curls between her long, incredible legs.

That had to be the thinnest chemise in creation. And he could already remember how it felt to be inside her, driving hard, buried deep—

"No," he growled, hanging on to the last bit of his self-control.

"You need to be in bed resting."

"If I get into bed with you when you're dressed like that, there will be no resting."

She arched one brow. "And if you go traipsing about the house, up and down the stairs, you might pass out and injure yourself even worse. At least in bed you can't hurt yourself."

"I wouldn't bet on that." He changed tactics, desperate to make her put her clothes back on. "Besides, your mother will come looking for us when she wakes. You don't want to shock her, do you?"

"When Mama dozes, she sleeps for hours if she's undisturbed, especially after she's been traveling."

"Yes, but what if one of the servants awakens her—"

"That's a chance we'll have to take. What happened to Alec the rule-breaker, Alec the rakehell who doesn't care about propriety? Come here, Alexander the Great . . . break some rules with me." Casting him a sultry smile, she wriggled her chemise off her shoulders and dropped it to her waist to bare her perfect breasts. "If you want to see more, you'll have to come inside."

Sweet God in heaven, see more? He wanted to tear her blasted chemise off with his teeth.

To hell with conscience and good intentions. This was *his* Katherine, in *his* bedchamber tempting him into *his* bed. He was only a man, and he wanted her. Striding through the doorway, he shoved the door closed behind him, then kicked off his shoes and advanced toward her in a trance.

But as he neared her, she jerked her chemise back up and scampered across the bed. Before he could react, she'd raced over to the door to turn the key in the lock. "There," she said in triumph as she knelt to slide the key under the door out of reach. "Now you *have* to stay in bed."

So that was her game, was it? Crafty wench. "I could call for Mrs. Brown."

"And she'll tell you the same thing I'm telling you—get into that bed."

"Not without you." He veered back toward her, stripping off his shirt and unbuttoning his trousers. "Now that you've started this, you had damned well better finish it."

"Don't come any closer, Alec," she warned as she left the door, giving him a wide berth, "you've had a bad head injury. You really need to rest."

He dragged off his trousers and threw them aside. "Take off your chemise, and get into the bed."

"You said you couldn't rest like that."

Damn it, this could go on all day, and he wasn't in the mood to dally. Edging close to the bed, he pretended to stagger. With a cry of alarm, she hurried to his side. He grabbed her and tossed her onto the bed.

"Alec, your head—"

"You wanted me in bed, didn't you?" he rasped as he covered her body with his.

She stared up at him in alarm. "I want you to rest."

"If you thought tempting me into bed, then abandoning me, would accomplish that, you don't know much about men, sweetheart." He bent his head to kiss her, but she turned her face aside, so he settled for scattering kisses over her cheek and her warm silky neck.

She went limp beneath him and twined her arms about his neck. "Don't blame me if you collapse in the morning."

"It was your idea." Nuzzling her ear, he then laved it with his tongue.

"I . . . couldn't think . . . of how else to get you back in bed."

"This is working very well."

"But Alec—"

"Shh, sweetheart." He nibbled her ear lobe. "I'm busy 'resting.' "

A choked giggle escaped her. "Oh, Alec, I missed you and your joking so much. Did you miss me?"

"Every hour of every day since I left." Then he captured her mouth with his.

Would he ever get enough of her, of this? It was all he could do not to take her right now, part her legs and bury himself inside her. But she was still barely initiated into the pleasures of the bedroom, so he settled for kissing her with all the fervor he'd kept banked for two days.

He would undoubtedly regret this later, but right now, he could no more push her away than he could stop breathing. He'd spent too many nights hungering for her, too many days craving her company.

When he was with her like this, he forgot all his sins . . . except for the one of wanting and needing her, far more than was wise. He ravaged her warm mouth and plundered her supple breasts through her chemise, storing up pleasures for when she punished him for his deceptions.

By the time he could bring himself to drag his lips from hers, they were both gasping for breath.

"Well," she whispered, eyes alight, "I think you did miss me."

He dragged up her chemise, then searched for the hot, juicy center of all her need. Reveling in the mew of a sigh she uttered when he stroked her, he muttered, "Apparently you missed me, too."

"Only every hour of every day since you left. That's the real reason I came here, you know."

He didn't want to be affected by her words, but he was. He'd never expected to find a wife who matched him desire for desire . . . who *needed* him. Her open affection humbled him.

And scared him out of his mind. Because he at last realized *this* was what he wanted: Katherine needing him despite everything, Katherine wanting him for who he really was.

Only she didn't know who he really was. She might not love him or claim to want more than a practical marriage, but she wanted a husband she could trust. And he'd already denied her that. Once she found out . . .

No, he wouldn't lose her. He couldn't. "Now that you're here, we can marry at once. Tonight, if you want." *If* he'd brought that license from London. "I'm sure the vicar in Ipswich would be happy to oblige us. We can send for him right away." He couldn't shake the feeling of impending doom . . . that if he didn't secure her as soon as possible, he'd lose her forever.

She gazed up at him through passion-glazed eyes. "Don't tell me you're getting a conscience about our . . . coupling before marriage. That's not like you."

"I want you to be mine, that's all."

She pulled his head down to hers. "I'm yours already."

You won't be if you find out the truth, he thought as he kissed her again. And that thought perversely fired his need even higher.

Sliding from the bed to shuck off his drawers, he pointed to her chemise. "You said if I came to bed, I could see the rest. Take it off, sweetheart. It was too dark in the orangery for me to see you well the last time."

She swallowed. "I-I don't know if I want you to see me well. I'm so thin and freckled, and my hair is too . . . red."

"I don't believe that." He might not have her blasted poet friend's gift for pretty words, but he could surely reassure her. "Come on, let me see you."

Sitting up, she dragged her chemise off over her head, then lay back down on the bed, looking so vulnerable it made him ache. "There, look your fill."

His breath quickened at the sight of her smooth alabaster skin. "My God, Katherine, you're perfect, absolutely perfect," he said in a husky voice.

With a frown, she reached for her chemise again. "You can't look at me if you're going to make fun."

Snatching it from her, he tossed it on the floor. "Have you no idea how beautiful you are?"

She eyed him askance. "You're the first to think it."

"Then the rest of them are blind." Climbing back onto the bed, he lay down beside her, then kissed her mass of curls spread out over the coverlet. "How could they not notice how lovely your hair is?"

"It's *red*, Alec."

"I know. It reminds me of the sea."

She lifted an eyebrow. "The last time I checked, the sea was green or blue. Decidedly not red."

"Except when the sun rises or sets." He twisted a curl around his finger. "On the Suffolk coast, it rises over the water. As a boy on holiday there, I used to watch it turn the sea to fire. And the fire ended in foam at the water's edge." He combed her tangled curls with his fingers. "Like your hair, all wild and tumbling."

A smile tugged at her lips. "And you claim you can't use pretty words like the poets."

"That's what you do to me—turn me into a poet." Her chuckle became a sigh when he trailed his hand down the side of her face to her jaw, then traced a line along the smattering of freckles on her upper chest. "And you know what they say about freckles—that they're fairy love bites."

Her eyes narrowed. "Who says that?"

He grinned. "Somebody must. Isn't that what they look like?"

A laugh bubbled out of her. "I don't know. What's a love bite?"

Bending his head, he sucked the skin low on her shoulder, then rubbed the red spot with his thumb. "That's a love bite."

"Oh," she whispered as she stared down at it.

"You see?" he said, kissing her freckles. "Fairy love bites everywhere." Then he pressed more kisses down the slope of her breast. "And as for being thin . . . believe me, you have the right amount of flesh in all the right places. Like here."

She moaned as he circled her nipple with his tongue. He sucked her breast until her nipple stood to attention, a sweet pearl he could lick and nibble all day. He lingered for a moment before dragging his open mouth down to her belly to dart his tongue inside her navel.

"And here." He planted a wet kiss to her belly. "Just enough flesh to make you soft, the way a woman should be."

As she stroked his hair, he slid lower until his mouth hovered over the patch of fiery curls that barely covered her silky petals. But when he pressed an open-mouthed kiss there between her legs, she gasped and tried to pull him away. "Alec . . . my goodness . . . what are you doing?"

He lifted his head to smile at her. "Breaking the rules."

Her eyes widened. "Ohh . . . so *that's* what's happening in the picture."

"What picture?"

Turning crimson, she stammered, "N-never mind."

"It's that blasted book again, isn't it? Now you've got me curious about it. Is there actually a picture of people doing this?"

"Well . . . yes . . . but I couldn't figure out why a man would—"

He scraped the rigid bit of her flesh with his teeth, and she arched into his mouth with another gasp. "So . . . *that's* . . . why . . ."

"Do you want more?"

He licked at her lightly. Though she blushed, she grasped his head and pressed it toward her cunny. He needed no more invitation to suck at her swollen bud, then thrust his tongue inside her.

The scent of her musk drove him mad, made him want to please her all the more. He reveled in how she writhed beneath him, uttering soft little cries that spurred him on. He'd give her this at least, this pleasure to remember after she discovered all his lies.

The more frenzied she grew, the more his cock stiffened until he thought he'd explode before she found her release under his mouth. But just as he feared he'd embarrass himself at any minute, her release hit her, making her shudder and convulse beneath him.

He gave her no time to come down. He couldn't—he wanted her too badly. Raising himself over her, he parted her thighs wide and drove into her damp warmth, sheathing himself inside her hot welcome with one deep thrust.

She caught at his shoulders with a cry. "Yes . . . like that . . . yes—"

Her long legs wrapped about his waist, sucking him deeper in, and he groaned. "By God, sweetheart . . . you're . . . incredible . . ."

"And you're definitely . . . Alexander the Great . . ."

A laugh tore out of him even as he pounded into her, losing himself, striving to conquer her so thoroughly she would never regret choosing him. And when his release neared, he held it ruthlessly back until he felt her shudder beneath him again, her body straining against him as she cried his name.

Only then did he let himself come, spilling himself inside her, fiercely determined to bind her to him for life, sure they could make a future together despite all his deceptions.

But as he collapsed atop her, drained and sated yet still wanting her, she whispered, "I love you, Alec."

And he knew he couldn't lie to her anymore.

Chapter Twenty-five

*Beware of scheming Mamas—they will
throw all your plans into disarray.*
—Anonymous, *A Rake's Rhetorick*

Katherine hadn't meant to say those words, hadn't
even realized she'd felt them until that moment. But
she'd said them, and she didn't regret it.

Until he drew back to stare at her in clear horror. "You
told me you didn't believe in love."

She blinked at him, her heart sinking. "I changed my
mind."

"You can't. You shouldn't."

This wasn't the reaction she'd expected. "Why not?"
she whispered, her contentment at their joining slowly
draining away.

With a groan, he rolled off her to lie on his back staring up at the ceiling that showed through the canopy
frame missing a canopy.

Feeling suddenly exposed, she sat up and reached for
the extra blanket that lay folded at the foot of the bed,
covering them both with it as she turned on her side to
look at him. "What is it, Alec? What's wrong?"

"You can't love me." The harsh words pummeled her tender heart. "You must not love me."

"It's not something I can turn on or off. It's how I feel." She swallowed down the fear rising in her throat. "But if you don't feel that way—"

"How I feel has nothing to do with it." He finally looked at her, and she saw a struggle in his eyes. "My God, how you're going to hate me."

"Don't be silly," she said, her fear growing. "How could I hate you when I just said I love you?"

"It won't be hard, trust me. There's something I—"

Before he could say more, someone tried the door, then pounded on it.

"Go away!" Alec called out as Katherine tensed up. "I'm ill!"

When a moment of silence passed, she relaxed . . . until she heard the lock being turned. Someone had found the key she'd thrust under the door.

Katherine dragged the covers up to her chin just as the door was flung open, and her mother stood there, looking surprisingly fierce.

With a curse, Alec sat up. "Hello, Mrs. Merivale."

"Don't you hello me, you . . . you fiend!"

"He's not a fiend!" Katherine protested.

Mama's furious gaze shifted to her daughter as she rounded the bed on Katherine's side. "You silly fool!" Mama snapped. "For a woman who prides herself on her clever mind, you can be amazingly stupid sometimes."

Alec glared at her mother. "Don't blame her for this—it's my fault. It's all my fault."

"Believe me, I know it," Mama retorted. "You made sure she had to marry you, didn't you? She might still have caught Sir Sydney, but you had to ruin her, you . . . you devil!"

Katherine grew more confused by the moment. Why was Mama bent on Sydney all of a sudden? She sat up, dragging the cover tightly about her breasts. "I *want* to marry Alec, Mama. You know that. We were going to marry in a day or two anyway, so I don't see why you're so angry."

"You don't see— My word, how can you be so blind?" Her mother hadn't looked this furious since she'd caught Papa in the stables with one of the dairy maids. "If I'd thought you would be up here with him doing this . . . I swear I would never have left you alone with him for one minute."

"Oh, please," Katherine said with a snort, "you've been trying to arrange my doing this ever since we met the man."

"Not after we got here, and I realized he must be a fortune hunter."

"Don't be silly, Alec isn't a—" She broke off, realizing that he wasn't leaping to defend himself. She turned to look at him, her blood chilling as she saw the alarm in his face. "Tell her, Alec. Tell her you didn't know about my fortune."

"I can explain, Katherine—"

"He has no money, and you expect a fortune upon your marriage," her mother interrupted. "Do you think that's just coincidence?"

"Perhaps," she whispered, though she began to see her mother's point. Especially when Alec was looking at her with such dread. "But you said you didn't tell anyone, Mama. So how could he have found out?"

"Oh, I don't know, girl," her mother said impatiently. "Perhaps he spoke to your father's solicitor or one of his creditors or—"

"Mr. Byrne." As the light dawned, Katherine's heart sank. She remembered when Alec had spoken privately to Mr. Byrne in the hall—could the man have explained then?

"Yes!" her mother cried. "Come to think of it, that night we were at Lady Jenner's ball, I saw him speaking to the man. I assumed it was one of those conversations gentlemen have about cricket and war and nonsense."

"You knew him even then?" Katherine asked Alec. This grew worse and worse. If Alec had known Mr. Byrne from the night he'd first met her— "You knew him even before you met him at our house and pretended *not* to know him?"

He winced. "Yes."

She thought she might be sick. All of his sweet words and courting had been for money? *Her* money?

"So . . . so you and Mr. Byrne plotted this from the beginning? Oh, of course you did." And she was every bit the fool Mama said. "He wanted his money; you needed a fortune. It was an alliance made in heaven."

"It wasn't like that," he protested.

"Oh?" Her hopes crumbled around her more with his every word. "You didn't court me for my fortune?"

"No! Not exactly. It was a factor, but—"

"I thought so," she whispered.

Dragging the blanket off him, she wrapped it around her and started to leave the bed, but he rose up on his knees, thoroughly naked, to catch her by the arm.

"Wait—" he began.

Mama's shriek cut him off. "My lord, please!" she protested as she covered her eyes.

He shot her a baleful glance. "Get out. I wish to speak to your daughter alone."

"Now see here—" Mama began, peeking at him from between her fingers.

"Out! Now! Or I swear I'll throw you out myself!"

"I'm going, I'm going." Mama's face was a mottled shade of red, though Katherine noticed she took one last glance at Alec naked before she vanished.

A hysterical laugh boiled out of her. Leave it to Mama to notice *that* about him, when she'd ignored the rest for so long.

She herself should have paid better attention. How blind she'd been. She'd guessed he was deceiving her, but she'd been so busy worrying about his fidelity that she hadn't considered any other reason for deception.

But now certain things came back to her—his gifts, the private box at Astley's, and the nice carriage, probably rented. He'd had no reason to pretend to be rich . . . except that he had to allay her suspicions. Because he knew she had a fortune, and he didn't want her to know he knew.

Oh, Lord, how would she bear it? This wasn't Sydney, whom she'd only thought she loved. This was Alec, *her* Alec. A fortune hunter, a deceiver, a man with no heart.

Tears sprang to her eyes, and she dashed them away. *I should brain him with the sculpture again, curse him.*

"Katherine—" he began.

"Why me?"

"What?"

As she gripped the blanket to her chest, she slid off the bed and turned to him, choking down the lump of raw hurt in her throat. "Why choose me? Surely there were other prettier heiresses."

His eyes blazed. "I wanted you. When I first saw you—"

"You thought, 'I can learn to tolerate the red hair and the lack of curves as long as she has a fortune.'"

"Blast it, it wasn't like that!" he roared as he slid off the bed after her. "Yes, Byrne suggested you, and yes, I needed your fortune, but it was your conversation with Sydney that made me want you. You were so . . . so . . ."

"Pathetic?" she whispered, mortified to the depths of her soul.

"Intriguing," he said fiercely. "Passionate and interesting and . . . full of life. I liked that you spoke your mind, that you were clever enough to see past Lovelace's evasions, that you were *real* when no one else in society was—"

"Especially you."

Pain slashed over his face. "Please believe me, sweetheart. Except for lying about knowing Byrne and deceiving you about my financial situation and my knowledge of your fortune, I did my best not to lie to you about anything else. The rest of it was the absolute truth. I wanted you from the moment I saw you."

"You wanted my fortune."

"I wanted *you*. I needed the fortune. It's not the same thing."

"How can you separate them?"

"Don't you understand? I had no choice—" he began, reaching out to grab her arm.

She snatched it free with a hiss. "Don't touch me! Don't you ever touch me again!"

He looked stricken. "That will be difficult once we're married."

She gaped at him. "You still expect us to marry? You took a harder blow to the head than I realized if you actually think I'd marry you now."

"Be sensible." He left the bed to jerk on his drawers. "You've been compromised, and you need the money as much as I do. I know you're upset, but in time—"

"You don't know a blessed thing about me if you think I'd live one day with you after this."

A cold stillness came over him as he faced her. "You don't mean that."

"I most certainly do."

"But what about your father's debts, what about—"

"I don't care about all that, don't you see? I'd rather rot in debtors' prison than stay with a man who made me think he cared for me when he only wanted . . ." She broke off with a sob and turned away, not wanting him to see her tears. Shaking with the effort to restrain them, she dragged on her chemise, then picked up her gown.

"Please, sweetheart, I do care," he said hoarsely. She felt him come up behind her, but when he slid his arms around her waist, she shoved them away.

"I know you can't believe this now," he went on in a rough whisper, "but I meant what I said about not being able to imagine anyone else as my wife. I wanted you from the day we met. And I swear I'll make this up to you for the rest of our marriage, if that's what it takes."

"We are *not* getting married!" She whirled on him, her anger so intense that just the sight of his handsome face notched it higher. "And your promises and . . . and lies won't work on me *this* time." Yanking her gown on, she fumbled with its fastenings. "You can forget about any marriage between us."

"You can't just throw away what we have together," he choked out.

The stark pain in his face gave her pause. But she knew better now than to believe anything he said. "And what exactly do we have?" Hastily, she slid on her shoes. "A collection of lies and deceptions, that's all."

"Katherine, I never meant to hurt you so badly."

His look of remorse only fired her temper higher. "No, you thought we would marry, and you would jolly me out of my anger with your seductions if I ever discovered what you and Byrne had plotted." When his guilty look told her she'd hit it right on the mark, she went on more coldly, "What a pity for you that you weren't alone in wanting my fortune. But at least Mama is honest about what she wants."

He stiffened. "So what do you mean to do? Marry Sydney? Who didn't fight for you, whose mother disapproves of you, who—"

"I don't know what I'll do," she snapped to stave off the cruel flow of his words. "But I'd rather make one of those awful marriages of convenience with an honest fortune hunter than marry a man like you."

His eyes turned deadly cold. "You mean a man who would do what he must to restore his estate, protect his tenants, and save his servants from poverty?"

She forced herself to ignore that very valid point. "You didn't have to lie to me about it. You should have told me you needed to marry a fortune—"

"And then you would have leaped eagerly into my arms?" he growled. "You, who won't trust any man because of your blasted father?"

"That's not true! I trusted Sydney—"

"Because he never got close enough to make you *not* trust him. You could always keep him at arm's distance. You liked him precisely because you knew he would never hurt you. But he wouldn't move you or challenge you or—"

"Leave Sydney out of this!" she cried, hating that he knew her so well.

"Why? He's your idea of the perfect man, isn't he? God forbid you should risk your heart on a man who breaks your blasted rules about how a courtship should run and what a husband must be."

"Don't you *dare* give me all that nonsense about how wonderful it is to break the rules and how dreary my life is because I follow them." She gave up on buttoning her gown and crossed her arms over her chest. "I don't mind your breaking the rules. I even admire you for it sometimes."

She choked back the tears burning in her throat. "But breaking rules is one thing, and breaking hearts is quite another. You broke my heart to get what you wanted, and for that I can't forgive you."

The fight seemed to drain out of him. "I went about this all wrong," he admitted in a low voice. "But I thought it was the best way to handle it. My parents married because of Mother's money, and they never had a real marriage because that always stood between them. I thought that if you and I got to know each other first, then once you found out—"

"It wouldn't matter? I wouldn't be hurt? Don't you understand? How can I ever separate the things you said to win me, from the things you said to win my fortune? I doubt even *you* can do it. And that's nothing to base a marriage on."

"Then what about basing it on love?" he bit out. "You said you loved me."

"That was when I thought I knew who you were. But I didn't know anything about you at all."

She turned toward the door, but he was at her side in

seconds, grabbing her arm to stay her. "I won't let you do this," he said fiercely. "You agreed to marry me, and I'll hold you to it. I won't let you simply walk out of my life, blast it."

She glanced up into the face she still found dearer than any other, knowing that what she felt didn't change her decision one whit. "Do as you please. Tell the world I shared your bed. Bring suit against me for breach of contract, so you can gain some of the fortune you need. But you'll never, ever, get me to marry you."

This time, when she wrenched free of him, he let her go. But the shocked expression on his face haunted her as she strode out into the hall.

That last glimpse of his face tortured her even as she dealt with Mama's protests that they couldn't leave, that Katherine had to marry the earl. And even after Mama had helped her finish dressing, and Katherine had convinced her to leave Edenmore, Alec's wounded gaze lingered in her memory as they were driving away in the carriage.

Especially after she made the mistake of taking one last look toward Edenmore as they thundered up the drive after dusk. For she could plainly see, through one of the upstairs windows, Alec watching them leave.

Without making any other protest.

Without storming after them on Beleza.

He was letting her go, after all. And that made her want to cry all the more.

Because a tiny part of her had wanted to believe he really did desire *her*, not her fortune. That he truly couldn't live without her. How stupid was that?

"You were a fool to let him bed you," her mother snapped, "but now that you have, you should certainly marry him."

"You have no say in this, Mama." She faced her mother with a grim look. "You have no say in my marital plans from now on. If you want to see any of Grandfather's fortune, you'll leave me to settle my affairs exactly as I please."

Her mother gaped at her. "B-But, my angel—"

"I'm through with letting you push me toward the men you think are best, whining about your life until I feel guilty enough to obey. You want that money? Fine. Let me make my own decisions about marriage, and *stay out of it.* Or I swear I'll give the entire amount to charity the minute it's mine."

When her mother blinked, then closed her mouth with a sullen sniff, Katherine felt a surge of triumph. She should have put her foot down long ago instead of seeking to escape her misery through Sydney, then Alec.

Alec had been right about one thing—it was *her* life, and she should be the one to decide how it should go. Family obligation should only go so far, especially when her family had made a hash of things long before she'd come along.

The way Alec's had.

Ruthlessly, she thrust that thought aside. She would *not* feel sympathy for that beast—she absolutely would not. He should have told her the truth instead of trying to pull the wool over her eyes until they married.

And then you would have leaped eagerly into my arms? You, who won't trust any man because of your blasted father?

She swallowed. If he had told her, would she have listened? Or would she have sent him packing?

She let out a sob. It didn't matter. He should have picked a woman who would have been glad to have an earl marry her for her fortune, instead of trying to deceive her to gain the same aim. Why didn't he?

I wanted you from the moment I saw you.

Stuff and nonsense! He chose her because of his friend Byrne. No doubt they'd made some nasty arrangement—Byrne would loan Alec money for the courtship if Alec made sure the Merivales' debts were paid.

Tears spilled onto her cheeks, and she brushed them away angrily. A pox on them both. As soon as she returned to London, she would give that Mr. Byrne a piece of her mind. And then she would forget all about the treacherous Earl of Iversley and his duplicitous seductions.

Even if it took half her life to manage it.

Chapter Twenty-six

If you want to live a life of debauchery,
never fall in love.
—Anonymous, *A Rake's Rhetorick*

The day after Alec watched the Merivales' hired carriage disappear into the night, he awoke to a splitting headache that had less to do with the blow to his skull than with the cheap brandy he'd drowned his sorrows in last night.

Not well enough, apparently. Because he could still feel that hollow emptiness in his chest where Katherine had ripped out his heart. He hadn't even known he had one, until she'd said in that sweet, innocent voice, "I love you." Right before she'd brought his world crashing down around his ears.

With a groan, he buried his face in the covers, then cursed roundly. He could still smell rose water on them, mingling with the scent of . . .

Burned coffee?

His head shot up. Emson was coming through the door with a tray bearing what Mrs. Brown probably considered to be a decent breakfast.

At least poison would put him out of his misery.

"Mrs. Brown knows you do not like her coffee, but she says it will give you strength, and I agree. You should eat something, my lord. You ate no dinner last night. If you still plan to return to London today, you shall need nourishment."

To beg creditors for more time, arrange for loans . . . begin courting another heiress. The thought churned his stomach, yet it was either that or give up Edenmore entirely.

Or get Katherine back.

No, after her parting words, that was impossible. Until then, he'd been sure he could eventually talk her round to seeing why he'd done what he did, to understanding that he really cared about her.

But if she believed he could be so callous as to spread nasty rumors about her chastity or sue her for breach of promise, she was right—she didn't know him at all. He'd be damned if he'd go begging her to take him back when she thought so ill of him.

She had reason to be upset, but he'd had a perfectly legitimate reason for what he did, too. Why couldn't she see that?

Emson put the tray on his writing table where he liked it, then brought his coffee to him. As Alec sipped the nasty brew, Emson drew a book out of his pocket. "I found this in your great coat, my lord. I thought you might want it."

Frowning, Alec took it from him. *The Rake's Rhetorick.* He'd forgotten all about that blasted book.

As Emson went to lay out his clothes, Alec thumbed through the chapbook, his temper flaring as he skimmed lines here and there. No wonder she thought ill of him. How could she trust any man after she'd read all this nonsense?

Never tell a woman the truth about what you want, not if you plan to get it.

He winced. All right, but he'd been justified in keeping the truth from her. He wasn't some rakehell bent on pleasure, blast it, doing whatever he must to gain the use of a woman's body.

No, just the use of a woman's fortune.

Damn his blathering conscience—what he'd done wasn't the same.

Lifting his coffee cup to his lips, he turned a page, started . . . and poured hot coffee down the front of his bare chest.

"God rot it all!" he swore as he thrust the cup onto his bedside table and swabbed coffee off himself with the coverlet.

Emson came running. "Good heavens, are you all right, my lord?" He whipped out a handkerchief the size of Ireland and began blotting Alec's chest.

Alec shoved his hand away. "It's fine, Emson. I merely . . . er . . ."

Too late. Emson was now staring at the book that still lay open to a picture of a man and a woman doing exactly what Alec and Katherine had done last night. Only these people were in a more . . . creative position, and the man was leering as he thrust into the woman with breasts like grapefruits.

"Good to see you indulging in light reading for a change," Emson remarked dryly.

Scowling, Alec shut the book with a snap. "It's not mine. I acquired it by accident."

"Of course, my lord," Emson said smoothly as he stuffed his coffee-soaked handkerchief back into his pocket. Then he delicately removed the book and placed it into the drawer of the bedside table. "All the same, perhaps we should spare the maids and Mrs. Brown any chance of exposure."

Impudent devil. "Thank you, Emson." Katherine had said the *Rhetorick* had pictures, but my God— No wonder the woman had known what to expect of him that day he'd made love to her in the orangery.

The thought of her finding this book in her father's effects and realizing what that said about the man's habits unnerved Alec. Could he blame her for being suspicious of men? Especially one who admitted to wanting her fortune.

"Will you have some breakfast now, my lord?" Emson asked.

"I suppose." Though he didn't know if he'd ever have an appetite again. Except for a certain winsome, fiery-haired miss—

No, she was gone. He had to get that through his thick skull.

Despair weighting him, he left the bed to walk over to his writing table and stare at the breakfast tray. It contained an apple, two boiled eggs, and a slice of what looked suspiciously like real bread rather than sawdust formed into bricks.

"No hemlock?" he said acidly.

"Fortunately for you, Mrs. Emson sends me breakfast every morning on the sly, and I thought it would suit you better. Only the coffee is Mrs. Brown's."

Emson's wife had been the lady's maid at Edenmore until the death of Alec's mother. Then the woman had married Emson, the valet-turned-butler who'd always fancied her. They'd both left service, and he'd probably never thought to return. But here he was, still waiting until Edenmore could afford another butler.

Alec sighed. The old man would be waiting a while longer. He pushed the tray aside. Even good food couldn't tempt him. "It might be better for everyone if you gave me hemlock."

"Nonsense. Your lady merely needs time to consider the situation rationally. Then I am sure she will return."

Alec gave a harsh laugh. "She won't. You don't know her. She has principles, and they don't bend for anyone. Certainly not for a bastard like me."

He'd meant "bastard" in a figurative sense, but when a long silence ensued, and Alec glanced over to find the hoary-headed servant staring oddly at him, a chill swept over him. "You know? About my . . ."

Emson nodded tersely. "I did serve your father for forty years, my lord."

A shiver ran down Alec's spine. "Who else knows?"

"Only me and my wife. It was hard not to notice when our mistress turned up with child, even though the master had not gone to her bed in months."

Alec sighed. Servants always seemed to know things before anyone else. "I suppose you also know who my real father is."

"Your mother told Mrs. Emson it was a certain . . . royal personage."

"She told me the same." That was something else he hadn't told Katherine, and she'd definitely deserved to hear it. "Odd, isn't it? The earl wasn't even my father, yet despite all my efforts to avoid his mistakes, here I am, right in his place. At least he managed to hold on to the woman he married for money."

Emson looked perplexed. "The old earl didn't marry your mother for money. He loved her then. Thought the sun rose and set in her."

Alec snorted. "Yes, I could tell from how he treated her."

"But it was not like that when they were courting. Your mother considered his lordship a very attractive prospect, and he thought her quite amiable. Yes, she had a fortune, but that was merely icing on the cake. She was young and pretty and made him laugh, something you know he rarely did. So he was sure that once they married, she would be the one to help him overcome his problem."

Alec glanced at him, perplexed. "What problem?"

Emson stiffened. "I beg your pardon. I thought you knew. Since you know all the rest, I thought somebody must have told you—"

"Told me what, damn it?"

Emson actually blushed. Alec didn't think he'd ever seen the man's papery cheeks turn pink. "The old earl could not"—he gestured to the drawer that held *The Rake's Rhetorick*—"attain the physical state required for those activities illustrated in your reading."

Alec gaped at him. "He was impotent?"

"I believe that is the term for it, my lord," Emson mumbled.

"How in God's name would you know such a thing about him?"

"I was his valet in his salad days, if you will recall. I slept right off his room for many years. And whenever he brought . . . er . . . ladies to his rooms, I was the one who . . . paid them. For services or nonservices, as the case may be. Not to mention that my wife was your mother's—"

"Enough." He'd have to watch what he told any valet he ever hired. "So in all the years the earl was married to my mother, he never—"

"Never, from what your mother said to my wife."

Alec wheeled away from the writing table, hardly able to take it in. He'd painted the old earl as the devil incarnate when the truth was far more complicated.

A sudden thought occurred to him. "That's why the old earl spent all that money on quack remedies, isn't it?"

Emson nodded. "He wanted a son very badly."

"His own son," Alec bit out. "Not another man's bastard."

"It was not merely that. He did love your mother enough to want to—"

"Love? That ass had no idea what love is. He was always calling her vulgar and cold, while she spent her nights crying."

"It was easier on his pride, I expect, to blame her." Emson shot him a veiled glance. "Some do say that it is the woman's fault if the man cannot perform his duties. So he may even have convinced himself that such was the case."

Alec bristled. "My mother was the sweetest, best—"

"I am not saying he was right, my lord, either in his beliefs or in his actions. Clearly in later years, he took the blame upon himself or he would not have sought cures. I am just saying it weighs sorely on a man when he cannot bed his wife."

"I suppose that's true." He sucked in a heavy breath. "And it probably weighs sorely on the woman, too."

"Yes. Unfortunately, after the old earl and your mother married, and he realized she was not . . . the solution to his problem, he lashed out at her. That wounded her feelings and made her uneasy around him, which in turn made him more bitter and on and on. It got worse until finally—"

"She let the Prince of Wales seduce her."

Emson nodded. "And then the marriage became as you knew it."

"With the earl always berating her and her believing she was of no worth." His jaw tightened. "And that her son was a reckless ne'er-do-well who would never be a credit to his name."

Alec glanced away. He couldn't believe he was talking about this with Emson. But then, who else was he supposed to talk to about it? The only other people who would understand were his half brothers, who weren't around, and—

Katherine. If she'd stayed, he could have told her. The woman who'd ached for him because he was "poor" and seemingly too proud to tell her might not have flinched at the idea that he was secretly a bastard because his father had been impotent. She might have understood and accepted it, as she'd done with so many other things about him—why he'd worked with horses, why he'd hidden his past . . . why he liked to break the rules.

But he'd driven Katherine away. And all because he'd been too much of a coward to trust her with the truth from the beginning.

Just like the old earl.

Alec stared blindly at his servant. "I thought it was the fortune that made it impossible for them to be close. He was always swearing that he wouldn't have married her if not for it."

Emson nodded. "The master was wrongheaded and too proud for his own good. Trouble is, his sort of pride has no place in love. A man must be humble enough to show his whole self, bad and good, to the woman he loves if he is to gain her trust."

"Which I didn't do," Alec said.

Emson shrugged. "You weren't marrying for love. You were marrying for money. That's different."

"I wasn't marrying only for—" He stopped short. He had been. His deceptions and manner of wooing had all been to lessen the risk of losing Katherine's fortune.

None of it had been to lessen the risk of losing her love. And now that he'd lost both, he saw that he'd put all his attention in the wrong place. Because losing her fortune didn't mean losing Edenmore. He could always find another heiress or borrow more money—assuming that Katherine kept silent about him in society, which he somehow knew she would.

But he didn't *want* another heiress. He only wanted Katherine. So losing her love meant losing it all, because without her . . .

The reality of what he'd done sank over him like a funeral shroud. Oh, God, how would he live without her? What did it matter if he restored Edenmore to a brilliant and efficient estate if he had no Katherine to share it with?

No Katherine to laugh at his puny jests, no Katherine to fuss over him, no Katherine to love.

He groaned. He loved her. Like an idiot, he'd gone and broken his own rule—not to fall in love with the heiress.

But she loathed him now. And too late, he understood what she'd been trying to tell him. *How can I ever separate the things you said to win me, from the things you said to win my fortune?*

He hadn't thought of it that way. He'd been too busy scheming to realize that his one deception would make her regard everything he'd said to her as a lie.

Even if it wasn't.

But how could she know that, when he'd never shown his true self? When he'd kept parts hidden purposely to deceive her? How could he expect her to know what was real and what wasn't?

He couldn't. That damned fortune of hers would always be between them, convincing her that he'd never really cared for her at all.

Unless he gave up the fortune.

The thought hit him like a low branch knocking a rider out of the saddle. If he gave up the fortune, arranged in the marriage settlement for the entire thing to go to her family, then she'd have no reason to balk anymore, no reason to distrust him. She would have to believe he'd meant every word he said.

And he'd forever lose his chance to restore Edenmore to what it had once been.

He could have one or the other: Katherine or Edenmore. Somehow he must find the strength to make the right choice.

Chapter Twenty-seven

❦

Sometimes a rakehell must take a wild risk
to get what he wants.
—Anonymous, *A Rake's Rhetorick*

The afternoon after they'd returned to London, Katherine went in search of her mother. As she approached the parlor, the blessed numbness she'd achieved since leaving Suffolk began to fade, and the sharp bite of pain to gnaw again at her belly.

She and Mama had barely spoken since their flight from Edenmore. Unfortunately, they couldn't continue that way forever.

Katherine entered the parlor to find her mother staring listlessly into the fire. A pang of sympathy hit her, which she squelched ruthlessly. It was Mama's fault she'd landed herself in this fix, promised in marriage to a man she should never have considered.

Not only Mama's fault, her conscience whispered.

She ignored it. "I spoke to the solicitor, Mama," she said in a businesslike tone. "He says Lord Iversley will have difficulty bringing suit against us for breach of contract, since he used deception to obtain my agreement to the marriage."

That wasn't all his cursed lordship had used. The "love bite" he'd left on her shoulder was proof of that. The thought of it fueled her temper. How could he have feigned interest so often? Every time he kissed her and held her and called her "senhora" . . .

She fought back the tears burning her eyes. Lord preserve her, when would she stop turning into a watering pot every time she thought of him?

Mama was staring at her with a sad little frown. "Katherine, my angel, are you sure it's so awful that his lordship is a fortune hunter? Perhaps you should give him another chance."

Katherine's anger welled anew. "Isn't that rather odd, coming from you? You're the one who doesn't want to share my fortune with any husband I take."

For the first time in days, Mama's own temper roused. "Now see here, little Miss Righteous and Noble. You have never lived with money. I *have*. When I was a girl, we lived very well. Papa never denied us anything we asked for."

"Until he died without leaving the money to you, the way you expected."

Her mother rose, eyes flashing. "Can you blame me? Do you know how many years I put up with your grandfather's carping about my poor choice of husband? I went from being his darling to being his disappointment. So yes, I wanted *something* in return." Her eyes narrowed. "And I wanted something better for you, too, whether you believe it or not. I wanted a husband who would *not* embarrass you, who'd treat you better than your father treated me."

"And you chose so well for me, too," she said bitterly.

"I didn't choose the earl, missy. And I certainly didn't

force you into any beds with him. You hopped into his bed all on your own."

Katherine swallowed. That was certainly true.

"Nor am I happy to learn he isn't rich, as Lady Jenner gave me to believe." She frowned. "No doubt she's another scurrilous friend of that Mr. Byrne."

"No doubt."

"But none of that matters now. It's done. We must learn to live with our disappointment. And if that means you marry a man who will use your fortune to better his estate, then so be it. I should think you'd prefer that to the alternative—dying in poverty as an old maid. Which is your only other choice now. Your prospects were never that good, but now that you've been seen in a compromising position by Lady Purefoy in the orangery, they're very bad indeed."

Katherine's chin trembled. "Surely there are still fortune hunters who don't care about such things. We can make an arrangement with one."

"You'd rather marry a man you don't know than a man you know and like?"

"Yes. I let my emotions become engaged, and look where that got me. I should have been sensible, not been swayed by soft words and sweet looks. And now I'm paying for it. Marrying a man I don't know, who won't care about me, would be infinitely sensible."

"But would he make you happy?"

"He'd make me happier than a man who . . . who *lies* to me. Who made me think he wanted me for myself, when all he wanted was my fortune."

"But my angel, isn't that exactly what you did to Sydney?"

Katherine bristled. "I did *not!*"

"You made him think you wanted him for himself. When you really wanted him so you could access your fortune."

"That's not true! I *loved* Sydney."

"Did you? Then why did you let Lord Iversley court you? Why did you accept his proposal of marriage and let him bed you? Your love for Sydney couldn't have been too strong if you tossed it aside for Lord Iversley's attentions."

Her first instinct was to strike back at her mother for putting her in such a cold light. "I tossed it aside because you wanted me to marry soon, and Sydney would not marry . . . well, he seemed not too eager, and . . ." She trailed off as the validity of her mother's words hit her. "No, that's not true. I mean . . . it is true, but Sydney did offer for me at the party. And I refused him."

Seeing herself through her mother's eyes, she felt ashamed. She'd used Sydney ill. Long before she'd fallen in love with Alec, she'd deceived Sydney about her feelings for Alec, merely to provoke her friend into marrying her. Just as Alec had deceived her about his own true feelings to tempt her into marrying him.

And she'd done it for what? To avoid trouble. How was that any different than Alec?

"I'm not saying you were wrong, mind you," her mother went on. "You wanted to marry Sydney so you could make all our lives more comfortable. But that was his lordship's reasoning, too. He wanted to make all his tenants' and his servants' lives more comfortable. So why do you blame him?"

"Because . . . because . . ." Because she loved him. And she wanted so badly for him to love her. She wanted to believe the sweet things he'd said and done, and now she couldn't. How could she live with a man whose every word she suspected?

She wasn't sure she could. One thing she did know—she'd behaved badly to Sydney. He'd deserved better from her.

Turning on her heel, she strode toward the door.

"Where are you going?" her mother said.

"I have to apologize to Sydney for how I've wronged him."

"Do you think he'll still have you?" her mother asked hopefully.

Katherine started to snap out a hot retort, but caught herself just in time. "It doesn't matter if he would, Mama. I could never marry him now. You were right—I never really loved him. And I treated him almost as badly as Alec treated me. But the answer to that isn't to marry him without loving him. That wouldn't be fair, either."

Now that she knew how much it hurt to be wanted for something other than oneself, she couldn't bear to think of anyone else suffering the same pain. And perhaps by seeking absolution for Sydney's broken heart, she could learn how to live with her own.

In a frenzy, Alec rode Beleza toward the Lovelace town house. This would probably be his last time to ride the Lusitano. If Draker came to London at Alec's summons, he'd soon arrive at Stephens Hotel to claim the horse.

But if Alec could get Katherine back, nothing else mattered. And since she had run right to Sydney upon her return to London, that was by no means certain.

When Mrs. Merivale had told him where Katherine was, he'd cursed a blue streak. Hearing that the woman he loved had turned to another man for comfort had briefly shaken his confidence. But Alec refused to lose her now.

At last he reached Lovelace's town house in Mayfair. Alec wasn't terribly surprised to find it a costly building of understated elegance. If he hadn't spent the last month assessing the price of improving his estate, he might not have realized just how costly. But as he dismounted and strode up the marble steps, he was painfully aware of the probable expense of procuring each finely crafted slab and hiring craftsmen talented enough to lay it so perfectly that no joint showed and not a single chip marred the surface.

This was what he meant to take Katherine away from? This easy wealth and secure position with a man whose temperament suited her?

Damned right he did.

Sydney might suit her in some ways, but the man didn't love her. And that kept Alec climbing those expensive marble steps, pushing past the footman in fine livery who tried to turn him away at the door, and striding through halls papered in silk until he located the drawing room.

He didn't know what to think when he saw Molly standing outside it. Katherine *was* here, and clearly she was alone with Sydney. He brushed past the maid and into the drawing room.

Where he found Katherine crying on Sydney's shoulder.

His low, involuntary moan drew their attention instantly. At the sight of him, Lovelace turned hostile, but Katherine's reaction was harder to read. She sat in the curve of the baronet's arm with her chin trembling, her nose red, and her eyes swollen by tears.

She'd never looked more lovely.

His heart twisted in his chest. It didn't matter that she was with Sydney. He refused to let her go. "Katherine, may I please speak to you alone?"

Lovelace stood to put himself between them. "Haven't you done enough? Can't you just leave her be?"

"This has nothing to do with you," Alec bit out. "Let me talk to her."

Katherine stood, her eyes now wary. "What do you want, Alec?"

"I told you—to speak to you privately."

"No. When we're private, you always . . . Whatever you have to say can be said in front of Sydney. He's my friend."

Alec choked back a string of jealous protests; they were certainly not the way to win her back. But must he say this in front of Lovelace, of all people?

Pride has no place in love.

Apparently he must. "First of all, I came to apologize."

"For which offense? Deceiving me about your true purpose? Conspiring with Mr. Byrne behind our backs? Wanting to marry me only for my fortune?"

His jaw tightened. "Everything but the last. I never wanted you only for your fortune, and that's the truth."

"You say that," she whispered, "but how can I ever believe it?"

"You can't. Which is why I want to marry you without your fortune."

Katherine blinked, then narrowed her eyes. "What do you mean?"

"I want you, Katherine, whatever the cost. I'll sign any marriage settlement you like—one that gives your fortune to your mother, or keeps it only in trust for our children, whatever you require." He added hoarsely, "Just say you'll marry me. That's all I want."

She tipped up her chin. "What about Edenmore? And your tenants and—"

"I've been thinking about all of that. I can't sell Edenmore because of the entail, but I can offer it to let. Someone else can take over the tenant farms in exchange for whatever income it provides. And if you and I can't live on the rents, then I can ride for Astley or even join the cavalry—I'm sure Wellington would offer me an officer's commission if I asked."

"What?" Sydney said. "Why the blazes would he do that?"

"Be quiet, Sydney," Katherine whispered, her eyes locked on Alec. "And your servants? What about Mrs. Brown and Emson and the rest?"

Heartened by her response, he stepped nearer. "The younger ones would work for whoever lets Edenmore. The older ones would have to be pensioned off."

"Using what for money?" Sydney sneered at him. "Your nonexistent officer's commission?"

Alec glared at him. "I have friends willing to loan me funds." He prayed they would, at any rate. "They'll help me see that the old earl's debts are paid, too, either by convincing his creditors to accept smaller monthly payments or advancing me the funds until I can repay them with the rents from Edenmore and my salary."

"Leaving you nothing to live on," Lovelace snapped.

Alec stiffened. "I know it would not be an easy life, but at least Katherine and I would be together."

Lovelace snorted, but Katherine drew nearer, her eyes huge in her face. "Why would you give up your estate for me?"

That was *not* something he wanted to say in front of a

sneering audience. "Please, sweetheart, give me five minutes alone with you. That's all I ask."

"Why?" Lovelace broke in before she could answer. "So you can twist her reason and blind her to your true character with kisses?" He turned to Katherine. "Dash it all, Kit, don't you see what he's doing? He knows that once he has you back in his snare, he can work on you until you admit that the fortune would make your life together much easier. Then it's one quick step to the altar, and he gets everything he wants. As usual."

When Alec saw Katherine's face cloud over once more, his temper flared. "Blast you, Lovelace, don't pretend you're protesting my suit because you care about *her*. We both know you wouldn't have fought for her at all, if anyone but I had entered the picture. But the fact that she loves a man you loathe grates on you, doesn't it? You hate that she thumbs her nose at your wealth, that even without money, *I'm* the one she prefers."

Lovelace's eyes narrowed. "And you only want her money. So I'll make you an offer here and now." He squared his shoulders. "I'll write you a bank draft for twenty thousand pounds."

"Sydney, no!" Katherine put in.

Lovelace ignored her. "I realize it's less than you'd hoped for, but it would certainly put a large dent in your debts. And you only have to walk away and leave her free. Just that."

It was Alec's turn to sneer. "Isn't it generous of you to give away twenty thousand pounds of her fortune to rid yourself of a rival?"

Lovelace drew himself up, the very picture of haughty elegance. "Unlike you, I've never wanted her fortune. I've already told her that if we marry, she can do with it as she pleases. But since she just refused my suit for the second time this week, it's unlikely I will ever get a chance at it anyway."

Lovelace balled his hands into fists. "So you see, this is *not* a case of me wanting something you have. I hope one day to convince her to marry me, but even if I can't, Katherine will always be my friend. So, yes, I'd do anything to keep her from you, but only because I know she deserves better. If all it takes to make her happy is paying you off, then the twenty thousand pounds is money well spent."

Alec was stunned speechless. Was the man mad? He'd pay such a sum for a woman who might never marry him? All this time, Alec had assumed that Sydney's feelings for Katherine didn't run deep, but now . . .

He glanced at Katherine, his blood chilling to see how expectantly she watched him, as if she actually thought he might take Lovelace's money. Suddenly he saw himself as they saw him—a low fortune hunter willing to do anything to get what he wanted, to trample over a long-standing friendship simply because it suited his needs and to ignore the welfare of the very woman he professed to love.

No wonder she didn't trust him. How could she, when she had a good man's example before her? A man who could give her more than Alec could ever hope to give her.

He tamped down a burst of pain as he realized what he must do. "Forgive me," he choked out. "It appears I have misunderstood everything, Lovelace. I thought you didn't care for Katherine the way she deserved. But I see now that you were simply more quiet about it. Keep your money—I won't trouble either of you anymore."

Lovelace's lips thinned. "You say that now, but I'd rather take no chances. I don't want Katherine forced to defend herself against a lawsuit. So take the money—it will buy you time to court another heiress."

It took all Alec's control not to put his fist through Lovelace's jaw. "I don't want another heiress. And I'm damned sure not going to bring any lawsuits. You'll have to accept my word as a gentleman for that. Believe it or not, I still have principles."

He turned to Katherine, who stared at him in shock. His heart lurched in his chest to think that this would be his last look at her. "Next time he asks for your hand, sweetheart, you should marry him. Because you were right that night on the gallery. He *is* the better man. And you deserve the best man England has to offer."

Turning on his heel, he left. At least he'd been spared the indignity of revealing his true parentage to her and suffering her contempt. Not to mention the ignominy of telling her he loved her, when she so clearly had lost all love for him.

Too bad pride was such a paltry consolation for having one's heart crushed.

Chapter Twenty-eight

〜✦〜

They say that reformed rakes make the best
husbands—but is there a woman alive who
could make a rake want to reform?
—Anonymous, *A Rake's Rhetorick*

Sydney had only a moment to relish his triumph before Kit started toward the door. He caught her just in time. "Let him go, for God's sake. You're finally free of him."

She cast Sydney a sad smile. "I don't want to be free of him. Not now that I know he truly cares for me."

"Because he refused my offer? Of course he did. He knew that would bring you to him as nothing else would, and then he'd have your fortune—"

"Sydney, my dear friend," she said in an indulgent tone, "he's not the monster you paint him. If you could only see what I've seen—how hard he's fighting to restore his estate, how well he treats his servants, how strongly he feels for his country. There are so many good things about him that you don't know."

"All I've seen is him being reckless and wicked and—"

"Yes, he's that too, sometimes. But then, so am I."

"Never. You're like me—you know what's right and proper and try to follow it."

She laughed. "After all these years, you know me so little."

"I know you well enough. Dash it all, you could never be happy with a man who wants you only for your fortune."

She removed his hand from her arm. "I'm going to tell you something I shouldn't. But I can think of no other way to put your mind at ease." She glanced away. "If Alec had wanted to ruin my chances with you forever, he could have. All he needed to say was the truth—that he and I have been . . . intimate."

Sydney gaped at her. "What?"

With a blush, she met his gaze. "Twice, as a matter of fact. Don't you see? If he'd wished to, he could have told you I wasn't chaste, and you would never have wanted to marry me. But he didn't. And more than anything else, that proves his sincerity." She took his hand and squeezed. "I only hope you won't think too ill of me for it."

"I could never think ill of you," he swore.

"Good. Because I want to remain your friend. But right now I must go."

"To him," he said bitterly.

She smiled. "Yes. I love him, you know. In a way that I never loved you. And perhaps in a way that you never loved me, either?"

He didn't answer.

"I thought so. But you deserve someone who truly loves you, whom you can truly love in return. I promise you, true love is better even than poetry."

Sydney swallowed. "Go on, then. Don't worry about me."

"Thank you." She stretched up to kiss his cheek. Then she was gone.

After she left, Sydney wandered the drawing room

aimlessly. He ought to feel bereft, but all he felt was relief. Iversley's refusal of the money had shaken his certainty that the man was wrong for her; Katherine's revelation had ground it to dust. She was right—he didn't know her.

Or perhaps he'd always known what she was . . . and that it wasn't what he wanted. No, he wanted something else entirely.

Someone else entirely.

His pulse began to race. He hadn't spoken to Jules since the day he'd left Napier House. The day Jules had demanded that Sydney choose a path once and for all: the trip to Greece and a life with Jules . . . or never seeing Jules again and trying to win Katherine back. Jules had said he could no longer bear to be with Sydney as a friend when he felt something different for him.

Sydney had chosen to leave. Because he'd been afraid to face his own true nature, his own wickedness.

Yet here were Katherine and Iversley both freely admitting theirs, willing to do almost anything to be together, even if it meant turning both their lives and their futures upside down.

It humbled him. Inspired him. Gave him hope.

He strode out into the hall and called to the footman on duty. "Have the carriage brought round, will you? And tell Mother that I've gone out to Lord Napier's estate."

Surely if Iversley could refuse a fortune and Katherine risk marrying a fortune hunter for love, then he could take a risk of his own.

Because Katherine was right. True love *was* better than poetry.

Katherine's heart thundered as the hackney coach approached the Stephens Hotel. What if Alec wasn't there?

What if he'd returned to Edenmore? Or worse yet, gone somewhere she'd never find him? But no, Sydney's footman had said he was on horseback. Alec couldn't have gone far.

Still, she should never have let Sydney delay her. She shouldn't have stood there gaping at Alec like a fool when he'd said those lovely words renouncing her fortune. But she'd been so stunned. She knew how badly he needed the money. And for him to give it up . . .

The hack shuddered to a halt. Thank goodness! Over Molly's protests, she ordered the maid to stay with the hack, then she jumped out without waiting for the driver to help her down. She raced into the hotel and halted as every eye stared at her, an unaccompanied lady. Never mind. She had to find Alec, even if it meant dealing with the secretive owner again on her own.

But if Alec had told the man of Katherine's defection, he would probably be even more stubborn than before. Then she spotted the footboy who'd delivered Alec's message when he'd left town. With a surge of relief, she hurried up to him.

"I need to see Lord Iversley. Is he here?"

"Well . . . I . . . the thing is—"

"Look," she said impatiently. "I know he lives here, I know he's poor, I know everything I need to know about him except where he is at this moment. And if you don't tell me, I swear I'll start wandering the halls screaming his name until *somebody* does." She'd already made a complete spectacle of herself; she might as well finish the job.

The servant blinked, then nodded. "This way, miss. He's in a dining room with his friends."

"Friends?" she asked as he led her through the halls.

"Mr. Byrne and Lord Draker."

Those two again. How strange that Alec should happen to be friendly with not one, but two of Prinny's by-blows. What could that possibly mean?

The boy opened the door to a room, but when she heard someone speak her name, she motioned to him to be silent, then waved him away. She stood outside the cracked open door, straining to hear their conversation.

"You might as well take Beleza now," Alec said. "I don't know when I can repay your loan."

"I'm not taking your horse," a man's gruff voice answered. It wasn't Mr. Byrne, so it must be the other one, the Dragon Viscount.

"Why not?" Alec answered. "I knew what I was doing when I offered her as collateral for the money to buy my tillers. With any luck, this crop will help me succeed with Edenmore, so I may be able to buy her back from you one day."

Katherine's heart twisted in her chest. He'd given up Beleza? Oh, her poor sweet darling. She started to push the door open and put an end to this right now when another voice arrested her, one she knew only too well.

"I don't understand why you can't marry another heiress. I know of a woman whose brother owes me money—"

"Absolutely not," Alec snapped. "If I can't have Katherine, I don't want another woman. You'll have to ask me for some other favor, Byrne, because marrying to help you get your money is no longer something I'm willing to do."

Her heart had begun to soar when one of the men said, "Wait a minute."

Before she could react, the door swung open, bringing her face-to-face with a bearded giant who bore a fierce scowl and hands that looked capable of crushing her with one blow.

"Who are you, skulking about, listening in on private conversations?" he growled.

This could only be the Dragon Viscount in the flesh. "I beg your pardon, but I—"

"Katherine?" Alec said. Coming up behind Lord Draker, he thrust the man aside. "For God's sake, stop scowling at her. You're scaring her to death."

Draker crossed his arms over his burly chest. "She was eavesdropping."

"I don't care." Alec's gaze never left her face. "What are you doing here?"

Gathering her courage, she stepped into the room. "You never answered my question. About why you'd be willing to give up my fortune if I'd marry you."

The leap of hope in his face sparked her own hope even higher. Then his expression changed to a troubled frown. "Before I do, I have to tell you something. No matter what happens between us, I'm done with keeping secrets from you."

She forced a smile. "That sounds ominous. I'm not sure I can take many more of your secrets."

"Forgive me, sweetheart, but this one's important." Shutting the door behind her, he nodded to his companions. "You know Byrne, and you've heard me speak of Draker. They're . . . well . . ."

"Your friends. Yes, I know."

"They're not just my friends, Katherine." He sucked in a deep breath. "They're my brothers. My half brothers."

She stared at him in complete bewilderment. "But that would mean—"

"That my father is His Highness. My mother had a short-lived affair with Prinny. I am the result."

She could hardly take it in. "Does the prince know?"

"Nobody knows except my brothers and two of the old earl's servants."

Yet he'd trusted her with the secret, too. He was Prinny's son. Oh, of course! That explained so much—why the previous earl had treated him cruelly, why he didn't like to discuss his parents ...

Why he was regarding her now with an air of expectant dread.

She cast him a reassuring smile. "It doesn't matter to me. I don't care who your father is. I don't care who your friends or your brothers are. I only care who you are."

Alec went still. Then, as if suddenly aware of their audience, he flashed his half brothers a glance. Muttering something about going in search of more brandy, they vanished past her into the hall.

As soon as the door closed behind his half brothers, she said, "*Now* will you answer my question?"

With his face alight, he stepped nearer. "Surely you know the answer."

"I need to hear the words."

"Very well." He laid his hands on her waist. "I love you, Katherine." He drew her close. "I love you." He bent his head toward her. "I will always love you."

As his lips met hers, her heart expanded near to bursting. His kiss was so tender, so loving, that she couldn't believe she'd ever thought to give him up.

When he pulled back, he added, "I think I began falling in love with you the minute you told me I was careless for turning my life into a cliché." His eyes darkened. "But when you tried to seduce me just to get me to rest, I knew I could never live without you."

She cupped his face in her hands, so happy she was beaming. "Oh, Alec, I love you, too. So very much."

"Enough to marry me?" he said hoarsely. "I have little to offer right now, but if we rent out Edenmore—"

"We are not renting out Edenmore." She looped her arms about his neck. "My fortune will give us all we need to restore it."

He scowled down at her. "I meant what I said—I don't want your money. I can take care of you on my own."

"If you think I'll let you march off to get yourself killed in the cavalry or go riding about Astley's ring with some other pretty senhora, think again."

That seemed to give him pause. Then he shook his head mutinously. "No, I can't. Lovelace will claim I used my kisses to gain your fortune."

"Why do you care what he says? I certainly don't."

He arched one brow. "You've changed your mind about him? You've decided he's not the better man after all?"

"Of course he's the better man." When Alec frowned, she added with a smile, "But I don't want the better man. I want Alexander the Great, who is reckless and wicked and does exactly as he pleases, who thinks that poetry is boring and that women should speak their minds. I want *you*, Alec. *And* my fortune. I refuse to marry you unless I can have both."

He began to smile. "Oh, you do, do you?"

"I'm not going to eat Mrs. Brown's cooking or put up with a sculpture of Lady Godiva in the bedroom because we can't afford anything else. So you might as well accept my fortune now."

His eyes gleamed down at her. "All right. But only under two conditions."

She eyed him askance. "Oh?"

"The first is that you set aside a substantial portion for our children."

She relaxed. "I wouldn't have it any other way." She smiled up at him. "And the second?"

"That you invite Senhora Encantador to join us from time to time."

She smothered a laugh. "I don't know. Senhora Encantador is very particular. She only likes rakehells."

"She'll have to settle for the son of a rakehell. And what about you? Will you take this wild and reckless by-blow of a notorious profligate to be your husband?"

"Yes, my great Alexander," she whispered, lifting her head for his kiss. "Most definitely yes."

Epilogue

*Some men are simply not cut out to
be rakehells.*
—Anonymous, *A Rake's Rhetorick*

*I*n her recently refurbished dressing room at Edenmore, Katherine frowned at her reflection in the new pier glass, the one that could show her entire form from head to toe. Perhaps she should have had it installed *after* her first child was born.

Then she wouldn't have to see herself in her chemise, looking like an olive on a stick, even at only five months along. What would she look like at nine months—a skewered melon? Surely that would test even Alec's insistence that she grew more beautiful by the day.

The door to her bedchamber opened, and her mother strolled in, already as comfortable at Edenmore as if it were her own home. She'd brought the children with her for this visit, probably so Katherine's new servants could look after them.

Katherine rubbed her belly with a smile. Funny how things like that didn't bother her anymore.

"Are you all right?" her mother asked.

"I'm fine, Mama."

Her mother led her to sit at the dressing table. "Then why are you standing, my angel? You mustn't risk any harm coming to his lordship's heir."

Katherine smothered a laugh. "It could be a girl, you know."

"Then you'll try again," her mother said soothingly.

They would be trying again no matter what—and most enjoyably. "I can't sit right now. I have to dress. Lord Draker and his sister could be here any minute."

Her mother lifted her eyes heavenward. "Your husband and his scurrilous friends. I suppose Lord Draker isn't so bad, and it's very good of you to offer to bring his sister out in society. But I shall never like Mr. Byrne."

"I don't know—I have a certain fondness for him." Part of her liked to think that he'd pointed Alec toward her not only to get his money, but because he thought them well suited. Of course, Mr. Byrne would ruthlessly deny such an accusation since he preferred to consider himself very wicked.

Like her husband. She smiled again as she stared down at her belly.

"Well," Mama said, "I suppose it's worth putting up with his lordship's friends to be a countess. But you really will have to speak to your husband about his pesky habit of riding out to the barley fields. That's no place for a gentleman."

"Is that where he is now?"

"He was. He rode into the new stables a few minutes ago, all sweaty." She shuddered. "I saw him out the window and came to warn you. Though he did look very pleased with himself."

"I'm so glad. He's had high hopes for that new strain of barley, and I know he wanted to be able to boast of it to Lord Draker when his lordship arrives."

"If you aren't careful, your husband will become one of those odd fellows who spends all his time at sheep-shearings and harvests."

Better that than spending it like Papa, with his mistresses and his gambling. "That's not very likely. Mr. Dawes will have the estate well in hand soon enough. And then Alec can do what he really wants."

"Return to London society?" Mama said hopefully. She was still waiting to make her grand debut as mother of a countess.

"Breed horses." Lusitanos and Suffolk punch horses, to be exact.

"He's buying more horses? But you already have several," her mother protested.

Katherine laughed. "My husband seems to think one can never have too many. And once he starts with his horses, you can forget about London."

Which she wouldn't mind in the least—she loved their life in the country. And once the baby was born, Alec said he'd teach her some riding tricks. Though the only time he'd tried, they'd ended up making love in the stables instead of riding.

She smiled down at her belly. "I wonder how big a pony your papa will buy for you, little angel?" she mused aloud.

"Angels don't need ponies," a male voice teased from behind them. "They have wings."

The glimpse Katherine caught of him in the tiny dressing table mirror was enough to make her heart swell with love. She turned on the stool to flash him a smile.

He answered it with a grin as he strolled into the room. "And here are two more angels, both looking lovely as usual."

Mama gave a girlish giggle. "Oh, go on with you, my lord." She headed for the door. "But I know when I'm not wanted. You young lovers are all the same." She paused in the doorway. "I did want to ask, however . . . Bridget is in dire need of a new pair of shoes, and there's—"

"Will fifty pounds cover whatever you and the children need?" Alec asked, knowing exactly how this worked.

"Oh, yes, my lord, thank you, my lord," she gushed, before sailing from the room with a smile on her face.

Katherine laughed. "You are such a soft touch."

He looked rueful as he walked up and bent to kiss her forehead. "It's really your money, you know."

"For now," she said tenderly. "But if your barley harvest is as fine as it looks to be, and your horse-breeding efforts are successful, we will soon have money of our own."

When his face lit up, she knew she'd chosen exactly the right thing to ease his pride. "Wait till you see the fields, sweetheart. Dawes says the barley has grown beyond his expectations. Next year we'll plant all the fields with it, and then—" He broke off. "But that's not what I came to tell you."

"Oh?"

Something dropped on the table behind her, startling her. Alec bent to brush her ear with his lips. "It's your turn to choose, sweetheart. Last time I chose."

She turned to stare longingly at *The Rake's Rhetorick.* "We can't. Lord Draker might arrive with his sister any minute. We're planning her debut, you know."

"She's waited this long for it; she can wait a few minutes more."

"A few minutes, hah! The last time we tried a position from the *Rhetorick,* it took us half an hour to achieve it."

He slid his hand inside her bodice to fondle her breast. "Ah, but it was a blissful half hour."

She sucked in a breath as his touch sparked fires. Even carrying his child hadn't curbed her craving for him. With a smile, she rose to slide her arms about his neck. "You're incorrigible, husband of mine."

"No more than you." Eyes gleaming, he swept his hot gaze down her. "As I recall, you also found the Swooping Eagle position blissful."

She stared up into the face of the man she loved more each day. "Yes, but I'm not so limber these days."

He grinned. "All right." Taking her by surprise, he lifted her onto the dressing table. "Then we'll have to use a position *I* created."

As he dragged her chemise up her legs, she couldn't help laughing. "Oh, and what is this called? The Dressing Table Dip? The Rakehell's Rocking Chair?"

He gazed at her with a warmly tender look. "I call it Iversley in Love."

"Ah, *that* one," she whispered as she gave herself up to his embrace. "I do so love the old favorites."

POCKET STAR BOOKS
PROUDLY PRESENTS

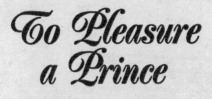

*To Pleasure
a Prince*

Sabrina Jeffries

Available in paperback spring 2005
From Pocket Star Books

Turn the page for a preview. . . .

$\mathcal{L}$ady Regina Tremaine closed the door to the library behind her, and a deep voice wafted down to her from above.

"I take it you got rid of Foxmoor's sister."

Startled, she glanced up to find the Dragon Viscount himself. Lord Draker stood on a little gallery that ran along the near side of the high-ceilinged room and contained more bookshelves. His impressively broad back was to her as he took down a volume and opened it with the care of a mother handling her babe.

It was the only careful thing about him. Everything else was haphazard—the raggedly trimmed hair that fell unfashionably below his collar, the fustian suit smeared in places with dust, and the scuffed boots.

Besides that, he was huge. No wonder everyone believed the rumor that he was actually Prinny's son and not the viscount's. He certainly had Prinny's height and large frame, but without the corpulence that plagued His Highness.

The shaggy-haired giant returned his book to the shelf, then squatted to remove one lower down, giving her an unprecedented view of his well-shaped behind and the impressive thigh muscles straining against the fabric of his ill-fitting trousers. Her mouth went dry. Even she could appreciate a fine male figure when she saw one.

"Well?" he asked. "Did Foxmoor's sister give you any trouble? I hear she's the troublesome sort."

The words jerked her back to the matter at hand. "No more troublesome than the average lady put off by a rude gentleman."

He stiffened, then rose to face her, and she sucked in a breath.

He was nothing like his rumored sire after all. For one thing, he wore an exceedingly unfashionable beard. His Highness would eat nails before he'd grow his whiskers that long. But the prince would certainly not mind having this man's body. A pugilist's meaty shoulders and burly chest tapered down to a surprisingly trim waist. Even his calves appeared to be well-turned, though his stockings . . .

She blinked and looked again. His stockings didn't match.

"Are you finished yet?" he snapped.

She jumped. "Finished what?"

"Looking me over."

Drat it, she hadn't meant to stare. "You can't blame me for being curious. Few people ever get to see Castlemaine, much less its owner."

"There's a reason for that." He turned his back on her to restore his book to the shelf. "Now if you'll excuse me—"

"I certainly will not. I wish to talk to you."

He removed another volume. "Like brother, like sister, I see. Can't take no for an answer."

"Not when the 'no' comes without an explanation."

"I don't need to explain why I'd refuse a caller. I believe that even social etiquette allows me to choose whom I'll see, especially when I'm busy."

"You're not busy; you're just a coward."

He whirled to face her, his scowl raining dragonly fury down on her. "What did you call me?"

Excellent, Regina—why not just slap his face with your glove?

But drat the man, he'd really roused her temper. "A coward. You're perfectly ready to slander my family to your sister, but God forbid you should state your objections to our faces."

A laugh echoed in the library. "You think you and your brother scare me?"

Her annoyance increased. "Simon said you refused to speak with him."

He returned to his books. "He knows perfectly well why I prefer to communicate through the Iversleys. And if they didn't sufficiently explain that I disapprove of his attempt to corrupt my sister—"

"My brother would never corrupt anyone!" she protested.

"I'll be happy to meet with him in person," he finished. He drew out another book, then flipped through it. "So tell Foxmoor he isn't going to soften me one whit by sending his sister here."

"He doesn't even know I've come. No doubt he would vigorously protest my interference."

Lord Draker turned to fix her with his hard gaze. "Then you should consider his wishes and stay out of this affair."

"I'm not here on my brother's behalf. I'm here to argue for your sister."

She didn't miss the subtle gentling in his features. "Louisa sent you?"

"Yes. She said you would never listen to her, since she's so inexperienced in society. But she hoped you might listen to someone who knows it well enough to point out the advantages of an alliance between her and my brother." Especially since the Iversleys upheld Lord Draker's refusal to let Simon near the poor girl.

His face closed up. "Louisa was wrong. My mind is set."

"What possible objection could you have to Simon's courting your sister? He's one of the most eligible gentlemen in London."

"I'm sure he is," he said, with an impatient wave of his hand. "Now if you'll excuse me, I have work to do."

Regina was *not* used to being dismissed or ignored. And to have this . . . this beastly devil do so was beyond the pale. "I'm not leaving until I hear some reason for your objection. Because I certainly can't see a good one."

"You wouldn't." He swept his gaze from the tip of her lilac hat to the points of her expensive kid shoes, and she would have sworn she saw admiration flicker in his gaze. Until he added with a sneer, "Your sort never does."

She bristled. Tired of craning her neck up at this obnoxious creature, she approached the stair that led up to the gallery. "And what sort is that?"

"A wealthy lady of rank moving in the highest circles of society."

She began to mount the little stairs. If he wouldn't listen, she'd trap him on the gallery and *make* him listen.

"Your sister is a wealthy lady of rank, moving in the highest circles of society."

He scowled at her. "She's only there until she finds a decent husband. I want a better life for her than that of a society chit—," he swept a contemptuous gaze over her, "—who spends her days dithering over which color of ball gown to wear."

Regina's temper rose even higher. She stepped onto the gallery and walked toward him. "I suppose you'd rather she marry a bushy-faced hermit like yourself. Then she can spend her days listening to him rebuff all her visitors."

The words hung in the air between them, turning it to frost. Sweet heaven, he had the most beautiful eyes she'd ever seen—a rich brandy-brown, with long, dusky lashes a shade darker than his hair.

A pity those eyes presently bored a hole through her skull. "Better that than spend it catering to Prinny and his ilk," he said.

The light dawned. "Oh, of course, I should have realized it from the first. You object to Simon because of his friendship with His Highness. You don't like your sister being around your father, after you took such great pains to throw the man out all those years ago."

"You're damned right I don't. And what's more—" He broke off suddenly. His frown disappeared, only to be replaced by a suspicious crinkling at the corners of his gorgeous eyes. "You do realize you just called me a bastard to my face."

"I did not!"

"In the eyes of the law, my father was the fifth Viscount Draker. And since you were clearly not referring to *him* . . ."

He had her there, drat him. Clever gentlemen were such a bother.

He went on smugly, "One would think a duke's daughter would know better than to throw salacious rumors about a man's parentage right in his face." He settled his hand on the gallery rail. "But then, we both know how thin is the facade of manners that you and your sort put so much stock in."

"I've had just about enough of your half-baked ideas about me and my 'sort,' you overgrown oaf." Pivoting on her heel, she headed back toward the little stair. "If you want to force Simon and Louisa to sneak around behind your back, then fine by me. Who cares if they're caught in some compromising position and tarred by scandal? I shall simply tell my brother to go right ahead setting up their secret meetings—"

"Stop!" he roared.

She halted near the stairs, a smile playing over her face.

He came up behind her. "What the devil are you babbling about?"

"Oh, no, I shan't trouble you with it—you're far too busy." She continued toward the stair slowly—very slowly. "Clearly I've taken up too much of your precious time already, so I'll be on my way."

She'd already reached the stairs when he grabbed her arm and swung her around to face him. "Not until you tell me what's going on, damn you."

Fighting a smile, she removed his hand from her arm. "Are you sure you can spare the time?" she said sweetly. "I don't know if I should impose."

He marched forward, forcing her to back down the stairs. "Your hints about 'secret meetings' had better be more than the figment of your imagination. Because if you think some paltry trick will gain you my attention—"

"Trick? Surely you don't think a woman who spends her time dithering over which gown to wear could trick a clever gentleman like yourself."

When he swore under his breath, she exulted. *Take that, you big lout.*

She was so busy congratulating herself that she didn't pay attention and missed a step. She stumbled and was about to tumble backward to the floor when his lordship snagged her about the waist.

For a moment they stood frozen, with only his broad arm beneath her back preventing her from hurtling down the stairs. Thank God he was strong.

And surprisingly clean, for all his rough looks. A faint scent of bay rum and soap wafted through her senses, making her wonder if he were not quite the oaf he seemed.

Then he dropped his eyes to where her pelisse had fallen open to reveal her low-cut bodice, and his gaze lodged there as if stuck.

Men often stared at her breasts—on occasion she'd even used that to her advantage. But for some reason, *his* staring unsettled her. He looked as if he wanted to devour them . . . then make her enjoy the devouring.

As her breasts pinkened beneath his gaze, she opened her mouth to rebuke him, then noticed the scar that crawled above his beard and onto his cheek. She'd heard he had a scar, but no one seemed to know how he'd got it or how bad it was. His heavy beard covered most of it, but the part that showed looked rather nasty. What had he done to gain such an awful scar, anyway? She shuddered to think.

He lifted his eyes to her face. Catching where her gaze was fixed, he scowled. "Watch your step, madam. You wouldn't want to go tumbling."

His thinly veiled threat sent a shiver along her spine.

He lifted her as if she weighed less than nothing and set her firmly on the floor two steps below, then descended to loom over her.

"Now, Lady Regina, you're going to explain exactly what you mean by my sister and secret meetings. Because you're not going anywhere until you do."

Ignoring how his low rumble of a voice sparked a peculiar quivering in her belly, she nodded. Apparently, she'd awakened the sleeping dragon.

Now she must figure out what to do with him.

As Foxmoor's sister strolled to the center of the library, Marcus followed, trying hard to keep his eyes in his head.

The woman moved as sweetly as a sonata. He couldn't take his eyes off her fine bottom, covered in what was undoubtedly a gown of the latest fashion. He'd give half his fortune to have that elegant bottom settled on his lap, where he could plunder every honey-perfumed, muslin-draped inch of her.

He scowled. As if a haughty female like her would let him within ten feet. Even after he'd rescued her from a near fall, she'd glared at him as if he meant to ravish her right there.

He'd wanted to. Who wouldn't, when a woman's luscious breasts were served up like that, begging him to dive in and enjoy?

And dash his brains out on the rocks. It could be no coincidence that the wily Foxmoor had sent his lovely sister to argue for him, no matter what the woman claimed. That's what they sent to appease a dragon, wasn't it? A beautiful young virgin?

But this virgin was braver than most. Not many society

misses would storm right into his study without an introduction, especially given the gossip about him. And while she might be a virgin, the woman was sophisticated enough that society had dubbed her "La Belle Dame Sans Merci"—the woman without mercy—after that poem by Chaucer about a heartless beauty.

He had best remember that she was what poets meant when they spoke of dying for love.

She was trouble.

"Well?" he snapped, wanting to get the damned woman out of his study before she put a siren's spell on him. "What's all this about secret meetings?"

Boldly she faced him. God help him, why must she be a blonde, too, his particular weakness? The curls peeking out from beneath her feather-adorned hat were as golden as the gilt edging on his favorite edition of *The Odyssey*. A pox on her and her fancy kind. He didn't need this right now.

She regarded him with cool composure. "Your sister and my brother are determined to see each other. If you don't consent to their courtship, they'll sneak around behind the watchful eyes of her guardians. Then they're sure to be caught in some compromising situation. That would harm Louisa more than my brother."

"Which is why she would never behave so recklessly."

"No?" Lady Regina stared him down. "I'm here precisely because she doesn't want to go behind your back until she's sure you can't be moved."

An alarm seized him that even Lady Regina's matter-of-fact tones could not banish. "You talked to Louisa about this?"

"I talked her *out* of it. She was ready to go along with my brother's plans, but I convinced her that even a duke is not above reproach in such matters and that if they were caught, the ensuing scandal—"

"Damn the scandal! I just don't want her anywhere near your brother and his confounded circle of friends!"

Her gray eyes hardened to steel. "Clearly Louisa doesn't share your aversion to His Highness."

That was the trouble. Louisa didn't even understand it. She'd been ten when their mother left. All she remembered of Prinny was an indulgent "Uncle George" who occasionally brought her treats. Marcus had worked hard to keep her from hearing rumors about the true nature of their mother's "friendship" with the man.

"I gather that you know Louisa well," he told Lady Regina.

"I consider her my friend, yes."

Damn, but the girl had landed in a pit of vipers. How could the Iversleys have allowed this? "Then you should know that she isn't wise enough to the ways of society to be a good choice for your brother."

"She makes him happy—that's all that matters."

He laughed bitterly. "Strange sentiments coming from you, madam."

She cocked her head, setting her ostrich feather aquiver. "What do you mean? You don't even know me."

"I know of you. Who hasn't heard of Lady Regina Tremaine, who despite refusing scores of gentlemen manages to acquire more marriage proposals with each passing year? Can't find one to make you happy, madam? Or just not one lofty enough to suit your family's fine lineage and high expectations?"

Color stained her cheeks. "I see you've been listening to idle gossip."

"It doesn't seem so idle, now that I've met you."

"I could say the same for the gossip about you."

"Oh? What do they say about me these days?" No one in society ever gossiped about a man to his face.

She skewered him with a sugared dagger of a smile. "They say you're a hard man with a foul temper. That you have secrets too dark to speak aloud, and that you will do anything to keep them."

He snorted. "They say that *you* enjoy putting upstarts in their places. That your sharp tongue has made you the darling of our corrupt society during the six or seven years since your come-out."

"Six," she corrected tightly. "And they say that *you* browbeat tradesmen and toss hapless messengers out on their ears for no reason."

Annoyed that her information was only half-right, he stalked toward her. "They say that some idiot poet is writing a poem to your heartlessness."

Her features grew more stony. "They say that William Blake, that daft artist, got the inspiration for one of his horrible dragon paintings from *you*."

He happened to own one of those "horrible dragon paintings." Blake himself had given it to him, but he'd thought it was Blake's idea of a joke. Until now.

Scowling, he bent his head until he was nose to nose with the impudent chit. "They say that you're a haughty bitch of a beauty who thinks the sun rises and sets for her because she's daughter to a duke."

When her glittering gaze met his, he thought he saw hurt in it. But that was absurd. Women like her did not hurt.

"They say you eat small children for breakfast," she countered. "With jam."

The deliberate absurdity of that last one startled him.

And he didn't like being startled. He glared down at her. "They call you La Belle Dame Sans Merci."

She thrust her face so close to his that her ostrich feather brushed his forehead. "They call *you* The Dragon Viscount. But that's because society entertains itself by attaching titillating names to those they fear, envy, or admire. It says nothing about either of our characters—as you, of all people, should know."

That astute assessment of society gossip gave him pause. Drawing back from her, he said sullenly, "You left out the worst of the gossip about me. That I bullied my mother and forced her to rely on the kindness of friends—your parents, for example. That I refused to honor the terms of my father's will. That I even used to beat her. Or had you not heard that, too?"

"I heard."

"Then why didn't you mention it?"

She thrust out her chin. "Should I? Is it true?"

That took him aback. No one had ever bothered to ask him. "You'll think what you want to, so it hardly matters what I say."

"It matters to me."

She said the words so sincerely, he almost believed her. Which infuriated him. "Think what you wish, then," he growled. "It makes no difference."

"Very well."

When she said nothing more, he cursed her for not indicating what she'd chosen to believe. Not that he cared what she thought. He didn't care in the least.

Then she had the audacity to smile and add, "I don't know how we got so far off the subject. This isn't about you or me. This is about Louisa."

Author's Note

The Prince of Wales (later, King George IV) had a number of mistresses during his lifetime, starting when he was eighteen. They ran the gamut of society, from actresses to married marchionesses. He was rumored to have had children by a few of them, some of whom were passed off as the children of the women's husbands (as in Lord Draker's case). He even showed two of his well-acknowledged by-blows a fatherly affection, making sure they were well settled in life. No one is completely certain how many bastards he fathered, but given his frequent liaisons, I suspect it was more than we know.

Although I did invent *The Rake's Rhetorick,* I based the title on a period book called *The Whore's Rhetorick,* which also included a reference to *L'Aretin Francais,* a set of prints of sexual positions. *La Carriola,* or "The Wheelbarrow," is the name of an actual print from an 1803 edition of that erotic work.

As for Alec and his riding skills, there were indeed British gentlemen who taught cavalry skills to the Portuguese during the Peninsular Wars. At least one of them was offered a position in Wellington's army later. Astley's Amphitheatre did exist and was the precursor to our modern circus. Demonstrations of cavalry maneuvers were as popular with audiences then as air shows are today. But although burlesque interludes were often performed at Astley's, I admit to having invented the one I called "The Angry Wife." I couldn't resist the chance to put my hero and heroine in a romantic embrace on a horse!

**Visit the Simon & Schuster
romance Web site:**

www.SimonSaysLove.com

**and sign up for our
romance e-mail updates!**

Keep up on the latest
new romance releases,
author appearances, news, chats,
special offers, and more!
We'll deliver the information
right to your inbox—if it's new,
you'll know about it.

POCKET BOOKS

2800.02

Visit
❖ **Pocket Books** ❖
online at

www.SimonSays.com

Keep up on the latest new
releases from your favorite
authors, as well as author
appearances, news, chats,
special offers and more.

SIMON & SCHUSTER
A VIACOM COMPANY
www.SimonSays.com

Pocket
Books

2381-01